THE CHESS COMPANION

The Most Instructive Games of Chess Ever Played
Practical Chess Endings
Logical Chess, Move by Move
An Invitation to Chess
  (*with Kenneth Harkness*)
Winning Chess
  (*with Fred Reinfeld*)

The
Chess Companion

♚

A MERRY COLLECTION OF

Tales of Chess and Its Players,

TOGETHER WITH A CORNUCOPIA OF

Games, Problems, Epigrams & Advice,

TOPPED OFF WITH

The Greatest Game of Chess

Ever Played

♚

SELECTED, ANNOTATED, AND BROUGHT

BETWEEN TWO COVERS BY

Irving Chernev

FABER AND FABER
3 Queen Square
London

First published in England in 1970
by Faber and Faber Limited
3 Queen Square London W.C.1.
First published in this edition 1972
Printed in Great Britain by
Straker Brothers Ltd., Whitstable
All Rights reserved

ISBN 0 571 10242 5 (Faber Paper Covered Editions)
ISBN 0 571 09315 9 (hard bound edition)

ACKNOWLEDGMENTS

I wish to express my thanks and appreciation to the authors, editors and publishers who permitted me to use the following material:

"The Hour of Letdown," from *The Second Tree from the Corner*, by *E. B. White*.
Copyright 1951 by E. B. White.
Originally appeared in *The New Yorker;* reprinted by permission of Harper & Row, Publishers, and by permission of Hamish Hamilton, Ltd., London.

"Fool's Mate" *by Stanley Ellin*.
Published originally in *Ellery Queen's Mystery Magazine* in November 1951.
Copyright 1951 by Davis Publications, Inc.
Reprinted by permission of Stanley Ellin and Curtis Brown, Ltd.

"The Ballad of Edward Bray" *by A. A. Milne*.
Originally appeared in *The Day's Play* in 1910.
Reprinted by permission of Methuen & Co., Ltd., Publishers.

"Last Round" *by Kester Svendsen*.
Originally appeared in *Chess World* in 1947.
Reprinted by permission of the author.

"Noblesse Oblige" *by J. L. Synge*.
Originally appeared in *Science: Sense and Nonsense*.
All rights reserved by the publishers.
Reprinted by permission of the publishers, W. W. Norton & Company, New York and Jonathan Cape, Ltd., London.

"The Man Who Sidetracked His Brains" *by Lord Dunsany*.
Published originally in *The Man Who Ate the Phoenix* and *This Week* Magazine.
Copyright 1940 by United Newspapers Magazine Corporation.
Reprinted by permission of Lady Dunsany and *This Week* Magazine.

"Pawn to King's Four," from *Happy Stories Just to Laugh At*, by *Stephen Leacock*.
Copyright 1943 by Dodd, Mead & Company.
Reprinted by permission of Dodd, Mead & Company and The Bodley Head, Ltd., London.

"Professor Pownall's Oversight" *by H. Russell Wakefield*.
Published originally in *They Return at Evening* by D. Appleton & Company.
Copyright 1928, 1955 by H. Russell Wakefield.
Reprinted by permission of Jessica Russell Wakefield.

"Slippery Elm," from *Rogues in Clover, by Percival Wilde*.
Copyright 1924, 1927 by Percival Wilde. Renewal copyright 1954 by Estate of Percival Wilde; © 1963 by Dana Marie Ross.
Published by Appleton & Company.

"Writers Who Have Changed Chess History" *by Harry Golombek*,
from *Chess Treasury of the Air*, edited by Terence Tiller.
Reprinted by permission of Penguin Books, Ltd.

"The Pride of the Eden Musée" *by John Kobler.*
    Originally appeared in *Afternoon in the Attic* and *The New Yorker.*
    Reprinted by permission of John Kobler.

I am indebted to Mr. Al Horowitz of *Chess Review* for permission to reprint many of my articles that appeared originally in that magazine. I am also grateful to Mr. Hayward Cirker, and to Dover Publications, publishers of *The Bright Side of Chess,* for permission to reprint material from that book.

This book is dedicated to
my dear granddaughter Celia Ann
with love

CONTENTS

PART ONE: *Chess in Fact and Fancy*

E. B. White
The Hour of Letdown   17

Stanley Ellin
Fool's Mate   21

A. A. Milne
The Ballad of Edward Bray   35

Kester Svendsen
Last Round   37

J. L. Synge
Noblesse Oblige   45

Anonymous
The King's Own   46

Lord Dunsany
The Man Who Sidetracked His Brains   49

Richard Garnett
The Rewards of Industry   51

Stephen Leacock
Pawn to King's Four   57

Lord Dunsany
The Three Sailors' Gambit   65

H. R. Wakefield
Professor Pownall's Oversight   73

Percival Wilde
Slippery Elm   85

John Kobler
The Pride of the Eden Musée   115

Harry Golombek
Writers Who Have Changed Chess History   127

PART TWO: *Chess Over the Board*

The Little World of Problems   151

End-Game Corner   155

Fantasia   162

Department of Serendipity   167

Remarkable Games   173

Ahead of Their Time   184

Curious Conclusions   192

Blindfold Beauties   198

Peripatetic Pawns   204

Happy Endings   209

All Sorts of Odds   215

The Galloping Knights   220

Queen Sacrifices   223

The Master at His Best   228

The Amazing Genius of Petrosian   257

Interlude   269

Epigrams and Advice   275

The Greatest Game of Chess Ever Played   281

Index to the Composers of the Problems, Puzzles
    and Endings   285

Index to the Players and Their Games   286

This Book is a Collection

of chess games, problems, puzzles, endings and short stories about chess and its players. The games range from 1760 to 1966 and illustrate almost every interesting idea ever shown on a chessboard. Most of the games will be, I think, new to you. Some may be familiar, but it would be hard to find a brilliancy by any great master, from Morphy and Anderssen to Fischer and Petrosian, that has not been printed before.

If you come across a game that is familiar to you (but delightful nonetheless) play it over once more, as you would read once again a favorite story reprinted in a new anthology.

New York, 1968   IRVING CHERNEV

*Chess, like love, like music, has the power
to make men happy.*

— TARRASCH

1

CHESS

in Fact and Fancy

by Various Writers

♛ ♛ ♛

by E. B. White

The Hour of Letdown

WHEN THE MAN CAME IN, carrying the machine, most of us looked up from our drinks, because we had never seen anything like it before. The man set the thing down on top of the bar near the beerpulls. It took up an ungodly amount of room and you could see the bartender didn't like it any too well, having this big, ugly-looking gadget parked right there.

"Two rye-and-water," the man said.

The bartender went on puddling an Old-Fashioned that he was working on, but he was obviously turning over the request in his mind.

"You want a double?" he asked, after a bit.

"No," said the man. "Two rye-and-water, please." He stared straight at the bartender, not exactly unfriendly but on the other hand not affirmatively friendly.

Many years of catering to the kind of people that come into saloons had provided the bartender with an adjustable mind. Nevertheless, he did not adjust readily to this fellow, and he did not like the machine — that was sure. He picked up a live cigarette that was idling on the edge of the cash register, took a drag out of it, and returned it thoughtfully. Then he poured two shots of rye whiskey, drew two glasses of water, and shoved the drinks in front of the man. People were watching. When something a little out of the ordinary takes place at a bar, the sense of it spreads quickly all along the line and pulls the customers together.

The man gave no sign of being the center of attention. He laid a five-dollar bill down on the bar. Then he drank one of the ryes and chased it with water. He picked up the other rye, opened a small vent in the machine (it was like an oil cup) and poured the whiskey in, and then poured the water in.

The bartender watched grimly. "Not funny," he said in an even voice. "And furthermore, your companion takes up too much room.

Why'n you put it over on that bench by the door, make more room here."

"There's plenty of room for everyone here," replied the man.

"I ain't amused," said the bartender. "Put the goddam thing over near the door like I say. Nobody will touch it."

The man smiled. "You should have seen it this afternoon," he said. "It was magnificent. Today was the third day of the tournament. Imagine it—three days of continuous brainwork! And against the top players in the country, too. Early in the game it gained an advantage; then for two hours it exploited the advantage brilliantly, ending with the opponent's king backed in a corner. The sudden capture of a knight, the neutralization of a bishop, and it was all over. You know how much money it won, all told, in three days of playing chess?"

"How much?" asked the bartender.

"Five thousand dollars," said the man. "Now it wants to let down, wants to get a little drunk."

The bartender ran his towel vaguely over some wet spots. "Take it somewheres else and get it drunk there!" he said firmly. "I got enough troubles."

The man shook his head and smiled. "No, we like it here." He pointed at the empty glasses. "Do this again, will you, please?"

The bartender slowly shook his head. He seemed dazed but dogged. "You stow the thing away," he ordered. "I'm not ladling out whiskey for jokestersmiths."

" 'Jokesmiths,' " said the machine. "The word is 'jokesmiths.' "

A few feet down the bar, a customer who was on his third highball seemed ready to participate in this conversation to which we had all been listening so attentively. He was a middle-aged man. His necktie was pulled down away from his collar, and he had eased the collar by un-buttoning it. He had pretty nearly finished his third drink, and the alcohol tended to make him throw his support in with the underprivileged and the thirsty.

"If the machine wants another drink, give it another drink," he said to the bartender. "Let's not have haggling."

The fellow with the machine turned to his new-found friend and gravely raised his hand to his temple, giving him a salute of gratitude and fellowship. He addressed his next remark to him, as though delib-erately snubbing the bartender.

"You know how it is when you're all fagged out mentally, how you want a drink?"

"Certainly do," replied the friend. "Most natural thing in the world."

There was a stir all along the bar, some seeming to side with the bartender, others with the machine group. A tall, gloomy man standing next to me spoke up.

"Another whiskey sour, Bill," he said. "And go easy on the lemon juice."

"Picric acid," said the machine, sullenly. "They don't use lemon juice in these places."

"That does it!" said the bartender, smacking his hand on the bar. "Will you put that thing away or else beat it out of here. I ain't in the mood, I tell you. I got this saloon to run and I don't want lip from a mechanical brain or whatever the hell you've got there."

The man ignored this ultimatum. He addressed his friend, whose glass was now empty.

"It's not just that it's all tuckered out after three days of chess," he said amiably. "You know another reason it wants a drink?"

"No," said the friend. "Why?"

"It cheated," said the man.

At this remark, the machine chuckled. One of its arms dipped slightly, and a light glowed in a dial.

The friend frowned. He looked as though his dignity had been hurt, as though his trust had been misplaced. "Nobody can cheat at chess," he said. "Simpossible. In chess, everything is open and above the board. The nature of the game of chess is such that cheating is impossible."

"That's what I used to think, too," said the man. "But there *is* a way."

"Well, it doesn't surprise me any," put in the bartender. "The first time I laid my eyes on that crummy thing I spotted it for a crook."

"Two rye-and-water," said the man.

"You can't have the whiskey," said the bartender. He glared at the mechanical brain. "How do I know it ain't drunk already?"

"That's simple. Ask it something," said the man.

The customers shifted and stared into the mirror. We were all in this thing now, up to our necks. We waited. It was the bartender's move.

"Ask it what? Such as?" said the bartender.

"Makes no difference. Pick a couple big figures, ask it to multiply them together. You couldn't multiply big figures together if you were drunk, could you?"

The machine shook slightly, as though making internal preparations.

"Ten thousand eight hundred and sixty-two, multiply it by ninety-nine," said the bartender, viciously. We could tell that he was throwing in the two nines to make it hard.

The machine flickered. One of its tubes spat, and a hand changed position, jerkily.

"One million seventy-five thousand three hundred and thirty-eight," said the machine.

Not a glass was raised all along the bar. People just stared gloomily into the mirror; some of us studied our own faces, others took carom shots at the man and the machine.

Finally, a youngish, mathematically minded customer got out a piece of paper and a pencil and went into retirement. "It works out," he reported, after some minutes of calculating. "You can't say the machine is drunk!"

Everyone now glared at the bartender. Reluctantly he poured two shots of rye, drew two glasses of water. The man drank his drink. Then he fed the machine its drink. The machine's light grew fainter. One of its cranky little arms wilted.

For a while the saloon simmered along like a ship at sea in calm weather. Every one of us seemed to be trying to digest the situation, with the help of liquor. Quite a few glasses were refilled. Most of us sought help in the mirror – the court of last appeal.

The fellow with the unbuttoned collar settled his score. He walked stiffly over and stood between the man and the machine. He put one arm around the man, the other arm around the machine. "Let's get out of here and go to a good place," he said.

The machine glowed slightly. It seemed to be a little drunk now.

"All right," said the man. "That suits me fine. I've got my car outside."

He settled for the drinks and put down a tip. Quietly and a trifle uncertainly he tucked the machine under his arm, and he and his companion of the night walked to the door and out into the street.

The bartender stared fixedly, then resumed his light housekeeping. "So he's got his car outside," he said, with heavy sarcasm. "Now isn't that nice!"

A customer at the end of the bar near the door left his drink, stepped to the window, parted the curtains, and looked out. He watched for a moment, then returned to his place and addressed the bartender. "It's even nicer than you think," he said. "It's a Cadillac. And which one of the three of them d'ya think is doing the driving?"

The introduction to "Fool's Mate" was written by Ellery Queen, on the occasion of this story's first appearance in Ellery Queen's Mystery Magazine.

The story won a prize, as did every short story Stanley Ellin ever wrote!
— IRVING CHERNEV

A new prize-winning story by the author of "The Specialty of the House," "The Cat's-Paw," "Death on Christmas Eve," and "The Orderly World of Mr. Appleby" is nothing short of an Event, with a capital E . . .

Some time ago, Stanley Ellin met a devotee of Dupin, Holmes, and EQMM, *and this devotee turned out to be one of the world's chess masters and possibly the greatest living authority on the game's history and literature. In a name, Mr. Irving Chernev, editor of* Fireside Book of Chess *(1949) . . .*

Mr. Chernev's home, we understand, groans with collected works on all phases and aspects of chess, from antiquity to modernity, and he mixes his deep erudition with wit and humor. Now, Mr. Ellin claims that he, Stanley Ellin, is but an indifferent player at the sport of Kings (and Queens), and that his only distinction in the game is the fact that he is one of the few players in all the world whom Mr. Chernev has never beaten — a distinction, Mr. Ellin hastens to explain, achieved only by his grimly refusing to play with Mr. Chernev. But while he obdurately avoided any test of prowess, Mr. Ellin was more than willing to talk about the game, and soon he found himself fascinated by chess lore — obscure points of history, psychological factors in playing, and anecdotes about famous competitors. It was inevitable, Mr. Ellin being what he is (a writer), and chess being what it is (one of the facts of life), that Mr. Ellin's exposure should lead to a head-on collision; and that this collision should assume, in its ultimate shape, the classical proportions of, on the one hand, an immovable (dead) body, and on the other, an irresistible (police) force.

by Stanley Ellin

Fool's Mate

WHEN GEORGE HUNEKER CAME HOME from the office that evening he was obviously fired by a strange excitement. His ordinarily sallow cheeks were flushed, his eyes shone behind his rimless spectacles, and instead of carefully removing his rubbers and neatly placing them on the strip of mat laid for that purpose in a corner of the hallway, he pulled them off with reckless haste and tossed them aside. Then, still wearing his hat and overcoat, he undid the wrappings of the package he had brought with him and displayed a small, flat, leather case. When he opened the case Louise saw a bed of shabby green velvet in which rested the austere black and white forms of a set of chessmen.

"Aren't they beautiful?" George said. He ran a finger lovingly over one of the pieces. "Look at the work on this: nothing fancy to stick away in a glass case, you understand, but everything neat and clean and ready for action the way it ought to be. All genuine ivory and ebony, and all handmade, every one of them."

Louise's eyes narrowed. "And just how much did you pay out for this stuff?"

"I didn't," George said. "That is, I didn't buy it. Mr. Oelrichs gave it to me."

"Oelrichs?" said Louise. "You mean that old crank you brought home to dinner that time? The one who just sat and watched us like the cat that ate the canary, and wouldn't say a word unless you poked it out of him?"

"Oh, Louise!"

"Don't you 'Oh, Louise' me! I thought I made my feelings about him mighty clear to you long before this. And, may I ask, why should our fine Mr. Oelrichs suddenly decide to give you this thing?"

"Well," George said uneasily, "you know he's been pretty sick, and what with him needing only a few months more for retirement I was carrying most of his work for him. Today was his last day, and he gave me this as a kind of thank-you present. Said it was his favorite set, too, but he wanted to give me the best thing he could, and this was it."

"How generous of Mr. Oelrichs," Louise remarked frigidly. "Did it ever occur to him that if he wanted to pay you back for your time and trouble, something practical would be a lot more to the point?"

"Why, I was just doing him a favor, Louise. Even if he did offer me money or anything like that, I wouldn't take it."

"The more fool you," Louise sniffed. "All right, take off your things, put them away right, and get ready for supper. It's just about ready."

She moved toward the kitchen, and George trailed after her placatingly. "You know, Louise, Mr. Oelrichs said something that was very interesting."

"I'm sure he did."

"Well, he said there were some people in the world who *needed* chess – that when they learned to play it real well they'd see for themselves how much they needed it. And what I thought was that there's no reason why you and I . . ."

She stopped short and faced him with her hands on her hips. "You mean that after I'm done taking care of the house, and shopping, and cooking your hot meals, and mending and darning, then I'm supposed to sit down and learn how to play games with you! For a man going on fifty, George Huneker, you get some peculiar ideas."

Pulling off his overcoat in the hallway, he reflected that there was small chance of his losing track of his age, at least not as long as Louise doted so much on reminding him. He had first heard about it a few months after his marriage when he was going on thirty and had been offered a chance to go into business for himself. He had heard about it every year since, on some occasion or other, although as he learned more and more about Louise he had fallen into fewer traps.

The only trouble was that Louise always managed to stay one jump ahead of him, and while in time he came to understand that she would naturally put her foot down at such things as his leaving a good steady job, or at their having a baby when times were hard (and in Louise's opinion they always were), or at buying the house outright when they could rent it so cheap, it still came as a surprise that she so bitterly opposed the idea of having company to the house, or of reading some book he had just enjoyed, or of tuning in the radio to a symphony, or, as in this case, of taking up chess.

Company, she made it clear, was a bother and expense, small print hurt her eyes, symphonies gave her a splitting headache, and chess, it seemed, was something for which she could not possibly find time. Before they had been married, George thought unhappily, it had all been different somehow. They were always in the midst of a crowd of his friends, and when books or music or anything like that was the topic of discussion, she followed the talk with bright and vivacious interest. Now she just wanted to sit with her knitting every night while she listened to comedians bellowing over the radio.

Not being well, of course, could be one reason for all this. She suffered from a host of aches and pains which she dwelt on in such vivid detail at times that George himself could feel sympathetic twinges go through him. Their medicine chest bulged with remedies, their diet had dwindled to a bland and tasteless series of concoctions, and it was a rare month which did not find Louise running up a sizable doctor's bill for the treatment of what George vaguely came to think of as "women's troubles."

Still, George would have been the first to point out that despite the handicaps she worked under, Louise had been as good a wife as a man could ask for. His salary over the years had hardly been luxurious, but penny by penny she had managed to put aside fifteen thousand dollars in their bank account. This was a fact known only to the two of them, since Louise made it a point to dwell on their relative poverty in her

conversations with anyone, and while George always felt some embarrassment when she did this, Louise pointed out that one of the best ways
to save your money was not to let the world at large know you had any,
and since a penny saved was a penny earned she was contributing as
much to their income in her way as George was in his. This, while not
reducing George's embarrassment, did succeed in glossing it with increased respect for Louise's wisdom and capability.

And when added to this was the knowledge that his home was always neat as a pin, his clothing carefully mended, and his health fanat-
ically ministered to, it was easy to see why George chose to count his
blessings rather than make an issue of anything so trivial as his wife's
becoming his partner at chess. Which, as George himself might have
admitted had you pinned him down to it, was a bit of a sacrifice, for in
no time at all after receiving the set of chessmen he found himself a
passionate devotee of the game. And chess, as he sometimes reflected
while poring over his board of an evening with the radio booming in his
ears and his wife's knitting needles flickering away contentedly, would
seem to be a game greatly enhanced by the presence of an opponent. He
did not reflect this ironically; there was no irony in George's nature.

Mr. Oelrichs, in giving him the set, had said he would be available
for instruction at any time. But since Louise had already indicated that
that gentleman would hardly be a welcome guest in her home, and since
she had often expressed decided opinions on any man who would leave
his hearth and home to go traipsing about for no reason, George did
not even think the matter worth broaching. Instead, he turned to a little
text aptly entitled *An Invitation to Chess,* was led by the invitation to
essay other and more difficult texts, and was thence led to a whole world
of literature on chess, staggering in its magnitude and complexity.

He ate chess, drank chess, and slept chess. He studied the masters
and past masters until he could quote chapter and verse from even their
minor triumphs. He learned the openings, the middle game, and the end
game. He learned to eschew the reckless foray which led nowhere in
favor of the positional game, where cunning strategy turned a side into
a relentless force that inevitably broke and crushed the enemy before it.
Strange names danced across his horizon: Alekhine, Capablanca, Lasker,
Nimzowitsch, and he pursued them, drunk with the joy of discovery,
through the ebony and ivory mazes of their universe.

But in all this there was still that one thing lacking: an opponent,
a flesh-and-blood opponent against whom he could test himself. It was
one thing, he sometimes thought disconsolately, to have a book at one's
elbow while pondering a move; it would be quite another to ponder even
the identical move with a man waiting across the board to turn it to his
own advantage and destroy you with it. It became a growing hunger,

that desire to make a move and see a hand reach across the table to answer it; it became a curious obsession, so that at times, when Louise's shadow moved abruptly against the wall or a log settled in the fireplace, George would look up suddenly, half expecting to see the man seated in the empty chair opposite him.

He came to visualize the man quite clearly after a while. A quiet contemplative man much like himself, in fact, with graying hair and rimless spectacles that tended to slide a bit when he bent over the board. A man who played just a shade better than himself; not so well that he could not be beaten, but well enough to force George to his utmost to gain an occasional victory.

And there was one thing more he expected of this man; something a trifle unorthodox, perhaps, if one was a stickler for chess ritual. The man must prefer to play the white side all the time. It was the white side that moved first, that took the offensive until, perhaps, the tide could be turned against it. George himself infinitely preferred the black side, preferred to parry the thrusts and advances of white while he slowly built up a solid wall of defense against its climactic moves. *That* was the way to learn the game, George told himself; after a player learned how to make himself invulnerable on the defense, there was nothing he couldn't do on attack.

However, to practice one's defense still required a hand to set the offense into motion, and eventually George struck on a solution which, he felt with mild pride, was rather ingenious. He would set up the board, seat himself behind the black side, and then make the opening move for white. This he would counter with a black piece, after which he would move again for white, and so on until some decision was reached.

It was not long before the flaws in this system became distressingly obvious. Since he naturally favored the black side, and since he knew both plans of battle from their inception, black won game after game with ridiculous ease. And after the twentieth fiasco of this sort George sank back into his chair despairingly. If he could only put one side out of his mind completely while he was moving for the other, why, there would be no problem at all! Which, he realized cheerlessly, was a prospect about as logical as an ancient notion he had come across in his reading somewhere, the notion that if you cut a serpent in half, the separated halves would then turn on each other and fight themselves savagely to death.

He set up the board again after this glum reflection, and then walked around the table and seated himself in white's chair. Now, if he were playing the white side what would he do? A game depends not only on one's skill, he told himself, but also on one's knowledge of his opponent. And not only on the opponent's style of play, but also on his character, his personality, his whole nature. George solemnly looked across the table at black's now empty chair and brooded on this. Then slowly, deliberately, he made his opening move.

After that, he quickly walked around the table and sat down on black's side. The going, he found, was much easier here, and almost mechanically he answered white's move. With a thrill of excitement chasing inside him, he left his seat and moved around to the other side of the board again, already straining hard to put black and its affairs far out of his mind.

"For pity's sake, George, what *are* you doing!"

George started, and looked around dazedly. Louise was watching him, her lips compressed, her knitting dropped on her lap, and her manner charged with such disapproval that the whole room seemed to frown at him. He opened his mouth to explain, and hastily thought better of it.

"Why, nothing," he said, "nothing at all."

"Nothing at all!" Louise declared tartly. "The way you're tramping around, somebody would think you can't find a comfortable chair in the house. You know I . . ."

Then her voice trailed off, her eyes became glassy, her body straightened and became rigid with devouring attention. The comedian on the radio had answered an insult with another evidently so devastating that the audience in the studio could do no more than roar in helpless laughter. Even Louise's lips turned up ever so slightly at the corners as she reached for her knitting again, and George gratefully seized this opportunity to drop into the chair behind black's side.

He had been on the verge of a great discovery, he knew that; but what exactly had it been? Was it that changing places physically had allowed him to project himself into the forms of two players, each separate and distinct from the other? If so, he was at the end of the line, George knew, because he would never be able to explain all that getting up and moving around to Louise.

But suppose the board itself were turned around after each move? Or, and George found himself charged with a growing excitement, since chess was completely a business of the mind anyhow — since, when one had mastered the game sufficiently it wasn't even necessary to use a board at all — wasn't the secret simply a matter of *turning oneself into the other player* when his move came?

It was white's move now, and George bent to his task. He was playing white's side, he must do what white would do — more than that, he must feel white's very emotions — but the harder he struggled and strained in his concentration, the more elusive became his goal. Again and again, at the instant he was about to reach his hand out, the thought of what black intended to do, of what black was surely *going* to do, slipped through his mind like a dot of quicksilver and made him writhe inwardly with a maddening sense of defeat.

This now became the obsession, and evening after evening he exercised himself at it. He lost weight, his face drew into haggard lines so that Louise was always at his heels during mealtimes trying to make him take an interest in her wholly uninteresting recipes. His interest in his job dwindled until it was barely perfunctory, and his superior, who at first had evinced no more than a mild surprise and irritation, started to shake his head ominously.

But with every game, every move, every effort he made, George felt with exultation he was coming nearer that goal. There would come a moment, he told himself with furious certainty, when he could view the side across the board with objectivity, with disinterest, with no more knowledge of its intentions and plans than he would have of any flesh-and-blood player who sat there; and when that day came, he would have achieved a triumph no other player before him could ever claim!

He was so sure of himself, so confident that the triumph lay beyond the next move each time he made a move, that when it came at last his immediate feeling was no more than a comfortable gratification, and an expansive easing of all his nerves. Something like the feeling, he thought pleasurably, that a man gets after a hard day's work when he sinks into bed at night. Exactly that sort of feeling, in fact.

He had left the black position on the board perilously exposed through a bit of carelessness, and then in an effort to recover himself had moved the king's bishop in a neat defensive gesture that could cost white dear. When he looked up to study white's possible answer he saw White sitting there in the chair across the table, his fingertips gently touching each other, an ironic smile on his lips.

"Good," said White pleasantly. "Surprisingly good for you, George."

At this, George's sense of gratification vanished like a soap bubble flicked by a casual finger. It was not only the amiable insult conveyed by the words which nettled him; equally disturbing was the fact that White was utterly unlike the man that George had been prepared for. He had not expected White to resemble him as one twin resembles another, yet feature for feature the resemblance was so marked that White could have been the image that stared back at him from his shaving mirror each morning. An image, however, which, unlike George's, seemed invested with a power and arrogance that were quite overwhelming. Here, George felt with a touch of resentment, was no man to hunch over a desk computing dreary rows of figures, but one who with dash and brilliance made great decisions at the head of a long committee table. A man who thought a little of tomorrow, but much more of today and the good things it offered. And one who would always find the price for those good things.

That much was evident in the matchless cut of White's clothing, in the grace and strength of the lean, well-manicured hands, in the merciless yet merry glint in the eyes that looked back into George's. It was when he looked into those eyes that George found himself fumbling for some thought that seemed to lie just beyond him. The image of himself was reflected so clearly in those eyes; perhaps it was not an image. Perhaps . . .

He was jarred from his train of thought by White's moving a piece. "Your move," said White carelessly, "that is, if you want to continue the game."

George looked at the board and found his position still secure. "Why shouldn't I want to continue the game? Our positions . . ."

"For the moment are equal," White interposed promptly. "What you fail to consider is the long view: I am playing to win; you are playing only to keep from losing."

"It seems very much the same thing," argued George.

"But it is not," said White, "and the proof of that lies in the fact that I shall win this game, and every other game we ever play."

The effrontery of this staggered George. "Maróczy was a master who relied a good deal on defensive strategy," he protested, "and if you are familiar with his games . . ."

"I am exactly as well acquainted with Maróczy's games as you are," White observed, "and I do not hesitate to say that had we ever played, I should have beaten him every game as well."

George reddened. "You think very well of yourself, don't you," he said, and was surprised to see that instead of taking offense White was regarding him with a look of infinite pity.

"No," White said at last, "it is you who thinks well of me," and then as if he had just managed to see and avoid a neatly baited trap, he shook his head and drew his lips into a faintly sardonic grimace. "Your move," he said.

With an effort George put aside the vaguely troubling thoughts that clustered in his mind, and made the move. He made only a few after that when he saw clearly that he was hopelessly and ignominiously beaten. He was beaten a second game, and then another after that, and then in the fourth game made a despairing effort to change his tactics. On his eleventh move he saw a devastating opportunity to go on the offensive, hesitated, refused it, and was lost again. At that George grimly set about placing the pieces back in their case.

"You'll be back tomorrow?" he said, thoroughly put out at White's obvious amusement.

"If nothing prevents me."

George suddenly felt cold with fear. "What could prevent you?" he managed to say.

White picked up the white queen and revolved it slowly between his fingers. "Louise, perhaps. What if she decided not to let you indulge yourself in this fashion?"

"But why? Why should she? She's never minded up to now!"

"Louise, my good man, is an extremely stupid and petulant woman . . ."

"Now, that's uncalled for!" George said, stung to the quick.

"And," White continued as if he had not been interrupted at all, "she is the master here. Such people now and then like to affirm their mastery seemingly for no reason at all. Actually, such gestures are a sop to their vanity — as necessary to them as the air they breathe."

George mustered up all the courage and indignation at his command. "If those are your honest opinions," he said bravely, "I don't think you have the right to come to this house ever again."

On the heels of his words Louise stirred in her armchair and turned toward him. "George," she said briskly, "that's quite enough of that game for the evening. Don't you have anything better to do with your time?"

"I'm putting everything away now," George answered hastily, but when he reached for the chessman still gripped between his opponent's fingers, he saw White studying Louise with a look that made him quail. White turned to him then, and his eyes were like pieces of dark glass through which one can see the almost unbearable light of a searing flame.

"Yes," White said slowly. "For what she is and what she has done to you I hate her with a consuming hate. Knowing that, do you wish me to return?"

The eyes were not unkind when they looked at him now, George saw, and the feel of the chessman which White thrust into his hand was warm and reassuring. He hesitated, cleared his throat, then, "I'll see you tomorrow," he said at last.

White's lips drew into that familiar sardonic grimace. "Tomorrow, the next day, any time you want me," he said. "But it will always be the same. You will never beat me."

Time proved that White had not underestimated himself. And time itself, as George learned, was something far better measured by an infinite series of chess games, by the moves within a chess game, than by any such device as a calendar or clock. The discovery was a delightful one; even more delightful was the realization that the world around him, when viewed clearly, had come to resemble nothing so much as an object seen through the wrong end of a binocular. All those people who pushed and prodded and poked and demanded countless explanations and apologies could be seen as sharp and clear as ever but nicely reduced in perspective, so that it was obvious that no matter how close they came, they could never really touch one.

There was a single exception to this: Louise. Every evening the world would close in around the chessboard and the figure of White lounging in the chair on the other side of it. But in a corner of the room sat Louise over her knitting, and the air around her was charged with a mounting resentment which would now and then eddy around George in the form of querulous complaints and demands from which there was no escape.

"How *can* you spend every minute at that idiotic game!" she demanded. "Don't you have anything to talk to me about?" And, in fact, he did not, any more than he had since the very first years of his marriage, when he was taught that he had neither voice nor vote in running his home, that she did not care to hear about the people he worked with in his office, and that he could best keep to himself any reflections he had on some subject which was, by her own word, Highbrow.

"And how right she is," White had once taken pains to explain derisively. "If *you* had furnished your home it would be uncluttered and graceful, and Louise would feel awkward and out of place in it. If she comes to know the people you work with too well, she might have to befriend them, entertain them, set her blatant ignorance before them for judgment. No, far better under the circumstances that she dwell in her vacuum, away from unhappy judgments."

As it always could, White's manner drove George to furious resentment. "For a set of opinions pulled out of a cocked hat that sounds very plausible," he burst out. "Tell me, how do you happen to know so much about Louise?"

White looked at him through veiled eyes. "I know only what you know," he said. "No more and no less."

Such passages left George sore and wounded, but for the sake of the game he endured them. When Louise was silent, all the world retreated into unreality. Then the reality was the chessboard with White's hand hovering over it, mounting the attack, sweeping everything before it with a reckless brilliance that could only leave George admiring and dismayed.

In fact, if White had any weakness, George reflected mournfully, it was certainly not in his game, but rather in his deft and unpleasant way of turning each game into the occasion for a little discourse on the science of chess, a discourse which always wound up with some remarkably perverse and impudent reflections on George's personal affairs.

"You know that the way a man plays chess demonstrates that man's whole nature," White once remarked. "Knowing this, does it not strike you as significant that you always choose to play the defensive – and always lose?"

That sort of thing was bad enough, but White was at his most savage those times when Louise would intrude in a game: make some demand on George, or openly insist that he put away the board. Then White's jaw would set, and his eyes would flare with that terrible hate that always seemed to be smoldering in them when he regarded the woman.

Once when Louise had gone so far as to actually pick up a piece from the board and bang it back into the case, White came to his feet so swiftly and menacingly that George leaped up to forestall some rash action. Louise glared at him for that.

"You don't have to jump like that," she snapped; "I didn't break anything. But I can tell you, George Huneker: if you don't stop this nonsense I'll do it for you. I'll break every one of these things to bits if that's what it takes to make you act like a human being again!"

"Answer her!" said White. "Go ahead, why don't you answer her!" And caught between these two fires George could do no more than stand there and shake his head helplessly.

It was this episode, however, which marked a new turn in White's manner: the entrance of a sinister purposefulness thinly concealed in each word and phrase.

"If she knew how to play the game," he said, "she might respect it, and you would have nothing to fear."

"It so happens," George replied defensively, "that Louise is too busy for chess."

White turned in his chair to look at her, and then turned back with a grim smile. "She is knitting. And, it seems to me, she is always knitting. Would you call that being busy?"

"Wouldn't you?"

"No," said White, "I wouldn't. Penelope spent her years at the loom to keep off importunate suitors until her husband returned. Louise spends her years at knitting to keep off life until death comes. She takes no joy in what she does; one can see that with half an eye. But each stitch dropping off the ends of those needles brings her one instant nearer death, and, although she does not know it, she rejoices in it."

"And you make all that out of the mere fact that she won't play at chess?" cried George incredulously.

"Not alone chess," said White. "Life."

"And what do you mean by that word *life*, the way you use it?"

"Many things," said White. "The hunger to learn, the desire to create, the ability to feel vast emotions. Oh, many things."

"Many things, indeed," George scoffed. "Big words, that's all they are." But White only drew his lips into that sardonic grimace and said, "Very big. Far too big for Louise, I'm afraid," and then by moving a piece forced George to redirect his attention to the board.

It was as if White had discovered George's weak spot, and took a sadistic pleasure in returning to probe it again and again. And he played his conversational gambits as he made his moves at chess: cruelly, unerringly, always moving forward to the inescapable conclusion with a sort of flashing audacity. There were times when George, writhing helplessly, thought of asking him to drop the subject of Louise once and for all, but he could never bring himself to do so. Something in the recesses of George's mind warned him that these conversational fancies were as much a part of White as his capacity for chess, and that if George wanted him at all it would have to be on his own terms.

And George did want him, wanted him desperately, the more so on such an evening as that dreadful one when he came home to tell Louise that he would not be returning to his office for a while. He had not been discharged, of course, but there had been something about his taking a rest until he felt in shape again. Although, he hastily added in alarm as he saw Louise's face go slack and pale, he never felt better in his life.

In the scene that followed, with Louise standing before him and passionately telling him things about himself that left him sick and shaken, he found White's words pouring through his mind in a bitter torrent. It was only when Louise was sitting exhausted in her armchair, her eyes fixed blankly on the wall before her, her knitting in her lap to console her, and he was at his table setting up the pieces, that he could feel the brackish tide of his pain receding.

"And yet there is a solution for all this," White said softly, and turned his eyes toward Louise. "A remarkably simple solution when one comes to think of it."

George felt a chill run through him. "I don't care to hear about it," he said hoarsely.

"Have you ever noticed, George," White persisted, "that that piddling, hackneyed picture on the wall, set in that Baroque monstrosity of a frame that Louise admires so much, is exactly like a pathetic little fife trying to make itself heard over an orchestra that is playing its loudest?"

George indicated the chessboard. "You have the first move," he said.

"Oh, the game," White said. "The game can wait, George. For the moment I'd much prefer to think what this room – this whole fine house, in fact – could be if it were all yours, George. Yours alone."

"I'd rather get on with the game," George pleaded.

"There's another thing, George," White said slowly, and when he leaned forward George saw his own image again staring at him strangely from those eyes, "another fine thing to think of. If you were all alone in this room, in this house, why, there wouldn't be anyone to tell you when to stop playing chess. You could play morning, noon, and night, and all around to the next morning if you cared to!

"And that's not all, George. You can throw that picture out the window and hang something respectable on the wall: a few good prints, perhaps — nothing extravagant, mind you — but a few good ones that stir you a bit the first time you come into the room each day and see them.

"And recordings! I understand they're doing marvelous things with recordings today, George. Think of a whole room filled with them: opera, symphony, concerto, quartet — just take your pick and play them to your heart's content!"

The sight of his image in those eyes always coming nearer, the jubilant flow of words, the terrible meaning of those words set George's head reeling. He clapped his hands over his ears and shook his head frantically.

"You're mad!" he cried. "Stop it!" And then he discovered to his horror that even with his hands covering his ears he could hear White's voice as clearly and distinctly as ever.

"Is it the loneliness you're afraid of, George? But that's foolish. There are so many people who would be glad to be your friends, to talk to you, and, what's better, to listen to you. There are some who would even love you, if you chose."

"Loneliness?" George said unbelievingly. "Do you think it's loneliness I'm afraid of?"

"Then what is it?"

"You know as well as I," George said in a shaking voice, "what you're trying to lead me to. How could you expect me, expect any decent man, to be that cruel!"

White bared his teeth disdainfully. "Can you tell me anything more cruel than a weak and stupid woman whose only ambition in life was to marry a man infinitely superior to her and then cut him down to her level so that her weakness and stupidity could always be concealed?"

"You've got no right to talk about Louise like that!"

"I have every right," said White grimly, and somehow George knew in his heart that this was the dreadful truth. With a rising panic he clutched the edge of the table.

"I won't do it!" he said distractedly. "I'll never do it, do you understand!"

"But it will be done!" White said, and his voice was so naked with terrible decision that George looked up to see Louise coming toward the table with her sharp little footsteps. She stood over it, her mouth working angrily, and then through the confusion of his thoughts he heard her voice echoing the same words again and again. "You fool!" she was saying wildly. "It's this chess! I've had enough of it!" And suddenly she swept her hand over the board and dashed the pieces from it.

"No!" cried George, not at Louise's gesture, but at the sight of White standing before her, the heavy poker raised in his hand. "No!" George shouted again, and started up to block the fall of the poker, but knew even as he did so that it was too late.

Louise might have been dismayed at the untidy way her remains were deposited in the official basket; she would certainly have cried aloud (had she been in a condition to do so) at the unsightly scar on the polished woodwork made by the basket as it was dragged along the floor and borne out of the front door. Inspector Lund, however, merely closed the door casually behind the little cortege and turned back to the living room.

Obviously the Lieutenant had completed his interrogation of the quiet little man seated in the chair next to the chess table, and obviously the Lieutenant was not happy. He paced the center of the floor, studying his notes with a furrowed brow, while the little man watched him, silent and motionless.

"Well?" said Inspector Lund.

"Well," said the Lieutenant, "there's just one thing that doesn't tie in. From what I put together, here's a guy who's living his life all right, getting along fine, and all of a sudden he finds he's got another self, another personality. He's like a man split into two parts, you might say."

"Schizoid," remarked Inspector Lund. "That's not unusual."

"Maybe not," said the Lieutenant. "Anyhow, this other self is no good at all, and sure enough it winds up doing this killing."

"That all seems to tie in," said Inspector Lund. "What's the hitch?"

"Just one thing," the Lieutenant stated: "a matter of identity." He frowned at his notebook, and then turned to the little man in the chair next to the chess table. "What did you say your name was?" he demanded.

The little man drew his lips into a faintly sardonic grimace of rebuke. "Why, I've told you that so many times before, Lieutenant, surely you couldn't have forgotten it again." The little man smiled pleasantly. "My name is White."

The Ballad of Edward Bray

(The author cannot lay claim to any technical knowledge of chess, but he fancies that he understands the spirit of the game. He feels that, after the many poems on the Boat Race, a few bracing lines on the Inter-University Chess Match would be a welcome change.)

THIS IS THE BALLAD of Edward Bray,
    Captain of Catherine's, Cambridge Blue —
Oh, no one ever had just his way
    Of huffing a bishop with KB2.

The day breaks fine, and the evening brings
    A worthy foe in the Oxford man —
A great finesser with pawns and things,
    But quick in the loose when the game began.

The board was set, and the rivals tossed,
    But Fortune (alas!) was Oxford's friend.
"Tail" cried Edward, and Edward lost:
    So Oxford played from the fireplace end.

We hold our breath, for the game's begun —
    Oh, who so gallant as Edward Bray!
He's taken a bishop from KQ1
    And ruffed it just in the Cambridge way!

Then Oxford castles his QBKnight
    (He follows the old, old Oxford groove;
Though never a gambit saw the light
    That's able to cope with Edward's move.)

35

The game went on, and the game was fast,
  Oh, Oxford huffed and his King was crowned,
The exchange was lost, and a pawn was passed,
  And under the table a knight was found!

Then Oxford chuckled; but Edward swore,
  A horrible, horrible oath swore he;
And landed him one on the QB4,
  And followed it up with an RQ3.

Time was called; with an air of pride
  Up to his feet rose Edward Bray.
"Marker, what of the score?" he cried,
  "What of the battle I've won this day?"

The score was counted; and Bray had won
  By two in honours, and four by tricks,
And half of a bishop that came undone,
  And all of a bishop on KQ6.

            .   .   .   .   .

Then here's to Chess: and a cheer again
  For the man who fought on an April day
With never a thought of sordid gain!
  England's proud of you, Edward Bray!

by Kester Svendsen

Last Round

THE OLD MASTER LOOKED DOWN at the board and chessmen again, although he had seen their stiff pattern times out of mind. While the tournament director was speaking he could wait. And as he waited the old questions rose once more in his mind. Could this be it, the perfect game, the thing of beauty, the work of art? Could there come out of this tension of minds, this conflict of wits, anything more than victory and defeat? This unknowing search for secret beauty! What was the perfect game of chess? Was Capablanca right? Was it a draw, with the board exhausted of pieces? Was it a smashing victory? Was it a thing of small advantages multiplied into attrition?

The director's voice seeped into his reverie.

"Final round . . . Rolavsky the Russian champion leading with seven points . . . draws against Henderson and Zettler . . . then six straight wins."

The thought of a perfect game faded. Win? Could he even draw? Could he hold off the faultless Rolavsky, whose countrymen had for years pooled their incredibly patient testing of every defense to the Queen's Gambit and the Ruy Lopez?

"His opponent half a point behind . . . no one else close enough."

The Old Master looked up at the other playing areas roped off in the center of the ballroom. Epstein and Creech, poised, repeating a tableau older than memory. Batchelor, bushy-haired and nervous, glancing at tiny Zeitlin, prepared to play as if the title were balanced. The others farther away, still figures drawn sharply together over the subtlest challenge in their lives. The huge demonstration boards against the wall, runners and movers waiting to record the play in each game. The crowd, impatient for the director to finish and for this game to begin.

"Ten years since he won a tournament . . . his entry invited frankly as a sentimental gesture to the spirit of his long career — now his amazing comeback against eight of the world's best . . . world's

championship vacated by the death of Alekhine . . . assured of second place, he has already done better than the old Lasker at Moscow . . . can this grand old man of chess snatch a full point from his ninth and last opponent, the unbeatable Russian? . . . He needs a win, Rolavsky only a draw."

Could he win? He lingered a moment over what a win would mean. The cash prize. Exhibitions. Tours. New editions of a champion's works. Contracts for others. No more the poverty of a chessmaster's life, articles and annotations for short-lived journals, books that barely paid their way, lessons to sharkish amateurs who wanted only to beat each other. How many masters, having given their lives to the game, had died penniless, like Alekhine?

"Additional drama . . . youth and age . . . the only player in the world with a plus score against Rolavsky . . . that famous fifteen-move surprise win of his at Bitzer Lake ten years ago." Bitzer Lake! The Old Master looked at the board again and wondered how he should open this time. Queen's Gambit?

"Like his countryman Frank Marshall, he has never played to the score, but has always sought to make each game a work of art."

A Lopez? Had Rolavsky been saving a defense for the Lopez ever since that savage encounter at Bitzer Lake? Could he meet it cold as Capablanca did Marshall's at New York and smash it? What to play? King pawn or queen pawn?

The voice stopped. The director was at his table, starting his clock. Two hours for thirty moves. The photographers near his table poised themselves as he moved his arm. He lifted his eyes to Rolavsky's face and saw etched in it the sharp memory of that defeat at Bitzer Lake.

Suddenly he felt tired, remembering the dilemma in which he had spent himself so many times in fifty years. Play for a win or play for perfection? There rose against him the ghosts of a hundred games and a dozen tournaments lost because he could never decide which he wanted. The clock at his elbow ticked insistently. King pawn or queen pawn? And, as ever, in a corner of his mind, the same old question. Could this be it, the work of art? He thought of Kieseritzky, remembered only as the loser of that ever-famous *partie* to Anderssen.

Rolavsky twisted a little, and somewhere out of the thousands of games and hundreds of players in the old man's memory there stirred a spark. The immortal Lasker playing his fourth move at St. Petersburg. Bishop takes knight, most drawish of all the variations in the Lopez, and there was Lasker needing a win but playing bishop takes knight against Capablanca. Psychological chess. Capablanca sweating away at the thought of a new wrinkle. Lasker sitting like a stone. Rolavsky twitched again, and suddenly the Old Master wasn't tired any more. Conviction freshened him like wine. He felt again as at every game, before the first move. He smiled at Rolavsky – and moved his pawn to king four. Photographers' flashes sprang at him. The audience riffled forward as Rolavsky duplicated the move. With no hesitation, the Old Master moved his queen pawn beside his king pawn and listened for the buzz from the spectators.

"*Center Game! . . . Is he playing the Center Game? . . . Mieses used to try it . . . but the queen moves too soon . . . hasn't been played in a tournament since Tartakower tried it at Stockholm against Reshevsky . . . is he crazy? Rolavsky will smash it to bits.*"

There was no good way to decline the capture even if Rolavsky had wanted to, but the younger man seemed a little slow as he took the pawn. The old man caught his eye again, smiled again, pushed his queen's bishop's pawn forward a square, then leaned back and waited for the avalanche.

It came with a rush, as of collapse at a distance. Rolavsky half rose from his chair.

"*Danish Gambit? . . . Danish Gambit! . . . Two pawns . . . who can give Rolavsky two pawns, development or no development? . . . What does he think this is, a skittles game? . . . Danish . . . not in a tournament since Marshall drew one with Capa twenty years ago.*"

Rolavsky stared across the board, tight-lipped in contempt. Then he took the second pawn.

For a moment the old man's mind drifted back to other ballrooms and hotels, the Crystal Palace, chop houses and concessions, the thousand places where he had paused before a board and moved a pawn or knight. The simultaneous play where he walked forever within a horseshoe of tables – fifteen, fifty, a hundred sometimes – moving a piece or being waved by, ever returning and ever wondering with each move if somewhere, in some single play, even on a greasy board with clumsy pieces, he might pluck the secret. The thick smoke, the bad food, the hours of walking, the stale people behind the tables straining for a win or a draw against the master and playing on even though a queen or a couple of pieces down. He remembered, too, the glittering tournaments at Margate, Hastings, San Remo, Monte Carlo, with jeweled women and royalty looking over his shoulder. He lived again that moment at Breslau when Marshall plunged his queen into a nest of Lewitzky's pawns, and the spectators, caught up in the excitement of the most elegant move ever made, showered the table with gold pieces. Slowly he forced these memories from his mind and, as he looked out over the spectators, moved his bishop to queen bishop four.

The crowd stirred uneasily, waiting for Rolavsky to take the third pawn and then hang on through the attack. The Old Master wondered

a little too. Rolavsky always took the pawn in the Queen's Gambit, probably because it wasn't a gambit at all. In the Danish he had to take the
first and could take the second, according to the books. Schlechter had
always taken the third too. But how lately had Rolavsky played against
a Danish? He was taking too long, that young wizard. Now it came:
knight to king bishop three. Development. Playing safe. The old man
advanced his knight to king bishop three and tapped the clock, as after
every move.

Rolavsky studied the board a long time. Again the spectators shifted
about. A few moves more, thought the Old Master, and he would know
whether to hope for a draw or a win. With an edge of sudden fear he
remembered that Tchigorin had once lost a game in eight moves, Alapin
in five. He jerked his mind about and worried the chessmen as they
waited for his turn. But Rolavsky was plainly hesitating now, as if trying to recall the best line. Surely the pawn was not poisoned. Yet, one
piece out to White's two. Even before Rolavsky's fingers touched the
bishop, the Old Master moved it mentally to bishop four. There it rested,
and a surge of power flowed into his mind. His reply was obvious, but
he lingered over it a while, probing with his imagination the mind of his
antagonist, that mind crammed with encyclopedic knowledge of standard openings, hundreds of variations in the Queen's Pawn. Was it
shaken a little now, that fine machine? The crowd seemed to think so.
A half-caught whisper: *"Why didn't he take the pawn? . . . Why not?"*

Why not? Was Rolavsky thinking of Bitzer Lake and the thrust of
rage with which he had swept the pieces to the floor at the fifteenth
move? Now the Old Master lifted his knight and removed the Black
pawn at bishop three. Rolavsky moved pawn to queen three; and as the
old man castled, it was obvious that White had ample compensation
for the pawn sacrificed. Again the muttering. *"Seven moves and Rolavsky on the defensive . . . unheard of . . . a Danish Gambit!"*

After long thought the Russian castled, and now the Old Master felt
himself moving into that strange trance of chess intuition. Attack.
Tempt a weakness. A combination, with the pieces piling up at one
spot, cleansing the board of each other's presence. Lines of play ran
through his head. The pieces on the board swirled into patterns, blended,
and stiffened into place eight or ten moves on. Tempt a weakness. But
would Rolavsky move his pawn? His whole queen side undeveloped?
The Old Master put his hand to the king's knight and a small sigh went
up from the spectators. *"One move . . . a single tempo . . . and Rolavsky's even . . . why didn't he pin the knight?"* A moment's hesitation, and then he placed the knight at knight five. There. Now would
Rolavsky move the pawn? The precisionist wouldn't. The arrogant refuter
of gambits would. Did there linger still a trace of something from the

third move? Would this Russian weaken? Rook and pawn, did he think, for bishop and knight?

Rolavsky studied the position almost interminably. Then he pushed his pawn to king rook three – then dropped his hand as if burnt, as if too late he had seen beneath the surface of the board a steady fire. And now the crowd was quiet, waiting, and there began to break into the Old Master's brain a long shaft of light. A combination, the moves tumbling over one another with sweet promise. A game of equilibrium, a perfect tension of pieces, everything held in suspense by a perpetual check from Black, a fantasy of eternal motion caught in the flowing lines of a knight's pendulum move. The perfect game of chess! He could force Rolavsky to play for a draw. Eagerly the Old Master took the bishop's pawn with his knight and waited for Rolavsky to retake with the rook. The combination was irresistible. But would Rolavsky see the knight check he himself would have to give, five moves later, to hold the draw? Would he take the draw that would give him the championship of the world?

Rolavsky retook with the rook, and the old man moved the king pawn down. The crowd, sensing something in the quick replies after so long a series of waits, rippled with comment. *"Why didn't he retake with the bishop? . . . If pawn takes pawn, the queen is lost . . . what's the old man after? . . . No, the rook is pinned . . . it won't run away."* At last Rolavsky switched the threatened knight to knight five. The Old Master moved the pawn to king six and found himself praying that Rolavsky would not take it with the bishop. The continuation darkened his mind: he takes with his bishop, I'll take with mine; he threatens mate, queen to rook five; I take the rook and check; he takes the bishop with the king; I check at bishop three with the queen; he goes to the knight square, then pawn to king rook three and he's lost. But lost in a brutal way after a blunt struggle. No charm there, no beauty, only a win. For a moment the Old Master cursed this insane undesire to win that had cost him so many a tournament; and he hoped that Rolavsky would take with the bishop. The pull of the title spun the chessboard before him as he thought of the fifty years he had divided his heart between fortune and perfection. He searched Rolavsky's face as the clock ticked off minutes. Two hours for thirty moves. Only a third of them made, and Rolavsky still looking at the board. Too long.

But now Rolavsky was moving his queen, and the old man saw it glide to rook five. The dreaded and then hoped-for continuation vanished from his mind and in its place came a sense of lightness and power. The pattern was forming. The tensions, threat and counterthreat, were moving toward that poetry of perpetual motion he had anticipated. He took the rook with his pawn. The Black king moved under it. He played his bishop to bishop four, covering the mate at rook two. The clock ticked as he listened for the beating of Rolavsky's heart and in a minute or two they seemed to focus, rising in tempo until at thunder pitch the Russian pulled away the bishop's pawn and dropped his knight on the square. The old man moved his queen to king two. The perfect game! He ran through the moves. Black knight to knight five, check. White king to the rook square. Black checking again with the knight. How tense the pieces looked! What a balance between White's accumulated force and the gyrations of the Black knight!

Rolavsky was sweating now, and the crowd was quiet. Twice the Russian's hand strayed to the board and twice he withdrew it. The old man went through the moves again. Then he looked up again from his dream to see in Rolavsky's eyes something that wrenched him. Bitzer Lake! The eagerness for revenge across the board shook him. Something in the game crumpled, and with it something in the old man's mind.

Rolavsky was bending over the board, demanding a win of his pieces. He didn't want a draw. The crowd jabbered, unmindful of frowns from the director, piecing out the perpetual check.

"Sure it's a perpetual . . . knight just moves back and forth . . . old man must be crazy . . . giving the championship away . . . why doesn't Rolavsky move?"

At last Rolavsky did, knight to knight five, discovering check. The Old Master pushed his king aside, and with it the illusion of fifty years. Rolavsky could check once more, demonstrate the perpetual to the referee, and then sweep the pieces into confusion as he rose. The Old Master waited.

But Rolavsky did not check. Slowly the old man's eyes moved from Rolavsky's face to the silent chessmen. They blurred; then the Russian moved — bishop to queen two.

As he stared at the move, the Old Master recognized a new defeat. There was no perpetual check. There never had been. Blindness! As if seeing the position for the first time, he painfully picked over the moves,

resisting each pull into the combination that deluded him. Had Rolavsky checked with the knight, Black would have lost. Knight checks, rook
takes knight, and if Black retakes, White mates at king eight. The Black
bishop had to move to queen two to protect the mating square. The old
man looked up again; and as he stretched his hand to the board, he
sensed rather than saw something else at the edge of Rolavsky's eyes.
He stopped his hand, and the gesture released the breath of the crowd
in a quiet sigh.

Once more he searched the position, wondering why he continued,
deaf to the reawakened swell of flurry beyond the ropes. Suddenly he
saw it, and everything else faded except the patterns of force formed by
the pieces as they moved into their predestined places. Again the testing
of each move, racked by the error of the first delusion, soothed by what
he saw unfolding on the board. Finally he pulled his queen rook to king
square. Rolavsky hurried his other knight to queen bishop three. And
now it was as if some inevitable force suddenly set in motion were lift-
ing the game away from both players. Or perhaps the old man had
realized that Rolavsky was but a chess piece too, to be moved and used.
Whatever the reason, only the moves remained. The Old Master traced
the final position in his mind. The rooks, side by side, one checking; the
other covering an escape square. The bishops, one checking, the other
covering an escape square. The rook on white and the bishop on black,
checking together, one from afar, the other only a diamond from the
Black king.

Here . . . here, this was it. There could be no mistake now. Out
of defeat, victory. Out of death, life. Out of the tangled emotions of this
fleeting game a beauty to endure forever. Those fifty tortured years of
his had not been in vain after all. This was perfection, a work of art,
an abstraction of force into an eternal tension utterly withdrawn from
its creators, from the moment, from the unmoved chessboard itself. A
superb sequence of power begun by the most daring stroke of all chess-
dom, the sacrifice of the most powerful piece, the queen. No . . . no,
not one queen but two! One queen, combiner of rook and bishop in its
motion, to die; from its sacrifice to come a new queen, itself to die still-
born, then the mate to be delivered by its divided functions, by bishop
and rook. Surely, the old man told himself, there was no greater beauty
than this. The victory was his. He had but to take it. With trembling
fingers he lifted his queen, moved it steadily down the file to king eight.

Someone in the crowd gabbled in astonishment. "*His queen? . . .
He's crazy . . . that square's twice covered . . . I can't see . . . no,
Rolavsky's time is almost gone . . . it's a trick . . . Bitzer Lake . . .
remember Bitzer Lake!*"

Rolavsky, with a wild look at the clock, swept the queen from the board with his rook. The old man took the rook, queening the pawn with the check. Rolavsky's hand faltered, moved again, and the bishop captured the second queen. Then with a loving movement, a long caressing gesture, itself somehow a part of the final position, the Old Master drew his bishop up to the queen pawn, removed it, left the bishop, and whispered, smiling gently above the file of the unmasked rook, a single word.

"Mate."

by J. L. Synge

Noblesse Oblige

◻◻◻ ONE EVENING Bloggs and Snogs were having a game of chess.
◻◻◻ They were well matched and it was an exciting game of thrust
and counterthrust. But luck turned against Snogs. He found himself
cornered, with checkmate only a few moves off. His bishops were lost.
He had his knights left, but at this moment they seemed useless. Immediate defeat stared him in the face.

Meanwhile Bloggs was glancing at his opponent, with elation at
his coming victory politely suppressed; for Bloggs was a gentleman of
the finest type. He saw Snogs move his hand towards one of his knights
and he wondered what move was coming. Then, to the amazement of
Bloggs, Snogs gave his knight a *bishop's* move on to the square where
Bloggs's queen stood. Snogs removed the queen from the board and
glanced up at Bloggs.

"That was a nice attack of yours, old man," he said. "Sorry to have
to spoil it like that."

Bloggs was taken aback. "Look here, old chap," he said to Snogs,
"you've made a bad mistake there. You moved your knight as if it were
a bishop!"

"I know I did," replied Snogs. "I had to do it; the situation was
getting too hot for me. After all," he went on, leaning back and lighting
a cigarette, "the moves in chess are just conventions. These chess pieces
are nothing but chunks of ivory. I make them do what I want them to
do. Why, once I was in a very bad fix, and I did this with my queen."
He took up his queen and moved it round the board in a circle. Then he
sat quietly smiling and puffing his cigarette.

Bloggs stared at him for a moment; then he got up and went out
of the room. When they met in the street two days later, Bloggs passed
with his head in the air.

That happened in 1930. In 1940 Bloggs was in London. As the
German bombers droned overhead, Bloggs sat playing his favourite game

with a friend (not Snogs of course). A bomb fell near by and broke the window. A tiny fragment of incendiary material, burning fiercely, flew in through the broken window and alighted on the chess board.

At that moment Bloggs had his hand on one of his knights and was about to make a move. He looked at the square on the chess board where the tiny fragment was burning. This square was *not* a knight's move away. If only his knight were a bishop, he could bring it down on the fragment and extinguish it!

The temptation was terrific. But suddenly he recalled the face of Snogs. Resolutely he executed the knight's move he had originally planned. The board burst into flames, the table caught fire and the whole room was consumed. Poor Bloggs was burned to death, and nothing now remains of him but the memory of a gentleman who always played the game.

The King's Own or Tumble Weed Opening

What is known as the Tumble Weed opening, so dubbed by E. P. Sharp, of Lincoln, Nebraska, chess editor of the State Journal, has received considerable vogue out West. It is also known as the King's Own opening, and was invented by the late W. H. K. Pollock, Irish champion, in the early nineties, when on this side of the Atlantic. Under the heading, "Queer Moves in Chess," Mrs. F. F. Rowland, editor of Pollock Memories, quoting the Baltimore News, of which Pollock was the chess editor for a number of years, explains the origin of this curious and extremely interesting debut, which outdoes even the Steinitz Gambit, as follows:

"Two or three years ago I showed Babson, the renowned problemist, a new opening which I had invented on the street. I called it the 'King's Own Gambit.' It was 1 P - K4, P - K4; 2 P - KB4, P x P; 3 K - B2! 'I'll try it on Short' (a strong player with whom he had had little success), said he, and he won eleven games straight at the opening."

This opening has recently been immortalized by an unknown bard, who has written a catchy poem around a game opened in this wise — a truly remarkable game and, in a way, a gem. The poem was sent to the St. Louis Globe-Democrat by Link Burnham, of Urbana, Ohio, with the remark: "I do not know where it came from or whether it has ever been published. A friend of mine sent it to me from Seattle, Wash." Mr. Foster, the chess editor of the Globe-Democrat, adds the comment: "The oddity of the opening and the plausibility of the move, as well as the jingle and rhyme, make the games and variations very readable — fine examples of the Tumble Weed Opening."

The text of the poem in question is appended herewith:

In Seattle, last summer, with nothing to do,
I went to the Chess Club, and there met a Jew
From New Orleans, a rabbi — no matter what name —
Perhaps you have met him, or heard of the same;

He's a player of note, and his problems in chess
Get some mighty good players in an awful bad mess.

He asked: "Do you play, sir?" I said: "Just a little."
"Well, sit you down here, and let's have a skittle."
He glanced round the room: "I judge by the looks
That you players here are not up in the books."
I replied with a laugh, and a gentle a-hem,
"No, we long, long ago got far beyond them."
With a shrug of his shoulders, the Whites he gave me,
"Make your opening," he said, "and we will soon see."
I played P to K's fourth, which he seemed to approve,
And replied with the same; 'twas a very good move.
The King's Bishop's Pawn I put out with some force,
And he took it at once, as a matter of course.
But judge the expression that came o'er his face
When I played out my King to K. B.'s second place.
"Oh, well," said the rabbi, "that looks a bit hazy,
If I'm any judge, the King's Gambit's gone crazy."
So he out with his Queen and he checked at R's five,
With the evident purpose to flay me alive.
With a soft, gentle push I interposed Pawn,
He took it with his, in a moment 'twas gone.
He thundered out "check" in such stentorian tones,
That it gave me the shivers a quake in the bones;
But I slipped the King over to Kt's 2d square,
Then he took my Rook's Pawn with his, and said "there,
You must take that with your Rook, and then it is plain
That my Queen takes the other one out in the main;
And with no Pawns on King's side, I must say I can't see
How you can prevent me Queening my three —
Should the game ever get to the point where they're needed."
"I don't think it will," I replied. But he heeded
Me not; and when he captured my little King's P
I brought out my Knight to the King's Bishop's three;
Next came Pawn to Queen's four, to free up his house,
I replied with my Queen's Knight, attacking his spouse,
Which he played to Kt's third, giving check to my King,
At the same time remarking "I'm on to this thing."
The King to Rook's square I quietly played,
And Q B to Kt's fifth he likewise essayed.
Not wishing that harm should come to my "hoss,"
I transferred King's Rook, from his second, across

To Kt's 2. He now thought to win at a canter,
So he took up his Queen, and at Rook's 4, instanter
He put her and checked; but I moved to Kt's square,
And he, little dreaming of the trap that was there,
Whipped off my poor Kt, as he laughingly said,
"That horse is of no use, so off comes his head."
My knight, he is gone — Oh, alas, 'tis too true,
But I'll interpose Bishop, and see what he'll do
"Well, if you want me to take all your pieces and done,
Shove 'em out and I'll capture them, every darned one."
So he grabbed the poor prelate at once by the neck,
And I somewhat surprised him with RxB, check.
Not till then did the truth dawn clear on his brain,
And he tried hard to save his fair Queen, but in vain.

"Now what kind of a game do you say you call that?"
"The KING'S OWN," I replied, "and I'll bet you a hat
You can't find it in any or all the chess books
You have studied," and I judged from his looks
That he somewhat doubted when I told him the same
Was a notion of Pollock's, who gave it that name.

The Man Who Sidetracked His Brains

"I KNEW A CASE," said the financier, "of a man with the most brilliant brains, who had finance at his finger tips.

"He was a man called Smoggs, utterly unknown of course. And I say 'of course,' because he never used his brains; or rather I should say he never made any use of them, which can be quite a different thing. He just sidetracked them, ran them down a siding that led nowhere; and he might have been as big a financier as any of us.

"Do you know what he did? Sit down and I'll tell you. He went and played chess. All the intellect that might have controlled, well, more than I can tell you, he wasted over a chessboard.

"It came gradually at first; he used to play chess with a man during the luncheon hour, when he and I both worked for the same firm. And after a while he began to beat the fellow, which he never could do at first.

"Then he joined a chess club, and some kind of fascination seemed to come over him; something like drink, or more like poetry or music; but, as I was never addicted to any of the three, I can't say. Anyway it completely got hold of him and he began to lose interest in things.

"He became a good player, there was no doubt of that, and he won a good many prizes. And the value of all the prizes he won in his life would have added up to about a hundred dollars. I've made a thousand times as much in an hour. And more than once. But that is all he ever got out of playing chess.

"Why! That man could have handled millions. He did dabble a bit in finance, as I dabbled a bit in chess; in fact we started together in the same firm, as I told you; but we both left our dabblings and went our different ways.

"And his way led nowhere. He could have done it though; he could have been a financier. They say it's no harder than chess, though chess leads to nothing. I never saw such brains so wasted."

"Well," said the warder, "I can't sit listening to you all day, but I see your point and I agree with it. There are men like that. It's a pity. but there are men just like it."

He locked the financier up for the night, and hurried back to his work.

by Richard Garnett

The Rewards of Industry

▢▢▢
▢▢▢ IN CHINA, under the Tang dynasty, early in the seventh century of the Christian era, lived a learned and virtuous, but poor mandarin who had three sons, Fu-su, Tu-sin, and Wang-li. Fu-su and Tu-sin were young men of active minds, always laboring to find out something new and useful. Wang-li was clever too, but only in games of skill, in which he attained great proficiency.

Fu-su and Tu-sin continually talked to each other of the wonderful inventions they would make when they arrived at man's estate, and of the wealth and renown they promised themselves thereby. Their conversation seldom reached the ears of Wang-li, for he rarely lifted his eyes from the chessboard on which he solved his problems. But their father was more attentive, and one day he said:

"I fear, my sons, that among your multifarious pursuits and studies you must have omitted to include that of the laws of your country, or you would have learned that fortune is not to be acquired by the means which you have proposed to yourselves."

"How so, Father?" asked they.

"It hath been justly deemed by our ancestors," said the old man, "that the reverence due to the great men who are worshiped in our temples, by reason of our indebtedness to them for the arts of life, could not but become impaired if their posterity were suffered to eclipse their fame by new discoveries, or presumptuously amend what might appear imperfect in their productions. It is therefore, by an edict of the Emperor Suen, forbidden to invent anything; and by a statute of the Emperor Wu-chi it is further provided that nothing hitherto invented shall be improved. My predecessor in the small office I hold was deprived of it for saying that in his judgment money ought to be made round instead of square, and I have myself run risk of my life for seeking to combine a small file with a pair of tweezers."

"If this is the case," said the young men, "our fatherland is not

51

the place for us." And they embraced their father and departed. Of their brother Wang-li they took no farewell, inasmuch as he was absorbed in a chess problem. Before separating, they agreed to meet on the same spot after thirty years, with the treasure which they doubted not to have acquired by the exercise of their inventive faculties in foreign lands. They further covenanted that if either had missed his reward the other should share his possessions with him.

Fu-su repaired to the artists, who cut out characters in blocks of hard wood, to the end that books might be printed from the same. When he had fathomed their mystery he betook himself to a brass founder, and learned how to cast in metal. He then sought a learned man who had traveled much, and made himself acquainted with the Greek, Persian, and Arabic languages. Then he cast a number of Greek characters in type, and putting them into a bag and providing himself with some wooden letter tablets of his own carving, he departed to seek his fortune. After innumerable hardships and perils he arrived in the land of Persia, and inquired for the great king.

"The great king is dead," they told him, "and his head is entirely separated from his body. There is now no king in Persia, great or small."

"Where shall I find another great king?" demanded he.

"In the city of Alexandria," replied they, "where the Commander of the Faithful is busy introducing the religion of the Prophet."

Fu-su passed to Alexandria, carrying his types and tablets.

As he entered the gates he remarked an enormous cloud of smoke, which seemed to darken the whole city. Before he could inquire the reason, the guard arrested him as a stranger, and conducted him to the presence of the Caliph Omar.

"Know, O Caliph," said Fu-su, "that my countrymen are at once the wisest of mankind and the stupidest. They have invented an art for the preservation of letters and the diffusion of knowledge, which the sages of Greece and India never knew, but they have not learned to take, and they refuse to be taught how to take, the one little step further necessary to render it generally profitable to mankind."

And producing his tablets and types, he explained to the Caliph the entire mystery of the art of printing.

"Thou seemest to be ignorant," said Omar, "that we have but yesterday condemned and excommunicated all books, and banished the same from the face of the earth, seeing that they contain either that which is contrary to the Koran, in which case they are impious, or that which is agreeable to the Koran, in which case they are superfluous. Thou art further unaware, as it would seem, that the smoke which shrouds the city proceeds from the library of the unbelievers, consumed by our orders. It will be meet to burn thee along with it."

"O Commander of the Faithful," said an officer, "of a surety the last scroll of the accursed ceased to flame even as this infidel entered the city."

"If it be so," said Omar, "we will not burn him, seeing that we have taken away from him the occasion to sin. Yet shall he swallow these little brass amulets of his, at the rate of one a day, and then be banished from the country."

The sentence was executed, and Fu-su was happy that the Court physician condescended to accept his little property in exchange for emetics.

He begged his way slowly and painfully back to China, and arrived at the covenanted spot at the expiration of the thirtieth year. His father's modest dwelling had disappeared, and in its place stood a magnificent mansion, around which stretched a park with pavilions, canals, willow trees, golden pheasants, and little bridges.

"Tu-sin has surely made his fortune," thought he, "and he will not refuse to share it with me agreeably to our covenant."

As he thus reflected he heard a voice at his elbow, and turning round perceived that one in a more wretched plight than himself was asking alms of him. It was Tu-sin.

The brothers embraced with many tears, and after Tu-sin had learned Fu-su's history, he proceeded to recount his own.

"I repaired," said he, "to those who know the secret of the grains termed firedust, which Suen has not been able to prevent us from inventing, but of which Wu-chi has taken care that we shall make no use, save only for fireworks. Having learned their mystery I deposited a certain portion of this firedust in hollow tubes which I had constructed of iron and brass, and upon it I further laid leaden balls of a size corresponding to the hollow of the tubes. I then found that by applying a light to the firedust at one end of the tube I could send the ball out at the other with such force that it penetrated the cuirasses of three warriors at once. I filled a barrel with the dust, and concealing it and the tubes under carpets which I laid upon the backs of oxen, I set out to the city of Constantinople. I will not at present relate my adventures on the journey. Suffice it that I arrived at last half dead from fatigue and hardship, and destitute of everything except my merchandise. By bribing an officer with my carpets I was admitted to have speech with the Emperor. I found him busily studying a problem in chess.

"I told him that I had discovered a secret which would make him the master of the world, and in particular would help him to drive away the Saracens who threatened his empire with destruction.

" 'Thou must perceive,' he said, 'that I cannot possibly attend to thee until I have solved this problem. Yet, lest any should say that the Emperor neglects his duties, absorbed in idle amusement, I will refer thy invention to the chief armorers of my capital.' And he gave me a letter to the armorers, and returned to his problem. And as I quitted the palace bearing the missive, I came upon a great procession. Horsemen and running footmen, musicians, heralds, and banner-bearers surrounded a Chinaman who sat in the attitude of Fo under a golden umbrella upon a richly caparisoned elephant, his pigtail plaited with yellow roses. And the musicians blew and clashed, and the standard-bearers waved their ensigns, and the heralds proclaimed, 'Thus shall it be done to the man whom the Emperor delights to honor.' And unless I was very greatly mistaken, the face of the Chinaman was the face of our brother Wang-li.

"At another time I would have striven to find what this might mean, but my impatience was great, as also my need and hunger. I sought the chief armorers, and with great trouble brought them all together to give me audience. I produced my tube and firedust, and sent my balls with ease through the best armor they could set before me.

" 'Who will want breastplates now?' cried the chief breastplate maker.

" 'Or helmets?' exclaimed one who made armor for the head.

" 'I would not have taken fifty bezants for that shield, and what good is it now?' said the head of the shield trade.

" 'My swords will be of less account,' said a swordsmith.

" 'My arrows of none,' lamented an arrow maker.

" ' 'Tis villainy,' cried one.

" ' 'Tis magic,' shouted another.

" ' 'Tis illusion, as I'm an honest tradesman,' roared a third, and put his integrity to the proof by thrusting a hot iron bar into my barrel. All present rose up in company with the roof of the building, and all perished, except myself, who escaped with the loss of my hair and skin. A fire broke out on the spot, and consumed one third of the city of Constantinople.

"I was lying on a prison bed some time afterward, partly recovered of my hurts, dolefully listening to a dispute between two of my guards as to whether I ought to be burned or buried alive, when the Imperial order for my disposal came down. The jailers received it with humility, and read 'Kick him out of the city.' Marveling at the mildness of the punishment, they nevertheless executed it with so much zeal that I flew into the middle of the Bosporus, where I was picked up by a fishing vessel and landed on the Asiatic coast, whence I have begged my way home. I now propose that we appeal to the pity of the owner of this splendid mansion, who may compassionate us on hearing that we were reared in the cottage which has been pulled down to make room for his palace."

They entered the gates, walked timidly up to the house, and prepared to fall at the feet of the master, but did not, for ere they could do so they recognized their brother Wang-li.

It took Wang-li some time to recognize them, but when at length he knew them, he hastened to provide for their every want. When they had well eaten and drunk, and had been clad in robes of honor, they imparted their histories, and asked for his.

"My brothers," said Wang-li, "the noble game of chess, which was happily invented long before the time of the Emperor Suen, was followed by me solely for its pleasure, and I dreamed not of acquiring wealth by its pursuit until I casually heard one day that it was entirely unknown to the people of the West. Even then I thought not of gaining money, but conceived so deep a compassion for those forlorn barbarians that I felt I could know no rest until I should have enlightened them. I accordingly proceeded to the city of Constantinople and was received as a messenger from heaven. To such effect did I labor that ere long the Emperor and his officers of state thought of nothing else but playing chess all day and night, and the empire fell into entire confusion, and the Saracens mightily prevailed. In consideration of these services the Emperor was pleased to bestow those distinguished honors upon me which thou didst witness at his palace gate, dear brother.

"After, however, the fire which was occasioned through thy instrumentality, though in no respect by thy fault, the people murmured, and taxed the Emperor with seeking to destroy his capital in league with a foreign sorcerer, meaning thee. Ere long the chief officers conspired and entered the Emperor's apartment, purposing to dethrone him, but he declared that he would in nowise abdicate until he had finished the game of chess he was then playing with me. They looked on, grew interested, began to dispute with one another respecting the moves, and while they wrangled loyal officers entered and made them all captive. This greatly augmented my credit with the Emperor, which was even increased when shortly afterward I played with the Saracen admiral blockading the Hellespont, and won of him forty corn ships, which turned the dearth of the city into plenty.

"The Emperor bade me choose any favor I would, but I said his liberality had left me nothing to ask for except the life of a poor countryman of mine who I had heard was in prison for burning the city. The Emperor bade me write his sentence with my own hand. Had I known that it was thou, Tu-sin, believe me I had shown more consideration for thy person. At length I departed for my native land, loaded with wealth, and traveling most comfortably by relays of swift dromedaries.

I returned hither, bought our father's cottage, and on its site erected this palace, where I dwell meditating on the problems of chess players and the precepts of the sages, and persuaded that a little thing which the world is willing to receive is better than a great thing which it hath not yet learned to value aright. For the world is a big child, and chooses amusement before instruction."

"Call you chess an amusement?" asked his brothers.

by Stephen Leacock

Pawn to King's Four

There is no readier escape from the ills of life than in a game of chess.
— FRANCIS BACON, AND EGGS

"PAWN TO KING'S FOUR," I said as I sat down to the chess table.

"Pawn to King's Four, eh?" said Letherby, squaring himself comfortably to the old oak table, his elbows on its wide margin, his attitude that of the veteran player. "Pawn to King's Four," he repeated. "Aha, let's see!"

It's the first and oldest move in chess, but from the way Letherby said it you'd think it was as new as yesterday . . . Chess players are like that . . . "Pawn to King's Four," he repeated. "You don't mind if I take a bit of a think over it?"

"No, no," I said, "not at all. Play as slowly as you like. I want to get a good look round this wonderful room."

It was the first time I had ever been in the Long Room of the Chess Club – and I sat entranced with the charm and silence of the long wainscotted room – its soft light, the blue tobacco smoke rising to the ceiling – the open grate fires burning – the spaced-out tables, the players with bent heads, unheeding our entry and our presence . . . all silent except here and there a little murmur of conversation, that rose only to hush again.

"Pawn to King's Four," repeated Letherby, "let me see!"

It was, I say, my first visit to the Chess Club; indeed I had never known where it was except that it was somewhere down town, right in the heart of the city, among the big buildings. Nor did I know Letherby himself very well, though I had always understood he was a chess player. He looked like one. He had the long, still face, the unmoving eyes, the leathery, indoor complexion that marks the habitual chess player anywhere.

So, quite naturally, when Letherby heard that I played chess he

57

invited me to come round some night to the Chess Club. . . . "I didn't know you played," he said. "You don't look like a chess player — I beg your pardon, I didn't mean to be rude."

So there we were at the table. The Chess Club, as I found, was right down town, right beside the New Commercial Hotel; in fact, we met by agreement in the rotunda of the hotel . . . a strange contrast — the noise, the lights, the racket of the big rotunda, the crowding people, the call of the bellboys — and this unknown haven of peace and silence, somewhere just close above and beside it.

I have little sense of location and direction so I can't say just how you get to the Club — up a few floors in the elevator and along a corridor (I think you must pass out of the building here) and then up a queer little flight of stairs, up another little stairway and with that all at once you come through a little door, a sort of end-corner door in the room and there you are in the Long Room. . . .

"Pawn to King's Four," said Letherby, decided at last, moving the piece forward. . . . "I thought for a minute of opening on the Queen's side, but I guess not."

All chess players think of opening on the Queen's side but never do. Life ends too soon.

"Knight to Bishop's Three," I said.

"Knight to Bishop's Three, aha!" exclaimed Letherby, "oho!" and went into a profound study. . . . It's the second oldest move in chess; it was old three thousand years ago in Persepolis . . . but to the real chess player it still has all the wings of the morning.

So I could look around again, still fascinated with the room.

"It's a beautiful room, Letherby," I said.

"It is," he answered, his eyes on the board, "yes . . . yes . . . It's really part of the old Roslyn House that they knocked down to make the New Commercial. . . . It was made of a corridor and a string of bedrooms turned into one big room. That's where it got the old wainscotting and those old-fashioned grate fires."

I had noticed them, of course, at once — the old-fashioned grates, built flat into the wall, the coal bulging and glowing behind bars, with black marble at the side and black marble for the mantel above. . . . There were three of them, one at the side, just near us, one down the end. . . . But from none of them came noise or crackle — just a steady warm glow. Beside the old-fashioned grate stood the long tongs, and the old-fashioned poker with the heavy square head that went with it.

"Pawn to Queen's Third," said Letherby.

Nor in all the room was there a single touch of equipment that was less than of fifty years ago, a memory of a half century. . . . Even the swinging doors, paneled with Russian leather, the main entrance on the right hand at the furthest end, swung soundlessly, on their hinges as each noiseless member entered with a murmured greeting.

"Your move," said Letherby. "Bishop to Bishop's Four? Right."
. . . Most attractive of all, perhaps, was a little railed-in place at the side near the fireplace, all done in old oak . . . something between a bar and a confessional, with coffee over low blue flames, and immaculate glasses on shelves . . . lemons in a bag. . . . Round it moved a waiter, in a dinner jacket, the quietest, most unobtrusive waiter one ever saw . . . coffee to this table . . . cigars to that . . . silent work with lemons behind the rails . . . a waiter who seemed to know what the members wanted without their asking. . . . This must have been so, for he came over to our table presently and set down long glasses of Madeira — so old, so brown, so aromatic that there seemed to go up from it with the smoke clouds a vision of the sunny vineyards beside Funchal. . . . Such at least were the fancies that my mind began to weave around this enchanted place. . . . And the waiter, too, I felt there must be some strange romance about him; no one could have a face so mild, yet with the stamp of tragedy upon it. . . .

I must say — in fact, I said to Letherby — I felt I'd like to join the club, if I could. He said, oh, yes, they took in new members. One came in only three years ago.

"Queen's Knight to Bishop's Third," said Letherby with a deep sigh. I knew he had been thinking of something that he daren't risk. All chess is one long regret.

We played on like that for — it must have been half an hour — anyway we played four moves each. To me, of course, the peace and quiet of the room was treat enough . . . but to Letherby, as I could see, the thing was not a sensation of peace but a growing excitement, nothing still or quiet about it; a rush, struggle — he knew that I meant to strike in on the King's side. Fool! he was thinking, that he hadn't advanced the Queen's Pawn another square . . . he had blocked his Bishop and couldn't Castle. . . . You know, if you are a chess player, the desperate feeling that comes with a blocked Bishop. . . . Look down any chess room for a man whose hands are clenched and you'll know that he can't Castle.

So it was not still life for Letherby, and for me, perhaps after a while I began to feel that it was perhaps just a little *too* still. . . . The players moved so little . . . they spoke so seldom, and so low . . . their heads so gray under the light . . . especially, I noticed, a little group at tables in the left-hand corner.

"They don't seem to talk much there," I said.

"No," Letherby answered without even turning his head, "they're blind. Pawn to Queen's Four."

Blind! Why, of course. Why not? Blind people, I realized, play chess as easily as any other people when they use little pegged boards for it. . . . Now that I looked I could see — the aged fingers lingering and rambling on the little pegs.

"You take the Pawn?" said Letherby.

"Yes," I said and went on thinking about the blind people . . . and how quiet they all were. . . . I began to recollect a play that was once in New York — people on a steamer wasn't it? People standing at a bar . . . and you realized presently they were all dead. . . . It was a silly idea, but somehow the Long Room began to seem like that . . . at intervals I could even hear the ticking of the clock on the mantel.

I was glad when the waiter came with a second glass of Madeira. It warmed one up. . . .

"That man seem's a wonderful waiter," I said.

"Fred?" said Letherby. "Oh, yes, he certainly is. . . . He looks after everything — he's devoted to the club."

"Been here long?"

"Bishop to Bishop's Four," said Letherby. . . . He didn't speak for a little while. Then he said, "Why practically all his life — except, poor fellow, he had a kind of tragic experience. He put in ten years in jail."

"For what?" I asked, horrified.

"For murder," said Letherby.

"For murder?"

"Yes," repeated Letherby, shaking his head, "poor fellow, murder. . . . Some sudden, strange impulse that seized him . . . I shouldn't say jail. He was in the Criminal Lunatic Asylum. Your move."

"Criminal Asylum!" I said. "What did he do?"

"Killed a man; in a sudden rage. . . . Struck him over the head with a poker."

"Good Lord!" I exclaimed. "When was that? In this city?"

"Here in the club," said Letherby, "in this room."

"What?" I gasped. "He killed one of the members?"

"Oh, no!" Letherby said reassuringly. "Not a member. The man was a guest. Fred didn't know him . . . just an insane impulse. . . . As soon as they let him out, the faithful fellow came right back here. That was last year. Your move."

We played on. I didn't feel so easy. . . . It must have been several moves after that that I saw Fred take the poker and stick its head into the coals and leave it there. I watched it gradually turning red. I must say I didn't like it.

"Did you see that?" I said. "Did you see Fred stick the poker in the coals?"

"He does it every night," said Letherby, "at ten; that means it must be ten o'clock. . . . You can't move that; you're in check."

"What's it for?" I asked.

"I take your Knight," Letherby said. Then there was a long pause — Letherby kept his head bent over the board. Presently he murmured. "Mulled beer," and then looked up and explained. "This is an old-fash-ioned place — some of the members like mulled beer — you dip the hot poker in the tankard. Fred gets it ready at ten — your move."

I must say it was a relief. . . . I was able to turn to the game again and enjoy the place . . . or I would have done so except for a sort of commotion that there was presently at the end of the room.

Somebody seemed to have fallen down . . . others were trying to pick him up . . . Fred had hurried to them. . . .

Letherby turned half round in his seat.

"It's all right," he said. "It's only poor Colonel McGann. He gets these fits . . . but Fred will look after him; he has a room in the building. Fred's devoted to him; he got Fred out of the Criminal Asylum. But for him Fred wouldn't be here tonight. Queen's Rook to Bishop's square."

I was not sure just how grateful I felt to Colonel McGann. . . .

A few moves after that another little incident bothered me, or per-haps it was just that my nerves were getting a little affected . . . one fancied things . . . and the infernal room, at once after the little dis-turbance, settled down to the same terrible quiet . . . it felt like eter-nity. . . .

Anyway — there came in through the swinging doors a different kind of man, brisk, alert, and with steel-blue eyes and a firm mouth. . . . He stood looking up and down the room, as if looking for some-one.

"Who is he?" I asked.

"Why that's Dr. Allard."

"What?" I said. "The alienist?"

"Yes, he's the head of the Criminal Lunatic Asylum. . . . He's a member here; comes in every night; in fact, he goes back and forward between this and the Asylum. He says he's making comparative studies. Check."

The alienist caught sight of Letherby and came to our table. Leth-erby introduced me. Dr. Allard looked me hard and straight in the eyes; he paused before he spoke. "Your first visit here?" he said.

"Yes . . ." I murmured, "that is, yes."

"I hope it won't be the last," he said. Now what did he mean by that?

Then he turned to Letherby.

"Fred came over to see me today," he said. "Came of his own voli-
tion. . . . I'm not quite sure. . . . We may not have been quite wise."
The doctor seemed thinking. . . . "However, no doubt he's all right
for a while apart from sudden shock . . . just keep an eye. . . . But
what I really came to ask is, has Joel Linton been in tonight?"

"No. . . ."

"I hope he doesn't come. He'd better not. . . . If he does, get some-
one to telephone to me." And with that the doctor was gone.

"Joel Linton," I said. "Why, he's arrested."

"Not yet . . . they're looking for him. You're in check."

"I beg your pardon," I said. Of course I'd read — everybody had —
about the embezzlement. But I'd no idea that a man like Joel Linton
could be a member of the Chess Club — I always thought, I mean
people said, that he was the sort of desperado type.

"He's a member?" I said, my hand on the pieces.

"You can't move that, you're still in check. Yes, he's a member,
though he likes mostly to stand and watch. Comes every night. Somebody said he was coming here tonight just the same. He says he's not
going to be taken alive. He comes round half past ten. It's about his
time . . . that looks like mate in two moves."

My hands shook on the pieces. I felt that I was done with the Chess
Club. . . . Anyway I like to get home early . . . so I was just starting
to say . . . that I'd abandon the game, when what happened happened
so quickly that I'd no more choice about it.

"That's Joel Linton now," said Letherby, and in he came through
the swing doors, a hard-looking man, but mighty determined. . . . He
hung his overcoat on a peg, and as he did so, I was sure I saw something bulging in his coat pocket — eh? He nodded casually about the
room. And then started moving among the tables, edging his way toward
ours.

"I guess, if you don't mind," I began. . . . But that is as far as I
got. That was when the police came in, two constables and an inspector.

I saw Linton dive his hand towards his pocket.

"Stand where you are, Linton," the inspector called. . . . Then
right at that moment I saw the waiter, Fred, seize the hand-grip of the
poker. . . .

"Don't move, Linton," called the inspector; he never saw Fred moving toward him. . . .

Linton didn't move. But I did. I made a quick back bolt for the
little door behind me . . . down the little stairway . . . and down the
other little staircase, and along the corridor and back into the brightly
lighted hotel rotunda, just the same as when I left it — noise and light
and bellboys, and girls at the newsstand selling tobacco and evening

papers . . . just the same, but oh, how different! For peace of mind, for the joy of life — give me a rotunda, and make it as noisy as ever you like.

I read all about it next morning in the newspapers. Things always sound so different in the newspaper, beside a coffee pot and a boiled egg. Tumults, murders, floods — all smoothed out. So was this. *Arrest Made Quietly at Chess Club*, it said. *Linton Offers No Resistance . . . Members Continue Game Undisturbed*. Yes, they *would*, the damned old gravestones. . . . Of Fred it said nothing. . . .

A few days later I happened to meet Letherby. "Your application is all right," he said. "They're going to hurry it through. You'll get in next year. . . ."

But I've sent a resignation in advance; I'm joining the Badminton Club and I want to see if I can't get into the Boy Scouts or be a Girl Guide.

by Lord Dunsany

The Three Sailors' Gambit

SITTING SOME YEARS AGO in the ancient tavern at Over, one afternoon in spring, I was waiting, as was my custom, for something strange to happen. In this I was not always disappointed, for the very curious leaded panes of that tavern, facing the sea, let a light into the low-ceilinged room so mysterious, particularly at evening, that it somehow seemed to affect the events within. Be that as it may, I have seen strange things in that tavern and heard stranger things told.

And as I sat there three sailors entered the tavern, just back, as they said, from sea, and come with sunburned skins from a very long voyage to the South; and one of them had a board and chessmen under his arm, and they were complaining that they could find no one who knew how to play chess. This was the year that the tournament was in England. And a little dark man at a table in a corner of the room, drinking sugar and water, asked them why they wished to play chess; and they said that they would play any man for a pound. They opened their box of chessmen then, a cheap and nasty set, and the man refused to play with such uncouth pieces, and the sailors suggested that perhaps he could find better ones; and in the end he went round to his lodgings near by and brought his own, and then they sat down to play for a pound a side. It was a consultation game on the part of the sailors, they said all three must play.

Well, the little dark man turned out to be Stavlokratz.

Of course he was fabulously poor, and the sovereign meant more to him than it did to the sailors, but he didn't seem keen to play, it was the sailors that insisted; he had made the badness of the sailors' chessmen an excuse for not playing at all, but the sailors had overruled that, and then he told them straight out who he was, and the sailors had never heard of Stavlokratz.

Well, no more was said after that. Stavlokratz said no more, either because he did not wish to boast or because he was huffed that

they did not know who he was. And I saw no reason to enlighten the
sailors about him; if he took their pound they had brought it on themselves, and my boundless admiration for his genius made me feel that
he deserved whatever might come his way. He had not asked to play,
they had named the stakes, he had warned them, and gave them first
move; there was nothing unfair about Stavlokratz.

I had never seen Stavlokratz before, but I had played over nearly
every one of his games in the World Championship for the last three
or four years; he was always, of course, the model chosen by students.
Only young chess players can appreciate my delight at seeing him play
first hand.

Well, the sailors used to lower their heads almost as low as the
table and mutter together before every move, but they muttered so low
that you could not hear what they planned.

They lost three pawns almost straight off, then a knight, and
shortly after a bishop; they were playing in fact the famous Three
Sailors' Gambit.

Stavlokratz was playing with the easy confidence that they say was
usual with him, when suddenly at about the thirteenth move I saw him
look surprised; he leaned forward and looked at the board and then at
the sailors, but he learned nothing from their vacant faces; he looked
back at the board again.

He moved more deliberately after that; the sailors lost two more
pawns, Stavlokratz had lost nothing as yet. He looked at me I thought
almost irritably, as though something would happen that he wished I
was not there to see. I believed at first he had qualms about taking the
sailors' pound, until it dawned on me that he might lose the game; I saw
that possibility in his face, not on the board, for the game had become
almost incomprehensible to me. I cannot describe my astonishment.
And a few moves later Stavlokratz resigned.

The sailors showed no more elation than if they had won some
game with greasy cards, playing amongst themselves.

Stavlokratz asked them where they got their opening. "We kind of
thought of it," said one. "It just come into our heads like," said another.
He asked them questions about the ports they had touched at. He evidently thought as I did myself that they had learned their extraordinary
gambit, perhaps in some old dependency of Spain, from some young
master of chess whose fame had not reached Europe. He was very eager
to find who this man could be, for neither of us imagined that those
sailors had invented it, nor would anyone who had seen them. But he
got no information from the sailors.

Stavlokratz could very ill afford the loss of a pound. He offered to
play them again for the same stakes. The sailors began to set up the

white pieces. Stavlokratz pointed out that it was his turn for first move. The sailors agreed but continued to set up the white pieces and sat with the white before them waiting for him to move. It was a trivial incident, but it revealed to Stavlokratz and myself that none of these sailors was aware that white always moves first.

Stavlokratz played on them his own opening, reasoning of course that as they had never heard of Stavlokratz they would not know of his opening; and with probably a very good hope of getting back his pound he played the fifth variation with its tricky seventh move, at least so he intended, but it turned to a variation unknown to the students of Stavlokratz.

Throughout this game I watched the sailors closely, and I became sure, as only an attentive watcher can be, that the one on their left, Jim Bunion, did not even know the moves.

When I had made up my mind about this I watched only the other two, Adam Bailey and Bill Sloggs, trying to make out which was the master mind; and for a long while I could not. And then I heard Adam Bailey utter six words, the only words I heard throughout the game, of all their consultations, "No, him with the horse's head." And I decided that Adam Bailey did not know what a knight was, though of course he might have been explaining things to Bill Sloggs, but it did not sound like that; so that left Bill Sloggs. I watched Bill Sloggs after that with a certain wonder; he was no more intellectual than the others to look at, though rather more forceful perhaps. Poor old Stavlokratz was beaten again.

Well, in the end I paid for Stavlokratz, and tried to get a game with Bill Sloggs alone, but this he would not agree to, it must be all three or none: and then I went back with Stavlokratz to his lodgings. He very kindly gave me a game: of course it did not last long but I am more proud of having been beaten by Stavlokratz than of any game that I have ever won. And then we talked for an hour about the sailors, and neither of us could make head or tail of them. I told him what I had noticed about Jim Bunion and Adam Bailey, and he agreed with me that Bill Sloggs was the man, though as to how he had come by that gambit or that variation of Stavlokratz's own opening he had no theory.

I had the sailors' address, which was that tavern as much as anywhere, and they were to be there all that evening. As evening drew in I went back to the tavern, and found there still the three sailors. And I offered Bill Sloggs two pounds for a game with him alone and he refused, but in the end he played me for a drink. And then I found that he had not heard of the *en passant* rule, and believed that the fact of checking the king prevented him from castling, and did not know that a player can have two or more queens on the board at the same time if he queens his pawns, or that a pawn could ever become a knight; and he made as many of the stock mistakes as he had time for in a short game, which I won. I thought that I should have got at the secret then, but his mates who had sat scowling all the while in the corner came up and interfered. It was a breach of their compact apparently for one to play chess by himself, at any rate they seemed angry. So I left the tavern then and came back again next day, and the next day and the day after, and often saw the three sailors, but none was in a communicative mood. I had got Stavlokratz to keep away, and they could get no one to play chess with at a pound a side, and I would not play with them unless they told me the secret.

And then one evening I found Jim Bunion drunk, yet not so drunk as he wished, for the two pounds were spent; and I gave him very nearly a tumbler of whiskey, or what passed for whiskey in that tavern at Over, and he told me the secret at once. I had given the others some whiskey to keep them quiet, and later on in the evening they must have gone out, but Jim Bunion stayed with me by a little table leaning across it and talking low, right into my face, his breath smelling all the while of what passed for whiskey.

The wind was blowing outside as it does on bad nights in November, coming up with moans from the south, towards which the tavern faced with all its leaded panes, so that none but I was able to hear his voice as Jim Bunion gave up his secret.

They had sailed for years, he told me, with Bill Snyth; and on their last voyage home Bill Snyth had died. And he was buried at sea. Just the other side of the line they buried him, and his pals divided his kit, and these three got his crystal that only they knew he had, which Bill got one night in Cuba. They played chess with the crystal.

And he was going on to tell me about that night in Cuba when Bill had bought the crystal from the stranger, how some folks might think that they had seen thunderstorms, but let them go and listen to that one that thundered in Cuba when Bill was buying his crystal and they'd find that they didn't know what thunder was. But then I interrupted him, unfortunately perhaps, for it broke the thread of his tale and set him rambling a while, and cursing other people and talking of other lands, China, Port Said and Spain; but I brought him back to Cuba again in the end. I asked him how they could play chess with a crystal; and he said that you looked at the board and looked at the crystal and there was the game in the crystal the same as it was on the board, with all the odd little pieces looking just the same though smaller, horses' heads and whatnots; and as soon as the other man moved the move came out in the crystal, and then your move appeared after it, and all you had to do was to make it on the board. If you didn't make the move that you saw in the crystal, things got very bad in it, everything horribly mixed and moving about rapidly, and scowling and making the same move over and over again, and the crystal getting cloudier and cloudier; it was best to take one's eyes away from it then, or one dreamt about it afterwards, and the foul little pieces came and cursed you in your sleep and moved about all night with their crooked moves.

I thought then that, drunk though he was, he was not telling the truth, and I promised to show him to people who played chess all their lives so that he and his mates could get a pound whenever they liked, and I promised not to reveal his secret even to Stavlokratz, if only he would tell me all the truth; and this promise I have kept till long after the three sailors have lost their secret. I told him straight out that I did not believe in the crystal. Well, Jim Bunion leaned forward then, even further across the table, and swore he had seen the man from whom Bill had bought the crystal and that he was one to whom anything was possible. To begin with his hair was villainously dark, and his features were unmistakable even down there in the south, and he could play chess with his eyes shut, and even then he could beat anyone in Cuba. But there was more than this, there was the bargain he made with Bill that told one who he was. He sold that crystal for Bill Snyth's soul.

Jim Bunion leaning over the table with his breath in my face nodded his head several times and was silent.

I began to question him then. Did they play chess as far away as Cuba? He said they all did. Was it conceivable that any man would make such a bargain as Snyth made? Wasn't the trick well known? Wasn't it in hundreds of books? And if he couldn't read books, mustn't he have heard from sailors that that is the Devil's commonest dodge to get souls from silly people?

Jim Bunion had leant back in his own chair quietly smiling at my questions but when I mentioned silly people he leaned forward again, and thrust his face close to mine and asked me several times if I called Bill Snyth silly. It seemed that these three sailors thought a great deal of Bill Snyth, and it made Jim Bunion angry to hear anything said against him. I hastened to say that the bargain seemed silly though not, of course, the man who made it; for the sailor was almost threatening, and no wonder for the whiskey in that dim tavern would madden a nun.

When I said that the bargain seemed silly he smiled again, and then he thundered his fist down on the table and said that no one had ever yet got the better of Bill Snyth and that that was the worst bargain for himself that the Devil ever made, and that from all he had read or heard of the Devil he had never been so badly had before as the night when he met Bill Snyth at the inn in the thunderstorm in Cuba, for Bill Snyth already had the damnedest soul at sea; Bill was a good fellow, but his soul was damned right enough, so he got the crystal for nothing.

Yes, he was there and saw it all himself, Bill Snyth in the Spanish inn and the candles flaring, and the Devil walking in out of the rain, and then the bargain between those two old hands, and the Devil going out into the lightning, and the thunderstorm raging on, and Bill Snyth sitting chuckling to himself between the bursts of the thunder.

But I had more questions to ask and interrupted this reminiscence. Why did they all three always play together? And a look of something like fear came over Jim Bunion's face; and at first he would not speak. And then he said to me that it was like this: they had not paid for that crystal, but got it as their share of Bill Snyth's kit. If they had paid for it or given something in exchange to Bill Snyth that would have been all right, but they couldn't do that now, because Bill was dead and they were not sure if the old bargain might not hold good. And Hell must be a large and lonely place, and to go there alone must be bad, and so the three agreed that they would all stick together, and use the crystal all three or not at all, unless one died, and then the two would use it and the one that was gone would wait for them. And the last of the three to go would bring the crystal with him, or maybe the crystal would bring him. They didn't think, he said, they were the kind of men for Heaven, and he hoped they knew their place better than that, but they didn't fancy the notion of Hell alone, if Hell it had to be. It was all right for Bill Snyth, he was afraid of nothing. He had known perhaps five men that were not afraid of death, but Bill Snyth was not afraid of Hell. He died with a smile on his face like a child in its sleep; it was drink killed poor Bill Snyth.

This was why I had beaten Bill Sloggs; Sloggs had the crystal on him while we played, but would not use it; these sailors seemed to fear loneliness as some people fear being hurt; he was the only one of the three who could play chess at all, he had learnt it in order to be able to answer questions and keep up their pretense, but he had learnt it badly, as I found. I never saw the crystal, they never showed it to any-one; but Jim Bunion told me that night that it was about the size that the thick end of a hen's egg would be if it were round. And then he fell asleep.

There were many more questions that I would have asked him, but I could not wake him up. I even pulled the table away so that he fell to the floor, but he slept on, and all the tavern was dark but for one candle burning; and it was then that I noticed for the first time that the other two sailors had gone, no one remained at all but Jim Bunion and I and the sinister barman of that curious inn, and he too was asleep.

When I saw that it was impossible to wake the sailor I went out into the night. Next day Jim Bunion would talk of it no more; and when I went back to Stavlokratz I found him already putting on paper his theory about the sailors, which became accepted by chess players, that one of them had been taught their curious gambit and the other two between them had learnt all the defensive openings as well as general play. Though who taught them no one could say, in spite of enquiries made afterwards all along the Southern Pacific.

I never learnt any more details from any of the three sailors, they were always too drunk to speak or else not drunk enough to be communicative. I seem just to have taken Jim Bunion at the flood. But I kept my promise, it was I that introduced them to the Tournament, and a pretty mess they made of established reputations. And so they kept on for months, never losing a game and always playing for their pound a side. I used to follow them wherever they went merely to watch their play. They were more marvelous than Stavlokratz even in his youth.

But then they took liberties such as giving their queen when playing first-class players. And in the end one day when all three were drunk they played the best player in England with only a row of pawns. They won the game all right. But the ball broke to pieces. I never smelt such a stench in all my life.

The three sailors took it stoically enough, they signed on to different ships and went back again to the sea, and the world of chess lost sight, forever I trust, of the most remarkable players it ever knew, who would have altogether spoiled the game.

It is difficult to write an adequate introduction to H. R. Wakefield's neglected classic. It is not only superlative fantasy writing, but a superlative chess fantasy. (And how many, or few, such can you name offhand?) To its devotees, chess is not only a game, it is a way of life. We believe it was this knowledge that enabled Mr. Wakefield to create his masterpiece of evil, little Professor Pownall, to whose warped soul chess was life itself . . . and destruction. This account of the Professor's error is taken from Mr. Wakefield's first and most important book, They Return at Evening *(Appleton, 1928).*

by H. R. Wakefield

Professor Pownall's Oversight

A NOTE BY J. C. CARY, M.D.:

About sixteen years ago I received one morning by post a parcel, which, when I opened it, I found to contain a letter and a packet. The latter was inscribed, "To be opened and published fifteen years from this date"; the letter read as follows:

Dear Sir,

Forgive me for troubling you, but I have decided to entrust the enclosed narrative to your keeping. As I state, I wish it to be opened by you, and that you should arrange for it to be published in the *Chess Magazine.* I enclose five ten-pound notes, which sum is to be used, partly to remunerate you, and partly to cover the cost of publication, if such expenditure should be found necessary. About the time you receive this, I shall disappear. The contents of the enclosed packet, though to some extent revealing the cause of my disappearance, give no index as to its method.

E.P.

The receipt of this eccentric document occasioned me considerable surprise. I had attended Professor Pownall (I have altered all names, for obvious reasons) in my professional capacity four or five times for minor ailments. He struck me as a man of extreme intellectual brilliance, but his personality was repulsive to me. He had a virulent and brutal wit, which he made no scruple of exercising at my and everyone else's expense. He apparently possessed not one single friend in the world, and I can only conclude that I came nearer to fulfilling this role than anyone else.

I kept this packet by me for safe keeping for the fifteen years, and then I opened it, about a year ago. The contents ran as follows:

The date of my birth is of complete unimportance, for my life began when I first met Hubert Morisson at the age of twelve and a half at Flamborough College. It will end to-morrow at six forty-five P.M.

I doubt if ever in the history of the human intellect there has been so continuous, so close, so exhausting a rivalry as that between Morisson and myself. I will chronicle its bare outline. We joined the same form at Flamborough — two forms higher, I may say, than that in which even the most promising new boys are usually placed. We were promoted every term till we reached the Upper Sixth at the age of sixteen. Morisson was always top, I was always second, a few hundred marks behind him. We both got scholarships at Oxford, Morisson just beating me for Balliol. Before I left Flamborough, the Head Master sent for me and told me that he considered I had the best brain of any boy who had passed through his hands. I thought of asking him, if that were so, why I had been so consistently second to Morisson all through school; but even then I thought I knew the answer.

He beat me, by a few marks, for all the great University prizes for which we entered. I remember one of the examiners, impressed by my papers, asking me to lunch with him. "Pownall," he said, "Morisson and you are the most brilliant undergraduates who have been at Oxford in my time. I am not quite sure why, but I am convinced of two things; firstly, that he will always finish above you, and secondly, that you have the better brain."

By the time we left Oxford, both with the highest degrees, I had had remorselessly impressed upon me the fact that my superiority of intelligence had been and always would be neutralised by some constituent in Morisson's mind which defied and dominated that superiority — save in one respect: we both took avidly to chess, and very soon there was no one in the University in our class, but I became, and remained, his master.

Chess has been the one great love of my life. Mankind I detest and despise. Far from growing wiser, men seem to me, decade by decade, to grow more inane as the means for revealing their ineptitude become more numerous, more varied and more complex. Women do not exist for me – they are merely variants from a bad model; but for chess, that superb, cold, infinitely satisfying anodyne to life, I feel the ardour of a lover, the humility of a disciple. Chess, that greatest of all games, greater than any game! It is, in my opinion, one of the few supreme products of the human intellect, if, as I often doubt, it is of human origin.

Morisson's success, I realise, was partly due to his social gifts; he possessed that shameless flair for making people do what he wanted, which is summed up in the word *charm*, a gift from the gods, no doubt, of jealousy, but these I fought, and on the whole conquered.

His success fascinated me. I had sometimes short and violent paroxysms
Neither, I believe. I simply grew profoundly and terribly used to him.
but one of which I have never had the least wish to be the recipient.

Did I like Morisson? More to the point, perhaps, did I hate him?

He became a Moral Philosophy Don at Oxford; I obtained a similar but inevitably inferior appointment in a Midland university. We used to meet during vacations and play chess at the City of London Club. We both improved rapidly, but still I kept ahead of him. After ten years of drudgery, I inherited a considerable sum, more than enough to satisfy all my wants. If one avoids all contact with women one can live marvellously cheaply; I am continuously astounded at men's inability to grasp this great and simple truth.

I have had few moments of elation in my life, but when I got into the train for London on leaving that cesspool in Warwickshire, I had a fierce feeling of release. No more should I have to ram useless and rudimentary speculation into the heads of oafs, who hated me as much as I despised them.

Directly I arrived in London I experienced one of those irresistible impulses which I could never control, and I went down to Oxford. Morisson was married by then, so I refused to stay in his house, but I spent hours every day with him. The louts into whom he attempted to force elementary ethics seemed rather less dingy but even more mentally costive than my Midland half-wits, and so far as that went, I envied him not at all. I had meant to stay one week; I was in Oxford for six, for I rapidly came to the conclusion that I ranked first and Morisson second among the chess players of Great Britain. I can say that because I have no vanity; vanity cannot breathe and live in rarefied intellectual altitudes. In chess the master surveys his skill impersonally, he criticises it impartially. He is great; he knows it; he can prove it, that is all.

I persuaded Morisson to enter for the British Championship six months later, and I returned to my rooms in Bloomsbury to perfect my game. Day after day I spent in the most intensive study, and succeeded in curing my one weakness. I just mention this point briefly for the benefit of chess players. I had a certain lethargy when forced to analyse

intricate end-game positions. This, as I say, I overcame. A few games
at the City Club convinced me that I was, at last, worthy to be called
master. Except for these occasional visits, I spent those six months
entirely alone; it was the happiest period of my life. I had complete
freedom from human contacts, excellent health and unlimited time to
move thirty-two pieces of the finest ivory over a charming chequered
board.

I took a house at Bournemouth for the fortnight of the Championship, and I asked Morisson to stay with me. I felt I had to have him near
me. He arrived the night before play began. When he came into my
study I had one of those agonising paroxysms of jealousy to which I
have alluded. I conquered it, but the reaction, as ever, took the form of
a loathsome feeling of inferiority, almost servility.

Morisson was six foot two in height; I am five foot one. He had, as
I impartially recognise, a face of great dignity and beauty, a mind at
once of the greatest profundity and the most exquisite flippancy. My
face is a perfect index to my character; it is angular, sallow, and its
expression is one of seething distaste. As I say, I know my mind to be
the greater of the two, but I express myself with an inevitable and blast-
ing brutality, which disgusts and repels all who sample it. Nevertheless,
it is that brutality which attracted Morisson; at times it fascinated him.
I believe he realised, as I do, how implacably our destinies were inter-
woven.

Arriving next morning at the hall in which the Championship was
to be held, I learned two things which affected me profoundly. The
first, that by the accident of the pairing I should not meet Morisson
until the last round, secondly, that the winner of the Championship
would be selected to play in the forthcoming Masters' Tournament at
Budapest.

I will pass quickly over the story of this Championship. It fully
justified my conviction. When I sat down opposite Morisson in the last
round we were precisely level, each of us having defeated all his opponents, though I had shown the greater mastery and certainty. I began
this game with the greatest confidence. I outplayed him from the start,
and by the fifteenth move I felt convinced I had a won game. I was just
about to make my sixteenth move when Morisson looked across at me
with that curious smile on his face, half superior, half admiring, which
he had given me so often before, when after a terrific struggle he had
proved his superiority in every other test but chess. The smile that I was
to see again. At once I hesitated. I felt again that sense of almost
cringing subservience. No doubt I was tired, the strain of that fortnight
had told, but it was, as it always had been, something deeper, something more virulent, than anything fatigue could produce. My brain

simply refused to concentrate. The long and subtle combination which I had analysed so certainly seemed suddenly full of flaws. My time was passing dangerously quickly. I made one last effort to force my brain to work, and then desperately moved a piece. How clearly I remember the look of amazement on Morisson's face. For a moment he scented a trap, and then, seeing none, for there was none, he moved and I was myself again. I saw I must lose a piece and the game. After losing a knight, I fought with a concentrated brilliance I had never attained before, with the result that I kept the game alive till the adjournment and indeed recovered some ground, but I knew when I left the hall with Morisson that on the next morning only a miracle could save me, and that once again, in the test of all tests in which I longed to beat him, he would, as ever at great crises, be revealed as my master. As I trotted back to my house beside him the words "only a miracle" throbbed in my brain insinuatingly. Was there no other possibility? Of a sudden I came to the definite, unalterable decision that I would kill Morisson that night, and my brain began, like the perfectly trained machine it is, to plan the means by which I could kill him certainly and safely. The speed of this decision may sound incredible, but here I must be allowed a short digression. It has long been a theory of mine that there are two distinct if remotely connected processes operating in the human mind. I term these the "surface" and the "sub-surface" processes. I am not entirely satisfied with these terms, and I have thought of substituting for them the terms "conscious" and "sub-conscious." However, that is a somewhat academic distinction. I believe that my sub-surface mind had considered this destruction of Morisson many times before, and that these paroxysms of jealousy, the outcome as they were of consistent and unjust frustration, were the minatory symptoms that the content of my sub-surface would one day become the impulse of my surface mind, forcing me to plan and execute the death of Morisson.

When we arrived at the house I went first to my bedroom to fetch a most potent, swift-working, and tasteless narcotic which a German doctor had once prescribed for me in Munich when I was suffering from insomnia. I then went to the dining-room, mixed two whiskies and soda, put a heavy dose of the drug into Morisson's tumbler, and went back to the study. I had hoped he would drink it quickly; instead he put it by his side and began a long monologue on luck. Possibly my fatal move had suggested it. He said that he had always regarded himself as an extremely lucky man, in his work, his friends, his wife. He supposed that his rigidly rational mind demanded for its relief some such inconsistency, some such sop. "About four months ago," he said, "I had an equally irrational experience, a sharp premonition of death, which lingered with me. I told my wife – you will never agree, Pownall, but there is something to be said for matrimony; if I were dying I should like Marie to be with me, gross sentimentality, of course — I told my wife, who is of a distinctly psychic, superstitious if you like, turn of mind, and she persuaded me to go to a clairvoyant of whom she had a high opinion. I went sceptically, partly to please her, partly for the amusement of sampling one of this tribe. She was a curious, dingy female, slightly disconcerting. She stared at me remotely and then remarked, 'It was always destined that he should do it.' I plied her with questions, but she would say nothing more. I think you will agree, Pownall, that this was a typically nebulous two-guineas' worth." And then he drained his glass. Shortly afterwards he began to yawn repeatedly, and went to bed. He staggered slightly on entering his room. "Good night, Pownall," he said, as he closed the door, "let's hope somehow or other we may both be at Budapest."

Half an hour later I went into his room. He had just managed to undress before the drug had overwhelmed him. I shut the window, turned on the gas, and went out. I spent the next hour playing over that fatal game. I quickly discovered the right line I had missed, then with a wet towel over my face, I re-entered his room. He was dead. I turned off the gas, opened all the windows, waited till the gas had cleared, and then went to bed, to sleep as soundly as ever in my life, though I had a curiously vivid dream. I may say I dream but seldom, and never before realised how sharp and convincing these silly images could be, for I saw Morisson running through the dark and deserted streets of Oxford till he reached his house, and then he hammered with his fists on the door, and as he did so he gave a great cry, "Marie! Marie!" and then he fell rolling down the steps, and I awoke. This dream recurred for some time after, and always left a somewhat unpleasant impression on my mind.

The events of the next day were not pleasant. They composed a testing ordeal which remains very vividly in my mind. I had to act, and act very carefully, to deceive my maid, who came screaming into my room in the morning, to fool the half-witted local constable, the self-important local doctor, and carry through the farce generally in a convincing mode. I successfully suggested that as Morisson had suffered from heart weakness for some years, his own Oxford doctor should be sent for. Of course I had to wire to his wife. She arrived in the afternoon — and altogether I did not spend an uneventful day. However, all went well. The verdict at the inquest was "natural causes," and a day or two afterwards I was notified that I was British Chess Champion and had been selected for Budapest. I received some medal or other, which I threw into the sea.

Four months intervened before the tournament at Budapest; I

spent them entirely alone, perfecting my game. At the end of that period I can say with absolute certainty that I was the greatest player in the world; my swift unimpeded growth of power is, I believe, unprecedented in the history of chess. There was, I remember, during this time, a curious little incident. One evening after a long profound analysis of a position, I felt stale and tired, and went out for a walk. When I got back I noticed a piece had been moved, and that the move constituted the one perfect answer to the combination I had been working out. I asked my landlady if anybody had been to my room: she said not, and I let the subject drop.

The Masters' Tournament at Budapest was perhaps the greatest ever held. All the most famous players in the world were gathered there, yet I, a practically unknown person, faced the terrific task of engaging them, one by one, day after day, with supreme confidence. I felt they could have no surprises for me, but that I should have many for them. Were I writing for chess players only, I would explain technically the grounds for this confidence. As it is, I will merely state that I had worked out the most subtle and daring variants from existing practice. I was a century ahead of my time.

In my first round I was paired with the great Russian master Osvensky. When I met him he looked at me as if he wondered what I was doing there. He repeated my name as though it came as a complete surprise to him. I gave him a look which I have employed before when I have suspected insolence, and he altered his manner. We sat down. Having the white pieces, I employed that most subtle of all openings, the queen's bishop's pawn gambit. He chose an orthodox defence, and for ten moves the game took a normal course. Then at my eleventh move I offered the sacrifice of a knight, the first of the tremendous surprises I sprang upon my opponents in this tournament. I can see him now, the quick searching glance he gave me, and his great and growing agitation. Every chess player reveals great strain by much the same symptoms, by nervous movements, hurried glances at the clock, uneasy shufflings of the body, and so forth; my opponent in this way completely betrayed his astonishment and dismay. Time ran on, sweat burst out on his forehead. Elated as I was, the spectacle became replusive, so I looked around the room. And then, as my eyes reached the door, they met those of Morisson sauntering in. He gave me the slightest look of recognition, then strolled along to our table and took his stand behind my opponent's chair. At first I had no doubt that it was an hallucination due to the great strain to which I had subjected myself during the preceding months: I was therefore surprised when I noticed the Russian glance uneasily behind him. Morisson put his hand over my opponent's shoulder, guided his hand to a piece, and placed it down with that slight screwing movement so characteristic of him. It was the one move which I had dreaded, though I had felt it could never be discovered in play over the board, and then Morisson gave me that curious searching smile to which I have alluded. I braced myself, rallied all my will power, and for the next four hours played what I believe to be the finest game in the record of Masters' play. Osvensky's agitation was terrible, he was white to the lips, on the point of collapse, but the Thing at his back – Morisson – guided his hand move after move, hour after hour, to the one perfect square. I resigned on move sixty-four, and Osvensky immediately fainted. Somewhat ironically he was awarded the first Brilliancy Prize for the finest game played in the tournament. As soon as it was over Morisson turned away, walked slowly out of the door.

That night after dinner I went to my room and faced the situation. I eventually persuaded myself, firstly, that Morisson's appearance had certainly been an hallucination, secondly, that my opponent's performance had been due to telepathy. Most people, I suppose, would regard this as pure superstition, but to me it seemed a tenable theory that my mind, in its concentration, had communicated its content to the mind of Osvensky. I determined that for the future I would break this contact, whenever possible, by getting up and walking around the room.

Consequently on the next day I faced my second opponent, Seltz, the champion of Germany, with comparative equanimity. This time I defended a Ruy Lopez with the black pieces. I made the second of my stupendous surprises on the seventh move, and once again had the satisfaction of seeing consternation and intense astonishment leap to the German's face. I got up and walked round the room watching the other games. After a time I looked round and · saw the back of my opponent's head buried in his hands, which were passing feverishly through his hair, but I also saw Morisson come in and take his stand behind him.

I need not dwell on the next twelve days. It was always the same story. I lost every game, yet each time giving what I know to be absolute proof that I was the greatest player in the world. My opponents did not enjoy themselves. Their play was acclaimed as the perfection of perfection, but more than one told me that he had no recollection after the early stages of making a single move, and that he suffered from a sensation of great depression and malaise. I could see they regarded me with some awe and suspicion, and shunned my company.

When I got back to London I was in a state of extreme nervous exhaustion, but there was something I had to know for certain, so I went to the City Chess Club and started a game with a member. Morisson came in after a short time – so I excused myself and went home. I had learnt what I had sought to learn. I should never play chess again.

The idea of suicide then became urgent. This happened three months ago. I have spent that period partly in writing this narrative, chiefly in annotating my games at Budapest. I found that every one of my opponents played an absolutely flawless game, that their combinations had been of a profundity and complexity unique in the history of chess. Their play had been literally super-human. I found I had myself given the greatest *human* performance ever known. I think I can claim a certain reputation for will power when I say the shortest game lasted fifty-four moves, even with Morisson there, and that I was only guilty of most minute errors due to the frightful and protracted strain. I leave these games to posterity, having no doubt of its verdict. To the last I had fought Morisson to a finish.

I feel no remorse. My destruction of Morisson was an act of common sense and justice. All his life he had had the rewards which were rightly mine; as he said at a somewhat ironical moment, he had always been a lucky man. If I had known him to be my intellectual superior I would have accepted him as such and become reconciled, but to be the greater and always to be branded as the inferior eventually becomes intolerable, and justice demands retribution. Budapest proved that I had made an "oversight," as we say in chess, but I could not have foreseen that, and, as it is, I shall leave behind me these games as a memorial of me. Had I not killed Morisson I should never have played them, for he inspired me while he overthrew me.

I have planned my disappearance with great care. I think I saw Morisson in my bedroom again last night, and, as I am terribly tired of him, it will be tomorrow. I have no wish to be ogled by asinine jurymen nor drooled over by fatuous coroners and parsons, so my body will never be found. I have just destroyed my chessmen and my board, for no one else shall ever touch them. Tears came into my eyes as I did so. I never remember this happening before. Morisson has just come in —

A FURTHER NOTE BY J. C. CARY, M.D.:

Here the narrative breaks off abruptly. While I felt a certain moral obligation to arrange for the publication, if possible, of this document, it all sounded excessively improbable. I am no chess player myself, but I had had as a patient a famous Polish master who became a good friend of mine before he returned to Warsaw. I decided to send him the narrative and the games so that he might give me his opinion of the first, and his criticism of the latter. About three months later I had my first letter from him:

My Friend,

I have a curious tale to tell you. When I had read through that document which you sent me I made some enquiries. Let me tell you the result of them. Let me tell you no one of the name of your Professor ever competed in a British Chess Championship, there was no tournament held at Pest that year which he states, and no one of that name has ever played in a tournament in that city. When I learnt these facts, my friend, I regarded your Professor as a practical joker or a lunatic, and was just about to send back to you all these papers, when quite to satisfy my mind, I thought I would just discover what manner of chess player this joker or madman had been. I soberly declare to you that those few pages revealed to me, as a chess master, one of the few supreme triumphs of the human mind. It is incredible to me that such games were ever played over the board. You are no player, I know, and, therefore, you must take my word for it that, if your professor ever played them, he was one of the world's greatest geniuses, the master of masters, and that, if he lost them his opponents, perhaps I might say his Opponent, was not of this world. As he says, he lost every game, but his struggles against this Thing were superb, incredible. I salute his shade. His notes upon these games say all that is to be said. They are supreme, they are final. It is a terrifying speculation, my friend, this drama, this murder, this agony, this suicide, did they ever happen? As one reads his pages and studies this quiet, this – how shall we say? – this so deadly tale, its truth seems to flash from it. Or is it some dream of genius? It terrifies me, as I say, this uncertainty, for what other flaming and dreadful visions have come to the minds of men and have been buried with them! I am, as you know, besides a chess master, a mathematician and philosopher; my mind lives an abstract life, and it is therefore a haunted mind, it is subject to possession, it is sometimes not master in its house. Enough of this, such thinking leads too far, unless it leads back again quickly on its own tracks, back to everyday things – I express myself not too well, I know – otherwise, it leads to that dim borderland in which the minds of men like myself had better never trespass.

I have studied these games, until I have absorbed their mighty teaching. I feel a sense of supremacy, an insolence, I feel as your Professor did, that I am the greatest player in the world. I am due to play in the great Masters' tournament at Lodz. I will write you when it is over.

Serge

Three months later I received another letter from him.

    J. C. Cary, M.D.
    My Friend,
    I am writing under the impulse of a strong excitement, I am unhappy, I am – but let me tell you. I went to Lodz with a song in my

brain, for I felt I should achieve the aim of my life. I should be the master of masters. Why then am I in this distress? I will tell you. I was matched in the first round with the great Cuban, Primavera. I had the white pieces. I opened as your Professor had opened in that phantom tourney. All went well. I played my tenth move. Primavera settled himself to analyse. I looked around the room. I saw, at first with little interest, a stranger, tall, debonair, enter the big swing door, and come towards my table. And then I remembered your Professor's tale, and I trembled. The stranger came up behind my opponent's chair and gave me *just that look*. A moment later Primavera made his move, and I put out my hand and offered that sacrifice, but, my friend, the hand that made that move *was not my own*. Trembling and infinitely distressed, I saw the stranger put his arm over Primavera's shoulder, take his hand, guide it to a piece, and thereby make that one complete answer to my move. I saw my opponent go white, turn and glance behind him, and then he said, "I feel unwell. I resign." "Monsieur," said I, "I do not like this game either. Let us consider it a draw." And as I put out my hand to shake his, it was my own hand again, and the stranger was not there.

My friend, I rushed from the room back to my hotel, and I hurled those games of supreme genius into the fire. For a time the paper seemed as if it would not burn, and as if the lights went dim: two shadows that were watching from the wall near the door grew vast and filled the room. Then suddenly great flames shot up and roared the chimney high, they blazed it seemed for hours, then as suddenly died, and the fire, I saw, was out. And then I discovered that I had forgotten every move in every one of those games, the recollection of them had passed from me utterly. I felt a sense of infinite relief. I was free again. Pray God, I never play them in my dreams!

                                                                    Serge

by Percival Wilde

Slippery Elm

1

WHEN THE MORAL ADVENTURES of William Parmelee, ex-card sharp and more or less unwilling corrector of destinies, are neatly collected into a volume dedicated to the advancement of honesty, this is one of the tales which will be omitted. At the very best, it will be relegated to an appendix, where readers under twenty-one may skip it, and thus avoid its corrupting influence; but in the volume proper it can have no place, for, being veracious, it relates how Parmelee, upon a certain most remarkable occasion, allied himself with the forces of evil, and how the only honest man in the tale fared badly.

This, of course, is all wrong. Axiomatic it is that honesty should be rewarded; that dishonesty should suffer; that morality, in the end, should triumph. If this does not invariably happen in life, it should most emphatically happen on the printed page. Granted that in the vicissitudes of modern civilization the good man – even so good a man as J. Hampton Hoogestraten – occasionally comes off second best, such episodes should be quietly hushed up, and not broadcast to undermine the virtue of the rising generation.

But when the said William Parmelee, ex-card sharp and corrector of destinies, stands face to face with the guardian of the pearly gates, the facts having to do with the downfall of that good man, J. Hampton Hoogestraten, will doubtless be investigated. Tony Claghorn will be interrogated, for Tony was a witness. Colonel Stafford, president of the Metropolitan Chess Club, will be examined mercilessly, for despite his seventy years and his snow-white hair, Stafford was an accomplice. The rank and file of the members, from Aalders to Zysser, will be questioned remorselessly, for they too, each and every one of them, took part in the dastardly plot. Little Reynolds will not be excepted – he least of all; and the great Niemzo-Zborowski himself will be in for a grilling. And that last may result in utter calamity, for Niemzo-Zborowski may not be permitted to pass the gates, and without him, there will be no chess in heaven – at any rate, no chess worth mentioning.

And while the many sinners concerned in the letting-down of J. Hampton Hoogestraten plead and parley at the great portals, the shade of that good man himself, smoking one of his infamous cigars, will stride into the blissful place unchallenged – maybe. And since that contingency is greatly to be feared, and since the facts in the case are more or less involved, it seems desirable to set them forth here and now, so that the matured opinion of mankind, rising upward like heated air, may reach the venerable guardian of the gate in good time, and thus prevent a miscarriage of justice.

Let the tale be passed from mouth to mouth; let there be an abundance of witnesses. Then, perhaps, the members of the Metropolitan Chess Club, with Colonel Stafford at their head, will march through the gates in battle formation, Aalders at one point of their phalanx, and Zysser at the other. And somewhere in the midst, concealed by their numbers, will march little Reynolds – and the great Niemzo-Zborowski – and Bill Parmelee himself.

And as for that good man, J. Hampton Hoogestraten – well, what about him?

2

He breezed into the Metropolitan Chess Club for the first time on a stormy night in February. He had applied for membership in writing, and as the check for a year's dues which had accompanied his application had been promptly honored at the bank, he had been duly elected. Like other chess clubs, the Metropolitan was none too affluent; an ability to pay the exceedingly modest sum which it charged for the privilege of belonging to it was sufficient recommendation for any candidate. Wherefore the application of J. Hampton Hoogestraten was acted upon with all expedition, and the secretary duly dispatched him the card which certified that he was entitled to all of the rights, immunities, and benefits of the organization, including the right of paying on the spot for coffee, cigars, and other refreshments as ordered.

J. Hampton Hoogestraten breezed in, poised his two hundred and twenty-eight pounds of oleaginous fat on the threshold, divested himself of a Fedora hat and a heavy overcoat provided with a quilted lining and a near-seal collar, and surveyed the long, narrow room which was the home of the Metropolitan Chess Club.

The walls were adorned with the photographs of dead and gone masters: Morphy, Steinitz, Paulsen, Anderssen, Zukertort, Blackburne, Pillsbury, Staunton, Tchigorin. Between them, suitably framed or incased, were the trophies which the club's team had won in hard-fought battles.

A score of chess tables, ranged in a long line, and each provided with its complement of chessmen and a chess clock, more than accommodated perhaps a quarter of the club's total membership. Had the night not been stormy, a larger attendance might certainly have been expected, and the dozen reserve tables stowed in nooks and crannies would have come into use. But upon the momentous occasion that J. Hampton Hoogestraten first honored the club with his presence, thirty men, at the outside, were revealed to his appraising glance.

There was a curious family resemblance among the thirty. Their foreheads were of more than average height; their hirsute adornments were uncommonly plentiful; their clothing uniformly careless. Young or old, tall or short, lean or well fed, there was a strangely similar patient look in the eyes of each. For an instant – but only for an instant – they looked up when the massive frame of J. Hampton Hoogestraten filled the doorway. Then they continued with their play.

Had they studied the new member closely, they would have observed a youngish middle-aged man of moderate stature, well upholstered as to the paunch, and rather bare as to the scalp, whose entire get-up radiated success. Not that J. Hampton Hoogestraten was a captain of industry, or even on the way to become one: far from it. His occupation, that of a salesman for a manufacturer of laundry soaps, provided him with a fair living and no more. But J. Hampton Hoogestraten believed to the innermost core of his being that success came inevitably to the man who looked the part. His clothing, therefore, consisted of garments of cheap material cut in ambitious imitation of the lines of expensive ones. A white vestee gleamed on either side of a brilliant tie; a huge pearl, guaranteed to defy any but expert inspection, topped a near-platinum scarf pin; patent-leather shoes shone on his large feet; and his pudgy hands, well manicured, twinkled with their load of shoddy jewelry.

He gazed about the room, discerned the dignified figure of Colonel Stafford, president of the club, seated in solitary dignity at a table, and he committed his first mistake. J. Hampton Hoogestraten marched over, smote the Colonel on the back in hearty he-man fashion, and extended a bejeweled paw.

"I'm the new member," he introduced himself, "my name is J. Hampton Hoogestraten. How about a little game?"

A blunder? Say rather a whole series of blunders. In the first place, the Colonel, who had earned his title at the head of a regiment in wartime, took himself seriously, and was a stickler for etiquette.

In the second place, the membership of the club, from time im-

memorial, had been neatly divided into fifteen classes, based on playing strength. For a newcomer, who automatically took his place at the
foot of the fifteenth class, to hint at a game with a man who was ranked
well up in the third class, before having himself fought his way within
striking distance, was a presumptuous violation of the club's most
sacred rule.

In the third place, the tactful thing to do, as a new member, would
have been to allow an old member to suggest a game. Indeed, once upon
the scene, J. Hampton Hoogestraten could hardly have avoided playing. But to his ebullient soul this modest procedure had not commended
itself. He had plunged in where angels feared to tread.

The Colonel raised his leonine head, gazed at the newcomer, and
reflected that had it been wartime, he would promptly have ordered
him to a week's kitchen police for insubordination. But no war being
on hand, the Colonel bowed gracefully to the inevitable, and resolved
to have his revenge by administering a merciless beating to the upstart.

"Sit down, sir," he commanded.

"Right you are," boomed J. Hampton Hoogestraten, and overflowed
into a chair. "I want to warn you in advance," he declared modestly,
"I'm good. I'm very good."

"Indeed?" murmured the Colonel, raising his eyebrows.

"Just that," said J. Hampton Hoogestraten.

The Colonel's self-control was admirable. "Perhaps I will learn
something from you," he said silkily.

J. Hampton Hoogestraten nodded vigorously. "I shouldn't be surprised," he admitted. If there was sarcasm beneath his opponent's remark, it had not touched him.

The Colonel had taken a white pawn and a black pawn in his
hands and had shaken them. He presented his closed fists to his antagonist. "Which will you have?" he inquired.

J. Hampton Hoogestraten indicated the Colonel's right hand. It
opened to disclose a white pawn.

"Lucky! Lucky right at the start!" declared the self-confessed good
man. He arranged his pieces, and played his opening move. "Lay on,
Macduff!" he invited.

That was precisely what the Colonel intended. Boiling with rage,
he would have defeated the new member in ten moves had that been
possible. It was not possible, for J. Hampton Hoogestraten's play speed-
ily disclosed that he was no novice. Indeed, before a dozen moves had
been made, the Colonel began to regret the careless assurance with
which he had managed his opening. J. Hampton Hoogestraten had
stated that he was good. He was; and the realization of that fact did
little to soothe the irate Colonel.

He realized that the task of winning would call for the best that was in him — and then a ghastly, pungent odor, strangely reminiscent of wartime, broke upon his consciousness. He sniffed; raised his head, glared at the newcomer.

"I beg your pardon!"

"Yes?" invited J. Hampton Hoogestraten.

Colonel Stafford pointed a quivering finger at the cigar which smoldered in his opponent's mouth. Its aroma, which was now reaching him in huge, deadly blasts, was paralyzing, and even though years of chess had made the Colonel immune to cigars of more than average frightfulness, he was compelled to place the object whose clouds billowed in his direction in a class wholly by itself.

"Mr. Hoogestraten," he demanded, "where did you get that gas bomb?"

As already indicated, Mr. Hoogestraten's hide was so tough that ordinary forms of sarcasm could make no impression on it.

"You mean this?" He waved the malodorous cigar. "I'll write down the name of the place where I buy them when I finish this game. And that won't take long. You've left your knight *en prise* — see?" He captured it with a swoop.

The Colonel choked. Overcome by the fumes with which his antagonist had attacked him, he had committed the blunder of leaving a piece on a square where it could be taken without compensation to himself. It was contrary to his usual careful method of play, and it was irritating that it should occur with his present opponent.

Against any other player, the Colonel would have resigned on the spot; the loss of a knight was more than enough to decide the issue. But a blind fury against J. Hampton Hoogestraten had seized him, and he played on, hoping against hope for a change for the better.

The change did not come. Instead, a bishop, neatly pinned, went to follow the knight, and even the veriest tyro could have seen that a castle was soon to follow.

The Colonel, outwardly calm, tipped over his king in token of surrender. He had been beaten by a fluke and by his own anger; and he had been beaten by a player who was certainly not his superior. He began to set up the pieces for a second game.

J. Hampton Hoogestraten surveyed him with a fishy eye.

"What are you doing?"

"We're going to have another game, aren't we?"

"What for?"

"My revenge, of course."

J. Hampton Hoogestraten pushed back his chair, and lighted a fresh cigar.

"Brother," he remarked to the president of the club, "go home, and study – study about six or seven years – and then, when you've learnt something about the game, I'll give you the odds of a rook and beat you. Don't make me waste more time on you now."

It was thus that J. Hampton Hoogestraten began his career as a member of the Metropolitan Chess Club.

3

Unnecessary it is to detail the steps by which Mr. Hoogestraten made himself the most unpopular individual who had ever entered the clubrooms. Indeed, they were not steps at all; with more accuracy they might have been termed a succession of sharp, sudden shocks.

There was something about his face that inspired dislike even before he opened his mouth. Its self-satisfied, smug, complacent air paved the way for an impression which was but too well confirmed when, between puffs at his infamous cigars, he sang his own praises. He was good; he admitted it, he proclaimed it, he gloried in it. What was worse, he proved it by taking a place in the third dozen.

He made enemies as naturally as soap makes suds. Colonel Stafford, too much of a gentleman to prejudice the club against the new member, said not a word to his discredit. But his silence could not affect the result.

There was the night, for instance, when Vanderberg and Strachan, players of but moderate strength, having concluded a particularly brilliant game, proudly replayed it for the benefit of the newcomer. J. Hampton Hoogestraten puffed at his overpowering cigar, blinked his little eyes, and when requested to state his opinion, remarked simply, "I think both of you were rotten."

Vanderberg, who had sacrificed a rook as the first move of what he considered a dazzling combination, recoiled as if struck by a whiplash.

"What do you mean?"

"What do you think I mean? Don't you understand plain English?"

J. Hampton Hoogestraten did not remove his cigar from his mouth as he set up the position.

"Here's where your combination started, isn't it? It took you fifteen moves more to lick him. Now, why didn't you do it this way?" To Vanderberg's consternation he demonstrated a shorter and simpler combination, which won the game in one third the time. "See? That's the way I would have done it."

It was Strachan's turn to take his medicine.

"I believe you said I played badly too."

"I didn't," corrected J. Hampton Hoogestraten. "I said you were rotten."

Strachan controlled himself enough to inquire, "And how so?"

Once more the bejeweled fingers of the good man flew over the chessboard.

"Look at that combination of his! Just look at it!"

"I couldn't find any flaw in it."

"No? Well, at this point you took his bishop —"

"It was a forced move."

"Forced nothing! If you hadn't taken it, you could have played this" — his pudgy fingers manipulated the pieces — "he would have played this — or this — or this, and either way you could have announced mate in three more moves."

The worst of it was that he was right, and that Vanderberg and Strachan were compelled to admit it. Had he stated his views more tactfully, he might have made worshipers of both men. As it was, he added two more to the considerable roll of those who hated him.

His tactics, when he discovered that chess might be made moderately lucrative, were what might have been expected of him. A stake of twenty-five cents a game was customary. By playing exclusively with weaker players, he might earn as much as three dollars in an evening. Under the club rules, he was compelled to concede a handicap to them; but it did not take him long to find out that he could still win pretty much as he pleased. Once sure of that, he no longer played with the men in his own class, but confined himself strictly to more remunerative chess.

Little Reynolds, for instance, had for years occupied an undisputed place at the foot of class fifteen — the lowest class. His only chance of winning, even his many friends admitted, was to seize a handful of pawns and ram them down an adversary's throat. He was entitled to large odds, but they did not help him; his games were lost so quickly that the disparity in material mattered not at all. Had he been able to survive twenty moves, his handicap might have decided the battle; as a rule, however, he would perpetrate some ghastly blunder before reaching that point, and would resign gracefully.

It was upon him, therefore, that J. Hampton Hoogestraten concentrated — at twenty-five cents a game. Playing him, Hoogestraten could run through a whole series of games in the time that one hard-fought, level game with a man of his own strength would have required. And it was more profitable, too.

During the day little Reynolds filled quite a place in the sun as the chief official of a huge trust company, at a salary that would have made J. Hampton Hoogestraten's eyes stick out. He cared nothing at all about the few dollars of which the soap salesman relieved him nearly every evening, but his fellow members, among whom he was popular, resented Hoogestraten's tactics bitterly.

We must not, however, discuss the advent of the good man without paying particular attention to the alleged cigars with which he was always well supplied. They were large, blunt, and liver-colored. They were ornamented with huge red-and-gold bands, and as Strachan, who was the club wit, pointed out, they would not have smelled so badly had their owner merely smoked the bands and not touched off the cigars.

There was something about their aroma which was indescribably devastating. It was heavy, penetrating, overpowering; and its effective range was great. Colonel Stafford, with memories of wartime, mentioned that it reminded him of a German offensive, and recommended the use of gas masks. Zysser, who ran a wholesale grocery establishment, murmured incoherently that it recalled thoughts of a Camembert cheese which had once gone very wrong. O'Neill, who was a mining engineer, swore that it was a variety of choke damp; and Beers, who was a physician, stated that in his professional opinion, it was twin brother to a fumigating agent sometimes used to combat the plague. Thereupon Strachan had voiced the general sentiment by declaring for the lesser of the two evils: the plague; and the club had emphatically endorsed him.

That it was a factor in Hoogestraten's success was undeniable. Strachan contended – and there was some truth in his contention – that the soap salesman, minus his cigars, would rank fifty numbers lower. The cigars themselves, he declared, were entitled to a place in the first class. The place which Hoogestraten occupied represented the average of his talents and his tobacco.

That it was difficult to play at anything approaching top form while inhaling whiffs of Hoogestraten's smoke was only too apparent to his clubmates. Brilliant combinations perished in the making; inspirations gasped and expired; ideas which might have won games died a-borning; and while his adversaries contended with his cigars, the soap salesman, hardened to them as a serpent to its venom, mowed down opponents who should have defeated him. It was unfair. It was unheard of. And coupled with his blatant personality, it was monstrously irritating.

It is hard to say how the movement started – movements which are the expression of a mass soul simply leap into existence – they do not properly start; but suddenly every one of J. Hampton Hoogestraten's fellow members found himself overflowing with a consuming desire to see J. Hampton Hoogestraten soundly and properly punished.

"Of course there are fellows in the club who can lick him," said

Strachan. "Macpherson can do it, and Golding can do it, and so can any of our first-string men. But to be licked by them isn't punishment; it's a compliment to have them play with you, and if you can make them work a little, you're satisfied. You don't expect to win."

"Quite so," said Colonel Stafford.

"What I'd like to see is something very much different," pursued Strachan. "I'd like to see Hoogie play a match with one of our tenth-raters —"

"Reynolds, for instance."

"Reynolds would be ideal. I'd like to see little Reynolds play him even, and knock the everlasting stuffings out of him."

"That," remarked Zysser, "would be my idea of Heffen on eart'l!"

"I'd like to see Reynolds stand him on his head," said Strachan savagely. "I'd like to see Reynolds turn him inside out and upside down. I'd like to see Reynolds make such a laughingstock out of him that he'll never dare to show his face in this club again. I'd like to see — I'd like to see Reynolds kerflummix him!"

"Rave on," said O'Neill, who was listening.

"It's a pipe dream," commented Beers.

"Too good to be true," sighed Vanderberg.

Strachan lowered his voice. "Boys," he said, "I don't know if it can be done."

"Neither do I," said O'Neill.

"Nor I," assented Vanderberg.

"You can search me," declared Beers.

Strachan hypnotized them with a long, lean forefinger. "Perhaps it can't be done at all. But if it's possible, if it's possible by hook or crook, I've heard of the one man in the whole world who can show us how to do it."

Colonel Stafford tugged hopefully at his mustache.

"What is he? A magician?"

But Strachan, fixing his eyes ecstatically upon the ceiling, did not appear to hear him.

"Boys," he inquired, "how many of you will join me in a petition to Bill Parmelee?"

4

Taken all in all, it was one of the strangest communications that Parmelee ever received. It arrived while he was enjoying a leisurely breakfast in Claghorn's apartment, and its arrival was timed to a second with his remark that here, at least, he felt safe from the regiment of his pursuers.

Much against his own inclinations, circumstances and his peculiar talents had forced Parmelee into a unique role: that of an expert on everything having to do with the devious and little understood arts of cheating. He had not deliberately adopted a profession so unusual that no name existed for it. Quite the contrary, he had made heroic efforts to escape when the trend of events had become evident. But Claghorn, singing the praises of his idol to his innumerable acquaintances in his many clubs, had discovered a surprisingly great demand for Parmelee's services.

Apparently scores of men, dabbling with games of chance, doubted the honesty of their opponents. Parmelee, possessing a past master's knowledge not only of the tricks of legerdemain but of the amazingly ingenious mechanical devices used to fleece unsuspecting victims, was in a position to help mightily. He did so, uncovering villainy where it was least expected and exposing one sharper after another — and with each adventure, his fame had spread.

The rural free delivery to his home in a little Connecticut village rarely deposited fewer than five or six appeals for assistance in his tin mailbox; even worse, would-be clients themselves, too often cranks, made the pilgrimage to his abode in such numbers that in order to have a moment's peace he had been obliged to invest in a pair of large and vicious dogs. He had not courted glory. It had come, and its unpleasant features were well to the front. In his friend's apartment, however, he felt safe. Here callers would not come. Here annoying letters need not be expected. He remarked as much, and then Tony, smiling broadly, handed him the petition of the Metropolitan Chess Club, addressed to Parmelee in his care.

Bill gazed at the superscription and looked inquiringly at his friend.

"Have you been saving this for me?"

Tony laughed. "It came with the morning's mail."

"Why didn't you destroy it?"

"Criminal offense, old man," exulted Tony. "You wouldn't ask me to commit a crime."

"No," said Parmelee, "I'll destroy it myself. Give me the letter." He turned it over and over, weighed it in his hand, held it to his ear and shook it. "There's not the least hope that this is nothing but a bill?"

"Not the least," smiled Tony.

With a sigh Parmelee slit it open, revealing three closely written sheets of foolscap and a check. Tony's eyes glittered as he spied the latter.

"Aha!" he exclaimed, rubbing his hands, "a client who pays in advance! A client who helps to build the Parmelee fortune! How much is it this time? A thousand? Five thousand? Ten thousand?"

Without a word Parmelee handed him the check.

Tony took it with a smile, glanced at it—examined it more closely with incredulous disbelief. "It's for – it's for –" he sputtered.

"The sum of twenty-nine dollars and fifty-five cents," chuckled Bill.

5

It took Tony a few seconds to recover his breath. "Is that – is that by any chance a fee?" he demanded horror-stricken.

"It seems to be," said Parmelee, who had glanced through the three sheets of foolscap.

"Twenty-nine dollars and fifty-five cents?"

"That's the amount that's mentioned in the letter."

"Are you joking?"

"Never more serious."

"Who on earth would insult you by offering you so little? Why, it's an outrage! Let me see that letter!"

Parmelee raised his hand. "Wait! I'm not through yet – and I'm enjoying reading it." He bent over it with more interest than he had displayed in hundreds of similar communications. "Aalders – Aalders," he read aloud, "did you ever hear of objects known as Aalders?"

"No," said Claghorn impatiently.

"Neither have I," Parmelee admitted. "Strange as it seems, Aalders must be a man's name." He scrutinized another signature. "Z-y; Z-y; Zysser, that's it! What under the sun is a Zysser?"

"Well, what is it?"

"I'd give a guess that it's another man's name. Yes, that's what it must be." He proceeded to the end of the communication, grinned happily, and handed the sheets to his friend. "Tony, read this. It's unique. It's in a class by itself. It deserves a medal."

Tony cast his eye over the closely written pages. Strachan, who had drawn up the petition, had been commendably brief.

In not more than a dozen sentences he had touched upon the coming of J. Hampton Hoogestraten, the personality of the man, his appearance, his manners, his egotism – his cigars. He had epitomized his history as a member of the Metropolitan Chess Club, his victories, his unpopularity. He had explained the object of the conspirators; he had expressed his conviction that Mr. Parmelee could help them to achieve that object if anybody could; he had hoped they would not be disappointed.

The devoted members of the club had taken up a collection, he added. They did not expect Mr. Parmelee to take their case without remuneration. He enclosed his personal check for the total, and mentioned the telephone number at which he could be reached.

The few words that Strachan had written occupied the upper half of the first sheet. The lower half — and two more sheets — were filled with the signatures of the subscribers. Strachan had led off munificently with three dollars. Reynolds, being a banker, and Colonel Stafford, being the president of the club and solicitous for its welfare, had contributed like amounts. Beers had added two dollars, and O'Neill and Vanderberg had donated one dollar each. A few members had taxed themselves seventy-five cents; more had contributed a half dollar; the rank and file had given twenty-five cents each, and a few poverty-stricken individuals, meaning well, but lacking funds, had scraped up ten cents apiece.

Tony read over the pages with growing indignation. "Twenty-nine dollars and fifty-five cents! It seems incredible," he said at length.

Bill laughed at his serious friend. "Add it up, Tony," he recommended, "perhaps Strachan has held out a nickel."

Tony crumpled up the sheets impatiently. "Let me answer them," he begged. "Let me tell them where they get off."

Parmelee shook his head gently. "What a mercenary soul you are!" he exclaimed. "Tony, if I were to write the Metropolitan Chess Club I'd say that their letter has more human interest in it than any other letter of the kind that I've ever read — and Lord knows I've received plenty! I'd say that I understood their feelings perfectly, because there have been times when I felt like that myself — only more so. And I'd thank them most sincerely because instead of asking me to expose somebody else's cheating, they're asking me to do some cheating myself. By George, what a relief! To be asked to cheat in a good cause!"

"Surely you're not going to take the case!" ejaculated Tony, aghast.

"Most surely I am."

"For twenty-nine dollars and fifty-five cents?"

"For the sheer fun of it! For the pleasure of helping regular fellows like Aalders and Zysser and Strachan and the rest of the men who had the blessed innocence to take up a collection for me! Twenty-nine dollars and fifty-five cents? I'll take it like a shot, and I'll be thankful. With it I'll get the eternal gratitude of the men who subscribed it. That's a whole lot better than pocketing some fat check and have the millionaire who signed it dismiss you from his mind because he knows that he has paid you in full."

"I think you're insane," said Tony candidly, "but if you want to do charity, I won't stop you." He handed back the letter. "I take it that you know a good deal about chess?"

Parmelee's eyes twinkled. "Tony, how much do you know about it?"

Tony scratched his head. "Well, I know that the game is played on a checkerboard; and I know that there are kings and queens; and I know some of the pieces when I see them. I know the pawns, because they're little; and I know the knights, because they have horses' heads. And I guess that's all."

Bill chuckled. "You know more about chess than I do!"

"You don't mean it!"

"I've tackled checkers — when I was a boy, I used to play across the counter in the grocery store back home — but I've never touched a chessman in my life." He glanced at his horrified friend with a smile. "Tony, you said there were kings and queens in the game."

"Yes."

"If that's so, it ought to come easy to me."

"Perhaps it won't be as easy as you think."

"All the better, then," said Parmelee sincerely. "I've had an advantage in every affair I've tackled in the past: I've known more about poker — or roulette — or gambling in general than the fellows whom I was fighting. This affair is different. I'm a greenhorn, and the advantage is with the other chap. He knows the game; I don't. I've got nothing to rely on but my wits. Tony," cried Bill, and threw up his arms in exultation, "for the first time I'm fighting against real odds, and I'm a good enough sport to relish it!"

His enthusiasm did not visibly move his unemotional friend. Tony glanced through the letter again.

"As I understand it, the members of the Metropolitan Chess Club want their very worst player to take on this man Hoogestraten on even terms, and they want you to work out some way for him to lick him."

"Exactly."

"You know nothing whatever about chess. Yet you are undertaking to teach a dub how to beat an expert." Tony raised his eyebrows. "May I ask how you are going to do it?"

Parmelee grinned cheerfully. "I'll be damned if I know," he admitted.

6

In response to a telephonic request, Strachan, who did not hesitate to sacrifice his ordinary business for the far more interesting business now on hand, came running to the apartment. He found Parmelee, divested of his coat, and with a wet towel bound around his head, reading up chess in the pages of Hoyle.

"You're going to help us?" he demanded eagerly.

"If you can be helped."

"Fine!" declared Strachan, "I know you'll turn the trick."

Parmelee smiled. "I wish I were as sure of it as you are." He dog-eared a page in Hoyle carefully, and closed the book. "Now," he demanded, "just how good is Hoogestraten?"

"He's in our third class."

"What does that mean?"

"It means that there are less than twenty-five men in the club — and that means in New York City — who are better."

"How much better are they?"

"Well, a man in our second class should win three out of five games from him."

"And your first-class men?"

"Four out of five."

"The first-class man wouldn't win every game?"

"He might — but I wouldn't bet on it. When you come to our top-notchers, Mr. Parmelee, our first three classes, you find that all of the men in them are good."

"So I see," assented Parmelee ruefully. "Now, the man whom you want to beat Hoogestraten —"

"Reynolds."

"Reynolds. How good is he?"

Strachan smiled. "It would be more like it to ask how bad he is. Mr. Parmelee, Hoogestraten can give him a rook and a knight and knock the tar out of him."

"A rook and a knight? What does that mean?"

Strachan gasped. "Mr. Parmelee, don't you understand chess?"

"Not a bit," said Bill cheerfully. "Now explain what you said."

Strachan was visibly shaken, but he composed himself manfully. "In terms of tennis," he translated, "it would mean that Hoogestraten could give him forty on each game and beat him a love set. In terms of golf Hoogestraten could give him two strokes a hole and come to the turn nine up. In terms of poker —"

"Now you're talking," said Bill.

"In terms of poker Hoogestraten could present him with a pair of aces on every deal and still wipe him out in an hour. In terms of billiards —"

"You needn't go beyond poker," Bill interrupted. "You've said enough to make it plain that Reynolds hasn't a chance in a million of winning on even terms —"

"No."

"— and when you asked me to think up some way in which he could do it, you handed me a man-sized job."

"If we could have worked out the answer ourselves, we wouldn't have gone to you," smiled Strachan.

"That occurred to me long ago," Parmelee admitted. "Let's get back to your first-class players, however. Nobody in the world, I take it, can beat them."

"Oh no!" said Strachan surprisingly, "you're forgetting the masters."

"I'll bite," said Bill. "What are masters?"

Strachan explained. There were players; there were good players; there were very good players; there were exceptionally good players — such as those in the first class at the Metropolitan. But far, far above them, inhabiting the heights, living, breathing, dreaming chess, were the few world geniuses who were to the ordinary expert what the siege gun is to the sporting rifle. They played serious games only with one another — for nobody else could extend them; they saved their efforts for international tournaments, where a dozen of their kind would gather and battle titanically; they took on ordinary first-class players eight or ten at a time simultaneously, and thought nothing of making a clean sweep of such a series.

Parmelee listened attentively. "What chance would Hoogestraten stand against one of these super-experts?"

"None," said Strachan flatly.

"He wouldn't win one out of five?"

"Not one out of ten," said Strachan, "not one out of twenty. Once in a while he might get a drawn game — but I'd give odds against that."

Parmelee rubbed his hands with satisfaction.

"Our next step is pretty clear: let's get one of these masters here, in the flesh, and let's ask him some questions."

Strachan frowned. "I know what you're thinking of, but it's no use," he said. "You want a master to coach Reynolds for the game. Well, it won't work. The more you try to teach Reynolds, the worse he plays."

"We'll talk to the master anyhow," Bill insisted. "Who are the top-notchers?"

"There's Alekhine," said Strachan.

"Send for him."

"He's in France."

"Who else is there?"

"Capablanca."

"Where's he?"

"In Cuba."

"Isn't there some master, guaranteed to be the real thing, right here in New York?"

"I'm afraid not," said Strachan. He interrupted himself. "No! Wait a minute! There's a chap who came here just a few days ago from Russia. He's negotiating with the club now: he wants us to engage him for an exhibition."

"Is he a real master?"

"He's one of the three or four greatest in the world," enthused Strachan. "He took first at Budapest; he came in second at Petrograd; he took another second at Christiania —"

"Can you reach him on the telephone?" Parmelee interrupted.

"Yes," said Strachan. "Of course he talks no English, but he'll find an interpreter."

Parmelee handed him the instrument.

"Tell him to bring the interpreter with him when he comes here."

He listened to Strachan's brief conversation with interest.

"What did you call him?" he inquired, as Strachan hung up the telephone with the remark that the master was on his way.

"Niemzo-Zborowski."

"Say it again."

"Niem-zo-Zbo-row-ski."

Parmelee chuckled. "If I had a name like that, I'd be able to play chess myself! I hope he lives up to it."

"You won't be disappointed."

He was not — least of all in the master's appearance. An amazingly round little man, two-fifths grin, and three-fifths hair, stood presently in the doorway, and smiled — and smiled — and smiled. A magnificent beard, luxuriant whiskers, an abundant mustache, and bushy eyebrows struggled for the domination of his countenance. But through them, like a light in a dense forest, broke the magic of his smile.

Strachan introduced him. "Well, will he do?" he demanded. "You can say anything you like before him; he doesn't understand a word of English."

Parmelee nodded gravely. "I like that grin. Once I saw a grin like that on a wrestler's face just before he broke his opponent's leg with a toe hold. I know what it means."

Zysser, the one and only Zysser of the Metropolitan Chess Club, who had accompanied the great man as interpreter, translated Parmelee's remark into explosive Russian.

The grin became still wider as Niemzo-Zborowski beamed his delight. A horizontal groove manifested itself along the front of the frock coat in which the chess master had encased his butterball of a body, and he bowed.

Parmelee turned to the interpreter. "Ask him if he won't sit down?"

Again Zysser imitated the sound of a string of exploding firecrackers, and Niemzo-Zborowski, bending at another unsuspected groove, eased himself into a chair.

Parmelee opened Hoyle to the page he had marked.

"I am going to ask you to translate a passage from this book into Russian," he said to Zysser. He read aloud: " 'The various moves which take place in the course of a game are recorded by a system of chess notation, the number of the move being given first, and then the pieces moved and the direction of their movement.' "

He waited while Zysser translated. Again Niemzo-Zborowski bowed.

"Ask him now," directed Parmelee, "if he is familiar with that system of chess notation."

Strachan interrupted. "That's an unnecessary question, Mr. Parmelee," he pointed out. "Every beginner is familiar with that system; he learns it, in fact, before he learns to play chess. As for Mr. Niemzo-Zborowski, he has played as many as twenty games at a time blindfold – that is, without sight of the boards or the men. It would have been impossible for him to have done that if he hadn't been familiar with the system of chess notation."

Parmelee nodded. "I stand corrected," he admitted, but he could not hide his satisfaction. "Now I have some other questions to ask."

The four men were deep in conference when Tony Claghorn, who had beaten a prompt retreat when his friend had begun on Hoyle, returned to the apartment. Through the crack of the door he heard explosive bits of Russian, and peering within, he saw four heads close together.

One head, however, seemed to dominate the others. Perhaps it was because its supply of hair easily surpassed the combined contributions of the remaining three; perhaps it was because a perpetual smile flickered over its features. The owner of the head was a foot shorter than his companions, but he took the center of the stage as inevitably as if spotlights had been focused upon him.

Tony did not lack an abundant share of curiosity, but the mysteries of chess, he realized, were far beyond him. Noiselessly he closed the door and shook his head.

7

The sequence of events at the Metropolitan Chess Club followed along lines distinctly military in character. Colonel Stafford, as president of the club, and as one greatly concerned with its welfare, consulted with Parmelee. As a result of that consultation, the Colonel took command, and organized a campaign.

Its first gun, and that surely a big one, was fired when Reynolds informed J. Hampton Hoogestraten, to whose support he had been contributing nightly for many weeks, that he had decided to abandon their customary games for a while.

"What's the big idea?" inquired the soap salesman. There were many other men whom he could beat in the club; but there was none who would continue losing to him at twenty-five cents a game as rapidly and as graciously as Reynolds.

"I have decided to spend at least a week studying by myself," said Reynolds. "I'm going to go home and lock myself up in my study. I'm going to take an armful of chess books with me, and I'm going to perfect my game."

In view of little Reynolds's great importance in the business world, and in further view of the monstrous salary which a week's devotion to anything but the affairs of his trust company would sacrifice, the statement was fishy on the face of it. But J. Hampton Hoogestraten could think only of the two or three dollars a night which the absence of his victim would cost him.

"You needn't go home to study," he said easily, "I'm teaching you by playing with you."

"Very kind of you, I'm sure, Mr. Hoogestraten."

"You have improved since I began," said the soap salesman magnificently. "Keep on, and you'll be an expert one of these days."

Little Reynolds actually blushed. "Now Mr. Hoogestraten, don't make sport of me," he begged.

"In any event, you can go on playing with me while you're studying."

Reynolds shook his head decisively. "No, Mr. Hoogestraten. I have made up my mind. I can't do both. I'm going to retire from the field, and when I come back, I hope you will find an improvement in my game."

Nothing that Hoogestraten could say could budge him from his determination, and the fat man, after exhausting his powers of persuasion and cajolery, ended by losing his temper. It was perfectly apparent to him that Reynolds had tired of their arrangement; that Reynolds would lose to him no longer; that Reynolds, in all probability, would never play him again. There was accordingly no reason why he should not insult Reynolds as grossly as he pleased.

"What's the good of your studying?" he said, giving full vent to the endearing qualities that had made him so beloved by his clubmates, "you've played twenty years, and you're rotten now. Study, and you'll only learn how to be rotten in more ways."

Reynolds kept his self-control admirably. "In that event the variety – when I come back – will make me a more interesting opponent," he said placidly.

"Huh!" sneered J. Hampton Hoogestraten, considerably beyond his depth, and again, "Huh!"

"If I can't get worse," said Reynolds craftily, "I may get better. Who knows? I've always been a great believer in study, Mr. Hoogestraten. A week of concentrated application may accomplish wonders."

Hoogestraten opened his eyes wide. It was only too evident that Reynolds was taking himself seriously.

Now the soap salesman was well aware that improvement in any game rested to a certain extent upon the mastery of its principles, but to an even greater extent upon natural aptitude. This last Reynolds lacked; and lacking it, was condemned for all eternity to remain a duffer. He had reached his zenith, such as it was, already. Nothing that either he or anybody else could do could cause him to rise higher.

This observation, perhaps, explains why J. Hampton Hoogestraten fell so readily into the trap which his clubmates had laid for him.

"I suppose you'll be such a great player when you come back," he snorted disdainfully, "that you'll be taking smaller odds from me."

"Of course, Mr. Hoogestraten."

"At the present odds you'll beat me."

"I hope to."

"Why don't you come out with the color? You hope to beat me at smaller odds."

"That too."

The eyes of the soap salesman narrowed. If he could tempt Reynolds, who had plenty of money, into betting —

"Perhaps," he ventured, "perhaps you are hoping to beat me on even terms."

Reynolds smiled diffidently. "I didn't like to say so before," he admitted. "It might have sounded like conceit. But since you ask me point-blank, I might as well admit that that is my ambition. You can beat me tonight, Mr. Hoogestraten. You can beat me badly. But a week from tonight, after I have devoted myself to the books for seven consecutive days, who can tell what will happen? You can be beaten, you know. I might be the man to do it."

"You wouldn't, by any chance, like to back that up with a little small change, Mr. Reynolds?"

"Why not? It would make the game more interesting."

"Just one game?" The soap salesman was plainly disappointed.

"That should be enough."

"Then how much of a side bet?" He paused, wondering how large an amount he might name.

"A dollar," said Reynolds.

"Two," said Hoogestraten.

"Five."

"Ten."

"Fifteen."

"Twenty."

"Twenty dollars," said Reynolds, following his instructions to the letter, "that will do nicely. And now I bid you good night, Mr. Hooge-straten."

The heart of the soap salesman leaped with joy as his prospective victim made his way out of the room. In a moment of idiocy, he felt, Reynolds had done an amazingly foolish thing, and he would benefit. That he himself had been cowardly and unfair occasioned him no concern. It was far more congenial to reflect that Reynolds would inevitably lose; that he might study his head off without endangering him.

Nevertheless he listened eagerly to reports on little Reynolds's progress as relayed to him nightly. This, the second part of Colonel Stafford's program, was referred to by the old gentleman as "breaking down the morale," and it began its insidious attack when Howells, a brief twenty-four hours after the match had been arranged, burst into the club with the startling news that he had spent the afternoon with Reynolds, and that Reynolds had beaten him in three consecutive games. Howells ranked two classes higher than Reynolds, and had never before, so he declared, lost to him.

Hoogestraten, puffing his rank cigar, bore the shock well. "You're not much better than Reynolds," he said ungraciously. "I can give you a rook any time and lick you."

"Yes, you can," admitted Howells, "but the point I'm making is different. I'm telling you that Reynolds, after a day's hard study, has improved so much that I can't beat him any more — and I used to. I'm wondering how good he'll be after he's studied a week."

Hoogestraten jingled his change pocket suggestively. "Are you wondering a dollar's worth?" he inquired.

"Yes," said Howells.

"I'll bet a dollar on Reynolds myself," Beers chimed in.

"Same here," said Aalders.

"I'll take five of that," said Strachan.

Hoogestraten had no desire to escape bets. He accepted twenty dollars' worth in a few minutes.

Yates, who topped the eleventh class, was selected to lead the assault the following night.

"Boys," he declared, "a most remarkable thing has happened. Reynolds phoned me to come to his house at five o'clock. I went. He played three games with me, and he made a clean sweep."

Hoogestraten managed to exhibit a placid exterior, though inwardly he was far from calm. In two days, according to reports, Reynolds had made progress which would have been sufficiently remarkable in two years. It was disturbing — very disturbing.

The soap salesman accepted a dozen more bets, and reflected that he was hazarding over fifty dollars. He began to be decidedly uneasy.

On the third day O'Neill succumbed. He ranked in the eighth class. "Study – concentrated study, that's how he does it," he explained. "He's sitting in his library with the shades pulled down, and soft green lights scattered around the room. He has a pot of black coffee on his desk, and a package of yeast tablets in his pocket. He has all the books that have ever been written on chess, and he's soaking up what's in them just as if he were a human blotter. He doesn't even leave the room for his meals: they're brought to his desk – and they consist of nothing but vitamins."

Had Hoogestraten possessed a sense of humor – which he did not – he would have seen through the conspiracy on the instant. Instead he inquired nervously, "Where can you get vitamins?"

"Imported from Scotland," answered O'Neill gravely, "they're small animals like squirrels – only furrier."

Hoogestraten accepted a few more bets that night, though he trembled in his boots. Common sense – such common sense as he possessed – told him that the whole affair was incredible; that no human being on earth could improve so rapidly and so consistently as Reynolds seemed to be improving. But the succession of assaults began to have its effect. What was unthinkable on the first day, was merely improbable on the second day. Quickly it became not only possible but reasonable.

Strachan, according to his own account, was bowled over like a tenpin by the invincible Reynolds on the fourth day, and when he suggested increasing his wager with Hoogestraten, the soap salesman, for the first time, demurred. The thought of the amount at stake no longer comforted him; it distressed him, and when Harbord, of the fourth class, and Forsythe, a really strong player, accustomed to battle Hoogestraten on even terms, were sunk without a trace on succeeding days, the fat man's agitation became very noticeable.

"Did he really beat you?" he asked Forsythe in the privacy of the cloakroom.

Forsythe, filled with Presbyterian scruples, would not tell a lie. "I didn't take a single game from him," he said quite truthfully.

It was then that Hoogestraten strolled casually into the clubroom, and made a determined, but unsuccessful effort to hedge his debts. He failed to relieve himself of a dollar of them. His fellow members, in unanimous agreement, declared that he, too, would fall before Reynolds. He believed it himself, and it did not need the knockout blow, deftly administered by Macpherson, to bring him to the depths of misery.

Macpherson, the finest player in the club, and a highly imaginative individual, put in an appearance twenty-four hours before the time scheduled for the great match, and his expression spoke volumes.

"Did he beat you?" chorused his audience.

Macpherson nodded sadly. Unlike Forsythe, he had no scruples against a lie — if in a good cause.

"Boys, he knocked the tar out of me. He told me to sit down at the chessboard, and he never looked at it. I called off my moves to him, and he called off his moves to me. Boys, there was never a minute that I had the advantage. He got the jump on me from the start, and he blew me off of the map."

"He beat you blindfold?"

"Ruined me," said Macpherson.

From a nearby corner came a heavy thud. J. Hampton Hoogestraten had collapsed.

8

The lengths to which high-principled men will go to avoid downright cheating are great. Colonel Stafford's elaborate campaign of demoralization had been undertaken in the hope that more decisive steps would not be necessary. If the soap salesman could be sufficiently terrified, calculated the Colonel, he would find some pretext to avoid the match. Despite the betting, no actual stakes had been posted. Hoogestraten would save his money — and would never dare show his face in the club again.

Until a few hours before the great game the Colonel's scheme was entirely successful. Unfortunately for him, however, it was altogether too successful. Hoogestraten, after a sleepless night, and in a state of panic, made a hurried trip to his physician. To him he confided his woes, and mentioned the amazing results of Reynolds' diet of vitamins. He had tried to purchase some himself, he admitted under seal of secrecy, but his butcher had been unable to supply them.

"The butcher?" repeated the physician in amazement. "Don't you know what vitamins are? You find them in fruits — fresh vegetables — salads —"

"Then they're not imported from Scotland? Small animals like squirrels — only furrier?"

"No, indeed!"

Hoogestraten slapped on his hat and walked into the street, feeling decidedly better. The fact that his tormentors had departed from the truth once, made it highly probable that they had done so more than once. He did not understand exactly what had happened; but he grasped enough to realize that he had been the victim of a conspiracy.

With that realization, the Colonel's campaign of demoralization ended in defeat. Indeed, he had barely remarked to the crowd that had

gathered for the match: "Gentlemen, I do not think that Mr. Hoogestraten will put in an appearance," when the door opened, and the
soap salesman, thoroughly and completely angry, marched into the
room.

He singled out O'Neill, author of the vitamin tale.

"I've been eating vitamins, too," he hissed, "imported from Scotland – small animals like squirrels – only furrier; and I'm ready to play
the game of my life!"

He discerned Reynolds, waiting at a table in the center of the room.
Somehow the sight of the little man in the flesh was less disconcerting
than the tales about him that had been relayed to him during the week.

He waddled over and plumped himself into a chair. "Come on," he
sneered.

Twenty feet away Colonel Stafford, observing developments, threw
up his hands and turned to Bill Parmelee. "I resign," he whispered,
"now it's up to you."

Now a game of chess, except to an expert, does not hold the visible
thrills of football – of tennis – of golf – or polo. There are no forward
passes; no cannonball services; no holes under par; no breathtaking
charges down the length of the field. Yet the huge audience – a hundred
and fifty at least – gathered around the contenders, took seats, or stood,
occupying every spot from which the chessboard was visible, testifying
to its interest by the sudden hush which fell upon it.

J. Hampton Hoogestraten opened his well-filled cigar case, lighted
one of his liver-colored cigars, moved, and the game was on.

Before replying, Reynolds, in his turn, produced a paper box,
opened it, and popped a tablet into his mouth.

"What's that?" inquired Hoogestraten suspiciously.

"Nothing but slippery elm," said Reynolds. "I'm hoping to neutral-
ize the effect of your tobacco."

The fat man grinned and puffed more vigorously. If any antidote
for his infamous cigars existed, he was anxious to put it to the test.

And in the background, understanding nothing of what was going
on, Tony Claghorn turned to Parmelee and whispered excitedly, "They're
off!"

"Hush!" said Bill. In pregnant silence he watched the first half
dozen moves, accompanied, on the one side, by furious blasts of smoke,
and on the other, by a rapid consumption of slippery-elm tablets.

Vanderberg was at his side. "How's the game going?" inquired Bill.

"Not well."

"What do you mean?"

"Reynolds has managed the opening badly – very badly," said Vanderberg.

With ill-concealed consternation Parmelee waited the ten minutes required to complete three additional moves. "Well?" he asked.

Vanderberg shook his head. "Worse and worse," he said. "Reynolds is playing like a novice, and Hoogie — well, Hoogie is playing chess. Reynolds is going to lose a bishop in a move or two." Even as he spoke, Hoogestraten, puffing like an engine, moved triumphantly. "Of course Hoogie sees his chance," Vanderberg pointed out. "If Reynolds doesn't brace up pretty soon, he'll be done for."

Parmelee, gazing helplessly at the game which was beyond his comprehension, saw his deep-laid plans crashing down to defeat. And then a thought, sharp and blinding as a flash of lightning, burst suddenly upon him. "Good Lord!" he exclaimed, "I know just what's happened! What a fool I was not to have thought of it!" He turned and dashed from the room.

It was Tony's turn to nudge Vanderberg. "How's it going?" he asked.

"Still badly." A groan came from the audience. "As I predicted," Vanderberg pointed out, "Reynolds has lost a bishop."

It was then, while Hoogestraten was gloating over the victory almost in his grasp, that an abrupt change came over the game. Reynolds moved, it seemed with new assurance, and Vanderberg, for the first time, found himself beyond his depth.

"What's the matter?" demanded Tony anxiously, "did he make a mistake?"

Vanderberg shook his head emphatically. "It's not a mistake: that's all I can tell you. It's either good — or it's extraordinarily good."

Hoogestraten seemed to share Vanderberg's opinion, for he gazed at his antagonist incredulously, and pondered his own next move well.

He moved. Reynolds moved — again a surprising move which disconcerted the fat man; and then, while the audience held its breath, it became apparent that Hoogestraten was meeting his match. No longer was the spectacle one of a strong player toying with an inferior; quite the contrary, the strong player, for all his strength, was as an infant in the mighty grip which his opponent was fastening upon him. He struggled; he called upon every weapon in his armory, but all to no avail. Relentlessly, mercilessly, brushing aside his resistance, the black pieces converged upon his weakest spot in a tremendous attack.

"What's happening?" gasped Tony. The very air was electric; the excitement in it was overpowering him.

But Vanderberg was in no condition to answer coherently. "Wonderful!" he whispered, "Wonderful! Marvelous! Amazing! Superb!"

Tony nudged his informant viciously. "Who's wonderful?" he demanded. "Which one?"

"Reynolds, of course!" crowed Vanderberg. "Of course, Reynolds!"

But for the uninterrupted crunch of Reynolds's strong white teeth on slippery-elm tablets, the room was still as death. Great beads of sweat began to roll from Hoogestraten's brow. His bejeweled hands trembled. He began to think of the tales of Reynolds's prowess which had come to him during the last week, and vitamins or no vitamins, he found himself believing.

His cigar, unnoticed, smoldered out, its vicious fumes first tapering off to a thin blue line, and then ceasing altogether; but Reynolds never suspended his continuous crunch. The only sound in the all-embracing silence, Hoogestraten found it curiously disconcerting.

He saw the attack, marvelously conceived and miraculously executed, pressing home. He realized its menace, and found himself helpless before it. He had won a bishop. In a dozen moves he found himself compelled to give it back, and saw the black forces marching on irresistibly toward victory.

He cursed himself for his stupid greed. Even on an apparently sure thing he had had no right to wager so heavily. To pay his bets would cripple him for weeks. And then an icy hand seemed to clutch his heart, as, looking ahead, he saw the end. First this; then this; then this and this; four moves, simple, beautiful, masterly, and their climax, his own checkmate. In an agony, he verified his calculations. There could be no doubt; four moves more, and then defeat.

His cigar case had fallen to the floor. Unthinkingly he ground his heel into the contents. And then, through the silence, came Reynolds's voice.

"Mr. Hoogestraten," it was saying, "if it's agreeable to you, I'll call this game a draw."

Agreeable to him? He leaped from his chair so vehemently that he upset it. "You're on!" he shouted. "You're on! It's a draw!" Then, to the audience, he tried to explain that in four more moves he would have been mated. Strangely enough, he found none to listen. After Colonel Stafford's brief declaration that all bets were off, interest in Hoogestraten had suddenly lapsed.

Only Strachan made his way to the fat man from the other end of the room.

"Mr. Hoogestraten," said Strachan, "our yearbook goes to press tomorrow."

"What of that?"

"In it our members are listed according to their classified playing strength. You will be listed at the foot of class fifteen — our lowest class."

Hoogestraten suddenly exploded. "Reynolds didn't beat me!" he expostulated.

Strachan corrected him pointedly. "You mean, you didn't beat Reynolds." He smiled happily. "It's a bit complicated, but I'll try to make it clear. If Reynolds had challenged you, and had beaten you, he would have taken a place above you in class three."

"Well?"

"That didn't happen. What did happen was that you challenged Reynolds and didn't win. You take a place below him in class fifteen. You needn't argue about it," he added encouragingly, "the directors have ruled on it already."

Hoogestraten grew pale. He had bragged about his chess to his friends, and to be listed publicly as the club's worst player was punishment more than he could bear. He would be the victim of numberless gibes – and he did not relish the thought.

"Mr. Strachan," he faltered, "isn't there some way in which my name can be kept out of the yearbook altogether?"

"Only one way, Mr. Hoogestraten," said Strachan mercilessly; "perhaps it will occur to you on your way home."

It did occur to Hoogestraten. In the morning he called up Strachan and resigned.

9

It was a jovial foursome that gathered around a table in a convenient restaurant half an hour after the match. In it were Parmelee and Claghorn, and Strachan and Niemzo-Zborowski. Zysser, the chess master's interpreter, had been lost in the confusion, wherefore Niemzo-Zborowski was silent. That, however, did not prevent his radiant grin, now more radiant than ever, from lighting up his face like a lamp.

"Why," demanded Tony, "why didn't Reynolds go on and lick that cad?"

Strachan looked at him reproachfully. "Mr. Claghorn, that would have been cheating. You forget that there was a great deal of money staked on the game. We didn't want to lose it; and we didn't want to win it unfairly. A draw was the one happy solution."

Tony glanced at him shrewdly. "Then the game, I take it, was not quite what it seemed?"

Parmelee laughed. "As you say, not quite."

"How so?"

"Well, Reynolds couldn't beat Hoogestraten – not in a million years."

"But I saw him –"

"You don't know what you saw. You saw Reynolds sitting opposite

Hoogestraten at the chessboard. You saw Reynolds handling the pieces and making the moves."

"What more was there to see?"

The conspirators exchanged delighted glances.

"Tony, old man, if you had gotten past the sentries, you might have seen Mr. Niemzo-Zborowski, sitting in a little room to one side, and playing that game for Reynolds! I got the idea out of Hoyle the day that the letter from the Metropolitan Chess Club arrived."

"Niemzo-Zborowski playing the game?" sputtered Tony.

"Why not?" asked Strachan. "Chess matches are played by mail — by telephone — by telegraph — by cable — by radio."

"There is a system of chess notation," Parmelee explained. "There's a kind of shorthand by which you can describe every move. When Hoogestraten moved, his move was reported to Niemzo-Zborowski. Niemzo-Zborowski worked out the answer on a second chessboard, and his move was telegraphed back to Reynolds."

"How telegraphed? It couldn't have been whispered. Hoogestraten would have overheard a whisper."

"It wasn't whispered."

"It couldn't have been signaled. Hoogestraten would have seen a signal."

"It wasn't signaled."

"Well, how was it done? Let me into the secret."

Again the conspirators exchanged delighted glances. Then, from his vest pocket, Parmelee drew a small, flat lozenge.

"This is how," he chuckled. "Hoogestraten's move was reported to Niemzo-Zborowski by word of mouth. One of the fellows near the door saw it, and passed it on. Niemzo-Zborowski's move was written down — in chess notation — on a slippery-elm tablet, and went from hand to hand until it reached Reynolds. Reynolds would glance at it — would make the move — and then he'd pop the tablet into his mouth and eat it! I'm no chess player, Tony; I don't even know the moves. But that was my idea, every bit of it!"

Niemzo-Zborowski understood no English, but the sight of the slippery-elm tablet, with a move scrawled upon its surface, explained the nature of the conversation. His grin became even wider, and emerging from the thicket of beard and whiskers about his mouth came a high-pitched, triumphant cackle.

But Tony was not yet completely satisfied. "If that's what you were doing, you low, unprincipled ruffians," he demanded, "how was it that the game started off so badly?"

Parmelee's smile vanished. "It started off so badly," he admitted, "that we might have lost it."

Strachan made a correction. "Any other man than Niemzo-Zborow-ski would have lost it," he said.

Parmelee nodded. "That's what they tell me. Well, I saw the pieces being moved, and I saw the slippery-elm tablets reaching Reynolds in plenty of time, and I knew something was wrong, but for the longest time I couldn't think what it was. Then, all of a sudden, the answer flashed on me, and I corrected things like a shot. I had found the mistake."

"What was it?"

Parmelee grinned nearly as widely as the chess master. "Different languages have different chess notations," he explained. "Mr. Niemzo-Zborowski was writing his moves in Russian!"

Tony's final observation did not come until the two friends were alone.

"An adventure in charity," he summed up. "We've had an entertaining evening, and you're ahead twenty-nine dollars and fifty-five cents."

Parmelee laughed. "I'm ahead nothing," he corrected. "Mr. Niemzo-Zborowski is a professional: he had to be paid to give his performance. I offered him twenty-five dollars. He asked fifty. I went up to twenty-six. He came down to forty-five. I went to twenty-seven. He said forty. We finally compromised —"

"At how much?"

"Twenty-nine fifty."

Claghorn went into a spasm of laughter. "So the net result, now that it's all over, is that you've made a nickel."

"Lost a nickel," corrected Parmelee gravely.

"How so?"

"I stood treat for a box of slippery-elm tablets," said Parmelee with a twinkle in his eye. "That cost a dime."

10

Sooner or later there will come a time when William Parmelee, ex-card sharp and more or less unwilling corrector of destinies, stands face to face with the guardian of the pearly gates, and when that time comes, the facts having to do with the downfall of that good man, J. Hampton Hoogestraten, will doubtless be investigated. Tony Claghorn will be interrogated, for Tony was a witness. Colonel Stafford will be examined mercilessly, for despite his seventy years and his snow-white hair, Stafford was an accomplice. The rank and file of the Metropolitan Chess Club, from Aalders to Zysser, will be questioned remorselessly, for they, too, each and every one of them, took part in the dastardly plot. Little Reynolds will not be excepted – he least of all; and the great Niemzo-Zborowski himself will be in for a grilling.

And while the many sinners concerned in the letting-down of J. Hampton Hoogestraten plead and parley at the great portals, the shade of that good man himself, smoking one of his infamous cigars, will stride into the blissful place unchallenged – maybe. And since that contingency is greatly to be feared, and since the facts in the case are more or less involved, it has seemed desirable to set them down here and now, so that the matured opinion of mankind, rising upward like heated air, may reach the venerable guardian of the gate in good time, and thus prevent a miscarriage of justice.

Let the tale be passed from mouth to mouth; let there be an abundance of witnesses. Then, perhaps, the members of the Metropolitan Chess Club, with Colonel Stafford at their head, will march through the gates in battle formation, Aalders at one point of their phalanx, and Zysser at the other. And somewhere in the midst, concealed by their numbers, will march little Reynolds – and the great Niemzo-Zborowski – and Bill Parmelee himself.

And as for that good man, J. Hampton Hoogestraten – well, what about him?

by John Kobler

The Pride of the Eden Musée

■■■ THE EDEN MUSÉE, a three-story architectural hodgepodge of
■■■ arches, pilasters, and ormolu at 55 West Twenty-third Street,
was opened to the public in 1884. For a year or more, as my grand-
mother used to tell me, a visitor to the place usually started off by paying his respects to the array of waxworks whose grisly charm made it
possible for the management to charge fifty cents admission and still
do a lively business. There were sixty tableaux in the waxworks section,
most of them stressing death in its spicier and more spectacular forms,
but, for the benefit of the high-minded and the chickenhearted, a few
patriotic displays of an inspiring nature were spotted along the way. If
the visitor's staying powers were up to it, he would struggle on to the
end; if his ears began to buzz, he could always fall out of line. In either
case, he was almost certain to wind up in the theater-café on the ground
floor, where, for a small additional fee, he could sit back and regain
his grip on himself by watching the performance of six-year-old Master
Walter Leon, a prodigy who wore his yellow hair in Fauntleroy ringlets,
dressed in velveteen and lace, and lisped as he gave lectures on topics
such as "Is Marriage a Failure?"

The sponsors of the Musée, a predominantly French syndicate
founded by a Count Kessler and headed by a New Yorker named Richard G. Hollaman, achieved a prose style as unctuous as an undertaker's
in describing their establishment. It was, their advertisements proclaimed, "a Temple of Art without rival in this country, affording to all
an opportunity for instruction, amusement, and recreation, without risk
of coming into contact with anything or anybody that is vulgar or offensive." James Huneker, the critic, writing in the *Times,* once called
the Musée the world's greatest assemblage of the "ludicrous and horrible." The public, tutored by its horse-car conductors, took to calling
the place the Moosie.

The tone of the Musée was stepped up in August 1886 by the

arrival of Ajeeb, billed as a chess-and-checkers-playing automaton. Ajeeb, whose body was made of papier-mâché and whose head was made of wax, was a larger than life-size likeness of a black-bearded Moor. Wearing a white turban and robe and a billowing red velvet cape, he enjoyed a thirty-year run at the Eden, during which he took on all comers, won nearly every one of his games, and wore out a series of more than a score of morose, brilliant, and frequently alcoholic little men who sweated through long afternoons and evenings inside him, guiding his right hand in the proper plays as they watched the board through a silk-covered slit in his midriff. My grandfather lost track of the number of times he vainly tried to vanquish Ajeeb. Throughout his career at the Eden, Ajeeb, grasping a hookah in his immobile left hand and wearing a stuffed cockatoo on his right shoulder, carried on in an atmosphere thick with theatrical abracadabra intended to support his owners' claim that he was a genuine automaton operated solely by a jumble of wires, cogs, flywheels, and pistons that were situated where the ordinary Moor keeps his lungs and stomach and were open to inspection, in a dim light, through a tiny door in his chest. All these works, which actually had nothing to do with the functioning of the dummy, were made of rubber. Judged by today's standards, Ajeeb was a fairly gimcrack mechanical fraud, but audiences then were not too fussy.

Ajeeb became the subject of earnest and for the most part fallacious theorizing by dozens of American and British newspapers and magazines, including the *Chess Monthly*, the *American Chess Bulletin*, the London *Quarterly Review*, and the *Cornhill Magazine*. One of the most widely accepted theories was that he was guided by some sort of remote control, probably electrical. A few of the enlightened persons who took to frequenting the Eden after Ajeeb's arrival seem to have been more impressed by his skill at chess and checkers than by how he functioned. There was O. Henry, for example, who, when he lived on Twenty-fourth Street, would frequently drop in at the Musée and challenge Ajeeb to a game of chess. Sometimes, when O. Henry found himself cornered, he would send an Eden attendant over to a Sixth Avenue saloon for a pint of Irish whiskey with which to clear his brain, and there are two versions of the scene that would follow. One has O. Henry gulping his tonic in full view of the red-eyed, thirst-ridden wretch inside Ajeeb; the other, and more charitable one, holds that O. Henry, while pondering a move, would slip the bottle under Ajeeb's robe and presently withdraw it, emptier by one snort. Another of Ajeeb's adversaries was Sarah Bernhardt, who played a game of chess with him on each of four trips she made to this country between 1886 and 1900. Christy Mathewson, the baseball player, liked to take him on too, and so did a number of Wall

Street men who used to spend an hour or two in the afternoon at the Musée on days when the Exchange was quiet.

Ajeeb was brought to this country from England by a couple named Mr. and Mrs. Charles Edward Hooper, who had designed and built him five years before and had already seen him through a long and prosperous run at the Crystal Palace. The Hoopers paid Hollaman a hundred dollars a week for the privilege of exhibiting their dummy and charged ten cents to anyone who wanted to see him in action. To play against him cost a dime for checkers and a quarter for chess. Mr. Hooper was a small, fragile, meek, quick-witted Englishman, the perfect specimen of an Ajeeb manipulator. His wife was a buxom Belgian beauty, hopelessly large for the work.

Ajeeb himself, by far the most impressive member of the trio, was ten feet high in all as he sat, erect, on a thronelike box. From the waist down he was mainly a mass of drapery. The game – chess or checkers, whichever the customer chose – was played on a board which rested on Ajeeb's lap, and his legs, which hung down as far as the bottom of the box, were completely hidden by his billowing robe. The box he sat on was four feet square and three feet high, and stood off the floor on four thick legs, so that spectators could look underneath and strengthen the illusion that no human agency was involved. The two front legs were hollow, although the spectators, of course, were not aware of it. The box could be opened at the rear, but this fact was concealed by Ajeeb's robe, which, like his legs, hung to the bottom of the box. When a game was to be played, Mr. Hooper squeezed himself feet first through the rear opening of the box, worked his legs part way into the hollow front legs, and then raised himself to a seated position in the box, his eyes on a level with the peephole in the dummy's middle. The customer, looking uncomfortably dwarfed, stood facing his towering opponent. The audience stood outside a rail fencing off the contestants.

Before a game, Mrs. Hooper pretended to wind Ajeeb up by turning a large key fitted to a plausibly noisy shaft in his right side. She then opened two six-by-eight-inch doors, one in the dummy's chest and the other at the same level in his back, and held a none too brilliant light at the back as if to give the spectators a good look at the tangle of rubber machinery. This called for great agility on Mr. Hooper's part. Just before his wife opened the doors, he had to twist to one side and lie along the bottom of the box. At the same time, he had to release a catch which dropped a shroud of black cambric over him as a precaution against players with especially strong eyes or suspicions. After Mrs. Hooper had closed the doors and announced that Ajeeb was ready to play, her husband would squirm back into position. Ajeeb was operated

by two levers – one, inside his right arm, controlling with great precision, the motion of the arm and of the thumb and forefinger with which
he handled the pieces, and the other, suspended from his gullet, producing the few but highly expressive gestures he made with his head.
Mr. Hooper would grab the first lever with his right hand and the second
with his left, squint through the peephole, and the game would be
on.

Ajeeb's manner while playing was imperious and deliberate and
gave no hint of the turmoil that was going on inside him. His right
arm swung over the board in a slow, graceful arc, pausing while the
papier-mâché thumb and forefinger closed on the piece to be played
and then moving it to the square where it was to be set down. He rarely
hesitated more than a second or two before moving. If a player tried to
cheat by moving the wrong way or by sneaking one of his opponent's
pieces off the board, Ajeeb would grandly sweep all the pieces off the
board and Mrs. Hooper would declare the game forfeit. If the player
was plainly a greenhorn and made a move forbidden by the rules, Ajeeb
would throw back his head in a gesture of mixed horror and scorn and
freeze in that position until Mrs. Hooper explained the game to the
novice and put things to rights. When Ajeeb played chess, he indicated
a check by nodding once and a checkmate by nodding three times. On
the infrequent occasions when it became apparent that he was going to
lose, he would concede the game by knocking over his king.

Before the next game started, Mrs. Hooper would open the doors
in the dummy again and once more her husband would have to duck.
Ajeeb's hours were from one to five every afternoon and from seven to
ten-thirty every evening. After each session had ended and the room
had been cleared, Mrs. Hooper locked the entrance and lifted the hem
of Ajeeb's robe, so that her husband, drenched with perspiration and
badly in need of a drink, could crawl out. All in all, it was a strenuous
life for a frail man, and in 1889, after three years of it in New York,
he began looking around for a substitute.

Hooper found a substitute in the person of Albert B. Hodges, a
twenty-nine-year-old statistician of Nashville, recommended by a mutual friend in St. Louis, who of course was in on the secrets of the hoax,
as an exceptionally swift and able chess-and-checkers player. Speed was
important, because the faster Ajeeb beat his customers the more dimes
and quarters came in. Hodges, who had a government job in St. Louis,
was told all about the new opportunity by the friend, and Mr. Hooper,
evidently feeling a nervous breakdown coming at any moment, engaged
him sight unseen, wiring him traveling expenses and instructions to
appear at noon four days later on the corner of Twenty-third Street and

Fifth Avenue, wearing a carnation. Mr. Hooper considered it advisable not to have a stranger wandering around backstage at the Eden until he had had a chance to size him up and swear him to secrecy. Hodges was easily sworn, but he sized up very poorly; in fact, he was almost prohibitively tall and stout. Mr. Hooper, however, was desperate. He hustled Hodges to the Musée and into Ajeeb, played him a practice game, and, an hour after the two men had met, told Mrs. Hooper to let in the day's first customers.

The only way Hodges could make himself fit was to lie on his side in the dummy's abdomen, and this allowed him to use only one eye at the peephole. By the end of a month he had become myopic and his head and muscles ached continually. He drank quantities of beer to ease the pain and this increased his girth. Even though Mr. Hooper morosely filled in for him one day a week, Hodges lasted only six months and then resigned to earn a normal living again as the chief accountant of Sailors' Snug Harbor. His successor was C. F. Burille, a Bostonian with the somewhat precious parlor-stunt knack of being able to solve sixty chess problems in an hour on paper. This didn't get him very far against Ajeeb's less effete opposition, and Mr. Hooper soon had to let him go.

The labor turnover inside Ajeeb presented a difficult problem. The professional life expectancy of an operator turned out to be just a little over one year. Mr. Hooper was always looking for players who were not only small and expert but sufficiently self-controlled to keep their temperaments and thirsts within bounds during working hours. Anonymity, an irksome thing for any professional chess or checkers player, was of course essential. After an Ajeeb operator had knocked off work and crept away to a bar, he had, on pain of dismissal, to say nothing about where he had been all day. On the other hand, the pay was from fifty to seventy-five dollars a week, which was more than most chess and checkers players could count on as a steady thing.

Only two or three men taller than five feet six or heavier than a hundred and thirty pounds stuck it out long in Ajeeb. Most of them were even smaller and slighter than that. At least two were consumptives, one had stomach ulcers, one was a dipsomaniac, and nearly all were anemic. The job was scarcely likely to improve their health. In summer the atmosphere inside Ajeeb was steamy, and its oxygen content always was low. This had such a soporific effect upon one Ajeeb operator, a fellow named Doc Schaefer, that he occasionally dozed off at his post while waiting for his opponent to move and had to be roused by a Musée workman hastily summoned to bang upon the dummy's throne under the pretense of repairing it. It is likely that opening the doors in Ajeeb's body before and after each game contributed as much to saving the life of the man inside as it did to the perpetration of the hoax. The head cold was an occupational disease among the Ajeeb workers, and a serious one, too, since an imperfectly strangled sneeze or cough would mean almost certain disaster for the whole venture.

The man who lasted longest inside Ajeeb was Harry Nelson Pillsbury, of Somerville, Massachusetts, a mental freak of startling capacities who wore wing collars and polka-dot four-in-hands, smoked Havana cigars, and drank a quart of whiskey a day. He worked Ajeeb from 1890 to 1900. He did, however, enjoy generous leaves of absence, to play in international chess competitions. He won twenty, several of them in Europe. His specialty, though one which he did not attempt with Ajeeb, was simultaneously playing ten games of checkers, ten of chess, and a hand of whist. A newspaperman who saw him compete in a chess tournament in Vienna in 1898, held as part of Emperor Franz Josef's Jubilee, wrote, "Pillsbury is a beardless young man, whose Anglo-American origin is easily read on his face. His profile is cameo-like, nobly cut; every movement is dignified and gentle eloquence. When Pillsbury sits at the board, he has an absolute stony calmness in his face; not a single muscle moves, only now and then will he wink a bit faster, when he feels himself slowly and satisfactorily nearing his goal."

Once, at the request of two college professors, Pillsbury took a memory test which consisted of repeating, as accurately as he could, a list of twenty-eight words and phrases which were read to him. Here, in its strange entirety, is the list: "Antiphlogistian, periosteum, takediastase, Plasmon, ambrosia, Threlkeld, streptococcus, staphylococcus, micrococcus, Mississippi, Freiheit, Philadelphia, Cincinnati, athletics, no war, Etchenberg, American, Russian, philosophy, Piet Potgelter's host, Salamagundi, Oomisillecottsi, Bangmamvate, Schlechter's Nek, Manzinyama, theosophy, catechism, Madjesoomalops." Pillsbury repeated it without error and without hesitation. Then he recited it backward. He repeated it again the next day, one way only. He died, insane, in Frankfort, Pennsylvania, in 1906.

After deducting the salaries of a barker and the operator and the hundred dollars a week they paid Hollaman, the Hoopers managed to clear a thousand dollars a month from Ajeeb. In 1895 they decided to sell out and go home to England. They found an eager buyer in Miss Emma Haddera, a ticket seller at the Musée who had long admired Ajeeb. She presently married James Smith, an assistant manager of the Musée, and gave him a half interest in the dummy. Miss Haddera died a few years later and soon afterward Smith presented his wife's share

to a divorcee named Mrs. Hattie Elmore, who had worked her way up
at the Eden from selling catalogues to costuming figures for the waxworks. Smith had tuberculosis of the bones and Mrs. Elmore, in return
for his generosity, took care of him until he died, after which she became the sole owner of Ajeeb. Hiring one chess-and-checkers expert
after another, Mrs. Elmore kept Ajeeb in operation until 1915, when
the Eden went bankrupt and closed, done in by the cinema. The honor
of being the last man to work in Ajeeb at the Musée went to Jesse B.
Hanson, who was further distinguished by being nearly six feet tall — a
giant by Ajeeb standards. He compensated for his height by weighing
only a hundred pounds and by his ability to coil up inside Ajeeb, somewhat like a rattler.

Ajeeb remained in being but went steadily downhill after the Eden
folded. Sam Gumpertz, the expansive gentleman who is now one of the
owners of Hamid's Million Dollar Pier in Atlantic City, got what might
be called his start by buying a controlling interest in the Musée's waxworks for fifteen thousand dollars and moving them to a museum which
he opened on Surf Avenue at Coney Island, also under the name Hamid's. Mrs. Elmore trailed along with Ajeeb. Finding it hard to pay the
high salaries asked by skillful chess players, she decided to confine the
dummy's activities to checkers. She hired, as the manipulator, a tiny,
consumptive Brooklyn boy named Sam Gonotsky, who also was a part-
time Western Union messenger and frequently wore his uniform while
on duty in Ajeeb. Gonotsky finally died, and shortly afterward Mrs.
Elmore had a disagreement with Gumpertz and moved Ajeeb a few
doors down Surf Avenue to a rival museum called the World of Wax,
where for several seasons she did a desultory business with the help of
fly-by-night checkers players. Meanwhile, she married a handsome,
three-hundred-pound Army drum major named Wethereall McKeever
and settled down with him in a frame house which they bought on
Avenue U in Brooklyn. In 1925 she retired and took Ajeeb home with
her. Her husband, whose size made it safe for him to show an indulgent
interest in the dummy, built him a shed on the front lawn and Mrs.
McKeever embroidered him a pretty Chinese robe. During the first year
of her retirement, she turned down six offers from showmen who
wanted to buy Ajeeb. "I just like to keep him around, fixed up nice,"
she told one of them.

The first chess-and-checkers-playing dummy was not Ajeeb. It was
Turk, who made his début in Austria in 1769, a little over a hundred
years ahead of Ajeeb. Turk had a career almost as illustrious as Ajeeb's
and was operating in the Chinese Museum in Philadelphia when he
was destroyed in a fire in 1854. Imitations of Turk, named Mephisto,

Hajeb, As-Rah, and so on, appeared briefly in various parts of the world and then dropped out of sight. Ajeeb was the last of the great dummies and, a modest amount of research has revealed, the only one to survive to this day.

In an effort to find out what ever happened to Ajeeb, who is now over seventy-five, and to those of his owners and manipulators who survived the experience, I learned that he had been moved from his shed on the McKeevers' front lawn and stored out in Queens, dissected into eight parts. Seven-eighths of him, done up in packing cases, rested in the back of a Cadillac touring car which was itself stored on blocks in an open-air parking lot in Astoria; the other eighth — his head — lay swathed in silk in a trunk in the Jackson Heights apartment of one of Ajeeb's two present owners, a man named Frank Frain, who, in his own words, has spent a great many of his forty-eight years "hovering on the fringes of the theatrical world." Ever since he was twelve, Frain had admired Ajeeb, and he has owned him for the past eighteen years. He used to make out fairly well with the dummy, moving him about the country in the Cadillac and exhibiting him, in both chess and checkers matches, at one-night stands in Masonic temples, Rotary Clubs, and state fairs, but during the war wasn't able to get enough gas and tires to carry on. Frain showed Ajeeb twice under highly distinguished auspices — one at the President's Birthday Ball at the Waldorf-Astoria and again, a few nights later, at an Aid to Britain party at the Astor. Shortly before, Ajeeb played an engagement in the basement of Hubert's Museum, the penny arcade and flea circus on West Forty-second Street.

Frain's partner, who did the work inside Ajeeb, was old Jesse Hanson, the skeletal six-footer who saw the dummy through the last days of the Musée. Of the more than twenty men who operated Ajeeb there, I found that only two were still alive — Hanson, and Albert Hodges, who was Mr. Hooper's first helper. Hodges, who gave up to take the accountant's job at Sailors' Snug Harbor, quickly succeeded in putting Ajeeb out of his life; Hanson was never able to. At eighty-two Hodges was married and lived with his wife in a cottage at 84 Valencia Avenue, in Stapleton, Staten Island. He had his last serious go at chess some thirty-seven years ago, when he won five and drew eight of a series of thirteen Anglo-American matches, played by cable. His weight went on increasing after he got out of Ajeeb, and he acquired the build of a Kodiak bear. Finally, his weight leveled off at a hundred and ninety pounds. He winced when he recalled the hours he spent inside Ajeeb.

Hanson was West, trying to get along by playing in checkers tournaments, wiring Frain for money when he ran short and waiting for the day he could operate Ajeeb again. He was described to me as a shy man, happiest when curled up inside the dummy, as he had been during a large part of the past twelve years.

Frain and Hanson bought Ajeeb from Hattie McKeever in 1932 for what Frain considered the bargain price of a thousand dollars. Mrs. McKeever could no longer afford to turn down an offer for sentiment's sake. Her drum-major husband had died in 1928, a mortgage on her Avenue U house was about to be foreclosed, and she had had to go back to work at Gumpertz's Coney Island museum. A bent and faded woman of sixty-four, she was on her old job of costuming wax horrors. Mrs. McKeever sold Ajeeb reluctantly, and Frain, who knew how attached one could become to the dummy, told her she could come over to Queens whenever she felt like it and see the old fellow. Unfortunately, Mrs. McKeever was never able to get away from the waxworks long enough to make the trip.

I found Frain to be a slight, jaunty man with a wedge-shaped head that was bald three-quarters of the way back, at which point a shock of gray hair rose from the skull like a fright wig. His normal conversation was conducted in a confidential shout, which was disconcerting when he got to describing the supernatural qualities he attributed to Ajeeb. "Why, one time," he yelled, "the pieces in those boxes in the Cadillac got to jumping up and down, so help my God! And three times, when I went to fix Ajeeb's head on him, I fell down like somebody shoved me!" It was a source of satisfaction to Frain, an Irish Catholic, that he had Ajeeb blessed at the shrine of Ste. Anne de Beaupré, in Quebec.

Frain was born in Passaic. When he was nine, his family moved to the Hell's Kitchen section of Manhattan, where his father ran a butcher shop. Young Frain went to Holy Cross School, on West Forty-second Street. Evenings he sold newspapers in front of the Eden Musée. One of his customers was James Smith, the assistant manager of the Musée who inherited Ajeeb from his wife, Emma Haddera, and passed him on to Hattie Elmore. Smith took a liking to Frain and occasionally asked the lad out to beer parties after the Musée had shut down for the night. Hanson was at one of these affairs, grew friendly with Frain, and gradually, over a period of weeks, let him in on the Ajeeb secret. Frain studied journalism at New York University for a short while and on the strength of that got a position as office boy at the *Scientific American*. After that he kicked around, doing odd jobs as a theatrical press agent, for twenty years or more. He always kept in touch with Hanson, who had become an itinerant checkers player.

Hanson became a quite distinguished man in his field. The record book of the Second International Checkers Match, in 1927, devoted twenty-five times to him, which was recognition equivalent to a whole column in *Who's Who*. He was born in Sacramento fifty-four years ago [that is, 1885] and he did nothing but play checkers after he was twelve. Before that he had driven a butcher's truck. When he was twenty-three, he went abroad, where he defeated some of the best checkers men of Germany, France, and England. After returning to this country, he went to work for Smith at the Eden. A lot of his best playing has been done in the name of Ajeeb, but he has won enough games as Jesse Hanson to be classed as one of the country's twenty ranking players. A bachelor with a mournful countenance and prominent ears, he was given neither to conversation nor easy companionship. He was never, by the way, what Frain considered a drinking man, but his partner conceded that "he takes a little whiskey now and then because he likes to feel his heart beat good and hard."

The most prosperous year Frain and Hanson had with Ajeeb was 1936, when they signed a contract with the Radio Corporation of America to take him on the road to advertise the company's Magic Brain radio. Ajeeb, with Magic Brain posters pinned on his robe and with Hanson inside, appeared in department stores, amusement parks, and hotels, while the partners incredulously split three hundred dollars a week and ten-cents-a-mile traveling expenses. They were authorized to give away every month a thousand dollars' worth of Magic Brain radios to people who beat Ajeeb, but in the whole tour they had to part with only eight $25 credit slips toward a radio – the prize for playing the dummy to a draw. Frain considers the trip a great success. "In Chicago, we outdrew Dizzy Dean, so help my God," he told me.

The Queens apartment which Frain shared with his wife and Ajeeb's head consisted of two rooms. Mrs. Frain, a dress designer, worked in a Brooklyn department store. Her husband spent most of the day away from home, hanging around Broadway and waiting for something to turn up. He said he had modernized Ajeeb considerably and spoke vaguely, but with pride, of an air-conditioning system which he had installed in the dummy. "The apparatus is all so mysterious that even genuine scientists don't ask questions for fear of embarrassing themselves," Frain said by way of warning to inquisitive laymen. When Frain had nothing better to do he got out Ajeeb's head and smeared its eyelids with vaseline, massaged its cheeks, and combed its long beard. He thought this helped preserve the lifelike expression he saw in the face. "The natural expression is intent, piercing, and friendly," Frain said, looking intent, piercing, and friendly himself. "When I set him up in the right light, with mirrors and drapes, there's a lot of controversy as to whether he is alive, so help my God." It was difficult to find out from Frain just who was waging this controversy. He had little patience with questions that did not concern

Ajeeb's past or, which was preferable, his future. Frain thought that eventually the dummy's supernatural powers would be of as great interest to the public as his chess-and-checkers playing. Fondly contemplating such a prospect, Frain shouted, as a lesser person might murmur, "I am a man of speculative nature!"

by Harry Golombek

Writers Who Have Changed Chess History

1. Philidor

CERTAIN BOOKS STAND OUT as great landmarks in the history
of chess literature and the playing of chess itself. They are not many;
you can count them on your fingers; but each one has changed the style
of chess played, not only in its period but in succeeding ages. Whether
we know it or not, whether we like it or not, our play has been strongly
influenced by these books to an extent far greater than is normally
realized.

In choosing such books there seems little point in going back to
what one might call the prehistory of chess; for example, the work of
Alfonso the Wise, of which I saw a most beautifully illuminated manu-
script in the Escorial on a free day during an international tournament
in Madrid; this can have had little influence on the course of chess.
Moving down nearer to modern times, we find that such writers as
Damiano and Ruy López produced books that were successful in their
lifetime but failed to retain public attention thereafter.

The first book that captured public interest and retained it for
a considerable length of time was Philidor's *Analyze des Échecs* which
was published and republished an extraordinary number of times, not
only in the eighteenth but also in the nineteenth century. Editions were
still being published and read in the 1850s and '60s, so the book had an
effective life of over one hundred years.

Before considering the book, just a few words about its famous
author. François-André Danican Philidor was born in 1726 and was already a fine player at the age of fourteen. He seems to have been equally
precocious at music and composed a motet that was performed at the
Chapel Royal in Versailles when he was eleven years old.

How often we've seen this curious link between chess and music.

In our own day there was the great composer Prokofiev who was also a
first class chess player; and Taimanov, the Soviet grandmaster, is also
a concert pianist. But of them all, Philidor seems to have been the most
outstanding, since he was equally celebrated in his lifetime as musician
and as chess player. How it seems to have worked with him is that he
took to chess as a profession whenever music failed to provide him with
a livelihood, as occurred increasingly during the latter portion of his
life.

Philidor spent a great deal of his time in England. It was in London
in 1747 that he overwhelmingly defeated Stamma in a match in which
he gave his opponent the odds of the move and also scored all draws as
a win for his adversary. He won eight out of ten games. Two years later,
at the age of twenty-three, he published his famous *Analysis of Chess*
in London and from then on divided his time as a chess player between
Paris and London – until the French Revolution. In 1793 he came to
London and stayed there, having published two enlarged editions of his
book, again in London, in 1777 and 1790. It was in London that most of
his celebrated blindfold displays took place and it was there, on August
31, 1795, that he died.

When he first appeared on the chess scene Légal was the acknowledged leading player in France, but Philidor soon passed him and was
in fact the world's best player for the last forty years of his life. Where
he excelled, both as a player and as a writer, was in his understanding
of the game. A contemporary refers to the "enterprise and spirit of Cun-
ningham, the brilliant promptness at resource of Salvio, and the comprehension and foresight of Philidor."

It was this quality of understanding that made his *Analysis of Chess*
so remarkable. In clear, simple language he presented the reader with
a complete picture of the game as it should be played by a master. He
made no concessions to other opinions and no doubt would have been
regarded as dogmatic had he lived and written today. But nobody before
his time, and precious few since, have been able to see the game of chess
as a whole, to conceive a theory about its basic strategy, and to put that
theory into practice with great success.

As I have mentioned earlier, he enlarged his book with successive
editions and it is the most enlarged version, that of 1790, which I am
describing now. He starts off with the King's Bishop's Opening and then
comes his celebrated Philidor Defense, though there are a couple of
acute differences from the version we know now. In the first place he
makes Black move first when considering this defense, and then he
recommends the variation *1* P - K4, P - K4; 2 N - KB3, P - Q3; *3* B - B4,
P - KB4; incidentally, it should be observed that Philidor never left his
analyses at the opening stages, but went right on with them to practically

the end of the game, so that he is concerned with the middle game as well as the opening.

He gives much about the King's Gambit in which he prefers the King's Bishop to the King's Knight Gambit; but he has these wise words to say about gambits in general:

> A Gambit, equally well attacked and defended, will not be decisive; it is true that he who gives the pawn has the pleasure of uniformly attacking, and a prospect of winning, which would be realized, if he on the defensive did not maintain the most undeviatingly good play for the first ten or twelve moves.

The word "undeviating" is the operative one here; you and I can maintain good play for quite a while; but "undeviatingly" — I'm not so sure.

A little later he has this colorful remark about the use of the king either in the opening or in the middle game:

> Charles XII of Sweden was observed, very characteristically, to move the king more than any other piece; but this conduct is seldom to be imitated, on account of the ruin which involves the whole community of pieces if the king meet with disaster.

Charles XII was the king who died in dubious battle after ravaging Europe and exhausting Sweden by a series of endless wars. Added point is given to the remark by the circumstances of his death; he died in the front line and, since he failed to leave instructions with the next in command, the battle was lost

In the second part of his book Philidor starts with the Queen's Gambit, otherwise called the Gambit of Aleppo, and he gives the following variation of the Queen's Gambit Accepted: *1* P - Q4, P - Q4; *2* P - QB4, P x P; *3* P - K4, P - K4; which he eventually brings to a drawn position. The next line is *1* P - Q4, P - Q4; *2* P - QB4, P x P; *3* P - K3, P - KB4; and this, in the first edition, he gave as in Black's favor; but in later editions he modified his opinion to the extent of regarding it as drawn.

He then returns to the King's Bishop's Game, and devotes much attention to the line *1* P - K4, P - K4; *2* B - B4, B - B4; *3* P - QB3, N - KB3; while the final part of the openings analysis concerns a variation of the Sicilian Defense that goes *1* P - K4, P - QB4; *2* P - KB4, N - QB3; *3* N - KB3, P - K3; *4* P - B3, P - Q4; *5* P - K5, P - B4.

I have mentioned all these lines with one specific purpose: to show you Philidor's intense preoccupation with pawns. His famous remark "Pawns are the soul of chess" forms the basis of his conception of the game and, when you come to think of it, we have moved back very near to this idea nowadays. Why, only the other day Hans Kmoch published a book *Pawn Power in Chess*, entirely à la Philidor.

That this was a conscious conception on Philidor's part is shown by his Preface to the first edition, where he says:

> My chief intention is to recommend myself to the Public, by a novelty no one has thought of, or perhaps ever understood well; I mean how to play the pawns: they are the very life of this game. They alone form the Attack and the Defense; on their good or bad situation depends the gain or loss of the party. A player who, when he has played a pawn well, can give no reason for his moving it to such a square, may be compared to a General, who with much practice has little or no theory.

Studded throughout the analysis are remarks – true to this day – that inculcate this pawn technique. For example, he has this to say about capturing with a pawn:

> When you have two bodies of pawns, and an opportunity of transferring a pawn from one body to another, the pawn should pass to the larger division, to concentrate them.

He continually emphasizes the value of center pawns. Apropos of one attacking line he says,

> None of the attacks of the adversary are dangerous, because they do not break your center.

This is a profound remark well worth thinking about. And again,

> It is policy to decline changing your king's pawn for the adverse king's bishop's, or your queen's pawn for the queen's bishop's; on account of the greater utility of the royal pawns; occupying the center, they preclude the adversary from the most advantageous posts.

If this appears a truism to you now, then it is only because Philidor said it so clearly; before his time nobody had even thought their way near to this.

But the *Analysis* is not just a book about the openings, or even about the openings as they affect the middle game. It also contains a most important end-game section. With Philidor, in fact, the scientific study of the end game commences.

The first edition contained only the celebrated analysis of the ending of rook and bishop against rook. This ending intrigues end-game experts to this very day, and was much discussed some years ago when Smyslov won with rook and bishop against Bronstein's rook, in a Soviet Championship tournament.

The later editions give much more about the endings: the mate with bishop and knight; a study of the rook and pawn against bishop,

showing when it is a win and when it is drawn; then comes a reversion
to the more elementary rook-mate, followed by an analysis of the queen-
against-rook-and-pawn, and the queen-against-rook endings.

There is a section about rook and pawn against rook; queen and
pawn against queen; and another celebrated analysis – the queen
against the advanced passed pawn on the seventh rank. Finally there
are some studies of knight against pawn; two pawns against one pawn;
and two isolated pawns versus two united pawns.

You will realize from this list that Philidor's *Analysis* represents a
great landmark in end-game as well as in opening theory.

2. Staunton

He achieved fame by winning a celebrated match against the
French champion Saint-Amant, became notorious for his avoidance of
a match with Paul Morphy, designed a set of chessmen that has become
standard and is still very much in use today, edited the first English
chess magazine, and by his originality and enthusiasm brought about
the first international chess tournament ever, at London in 1851. This
remarkable man was Howard Staunton, the only British chess master of
whom it could be said that at one time he was the world's leading player.

He himself believed that his chief life work and claim to subsequent
fame lay in his edition of Shakespeare. But if there is a reference to it
nowadays it's only in a variorum footnote which starts off something
like "Staunton wrongly surmises," and so on. The fact is that, though he
was widely read in Elizabethan drama, those powers of analysis that
distinguished him over the chessboard seemed to desert him when he
was considering a Shakespearean text. No, if Staunton is remembered
for his literary labors it is in the field of chess journalism and chess
authorship. His *Chess Player's Handbook*, and, to a lesser extent, his
Chess Praxis, constitute his monuments more lasting than bronze. When
all is said and done this was only just, however ironic this may seem in
view of Staunton's contrasting attitude toward chess and literature.

He was born in 1810 and thus followed on soon after Philidor,
whose teachings by the way he seems to have understood not only more
than anyone in his own day, but better than most subsequent chess
writers. His death came in 1874, by another ironic twist of fate on June
22, which happened to be the anniversary of Morphy's birth. So, they
may not have had a match in life but they did meet in death. Staunton
was that rare bird among great chess players, a late learner; he was
nearly twenty before he knew how to play and in his middle twenties
before he became a really good player. But, by 1840 when he won a
match against Popert in London, he had established himself as one of

England's leading players. In 1843 came his victory over Saint-Amant, in a match in Paris, by eleven wins to six and four draws. Three years later he won matches against both Horwitz and Harrwitz and it was round about this time that he might have been reckoned the world's leading player.

Meanwhile, Staunton had become well known as a chess writer. In 1841 he founded the *Chess Player's Chronicle* and continued to edit it till 1852. This first series still makes interesting reading; but one thing becomes very evident when you glance through the *Chronicle*. Staunton regarded his readers as either enemies or friends, and the warmth of his language was such that the first class increased more rapidly than the second. To give an example, reference to George Walker's writings as "idle puerilities" was hardly calculated to endear him to a fellow author.

In 1847 there came his first and greatest work on chess, *The Chess Player's Handbook*. It was at once an immense success and remained so throughout his lifetime and long after. In between the years 1847 and 1935 it was republished twenty-one times. Two years later, in 1849, he published his games in a book called *The Chess Player's Companion*, and it was in that year that he designed his Staunton chessmen. Chess sets are still being produced on this design, and I for one have never seen a better.

In 1854 he sold his *Chess Player's Chronicle*, and commenced work on his edition of Shakespeare. He was engaged on this for the next six years, so it was no empty excuse when he pleaded absorption in literary work as a reason for not giving Paul Morphy a match. I don't want to intrude on a controversy that has gone on through the ages. Briefly, Staunton would have certainly lost the match; but his name would have smelled sweeter had he somehow or other found time to play it.

One more book by Staunton remains to be mentioned, his *Chess Praxis*, published in 1860. This was, to quote the title page, "A supplement to the *Chess Player's Handbook* containing all the most modern improvements in the openings, illustrated by actual matches, etc., in England and France." In this work, at any rate, he acknowledged Morphy's greatness.

From then on Staunton busied himself more and more with Shakespearean studies and apart from fresh editions of his *Chess Player's Handbook* made no further contribution to chess literature.

But, had he written only this one book, it would have been enough to put him among the classic writers on the game. It was not especially original. As he acknowledges in the preface, he owed a great debt to the German *Handbuch* of Bilguer and von der Lasa. Nor did he make any great pretensions; for he says:

Adopting the common basis founded by the earlier writers, López, Salvio, Greco, Cozio, Lolli, etc., and super-adding the important discoveries brought to light in the works of Bilguer and Jaenisch, I have aimed only at producing an instructive compendium available by the large majority of English players to whom those works are inaccessible.

But he added a considerable amount of his own analyses — again, as the preface says, "In my labours of collation and compression, I have subjected every variation to the test of repeated investigation." Nor was it just what he added that counted, it was the cunning way in which he arranged existing material that really mattered. The result was an ideal manual of the game, limited of course to the knowledge of chess existing at the time. With only small differences, all subsequent manuals have followed his model. The language too in which he expresses himself is natural and vigorous, simple and clear, and more direct in its approach to the reader than one might have anticipated. He makes no statement which he does not attempt to prove, shirks no issue and abounds in common-sense remarks.

Staunton divides the *Handbook* into six sections, or "books," as he calls them. The first book is elementary, and in fifty-seven pages he neatly gives the beginner all he needs to know. It should be observed that he makes few concessions. He writes for the adult intelligence; but all the same, the instructions are clear enough and unambiguous.

Book Two contains the analysis of what Staunton calls the King's Knight's Opening. That is, any opening starting 1 P-K4, P-K4; 2 N-KB3. So this section includes the Philidor and Petroff Defenses, the Giuoco Piano, the Evans Gambit, the Ruy López, the Scotch Game and Gambit and the Ponziani.

The method of presentation is to give a synopsis at the beginning of the book; then an analysis of the opening in question, starting off with a survey of its origin and history; and finally, at the end of the analysis, a set of illustrative games. This is about as neat and comprehensive a method as can be imagined, and Staunton has done especially valuable work in his classification and nomenclature of the openings.

There is, of course, considerably more to the book than this purely formal side, as indeed there must be to any chess book of value. Staunton, like Philidor before him, had a conception of the game which he endeavored to convey to the reader. Running through the work one can discern continual emphasis on two positional points. The first is on solidity; for example, he recommends the Giuoco Piano as an opening that usually generates games of the most solid and instructive kind. The coupling of the words "solid" and "instructive" is significant. Nor do we go far wrong if we equate Staunton's *solidity* with our modern *soundness*.

The other strain clearly to be discerned is a dislike for a constricted position or for a position in which one side enjoys noticeably less control of space than another. Here Staunton anticipates Tarrasch in a quite startling manner. For instance, he condemns the Philidor Defense for Black since "play as he can afterwards, if the best moves are adopted by the first player, he will always have a very insecure or a very constrained game." Similarly, he condemns the Berlin Defense to the Ruy López on the grounds that it leaves Black's K bishop locked in. Incidentally, it's a sign of the times when the work was written that out of the 135 pages devoted to Book Two, Staunton gives only nine to the Ruy López, though, to give him his due credit, he does state that it is a variation which seems to merit a more favorable judgement than has been passed on it by the generality of subsequent writers.

The third book contains the King's Bishop's Opening, that is, all openings starting with *1* P - K4, P - K4; 2 B - B4. This he gives largely in deference to Philidor, who favored this type of opening. But it is quite apparent that Staunton does not think much of it.

Book Four must have been the most popular section at the time, since Staunton analyzes in it the King's Gambit, with no less than 109 pages. Staunton describes it in the opening chapter in these words:

> This admirable opening in which is comprehended every variety of the game, beginning with *1* P - K4, P - K4; 2 P - KB4, gives birth to the most intricate and beautiful combinations of which the chessmen are susceptible.

Should we say with Molière, *"Nous avons changé tout cela,"* or should we remember that Spassky brilliantly beat Fischer with a King's Gambit at Mar del Plata?

Book Five is concerned with the Queen's Gambit and what Staunton terms the Irregular Openings. In this classification come the half-open defenses and the English Openings. Staunton calls the Sicilian the best possible reply to *1* P - K4, and terms the English "this fine opening." Both remarks reflect his own practice.

The final section of the *Handbook*, Book Six, deals with the endings. It is a large section containing 112 pages and it starts off,

> To play with corectness and skill the ends of games, is an important but a very rare accomplishment, except among the magnates of the game.

It is a melancholy reflection that this state of affairs hasn't altered much in the last 120 years in this country.

His treatment of the end game is much more systematic than that of his great predecessor Philidor, and yet one gains the impression that his heart was not in it, certainly not so much as Philidor's. It is in the openings rather than the endings that Staunton's chief interest lies, and manual writers have followed him in the tradition ever since.

The edition from which I have been quoting is the first, published in London in June 1847. My copy is a tattered one which I bought as a boy some thirty-five years ago for the sum of one shilling. It was a good buy.

3. Lasker

Emanuel Lasker was perhaps the most remarkable man ever to achieve eminence in the chess world. The phrase that his biographer, Dr. Hannak, once used about him — the Michelangelo of the chess world — was well deserved. His gifts and interests were so varied. He was world chess champion for twenty-seven years — from 1894, when he beat Steinitz, till 1921, when he lost to Capablanca. His tournament record was an amazing one. Over a long period he was almost invariably first, above such players as Capablanca, Rubinstein, Alekhine, to mention only a few. He preserved his chess powers to such a degree that he was one of the world's leading players almost to the end of his life. In 1935, at the age of sixty-seven, he was second to Botvinnik and Flohr at Moscow, half a point behind them and half a point ahead of Capablanca.

He was a fine mathematician, of a caliber sufficient to be praised by Einstein. A great deal of his life was spent in studying philosophy and he published many works on the subject. He wrote on political and social themes and composed a play. He was greatly accomplished in indoor games — bridge, Go, dominoes, and many others.

His literary output was prolific, on a wide range of subjects, and he was just as varied in his writings on chess. But the book which I regard as most important of all was his *Common Sense in Chess*, a small work of 141 pages, published in London and Berlin in 1896. This was a product of a lecture tour he made in England in 1895, and reads very much like a series of easy talks. It was at once a great success and was published again all over the world in ensuing years, in St. Petersburg in 1897, in America and Germany, in Spain and Mexico, and elsewhere.

Small as the book was, it had, and still has, a most important influence on the way chess was and is played. That it was, to quote the preface, "an attempt to deal with all parts of a game of chess by the aid of general principles" could not be called new. After all, this had been the aim of both Philidor and Steinitz. But his vision of the game was very different. He saw chess as a struggle between two intellects; for, as he goes on to say, "the principles laid down are deduced from considerations concerning the nature of Chess as a fight between two brains."

In the opening part of the book he attacks and denies two opposing schools of thought as regards chess.

> Chess [he says] has been represented, or shall I say misrepresented, as a game – that is, a thing which could not well serve a serious purpose, solely created for the enjoyment of an empty hour. If it were a game only, Chess would never have survived the serious trials to which it has, during the long time of its existence, been often subjected.

So much for that tedious old saying often trotted out by those who, poor devils, know no better, "Chess is only a game."

But then Lasker swings away to attack a different and more substantial body of opinion.

> By some ardent enthusiasts [I am sure he must have had Steinitz in mind here] Chess has been elevated into a science or an art. It is neither; but its principal characteristic seems to be – what human nature mostly delights in – a fight.

He qualifies this a little by adding that it is "a fight in which the scientific, the artistic, the purely intellectual element, holds undivided sway." Now this is very far from the view Steinitz held of chess; and I myself do not see how we could say that either one or the other was the right view. The controversy rages to this very day, Botvinnik being very much of Steinitz's way of thinking and Tal just as emphatically on Lasker's side. Perhaps it all boils down to a question of differing temperaments; and certainly both standpoints are perfectly valid.

Once he has laid down his chief principle, Lasker proceeds to cases; and the first point he makes is the necessity for development. It is as though Lasker was inhabited by two spirits, neither necessarily contradicting the other. The philosophic one enunciates first principles, and the prosaic deals with the practical side of the game. Thus he says that it should not take more than six moves as a rule to develop one's pieces and illustrates this by giving some brevities in which players come to grief through lack of development. There is a nice description of the disarray due to faulty development:

> The losing side had the greater part of his army in positions where they had no bearing whatever upon the questions at issue. They might have been just as well anywhere else but on the board.

He formulates the following four rules of development, drawn from his own experience over the board:

> 1. Do not move any pawns in the opening of a game but the K and Q pawns.
> 2. Do not move any piece twice in the opening, but put it at once

upon the right square. [How we all wish we could invariably achieve this.]

3. Bring your Knights out before developing the Bishops, especially the QB.

4. Do not pin the adverse KN [by B - KN5] before your opponent has castled.

I can think of specific instances in which these rules do not work; in the Queen's Gambit, for example, you just have to pin the opposing KN more often than not. But, by and large, you cannot go far wrong with these principles of development.

In the second chapter, Lasker has a look at the Ruy López; and it's interesting to see that he does not like the Steinitz Defense (3 .... P - Q3) since he does not want to shut in his KB. In this section he has a very important passage about gambits.

> When you are conscious not to have violated the rules laid down you should accept the sacrifice of an important pawn. If you do not, as a rule the pawn which you have rejected will become very troublesome to you. Do not accept the sacrifice, however, with the idea of maintaining your material advantage at the expense of development. Such policy never pays in the end. By far the better plan is to give the pawn up after your opponent has made some exertions to gain it.

Lasker considers other forms of the Ruy López in his third chapter and starts off with a brilliant remark in which his common sense has almost poetic force:

> Truth derives its strength not so much from itself as from the brilliant contrast it makes with what is only apparently true. This applies especially to chess, where it is often found that the profoundest moves do not much startle the imagination.

It is curious that Réti was to develop a very similar theme many years later, though neither he nor Lasker would have been particularly pleased to discover they were thinking along similar lines.

Common sense keeps on breaking out in this book, or perhaps flowering is the right word. A few pages later, after some fairly exhaustive analysis, Lasker warns against learning parrot-fashion.

> My object, in thus diving down into the depths of this position, is not by any means to provide your memory with ballast. All I want to show is that the superior position will perforce become overpowering, whichever turn you may try to give the game.

How often we've seen these ballast-laden players whom not even Lasker can help and who, once they have left the opening, either sink helplessly in the middle game or drift upon the rocks in the ending.

In Chapter Four he deals with the Evans Gambit, and recommends his own Lasker Defense to the gambit; while in Chapter Five he roundly condemns the King's Bishop's Gambit as directly contravening his second principle of development – the one that said that knights should be developed before bishops. Again he uses the weapon of common sense in most eloquent fashion:

> By what right should White, in an absolutely even position, such as after move 1, when both sides have advanced P - K4, sacrifice a pawn, whose recapture is quite uncertain, and open up his K side to attack? And then follow up this policy by leaving the check of the Black queen open? None whatever! The idea of the gambit, if it has any justification, can only be to lure Black into the too violent and hasty pursuit of his attack. If, therefore, we can obtain by sound and consistent play, the superiority of position, common sense triumphs over trickery, and rightly so.

Chapter Six, on the French Defense, is, I think, the weakest part of the book. Under the influence of his fourth rule of development, which condemns *B - KN5* before the opponent castles, he follows the Steinitz line. Even this section, however, contains some wise remarks. For example, he says about close games in general,

> The rules of quick development, as already laid down, require *one* amendment, viz. do not obstruct your QBP by your QN (unless you wish to open the game at once by *P - K4*), and advance that pawn as early as you can to QB4.

This sentence alone contains more instruction than many a book that we see turned out by the dozen nowadays.

Chapters Seven and Eight, which deal with the attack, and Chapter Nine on the defense, are all most valuable sections of the book. He defines the attack as "that process by means of which you remove obstructions." Like the rest of the chapter this is persuasively direct. It's interesting to see that he uses Morphy's game against Paulsen, with the celebrated queen sacrifice, as an illustration. What a fascination this game has held for all the great players of the last hundred years!

Where common sense comes into the attack most strongly is shown in his rule:

> Don't attack unless you have some tangible superiority, either in the stronger working of your pieces, or in longer reach. With the corollary: if you do, the reaction will place your army in a critical position, and the inevitable counter-attack will find you in disorder.

You and I know those players whose brilliance far exceeds their common sense, and whose attacks are made irrespective of whether the position warrants any attack. However, I'll mention no names, partly out of kindness and partly out of fear — who knows, I might be meeting one in the British Championship.

Lasker was one of the best end-game players the chess world has ever seen, so it is little wonder that his last three chapters, which are concerned with the endings, should be so good. There is no padding here, and no highfaluting verbiage. Consider this remark on pawns: "A pawn move without a clearly defined purpose is to be blamed." This is the height of common sense, even if it is a trifle severe for us lesser mortals. This is a work whose importance is such that, even now, it can hardly be reckoned out of date.

4. Réti

When I was in Moscow, in March 1960, I met a living remembrance of things past at the Central Chess Club. The occasion was the opening ceremony of the world championship match between Botvinnik and Tal. Inevitably, some speeches were made; but the Russians have a delightful habit of making these events beguiling by holding a concert; ballerinas perform solo dances; famous singers sing arias, and distinguished musicians play the piano or the violin. One of the items this time was a prelude for pianoforte dedicated to Tal and Botvinnik. Afterward I was introduced to the composer, who, surprisingly enough, wasn't a chess player. His connection with the chess world was that his wife was the former Mrs. Réti. Despite the passage of some thirty-five years since the remark was made, on looking at her I realized what was meant when it was said that Réti may not have won a beauty prize over the board at Moscow 1925, but he had come away with one all the same. For this was the beautiful Russian girl whom he had met and married in Moscow that year.

Réti left a great impression behind him in Moscow, and his writings are still rightly regarded by Soviet chess experts as the most important of their kind in this century. When one considers that only two books by him appeared in his lifetime, and that a further two were published posthumously, one is amazed that such a small output should have had such a great effect. Of Réti, almost more than of anyone, it could be said that here was a writer who indeed changed the whole course of chess history. His art was great though his life was short. Born at Pezzinok, near Bratislava, in what is now Czechoslovakia, on May 28, 1889, he died of scarlet fever in a Prague hospital on June 6, 1929. So he was only forty when he died, and his life was cut short just at the height of his literary career. His best period as a player was already past;

for, after winning the great international tournament at Gothenburg in 1921 and achieving further successes in the early 1920s, he had been tending more and more to devote his energies to writing rather than playing.

Réti's first book we really owe indirectly to one Franz Gutmayer. The worthy Franz belonged to the perennial breed of hack chess writers of which we have some notable examples living today. The laws of libel prevent me from mentioning names, but no doubt the reader, like the Lord High Executioner in *The Mikado,* will have his little list.

Gutmayer was horribly prolific, another characteristic trait, and wrote books on all sorts of chess subjects: *The Way to Chess Mastership, The Secrets of the Art of Combination, My System,* and many others. He distressed and annoyed Réti for two particular reasons. One was that his books were widely read and the other was that he understood little about what he was writing. Understanding as little as he did, Gutmayer had one infallible recipe – if a master was dead he was great, and, if he was alive, then, by the same reasoning one was forced to suppose he could not be as good as those dead. Trying to be as fair to him as was possible, Réti wrote,

> This Gutmayer, who might perhaps in fifty years' time be so far advanced as to comprehend Steinitz, has at present achieved this much at least – a partial understanding of Morphy.

But, alarmingly, Gutmayer projected a whole series of books designed to show what the great masters of the past, in particular Morphy, had contributed to the game. This, Réti found intolerable; he wrote first a series of articles proving that Gutmayer did not really understand the subject and then, driven on by the intrinsic interest of the theme, a little book of 121 pages that was published in Vienna in 1922 under the title of *Die Neuen Ideen im Schachspiel* (New Ideas in Chess). An enlarged version of this book was translated into English by John Hart, and published by Bell in London, 1923. It was an instantaneous success; a second edition appeared the following year, and it was republished with a new foreword by myself, twenty years later. It contains 181 pages, it is a sheer joy and delight to read from beginning to end, and nothing to approach it has been written either before or since. Its readability is naturally a virtue, but its chief value lies in the deeper understanding it gives to the reader of the game of chess, especially in its strategic aspects. In fact, given a promising young player who already plays good chess but needs just that little something extra necessary to bring him along to master strength, I would say that reading and study of this book might well provide this final spur.

The first chapter deals with the development of positional play.

Réti describes the dark ages that prevailed till the middle of the nine-teenth century, until the advent of Morphy, in fact, when there was a sole preoccupation with the combination and other aspects of the game were grossly neglected. But he has an interesting footnote: "An exception was the great chess philosopher, A. D. Philidor, who was too much in advance of his time to be properly understood." But don't imagine that Réti underestimates the beauty of Anderssen's combinations. He gives the famous instance of his wonderful combination against Du-fresne and explains exactly where the beauty lies.

There follows a wise section on combinations in their relation to positional play with an important passage that seems specially designed to dash the layman's idea of the great chess player:

> Those chess lovers [he writes] who ask me how many moves I usually calculate in advance, when making a combination, are al-ways astonished when I reply, quite truthfully "as a rule not a sin-gle one."

And later on he specifies his chief aim in writing:

> Speaking generally the essential object of this work is to deal not with exact combinations but with all kinds of considerations relat-ing to the development and evolution of the strategic mind.

One wonders whether here he is not perhaps exorcizing the ghost of Gutmayer, who, you may remember, did write a book on the art of com-bination.

Then Réti comes to Paul Morphy who was, he says, the first posi-tional player and demonstrated the principles for the treatment of open positions. This chapter has been much criticized and disparaged by recent writers who unite sophistication and ignorance to a curious and astonishing degree. But it must be said that a study of Morphy's games bears out exactly what Réti says about Morphy's being more at home in open than in close positions. How important this chapter is, appears in this remark on the section dealing with the opening:

> Another of Morphy's perceptions, which becomes clear in a large number of his games, is that superior development increases in value, in proportion as the game is more open.

Obvious, do you think? But only after Réti has said it.

In the next chapter he deals with the man whom he terms "the greatest representative of the scientific tendency in chess – Wilhelm Steinitz," and by argument and illustration he shows the difference in approach to chess between Steinitz and Morphy. His theme here is that Steinitz was responsible for the discovery of the principles of dealing with close positions, just as Morphy found those for open positions.

This is followed by a chapter on the Steinitz school in which Réti shows how Tarrasch developed Steinitz's theories and extended them to wider fields. He gives a passage that contains a remarkably generous tribute to Tarrasch, all the more so when one realizes that Réti himself was one of the leaders of a school directly in reaction against Tarrasch's teachings. There's a certain piquancy in the passages about the inimitable Emanuel Lasker as he describes him, when one remembers how Réti always found him his most redoubtable adversary over the board. It is in this section that he has a wonderful description of chess at its best — "It is the triumph of the intellect and genius over lack of imagination; the triumph of personality over materialism."

Under a section headed "Americanism in Chess" he makes an interesting contrast between the romanticism of Charousek, as representing European intellectual life, and the colossal efficiency of Pillsbury, typical of the best in America. Pillsbury's games, he says, "show astonishingly big lines in their undertakings and have a refreshing effect upon their onlooker through the energy in their execution." Incidentally, this whole section is an addition and is not to be found in the original German version.

It is when Réti comes to describe Schlechter and his style of play that he rises to his greatest poetic heights. Schlechter was a Viennese and so, for all his Czechoslovak nationality, was Réti too, in spirit. "Vienna," he says, "has an old chess tradition, because chess is particularly the game of the unappreciated, who seek in play that success which life has denied them." I could really quote the entire section about Schlechter since it is all pure gold; but I'll content myself with the final paragraph:

> By the time we shall have grown weary of the blatant combinations of the old masters and the over-subtle positional plans of the new ones, we shall still delight in immersing ourselves in Schlechter's games, in which, side by side with the greatness and simplicity of nature, the grace and airiness of Viennese music are often reflected.

To reinforce his argument, Réti gives the beautiful game between Schlechter and John with its famous "broad design."

Chapter Four, headed "The Perfecting of Chess Technique," brings us to quite a different era, in which the heroes are first Rubinstein and then Capablanca. Rubinstein he regards as the greatest artist among chess players — perhaps the greatest compliment Réti could pay. And he gives us this serene passage:

> While in all of Schlechter's beautiful games there is to be found playful delight comparable to the joyful dance, and while with

Lasker a dramatic struggle captivates the onlooker, with Rubinstein all is refined tranquillity.

Before discussing Capablanca he reverts to what he calls an old question. What is chess, a game or a science? While admitting that chess is a fighting game, Réti seems to lean more to the theory that it is also an art.

Capablanca represents to him the beauty of modern technique and he illustrates this by a number of apposite games showing the same magnificence and precision as in the marvelous works of modern technique.

The remaining sixty pages are devoted to the new ideas in chess, and he borrows Tartakower's ingenious phrase "the hypermodern style" to describe the elasticity of thought which he, and his colleagues, Breyer and Nimzowitsch, used in their conception of the game.

It is the aim [he says] of the modern school, not to treat every position according to one general law, but according to the principle inherent in the position.

When you come to consider this sentence you realize how fresh an approach is necessary, to play as Réti required. And the natural counterpart to this is Breyer's joke, which Réti reproduces here. Under the heading of "A complicated position," he gives the initial position on the chessboard. But Réti takes it seriously, and goes on to discuss which is the better first move: *1* P - K4 or *1* P - Q4, finishing up with this deep remark: "The opening is the hardest part of the game; for it is very difficult at that point to get to know what is really going on."

Then comes a section on Alekhine, with a description of a typical Alekhine combination as one in which it is the final move that takes his opponent's breath away. A section about that extraordinary genius Breyer is of great value as regards the hypermodern way of thought, and his premature death moves Réti to say, "A new Steinitz was all too soon snatched from us." The remaining players considered are Bogolyubov, "a true artist"; Tartakower, "a child of his time," and what were then the youngest masters – Grünfeld, Euwe, and Sämisch. Lastly he talks about symbolism in chess, and I leave Réti with the final words: "In the idea of chess and the development of the chess mind we have a *picture* of the intellectual struggle of mankind."

5. Nimzowitsch

In the early years of this century, round about 1906 and 1907, two young chess masters were breaking their way into the international arena – Aron Nimzowitsch of Riga, in Latvia, and David Przepiorka of

Warsaw, in Poland. They had much in common: for one thing they were both Jewish, and for another they had a passionate devotion to chess as a game in which they could exercise their great combinational gifts. But despite these mutual interests, and although they were continually coming across each other in the chess world, a certain coldness seemed to exist between them. Now, you couldn't say Przepiorka was responsible for this. He was the most amiable of chess masters, and I well remember the friendly conversations we shared at my first international team tournament, at Warsaw, 1935. It was Nimzowitsch who wouldn't speak to Przepiorka and refrained from shaking him by the hand or even from saying hello when they met.

This state of affairs went on for many years – until the year 1930, when both were playing in an international tournament at Liège. Then at last, when Przepiorka had won a most brilliant game, the ice melted. Nimzowitsch congratulated him warmly, shook him by the hand, and told him how much he had admired the beautiful conception with which Przepiorka had crowned his brilliancy. Now was the moment for Przepiorka to discover the reason for their strained relations. "Tell me, grandmaster," he said, "why haven't you spoken to me all these years?" "Oh," replied Nimzowitsch, "I always thought you were a member of the Tarrasch school."

This showed how earnestly Nimzowitsch believed in the truth of his own theories. Until Przepiorka had demonstrated by actual play that he too followed these theories Nimzowitsch had classed him as a member of the enemy camp and, as such, practically criminal and certainly antisocial. This little story links up with a passage toward the end of his greatest book, *My System*. His is writing about the line 1 P - K4, P - QB4; 2 N - KB3, N - KB3; and he says,

> I tried it on Schlechter; and in the book of the Congress we find the following note to this move by Tarrasch: "Not good, since the Knight is at once driven away, but Herr Nimzowitsch goes his own road in the openings, one, however, which cannot be recommended to the public."

This must have hurt Nimzowitsch grievously at the time, and he goes on to say,

> Ridicule can do much, for instance embitter the existence of young talents; but one thing is not given to it, to put a stop permanently to the incursion of new and powerful ideas. The old dogmas, such as the ossified teaching on the center, the worship of the open game, and in general the whole formalistic conception of the game, who bothers himself today about these? The new ideas, however, those supposed byways, not to be recommended to the

public, these are become today highways, on which great and small move freely in the consciousness of absolute security.

Poor Tarrasch, you might feel, after all this. But you needn't worry — Tarrasch gave as good as he got, and posterity, at any rate, can reconcile the two warring schools by awarding a measure of truth to each one. In his milder moments even Nimzowitsch would admit that Tarrasch was both a great player and a great teacher, though he still maintained that some of his teaching was deceptive.

He himself formulated his theories late in his rather brief life — he was born in Riga on November 7, 1886, and died at Copenhagen on March 16, 1935. He relates that in his earlier chess career he was solely interested in combination play. After discovering from bitter experience that this was not enough against masterly opposition, he retired for a while from active play and worked out his own highly original ideas on the game. He rejoined the fray, and his tournament successes came in the post-First World War period. They were notable: a first at Copenhagen, 1923, ahead of Tartakower and Spielmann; an equal first with Rubinstein at Marienbad, 1925; two firsts in 1926, at Dresden above Alekhine and at Hanover above Rubinstein; a couple of equal firsts in 1927, and a first at Berlin 1928 ahead of Bogolyubov; and, the climax of all, first at Carlsbad 1929 in front of Capablanca, Spielmann, Rubinstein, Tartakower, Bogolyubov, and Vidmar. A wonderful record that should have earned him the right to a match for the world championship. But the financial backing for such a match was never forthcoming; and instead, Alekhine played a couple of meaningless matches against Bogolyubov.

Nimzowitsch's writings roughly correspond with this period of tournament successes. From 1921 to 1930 he published a number of stimulating articles in *Kagans Neueste Schachnachrichten* (*Kagan's Latest Chess News*); and in 1925 came his first monograph *Die Blockäde*, published in Berlin, 1925. In the same year came his most celebrated work, *Mein System*.

Before going on to consider *My System*, let me say a word or two about his contributions to opening theory. These were of such importance that it is difficult to think of anyone who had a comparable influence in our time. I have already mentioned one line in the French Defense that stemmed from him; but there were also others in this same defense. To Winawer's line *1* P - K4, P - K3; 2 P - Q4, P - Q4; 3 N - QB3, B - N5 he made such a considerable contribution that the line is now known on the Continent as the Nimzowitsch variation. From him too stems the entire modern theory of the advance line *1* P - K4, P - K3; 2 P - Q4, P - Q4; 3 P - K5. Another intriguing defense he invented was the Nimzowitsch Defense to the King's Pawn: that is, *1* P - K4, N - QB3.

But beyond all question the most important was the Nimzowitsch Defense to the Queen's Pawn, sometimes known under the barbarous and illogical title of the Nimzo-Indian — that is, 1 P - Q4, N - KB3; 2 P - QB4, P - K3; 3 N - QB3, B - N5. Since he introduced this into master chess the line has become one of the most popular defenses of all. Naturally, there have been many additions and refinements made to this defense since his death, but it must be admitted that the broad lines laid down by Nimzowitsch have never been altered or improved.

The fundamental ideas of these openings are to be found in *My System*, a book so rich in ideas that I rather despair of being able to give you an adequate notion of its content in the space available.

What makes the book so valuable? Well, in the first place the originality and subtlety of the mind that produces these ideas; and in the next place the extraordinary manner in which they are treated and conveyed to the reader. There is a quality of vivid color in Nimzowitsch's writing that's all his own, and a boisterous type of humor that practically forces his ideas on the reader with much more power than the normal didactic methods — as Nimzowitsch himself says, "true humor often contains more inner truth than the most serious seriousness." In consequence, Nimzowitsch's ideas not only have wit in them, but are wittily expressed. Here I suppose the nearest parallel is Tartakower; but on reflection I can't find a true parallel to the Nimzowitschian mind in chess literature. No, for a comparison one must go to the poets — to some mind combining the witty depth of John Donne with the colorful originality of Robert Browning. How Browning would have delighted in Nimzowitsch's mysterious rook move, and how Nimzowitsch would have enjoyed the humor of Donne's "busy old fool, unruly sun" especially if for "sun" he could have substituted "Tarrasch."

My System is divided into two parts: Part One is devoted to the elements of chess strategy, and Part Two is a more advanced section about positional play. The two portions are not mutually exclusive. Many of the ideas in the first part appear in more highly developed form in the second; but Part One is certainly simpler and easier to understand at a first reading. In the first chapter he deals with the center and with development — rather like a more sophisticated Steinitz, who might well have written, as Nimzowitsch does, that "a center pawn should always be taken if this can be done without too great danger." Next comes an instructive chapter on open files, starting off with the proud boast, "the theory of open files, which was my discovery, must be regarded as one of the polishing stones of my system." The natural follow-up is his celebrated chapter on the seventh and eighth ranks, with its description of the "seventh rank absolute" — "by which we mean," he says, "that our control is such that the enemy King is shut in behind it."

Perhaps it is when he comes to deal with the passed pawn that Nimzowitsch is at his best. The chapter is full of such instructive remarks as, "every healthy, uncompromised pawn majority must be able to yield a passed pawn." Vitally important is his theory of the blockade here.

A short but highly interesting chapter on exchanging is followed by one of the elements of end-game strategy, where perhaps Nimzowitsch is not at his best. This is essentially a book about the middle game and the openings as they affect the later stages of play. He recovers his real interest in the next three chapters, those of the pin, discovered check, and the pawn chain. This last is something very much after his own heart and the chapter on discovered check, though short, is, as he says, "rich in dramatic complications." Let me just give you the pleasant little game (Ruy López) he won against a certain Ryckhoff: *1* P - K4, P - K4; *2* N - KB3, N - QB3; *3* B - N5, N - B3; *4* O - O, P - Q3; *5* P - Q4, N x P; *6* P - Q5, P - QR3; *7* B - Q3, N - B3; *8* P x N, P - K5; *9* R - K1, P - Q4; *10* B - K2, P x N; *11* BP x P, B x P; *12* B - N5 double check and mate.

With the second part of the book, that on position play, we have Nimzowitsch in his most subtle vein. Here we find his famous theories of prophylaxis and overprotection, and perhaps his greatest theme, that of the doubled pawn and restraint. It is no exaggeration to say that this theme has dominated the whole theory of the defense to the Queen's Pawn. There are such whiplash remarks as "First restrain, next blockade, lastly destroy," and such illuminating passages as

There is no such thing as an absolute freeing move. A freeing move in a position in which development has not been carried far, always proves to be illusory, and, vice versa, a move which does not come at all in the category of freeing moves can, given a surplus of tempi to our credit, lead to a very free game.

There is a masterly chapter on the isolated queen's pawn, and a still more magnificent one on maneuvering against weaknesses: here occurs the description of play on two wings,

We engage one wing, or the obvious weakness in it, and thus draw the other enemy wing out of its reserve, when new weakness will be created on that reserve wing, and so the signal is given for systematic manoeuvring against two weaknesses.

Finally, there are fifty illustrative games, all abounding in humor and imagination. My two favorites and, I suppose, those of most people are the Sämisch game with its wonderful *Zugzwang*, and that against Johner, one of the greatest of all blockading games.

2

CHESS

over the Board

by Irving Chernev

THE LITTLE WORLD OF PROBLEMS

A LITTLE delicacy by Kipping. White is to play and mate in two moves.

A charming under-promotion. Black with a preponderance of a Queen; two Rooks, two Bishops, a Knight and eight Pawns is completely helpless against the threat of a smothered mate next move!

SOLUTION:

1   **P - Q8 (N)!**

HERE is an easy but pretty two-mover by Gilberg. White mates in two.

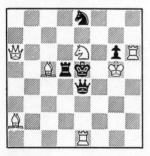

SOLUTION:

1   **Q - B1**   K x N dis. ch.
2   **Q - B5** mate!

Black's Queen, Rook and Pawn are pinned and unable to capture the impudent Queen.

WHITE moves and mates in three. This one is by Dobrusky.

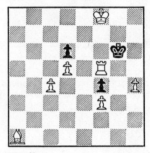

SOLUTION:

1   **B - R8**   K x R
2   **K - N7**   K - K4
3   **K - N6** mate

WHITE moves and mates in three. This problem is by Cheron.

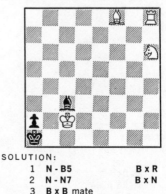

SOLUTION:

1   **N - B5**   B x R
2   **N - N7**   B x N
3   **B x B** mate

ANYONE can win with a Queen, two Rooks, two Bishops, two Knights and eight Pawns against a lone King. But the trick here is to force mate in no more than two moves. The problem is by O. Wurzburg.

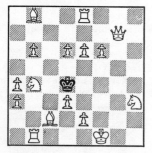

SOLUTION:

Believe it or not, there is only one way to force mate in two moves in this remarkable position. The key move is

1   R - Q1

FOR that long subway ride, try this miniature, by Shinkman, on your pocket board. White is to move and mate in three, and the only hint you get is that the key move is startling.

SOLUTION:

The first (key) move is magnificent!

1	N - R8!		K - Q3
2	K - Q4		K - B3
3	Q - Q5 mate		

TRY this little one by Dawson, mate in one; but, after you mate, remove the mating piece (and anything it has captured) and mate again and again. Keep on doing this till you have mated twelve times!

SOLUTION:

1 N x P mate		
Remove N(B7),	2	N x N mate
" N(N6),	3	P x BP mate
" P(B4),	4	P - B4 mate
" P(B4),	5	P - B4 mate
" P(B4),	6	R x N mate
" R(B5),	7	P x P mate
" P(Q4),	8	P - Q4 mate
" P(Q4),	9	P - Q4 mate
" P(Q4),	10	B - B4 mate
" B(B4),	11	R x R mate
" R(K1),	12	Q - K4 mate

THERE are only two lines of play in this little problem of Loyd's, but they show the pawky humor of this genius. White moves and mates in three.

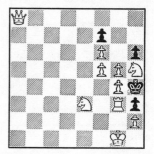

SOLUTION:

1   Q - KR1   K x P

2   N - N2   P x N
3   P - R4 mate

Or *1* .... P x P, 2 Q - N2, P x Q, 3
N x P mate.

STEINITZ once said, "If a man wanted
to solve one of Loyd's problems by
analyzing every possible move on the
board, he would naturally get the solution, but only on his last trial — not
before!" This is in keeping with Loyd's
own statement, "My theory of a key
move is always to make it just the re-
verse of what a player in 999 cases
out of 1000 would look for."

The hallmarks of Loyd's genius were
the startling originality of his key
moves and the fertility of his invention. Loyd was not afraid of being
unconventional if he could thereby
illustrate a remarkable concept. Sometimes, though, the problem was sub-
ordinate to the story behind its creation. . . .

Loyd composed this problem in 1858
at the Morphy Chess Rooms: White
to play and mate in five moves.

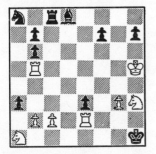

This is how Loyd tells the story: "It
was quite an impromptu to catch old
Dennis Julien, the problemist, with.
He used to wager that he could analyze any position so as to tell which
piece the principal mate was accomplished with. So I offered to make a
problem, which he was to analyze and
tell which piece did not give the mate.
He at once selected the Queen Knight

Pawn as the most improbable piece,
but the solution will show you which
of us paid for the dinner."

SOLUTION:
1   P - QN4   ....

Threatening 2 R - Q5 or 2 R - KB5,
followed by mate on the first rank.
(Not at once *1* R - Q5 as *1* .... R -
B4 then pins the Rook.)

1   ....   R - B4 ch
2   P x R   ....

Threatens 3 R - N1 mate.

2   ....   P - R7
3   P - B6   B - B2

Intending to reply to 4 R - Q5 with 4
.... B x P or to 4 R - KB5 with ....
B - B5. In either case, the Bishop
would delay the proceedings one move
and so make mate in five impossible.

4   P x P   Any
5   P x N (Q) mate

Thus the Pawn, which seemed in the
initial position to be a bystander, becomes the chief actor in mating the
King!

IN THIS one, by J. Halumbirek, White
moves and mates in six.

SOLUTION:
1   P - R3!   ....

Not *1* P - R4, P - R4, 2 P - R5, P - R5,
3 P - R6, P - R6, 4 P - R7, P - B6, 5
P - R8(Q) — Black is stalemated!
The first move is all you need of the
solution — the rest plays itself.

HERE is a little problem of which Kurt Richter says, "There's no hope for anyone who doesn't get a smile of pleasure out of this composition." White plays and mates in seven. This problem is by K. Piltz.

SOLUTION:

It is clear that White must capture the Queen Rook Pawn. But how does he do this without giving too much freedom to Black's pieces in the corner?

1	R - R1	P - R3
2	R - KB1	P - R4
3	R - R1	P - R5
4	R - KB1	P - R6
5	R - R1	P - R7
6	R - KB1	P - R8 (Q)
7	R x Q mate	

♛

END-GAME CORNER

THERE is a quality of simple refinement about this ending of Selman's which is extremely attractive. White is to play and win:

SOLUTION:

| 1 | K - R5 | .... |

Planning to win the Bishop by the zigzag route — 2 K - N6 and 3 K - R7.

1	....	B - N2
2	K - N6	B - B1
3	K - B7	B - Q3
4	N - N5	B - N1
5	B - K4 mate!	

♚

WHITE is to play and win. This is one of my favorite bits of Rinck.

SOLUTION:

1	P - N6	N - K3
2	P - N7!	....

Black must not touch this Pawn, as the Queen Pawn then pushes on to the seventh and then the eighth.

2	....	N - K2!
3	P - B5!	....

If 3 P x N, N x NP, 4 P - B5, N - K1.

| 3 | .... | N x NP |

Now Black is ready to answer 4 P x N with 4 .... N - K1, drawing.

| 4 | P - B6! | .... |

Here we have a pretty picture!

4	....	N - K1
5	P - B7 and wins	

♚

HERE is a little ending by Selesniev, with a surprise twist. White is to play and win.

SOLUTION:

| 1 | P - Q7 | .... |

The only move to win. On 1 R - Q1, R - KR7, 2 P - Q7, R - R8 ch, 3 K - K2, R x R, 4 K x R, K - B2, and Black draws.

1	....	K - B2
2	P - B8 (Q) ch!	....

Giving up that beautiful Queen?

| 2 | .... | K x Q |

Black gratefully captures.

| 3 | 0 - 0 - 0 ch | .... |

White snips off the Rook next move and wins.

♛

155

HERE is a cute little ending by J. Fritz. White is to play and win.

SOLUTION:

1 K - N3	N - N5

If 1 .... B - R6, White wins by 2 N - B7 ch, followed by 3 P - B7.

2 P - B7	B - B5 ch!
3 K x B	N - Q4 ch
4 K - K5	N x P
5 K - Q6	N - K1 ch

If 5 .... N - R1, Black's Knight falls after 6 K - B6.

6 K - K7	N - N2

Or 6 .... N - B2, 7 B - B4, and again the Knight is caught.

7 K - B8	N - R4
8 N - B7 mate!	

A delightful King wandering.

♛

ENDINGS with the heavy pieces often turn out to be heavy-handed, but not when Rinck directs their movements. Witness the graceful turnings and twistings of the performers in this Rookery. White plays and wins.

SOLUTION:

1 R - B5 ch	K - K1
2 R - K7 ch	K - Q1
3 R - Q7 ch	K - B1

After 3 .... K - K1, White has 4 R - QR5, R - N3 ch, 5 K - B7, and mate comes by R - R8.

4 R - B5 ch	K - N1
5 R - N5 ch	K - R1

Or 5 .... K - B1, 6 R - B7 ch, K - Q1, 7 R - N8 mate.

6 K - B7	R (N6) - N4
7 R - Q8 ch	K - R2

On 7 .... R x R, 8 R x R, Black's Rook is attacked while his King faces a threat of mate.

8 R - N7 ch	K - R3
9 R - Q6 ch	K - R4
10 R - R7 ch	K - N4
11 R - N6 ch	K - B4
12 R - R5 mate	

♛

White is to play and win. A prize-winner by Clausen.

SOLUTION:

1 P - Q4	....

Threatens mate on the move.

1	K - B5
2 Q - R2 ch	K - N4

If 2 .... K - Q6, 3 Q - K2 ch, K - B6, 4 Q - B2 mate.

3 Q - N3 ch	K - B3

If 3 .... K - R4, 4 Q - N4 ch, K - R3, 5 Q - R4 ch, K - N2, 6 Q - N5 ch, K - R1, 7 Q - R6 ch, K - N1, 8 Q - R7 ch, K - B1, 9 Q - R8 mate.

THE CHESS COMPANION

4 **B - K7!!**   **Q x B**

Else mate, by 5 P - Q5 ch.

5	**P - Q5** ch	**K - Q3**
6	**Q - N4** ch	**P - B4**
7	**P x P** e.p. ch	**K - K3**
8	**Q x Q** ch	**K x Q**
9	**P - B7** and wins	

The beauty of the solution harmonizes with the classic simplicity of the setting.

♛

AN ATTRACTIVE miniature taken from my "little black book," featuring delicate timing by the White forces. It is composed by L. Prokes. White is to play and win.

SOLUTION:

1	**P - N7**	**N - Q3** ch
2	**K - Q4!**	....

It is important that White "lose a move" and get to Q5 in two moves.

2	....	**N x P**
3	**K - Q5**	....

Zugzwang! Black's Knight is a prisoner. His King can move but only away from the Pawn!

3	....	**K - N2**
4	**N - Q8!**	....

A gift which enriches the giver.

4	....	**N x N**
5	**P - K7** and wins.	

♚

IN THIS ending, by Bron, White is to play and draw. It won't spoil the story to tell you that the last move is a stunning surprise.

SOLUTION:

1 **B - B6**   ....

Threatening mate on the move.

1	....	**B - Q6** ch
2	**P - K4**	**Q - Q1**

The best defense.

3	**R - R5** ch	**K - N1**
4	**B - Q5** ch	....

Apparently White has an easy draw, as he wins the Queen after 4 .... K - B1, 5 R - R8 ch.

4 ....   **Q x B**

Black gives up his Queen! White's Pawn is pinned, and, if 5 R x Q, B x P ch, 6 R - B5, P - R6, and Black wins.

5 **R - R8** ch!!   **K x R**

And White draws by stalemate! This and thousands of other beautiful last-minute rescues are a powerful argument against abolishing the draw by stalemate.

♚

ANOTHER Selman ending which has a morbid touch specifies that White is to play and draw.

SOLUTION:

1	B - K6 ch	
2	B x R	P x B
3	N - N5 ch	P x N
4	P - Q4	P - N7 ch

Or 4 .... P x P and White is stale-mated.

5	K - N1	P - N6
6	P - B3	P - N5
7	P - B4	....

And now Black is stalemated. Curious how Black's King is buried alive!

TRY THIS little end game in which Black's Knights betray his Queen. Its composer is Kuznetzov. White is to play and draw.

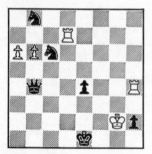

SOLUTION:

1	P - R7	Q - N7 ch

Black must drive the King off. If 1 .... Q - R6, then 2 R x P ch, and mate follows.

2	K - R1	Q - R8
3	P - R8 (Q)	Q x Q
4	R x P ch	K - B7
5	R - B7 ch	K - N6
6	R - QR7!	N x R
7	P - N7	Q x P
	Stalemate!	

THE FOLLOWING composed ending by M. Libiurkin is one of the prettiest compositions I have run across in a long time. White is to play and draw. I still marvel at the delicate balance maintained from the very first move to the last.

SOLUTION:

Black has two Pawns on the seventh, ready to queen. How does White stop both of them from advancing? If 1 K - N2, P - B8 (Q) ch, 2 K x Q, P - R8 (Q), Black wins.

1	N - N3 ch	K - R5
2	K - N2	P - B8 (Q) ch
3	K x Q	B - K5!
4	N - R1!!	B x N
5	B - R3!!	B - B3
6	B - N2!	B x B
7	P - Q7	P - R8 (Q) ch

After sacrificing his Knight and his Bishop, White lets his opponent queen with a check!

8	K - Q2!	Drawn

There are no more checks, and the Pawn cannot be stopped by the Queen or the Bishop.

IN THIS ONE, by Valvo, White is to play and win.

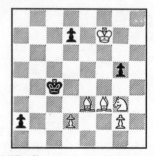

SOLUTION:

1	B - Q4	K x B
2	N - K2 ch	K - K4

If 2 .... K - B4, then 3 N - B1, P - R8 (Q), 4 N - N3 ch; or if 2 .... K - B5, then 3 B - Q5 ch, K x B, 4 N - B3 ch, and White wins.

| 3 | P - Q4 ch | K - Q3 |

If 3 .... K - B4, then 4 P - N4 mate.

| 4 | N - B3 | P - R8 (Q) |
| 5 | N - N5 mate | |

IN THIS ONE, by Sarychev, White is to play and draw. Note that he must lose one of his Bishops.

SOLUTION:

| 1 | P - N3 ch | B x P |

If 1 .... K x P, then 2 B - K5 ch.

2	B - B1 ch	K - N5
3	B - R1!!	R - N8
4	K - N2!	R x B
	Stalemate!	

HERE is one of the most delightful endings that I've come across in many a moon. It is a composition by Libiurkin and Bondarenko and features a surprise move which will hit you like a shot! White is to play and win.

SOLUTION:

| 1 | N - R4 | K - N8 |
| 2 | N - B3 ch | .... |

Clearly, White must eliminate that dangerous Rook Pawn.

2	....	K - N7
3	N x P	K x N
4	P - K5	B x P

Now what? 5 K x B, of course!

| 5 | K - K6!! | .... |

Remarkably enough, 5 K x B leads only to a draw. After 5 K x B, K - N6, 6 K - Q6, K - B5, 7 K - B7, K - K4, 8 K - N8, K - Q3, 9 K x P, K - B2, 10 K - R8, K - B1, 11 P - R7, K - B2 stalemate.

5	....	K - N6
6	K - Q7	K - B5
7	K - B8	B - B2
8	K - N7	....

White wins by taking the Rook Pawn, returning to N7 and then simply queening his passed Pawn.

VERY often the question of whether to capture or not to capture is not one to be decided by instinct or inspiration, but can be resolved by simple arithmetic. Take this position by Vlk. White is to play and win.

SOLUTION:

| 1 | K - N8 | R - B3 |
| 2 | R - B6 | .... |

Should Black capture? No! — after 2 .... R x R, 3 P x R, P - B5, 4 P - B7, P - B6, 5 P - B8 (Q), White wins.

| 2 | .... | P - B5 |

Should White capture? No! — after 3
R x R, P x R, 4 P - N6, P - B6, 5 P -
N7, P - B7, 6 P - N8 (Q), P - N8 (Q),
White draws, at best.

    3   **R - R6 ch!**   ....

Should Black capture? No! — after 3
.... R x R, 4 P x R, P - B6, 5 P - R7,
P - B7, 6 P - R8 (Q) ch! and White
wins.

    3   ....   **K - N2**

Should White capture? Yes, for now
the combination clicks mathematically as well as chessically.

    4   **R x R**   **P x R**
    5   **P - N6**   **P - B6**
    6   **P - N7**   **P - B7**
    7   **P - N8 (Q) ch**

White wins.

WHITE is to play and draw in this exquisite ending by Korteling.

SOLUTION:

Obviously, if White plays *1* R - KN4,
Black replies: *1* .... B - B3 ch, followed by 2 P - N7, 3 .... P - R4 and
4 ..... P - R5. The unhappy Rook
cannot then hold the position.

    1   **R - Q8 ch**   **K - N2**
    2   **R - Q3**   **B - B3 ch**
    3   **K - N4**   **P - N7**
    4   **R - N3 ch**   **K - B3**
    5   **K - B5!**

The attack on the Bishop is an important finesse which gains a move
for White's King.

    5   ....   **B - N2**
    6   **K - Q4**   **P - R4**
    7   **K - K3**   **P - R5**

Where can the Rook move? Answer:
he doesn't!

    8   **K - B2!!**   **P x R ch**
    9   **K - N1!**   ....

Drawn! Black can only choose between stalemating White or losing
both Pawns.

THE ENDING is by Lazard and it won
Second Prize in a competition. White
is to play and draw.

At first glance, one would not give
much for White's chances. His Bishop
is attacked and he dare not move it
away. But there is hope in the
crowded position of Black's King.

SOLUTION:

    1   **N - K4 ch!**   **K - R5**

On *1* .... P x N, 2 B - K1 mate!

    2   **N - N3!**   **Q - KB1**

Clearly, if 2 .... K x N, 3 B - K1
mate; and, if 2 .... P x N, 3 B - N6,
Q - R8 ch, 4 B - N1, and Black cannot
win! And, on other moves, White has
3 N - B5 mate.

    3   **B - K1**   ....

Now White threatens mate again, by
a double check.

    3   ....   **P x N**
    4   **B - B2!**   **P - Q5**
    5   **B x QP**   **P - B4**
    6   **B x P**   **Q - B8 ch**
    7   **B - N1**   **Q - B7**
    8   **B x Q**   **P x B**
    9   **P - N3 ch**   **Any**

               Stalemate

CUTE yet not too difficult is this end-game study by Selesniev. White is to play and win.

SOLUTION:

1	P - R3 ch	
2	P - R4 ch	K - N5
3	R - KB8	R - N7 ch
4	R - B2	R x R ch
5	K x R	P - R7
6	P - N8 (Q)	P - R8 (Q)
7	Q - QB8 mate	

HERE is an ending which will brighten your day. It was composed by J. Terho. White is to play and draw.

SOLUTION:

1	B - N1	P x P
2	K - R4	P - R7
3	N - N5!	P - R8 (Q) ch

If 3 .... P x B (Q), then 4 N - B3 ch wins for White.

| 4 | K x P | .... |

The natural 4 N - R3 fails after 4 .... Q - R7.

| 4 | .... | K - B3 |

The Queen must stay put.

5	N - R3	K - N3
6	K - R4	

And Black can make no headway, as White's King shuttles from R4 to N3 and back again.

IN THIS clever composition by P. Heu-acker, White is to play and win, although his prospects of doing so look very slim.

SOLUTION:

Obviously White's only chance lies in his passed Pawn. He cannot push on by 1 P - R7 as 1 .... P - K5 would be the reply.

1	B - R7!	B - R8

Of course not 1 .... B x B, 2 P - R7.

2	K - N1	B - B6
3	K - B2	B - R8
4	B - Q4!	....

A pretty offer; if 4 .... P x B, 5 K - Q3, followed by 6 P - R7, wins for White.

4	....	B x B
5	K - Q3	....

Threatening to continue with 6 K - K4 and 7 P - R7.

5	....	B - R8

Hoping for 6 P - R7, P - K5 ch as the Bishop then guards the Queening square.

6	K - K4!	....

Blockade! Black's own Pawn keeps his Bishop a prisoner, and White's Pawn is free to advance to the Queening square.

FANTASIA

MORE than a hundred years ago conditional problems were greatly in vogue. One of my favorites is this pretty composition of Mendheim's: White is to mate in nine moves *with the Pawn at his N2*.

SOLUTION:

1	P - N6 ch	K - R1
2	B - R6	P x B
3	P - N7 ch	K - R2
4	N - B3	P - R4
5	P - N5	P - R5
6	P - N6 ch	K - R3
7	P - N4	P - R6
8	P - N5 ch	K - R4
9	P - N4 mate	

IN THIS one, composed by T. M. Brown, White mates in eight without capturing any Black Pawns.

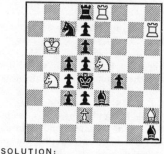

SOLUTION:

1	N(K5) - B6 ch	P x N
2	P x B ch	P x P

3	R - R4 ch	B - K5
4	R(R4) x B ch	P x R
5	B - K5 ch	P x B
6	R x R ch	N - Q4
7	R x N ch	P x R
8	N - B6 mate	

THIS ONE, by K. Flatt, calls for self-mate in ten.

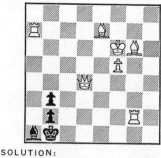

SOLUTION:

1	B - B8	K - B8
2	Q - Q2 ch	K - N8
3	R - R7	K - R7
4	B - R5	K - N8
5	B - N8	K - R7
6	K - N7	K - N8
7	P - B6	K - R7
8	P - B7	K - N8
9	B - N6 ch	K - R7
10	Q - R6	P - N8 mate

AND IT CAME TO PASS in the reign of King Al-ya-keen that there dwelt in the land a comely youth who was skilled in the ancient art of chesse-play. Enamored as he was by its subtle witchery, he yet found it in his heart to be beguiled by the beauty of the daughter of the Court Wizard and Soothsayer, El-oyd. So enchanted was the youth with her charms, that he besought her hand in marriage from the Old Magician, her father.

"You may have my consent," said the Wizard, "if you will answer me this riddle of chesse-play which has been troubling me sorely." He thereupon set forth on the chesse-board all the pieces in battle array, as they are at the beginning of an encounter. "Move both White and Black in such manner," said he to the youth, "that, when four moves shall have been played by each side, White's King shall have been checkmated by a discovery."

So swayed by love for the fair maiden was this youth (and mayhap so well-versed in the wiles of his art) that he needed but a moment to tear away the veil of the riddle and reveal its mystery.

SOLUTION:
Set the board up as at the beginning of play, and then

1	P - KB3	P - K4
2	K - B2	P - KR4
3	K - N3	P - R5 ch
4	K - N4	P - Q4 mate

LET US turn to a bit of Fairy Chess. In this problem by Chernev the conventions are suspended. Black is to play first and *help* White to mate in three moves.

SOLUTION:

1	....	Q - R2 ch
2	N - K7	B - N2
3	N - Q5	R - QN1
4	N - B7 mate	

IN THIS problem, composed by Kovacs, Black moves first, and Black and White collaborate to stalemate Black in five moves.

SOLUTION:

1	....	R - R8
2	K - Q5	R(N8) - N8
3	K - B4	Q - KB8
4	K - N3	K - K8
5	K - B2	

And, *mirabile dictu*, Black has no move.

THE FOLLOWING are maximummers. This frightening term means that Black must make only his longest possible moves.

In the first, White is to play and mate in six moves.

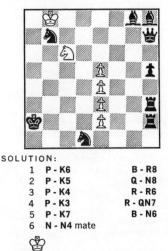

SOLUTION:

1	P - K6	B - R8
2	P - K5	Q - N8
3	P - K4	R - R6
4	P - K3	R - QN7
5	P - K7	B - N6
6	N - N4 mate	

IN THIS problem, composed by Lommer, Black is to play and help White to checkmate in five moves. Hint (and this will confuse the issue): White does not move his King or his Knight.

SOLUTION:

1	....	P - R8 (R)
2	P - N5	R - R1
3	P - N6	R x N
4	P - N7	R - QR1
5	P - N8 (Q)	R - R8
6	Q - N3 mate	

♛

HOW they ever reached this position, no one will ever know, but here it is, with the Expert as White ready to move and mate the Dub.

"Hold on!" said the Dub. "Anyone can mate with one of the Rooks. How about doing it the hard way?"

"How do you want to be mated?" asked the Expert.

"Mate me with your Pawn, but —"

"But what?"

"But don't move your King!"

The proposition looked impossible,

even to the Expert (who was tempted to call in his brother, Mycroft), but he thought a while and then said, "I'll do it on one condition. If you promise to promote your Pawn to Queen when it reaches the last square, I will then mate you in three moves — with the Pawn."

Dear Reader: How did he do it?

SOLUTION:

1	R - K7	P - Q4
2	R - Q7	P - Q5
3	R - Q6	P - Q6
4	R - Q5	P - Q7
5	R - Q3	P - Q8 (Q)
6	R - R3 ch	Q - R5
7	R - R7 ch	Q x R ch
8	P - N7 mate!	

♛

THIS one is for the graduating class: Play the shortest game ending in stalemate.

This is how Sam Loyd does it:

1	P - K3	P - QR4
2	Q - R5	R - R3
3	Q x QRP	P - R4
4	Q x BP	QR - R3
5	P - KR4	P - KB3
6	Q x QP ch	K - B2
7	Q x NP	Q - Q6
8	Q x N	Q - R2
9	Q x B	K - N3
10	Q - K6	....

Stalemate after only ten legal moves! As Dawson says, "A wonderful result!"

The final position

♛

IN THIS position by Leathem, both players have vowed to keep on checking until one of them is mated. Warning to the reader: Don't try to solve this or you will go mad.

SOLUTION:

1	P - B7 ch	N(K1) x P ch
2	NP x N ch	N x P ch
3	P x N ch	K - K2 dis. ch
4	P - KN8 (N) ch	R x N ch
5	RP x R (N) ch	Q x N ch
6	P - KB8 (B) ch	Q x B ch
7	Q - K8 ch	Q x Q ch
8	P - Q8 (Q) ch	Q x Q ch
9	P - B8 (N) ch	R x N ch
10	P x R (N) ch	Q x N ch
11	B - N8 dis. ch	B x R ch
12	N - Q5 ch	B x N ch
13	N - B6 ch	B x N ch
14	R - N7 ch	Q x R mate

♛

IN THIS one, too, White is to play and mate in six moves.

SOLUTION:

1	P - N4	Q - QR8
2	P - K5	Q - R1
3	B - R7	B - R3

4	P - N5	R - N8
5	B x R	P - B4
6	P x P e.p. mate	

♚

MULTIPLE PROBLEM

IN THIS little promotion problem by Hanneman, White is to mate in one, two, three or four moves. How many of these can you find?

SOLUTION:

Mate in one by

1	P - K8 (Q) mate	

Mate in two by

1	P - K8 (R) ch	K - Q2
2	R - K7 mate	

Mate in three by

1	P - K8 (B)	P - Q4
2	K - B6	P x P
3	B - Q7 mate	

Mate in four by

1	P - K8 (N)	K - Q2
2	N - N7	P - Q4
3	P - K5	P - Q5
4	P - K6 mate	

♛

ONE OF Sam Loyd's famous puzzles is this:

Play a game of seventeen moves where all the pieces, except the Kings, come off the board.

SOLUTION:

1	P - QB4	P - Q4
2	P x P	Q x P
3	Q - B2	Q x NP
4	Q x BP	Q x N
5	Q x NP	Q x RP
6	Q x N	Q - K4

7	Q x B ch	R x Q
8	R x P	Q x NP
9	R x R	Q x RP
10	R x N	Q x P ch
11	K x Q	R x B
12	R x NP	R x N
13	R x P	R x B
14	R x B ch	K x R
15	R x P	R x P
16	R x P	R x P ch
17	K x R	K x R

The final position

DEPARTMENT OF
SERENDIPITY

FOR A good many years I've kept an eye out for unusual problems, puzzles and endings. These might be conventional compositions, conditional problems, help-mates, self-mates, or the lighter forms of retrograde analysis. My standards were simple: if I liked an idea, and could hardly wait to show it to a friend, it was worth jotting down immediately in my little black notebook.

Here then are some positions that have amused, pleased and sometimes bewildered me. Let me share these happy discoveries with you.

THIS problem, by Adamson, calls for the construction of a position in which there can be ten discovered checks in succession.

SOLUTION:
This is the position:

And this is the play:

1	R - N2 dis. ch	N - Q6 dis. ch
2	N - B4 dis. ch	N(Q2) - K4 dbl. ch (incl. dis. ch)
3	K - N3 dis. ch	P x B dis. ch
4	B - N5 dis. ch	N x R dis. ch
5	N - K3 dis. ch	N(K4) - Q6 dis. ch

Q.E.D.

IN THIS one, by Tolosa, White is to mate in less than a move.

SOLUTION:
Lift the King in the air, discovering check and mate. *Do not set the King down,* as then Black can move out of check.

IN THIS one, by Orlimont, White mates in three moves.

SOLUTION:

1	R x P ch	K - Q5
2	P x B (N)	K - Q4
3	R - Q3 mate	

(The hard part at this point is to avoid saying something about a Knightmare.)

IN THIS one, by Moravec, White mates in two moves.

SOLUTION:

In order to force mate in two, we must know what Black's last move was. If Black's last move was with King or Rook, then he may not castle as a defense, and White mates in two by

1   K - K6   Any
2   Q - R8 mate

If Black's last move was P - K4, the solution is

1   P x P e.p.   Any
2   Q mates

A simple, but pleasing bit of retrograde analysis.

IN THIS one, by Kovacs, White mates in two moves.

SOLUTION:

1   N - B6
If 1 . . . . P - QR8(Q), 2 B - R6 mate
If 1 . . . . P - QN8(Q), 2 B - N7 mate

If 1 . . . . P - QB8(Q), 2 B moves, mate
If 1 . . . . P - Q8(Q), 2 B - Q7 mate
If 1 . . . . P - K8(Q), 2 B - K6 mate
If 1 . . . . P - KB8(Q), 2 B - B5 mate
If 1 . . . . P - KN8(Q), 2 B - N4 mate
If 1 . . . . P - KR8(Q) ch, 2 B - R3 mate

Both setting and solution are aesthetically pleasing.

IN THIS one, by Reichhelm, White mates all ten Kings in one move.

SOLUTION:

1   N - K5 mate, mate, mate,
         mate, mate, mate,
         mate, mate, mate,
         mate.

IN THIS one, by Gereben, White mates in four moves.

SOLUTION:

1   B - N5   K x B
2   N - K6   K - R4

| 3 | N - Q4 | P - N4 |
| 4 | N - B6 mate | |

IN THIS one, by Hanneman, White plays and forces Black to mate in four moves.

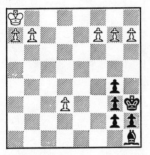

SOLUTION:

1	P - QN8 (B)	K - R5
2	P - R8 (Q) ch	K - N4
3	P - N8 (R) ch	K - B4
4	P - B8 (N)	P - N8 (Q) mate

The underpromotions are attractive.

THIS IS the position after White's sixteenth move. How did the game go? The problem was composed by Fabel.

SOLUTION:

1	N - QB3	P - QN4
2	N x P	N - KB3
3	N x RP	N - K5
4	N x B	N - B6
5	N x P	P - QB3

6	N x P	N - N8
7	N x N	R - R6
8	N x P	P - N4
9	N x B	Q - Q3
10	N x P	K - Q2
11	N x P	R - KR5
12	N x P	R - QB5
13	N x Q	K - B3
14	N x R	K - N4
15	N x R ch	K - R5
16	N x N	

and we have the position above. A seemingly impossible task, accomplished by one White piece!

THIS is one of the most amazing endings I have ever seen, the final position being almost incredible! It was created by Sarychev. Unless you are a master solver of problems and endings, I would advise you not to tackle this compositon, as it is quite difficult. But *do* play over the solution, as it is an eye-opener! White is to play and draw.

SOLUTION:

| 1 | B - K3 | .... |

Attacks one Knight, and threatens to check and win the other.

| 1 | .... | N - Q6 ch |
| 2 | K - B3 | N - K8 |

If 2 .... N - N7, 3 B - B1.

| 3 | B - Q4 | N - B4 |
| 4 | B - KB2 | N - B6 |

If 4 .... N - KN7, 5 B - B2, N(B4) - K6, 6 B x N, N x B, 7 B x P, and White draws.

5	B - B2	N - Q3
6	B x P	N - N4

Threatens to win one of the Bishops.

7	B - QB5	N - N2
8	B - K7!	N x B
9	K - N4	
	Draw!	

All three of Black's pieces are paralyzed! White simply moves his King up the board, and captures the Bishop, and draws against the two Knights.

NOW for an old-fashioned conditional problem, this one by Horwitz. White to play, mates with the Knight, in ten moves, without capturing any Black Pawns, or permitting them to move.

SOLUTION:

1	R - KN6	K - R2
2	R - N8	K - R3
3	R - R8 ch	K - N3
4	B - R3	K - B3
5	R - R6 ch	K - K4
6	R - Q6	K - B5
7	K - K7	K - K4
8	B - B1	K - B5
9	N - B2	K - K4
10	N - Q3 mate	

IN THIS one, by Rubin, White is to play and force Black to mate in five moves.

SOLUTION:

1	B - R6	P x P
2	B - N5	P x P
3	B - B4	P x P
4	B - Q3	P x P
5	B - K2	P x P mate

IN THIS one, by Kemp, White is to play and mate in six moves — with Black's help!

SOLUTION:

1	P - N4	K - N2
2	P - N5	K - B3
3	P - N6	K - K4
4	P - N7	K - Q5
5	P - N8 (Q)	K - B6
6	Q - N2 mate	

A suicide complex!

IN THIS one, by Grasemann, White mates in six moves.

SOLUTION:

1	Q - R3 ch	K - K7
2	Q - B1 ch	K x Q
3	B - R3 ch	K - K7
4	B - B1 ch	K x B
5	N - B5	Any
6	N - N3 mate	

THE next problem, devised by Mortimer, has baffled many a solver. In fact, the better the player, the more trouble he has finding the right moves!

The task is: Set the pieces up as at the start of a game, and reach the diagramed position in four moves.

SOLUTION:

1	N - KB3	P - Q4
2	N - K5	N - KB3
3	N - B6	KN - Q2
4	N x N	N x N

The hidden point is that it is Black's Queen Knight that disappears, not the King Knight!

THIS one illustrates a situation where Black has forty-nine legal moves. The stipulation is that White is to make one move that reduces Black to immobility. Shinkman is the composer.

SOLUTION:

1   B x Q Stalemate!

IN THIS problem, by Wolff, White mates in three moves with the Rook at R5, without moving the Rook!

At first glance it seems impossible to clear (by force) the six pieces between the Rook and Black's King in three moves — but let us see!

SOLUTION:

What was Black's last move? Obviously it could only have been P - B4. Then

1	P x P e.p.	P - K5
2	N - K3	K x P
3	K x QP mate!	

IN THIS, another one by Shinkman, none of Black's pieces can move. The stipulation is that White is to make one move that will allow his opponent the greatest degree of freedom.

SOLUTION:

1   N(N4) x BP

After this stroke, Black can move any of twelve pieces and Pawns.

REMARKABLE GAMES

ONE of the perennial ancedotes of musical literature is the story of the infant prodigy. The young genius first amazes his family and friends by his incredible skill at the piano, or the violin. He is immediately dispatched to the local maestro (played by Paul Muni) for formal musical instruction. After hearing the youngster play, the kindly Kapellmeister wipes away a suspicious moisture from a myopic eye, and declares solemnly that there is absolutely nothing he can teach the boy. No one in the world can instruct him properly but Ignatz Spoldoni, last pupil of the last pupil of the immortal Franz Liszt. It turns out that the great Spoldoni is now seventy-eight years old, has given up teaching, doesn't take any new pupils, charges fifty dollars an hour, and hates all children. Much against his will, Spoldoni finally consents to listen to the *wunderkind.* It takes only three pizzicati and a tremolo to make Spoldoni leap into the air, and swear that never in all his long dull life has he ever heard such virtuosity. From now on, he says, he will take the boy under his protective wing. As for money, "Poof! How can anyone dream of asking compensation where such a remarkable talent is concerned?" Besides, payments would be moderate, on a long-term plan, and would involve nothing more difficult than signing over the father's pay check every week.

The world of chess also has its legends of child-wizards and unknown masters. One of these child-wizards was Capablanca, who learned the moves of chess at the age of four, by watching his father play. At twelve he won the championship of Cuba, and at twenty-one he beat the United States champion Frank Marshall, one of the world's leading masters, by an amazing score — eight wins to one! Two years later, Capa was invited to play at San Sebastian in one of the strongest international tournaments ever held. He came in first ahead of such giants as Rubinstein, Tarrasch, Nimzowitsch, Vidmar, Marshall and Schlechter. It is no wonder that Lasker once said, "I have known many great masters, but only one genius — Capablanca."

This, then, is the story of Supermaster and his Unknown Rival:
On November 20, 1925, in the Leningrad Conservatorium (this is reported by J. Rochlin), the world's champion, José Raoul Capablanca, gave a simultaneous exhibition. He came for one day from Moscow, where he was taking part in the great international tournament. The Cuban genius was opposed by thirty players. The play lasted for seven hours without a break. Capablanca lost four games, and one of them was to a little-known youth. After the play, Capablanca asked the organizer, "What grade does the boy in spectacles belong to?" He was told that he was a "B" grade player, Misha Botvinnik.
Capablanca laughed and said, "This youngster plays with the confidence of a master. He will go far."
This is the score of their historic game:

Leningrad, 1925
QUEEN'S GAMBIT DECLINED

CAPABLANCA BOTVINNIK

	White	Black
1	P - Q4	P - Q4
2	P - QB4	P - K3

3	N - QB3	N - KB3
4	B - N5	QN - Q2
5	P - K3	B - N5

The other contestants stuck to book as long as possible. Misha is not content to equalize but goes gunning for a win.

| 6 | P x P | P x P |
| 7 | Q - N3 | P - B4! |

Black guards his Bishop, disputes the center and clears the way for .... Q - R4.

| 8 | P x P | .... |

Intending to castle Queen side, and bear down on Black's isolated Queen Pawn.

8	....	Q - R4
9	B x N	N x B
10	0 - 0 - 0	0 - 0
11	N - B3	....

It is risky to go in for 11 N x P, N x N, 12 Q x N, as 12 .... B - K3 gives Black a powerful attack.

| 11 | .... | B - K3 |
| 12 | N - Q4 | QR - B1 |

Black threatens 13 .... R x P.

| 13 | P - B6 | .... |

White gives up a Pawn, as the alternative 13 K - N1, B x N, 14 Q x B, Q x Q, 15 P x Q, N - K5 is not a pleasant prospect.

13	....	B x N
14	Q x B	Q x P
15	B - Q3	P x P
16	K - B2	P - B4
17	N x B	....

17   ....   Q - R5 ch!

Avoiding the mechanical 17 .... P x N after which 18 R - R1, P - Q5, 19

Q - B4, Q x Q, 20 B x Q saves White.

18	P - N3	Q - R7 ch
19	Q - N2	Q x Q ch
20	K x Q	P x N
21	P - B3	R - QB2

Black now plans the Pawn push, ... P - B5, which will give him a passed Pawn. If he is opposed on the Queen Bishop file, he is ready to continue with .... KR - B1, N - K1, N - Q3 and then irresistibly .... P - B5.

22	R - R1	P - B5
23	P x P	P x P
24	B - B2	R - N1 ch
25	K - B1	N - Q4
26	R - K1	P - B6!

Every move a picture! The fourteen-year-old boy plays the ending as though he were Capablanca!

27	R - R3	N - N5
28	R - K2	R - Q1
29	P - K4	....

A little trap. If Black tries to win a piece by 29 .... R - Q7 (attacking the Bishop), White does not oblige with 30 R x R, P x R ch, 31 K x P, R x B ch, but turns the tables with 30 R x BP!

29   ....   R - B3!

The Rook is now protected by the Knight, and invasion at Q7 is threatened.

| 30 | R - K3 | R - Q7 |
| 31 | R(K3) x P | .... |

Desperation — but any Bishop move would lose to the pretty reply, 31 .... P - B7!

| 31 | .... | R x B ch |
| 32 | R x R | R x R ch |

Resigns

And that boy, my dear children, eventually became world's champion. . . .

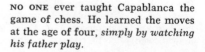

NO ONE ever taught Capablanca the game of chess. He learned the moves at the age of four, *simply by watching his father play.*

By the time Capablanca was twelve, his admirers, anxious to test his skill in serious play, arranged a match for him with Juan Corzo, champion of Cuba. In the course of the match (which he won) Capablanca turned out one game that was truly magnificent. Of it Reinfeld says: "This game is perhaps the most remarkable of Capablanca's career; the arduous jockeying for position in the middle game, the delightful and carefully calculated Queen sacrifice and the ensuing accurate endgame play – all are worked out with a skill which is astounding in one so young."

My own opinion: This game is the finest ever played by a chess prodigy. It surpasses every performance by the other great prodigies – Morphy, Reshevsky, Fischer and Petrosian.

Havana, 1900
QUEEN PAWN OPENING

CAPABLANCA	CORZO
White	Black
1 P - Q4	P - Q4
2 N - KB3	P - QB4
3 P - K3	N - QB3
4 P - QN3	P - K3
5 B - N2	N - B3
6 QN - Q2	P x P
7 P x P!	....

The proper way to recapture; White gets a grip on the strong point K5 and also opens the King file for the use of his Rook later on.

7	B - Q3
8 B - Q3	0 - 0
9 0 - 0	N - KR4
10 P - N3	....

This prevents an incursion by the Knight at Black's B5.

10	P - B4
11 N - K5	N - B3
12 P - KB4	B x N
13 BP x B	N - KN5
14 Q - K2	Q - N3
15 N - B3	B - Q2

The Bishop must be brought out if only to establish communication between the Rooks. Its prospects look bleak, though, with so many Pawns blocking its path.

16 P - QR3	....

This prevents 16 .... N - N5, followed by the removal of one of White's Bishops.

16	K - R1
17 P - R3	N - R3
18 Q - B2	N - B2
19 K - N2	P - N4

This attempt to attack leaves Black with a minute weakness on the long diagonal. But who would suspect danger from White's harmless-looking Queen Bishop?

20 P - KN4!	N - K2
21 Q - K3	R - KN1
22 QR - K1	N - N3
23 P x P	N - B5 ch
24 K - R2	N x B
25 Q x N	P x P
26 P - B4!	....

The idea of this is to rid the board of Black's Queen Pawn. White's center Pawns could then advance and open the long diagonal for the Bishop.

26	Q - K3
27 P x P	Q x P
28 P - K6!	....

The combinations begin! If now 28 .... B x P, then 29 R x B, Q x R, 30 P - Q5 dis. ch wins Black's Queen.

28	B - N4

This is the position:

29 Q x B!	....

Brilliant, forceful and decisive – the way of a genius! There may have been "a much simpler win," as a commentator says, by 29 Q - Q2, B x R, 30 P x N, Q x BP (if 30 .... Q x N, 31 P - Q5 ch!, R - N2, 32 R - K8 ch and wins), 31 P - Q5 ch, R - N2, 32 N x P, Q - N3, 33 R - K7, R - KN1, 34 N - B7 ch, and White wins. We may be grateful, though, that Capablanca, who saw this line of play, preferred the Queen sacrifice, as that was the continuation he had in mind when he played 28 P - K6.

29	....	Q x Q
30	P - Q5 dis. ch	R - N2
31	P x N	P - KR3

Against 31 .... R - KB1, Capablanca would have proceeded, he says, as follows: 32 N - Q4, Q x QP, 33 R - K8, Q x BP, 34 R x R ch, Q x R, 35 N x P, and White wins.

| 32 | N - Q4 | Q x R |

Painful but necessary. The alternative is 32 .... Q - Q2, after which Capablanca would force a beautiful win (as he points out) by 33 N x P, Q x BP, 34 B x R ch, K - R2, 35 R - K7, and Black must give up his Queen, as 35 .... Q x P loses by 36 B - K5 ch, K - N3, 37 R - N7 ch, K - R4, 38 N - N3 ch, K - R5, 39 R - B4 ch, P x R, 40 R - N4 mate!

33	R x Q	R x P
34	R x P	R x R
35	N x R dis. ch	K - R2
36	N - K7!	....

Cleverly preparing the advance of the Queen Pawn! The Knight and Bishop control the exits and prevent Black's King from approaching the Pawn.

36	....	R - KB1
37	K - N2	P - KR4
38	P - Q6	P - N5
39	P x P	P x P
40	B - K5	K - R3
41	P - Q7	....

Threatens 42 B - B7 and 43 P - Q8 (Q).

| 41 | .... | R - Q1 |
| 42 | N - N8 ch! | R x N |

Or 42 .... K - N3, 43 N - B6, K - B2, 44 B - B7, and Black must give up his Rook.

43	B - B6	K - N3
44	P - Q8 (Q)	R x Q
45	B x R	P - N4
46	K - B2	K - B4
47	K - K3	K - K4
48	K - Q3	K - Q4
49	K - B3	P - N6
50	B - R4	P - N7
51	B - B2	P - R4
52	P - N4!	K - K5
53	B - N6	....

Of course not 53 P x P, K - Q4, after which White cannot win, as his Bishop does not control the Rook Pawn's queening square.

53	....	K - Q4
54	K - Q3	K - B3
55	B - N1	K - Q4
56	B - R2!	K - B3
57	K - Q4	P - R5
58	K - K5	K - N3
59	K - Q5	K - R3

Hoping for the natural move 60 K - B6, when 60 .... P - N8 (Q), 61 B x Q allows Black to escape with a draw by stalemate. But Capablanca was not to be caught by traps, either as a child prodigy or in his entire chess career.

| 60 | K - B5! | Resigns |

A typical Capablanca game — a masterpiece!

♚

Moscow, 1935

QUEEN PAWN OPENING

GERASSIMOV   SMYSLOV
White   Black

1	P - Q4	P - Q4
2	N - KB3	N - KB3
3	P - K3	P - K3
4	B - Q3	P - B4
5	P - QN3	N - B3
6	B - N2	B - Q3
7	0 - 0	Q - B2

Black prevents the establishment of an outpost by 8 N - K5.

8	P - QR3	P - QN3
9	P - B4	B - N2
10	N - B3	P - QR3
11	R - K1	BP x P
12	KP x P	0 - 0

13	N - QR4	B - B5
14	N - K5	P x P
15	P x P	N x N
16	P x N	Q - B3!
17	B - KB1	....

White guards against mate. His reluctance to simplify by 17 Q - B3 may be understood by the fact that he was facing an opponent playing in his first tournament who was likely to lose his way in a complicated position. (Did *he* have a wrong number!)

17	....	KR - Q1
18	Q - N3	N - N5
19	P - R3	....

| 19 | .... | R - Q6! |
| 20 | Q x P | .... |

Capturing the Rook means being mated or losing material: 20 B x R, Q x P mate or 20 Q x R, B - R7 ch, 21 K - R1, N x P ch, followed by 22 .... N x Q.

| 20 | .... | R x KRP |
| 21 | B - Q4 | .... |

Obviously, 21 Q x Q fails after 21 .... B - R7 ch, 22 K - R1, N x P mate.

21	....	B - R7 ch
22	K - R1	B x P dis. ch
	Resigns	

If 23 K - N1, B - R7 ch, 24 K - R1, B - B2 dis. ch, followed by 25 .... B x Q.

Beautiful play by the fourteen-year-old Smyslov, strategically and tactically.

FOR years I've told every player I could buttonhole about an extraordinary game of Alekhine's. In this game, which he played in 1915 against Gregoriev, there appeared at one time five Queens on the chessboard! Such a position, I thought, must be unique in the history of recorded chess. For years I was happy that such a fantastic situation had occurred in an actual game and not as the result of the imaginings of a problem composer.

And then the blow fell! Casually glancing through a volume of *Tijdschrift van den Nederlandschen Schaakbond* (Dear Reader, there *is* such a magazine) for 1913, I came across this game:

Winschoten, 1896
RUY LOPEZ

J. D. TRESLING   L. BENIMA
White   Black

1	P - K4	P - K4
2	N - KB3	N - QB3
3	B - N5	P - QR3
4	B - R4	N - B3
5	N - B3	B - K2
6	0 - 0	P - QN4
7	B - N3	P - Q3
8	P - Q3	....

Everybody knows this ancient trap: 8 P - Q4, P x P, 9 N x P, N x N, 10 Q x N, P - B4, followed by 11 .... P - B5, winning a piece (Noah – Japeth, Ararat, B.C. 2349).

8	....	B - K3
9	Q - K2	Q - Q2
10	N - Q5	B x N
11	P x B	N - QR4
12	P - Q4	N x B
13	RP x N	P - K5
14	N - Q2	0 - 0
15	P - QB4	KR - K1
16	N x P	N x N
17	Q x N	B - B3
18	Q - Q3	Q - N5
19	B - K3	P - N5
20	P - B4	P - KR4
21	P - R3!	Q - Q2
22	P - KB5	Q - K2
23	QR - K1	P - R4

| 24 | K - R1 | .... |

Not 24 B - N5 at once, as Black saves himself by 24 .... B x P ch, 25 Q x B, Q x B.

24	....	Q - K5
25	Q - Q1	P - B4
26	P x P	B x P
27	R - B4	Q - K2
28	Q x P	B - B3

If 28 .... P x P, then White wins with 29 R - R4, P - B3, 30 Q - R7 ch, K - B2, 31 Q - N6 ch, K - N1, 32 R - R7, Q - KB2 (to stop 33 Q - R5) 33 R - R8 ch. Nor does 30 .... K - B1 avail: 31 Q - N6, Q - KB2, 32 B x P ch and mate follows.

| 29 | P x P | Q x P |

Black threatens 30 .... R x B.

| 30 | Q - B3 | .... |

White guards Rook and Bishop and his Queen Pawn as well, threatening P - B5.

30	....	R - K4
31	R - K4	R x R
32	Q x R	Q - N6

Black hopes to follow with .... B - K4.

33	B - B4!	Q x NP
34	P - Q6	R - KB1
35	P - B5	P - R5
36	P - B6	P - R6
37	B - K5	B x B
38	Q x B	P - R7
39	P - Q7	Q - R6
40	P - B7	P - N6
41	P - Q8 (Q)	P - N7
42	P - B8 (Q)	P - N8 (Q)

This is the position; it makes a pretty picture:

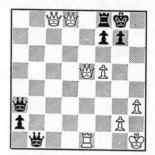

White mated in three moves by *43 Q x R ch, Q x Q, 44 Q x Q ch, K x Q, 45 Q - K8 mate.*

So the next time someone says something about a remarkable Alekhine game with five Queens on the board, just toss off casually, "Oh! yes, a bit like Tresling — Benima, Winschoten, 1896." You will quickly get a reputation for erudition.

THE popular conception of opening play as it is treated in "the books" is that it consists of a series of strong but incredibly dull moves in each form of debut, leading at about the fifteenth move to a position which is comparatively equal for practical purposes but completely boring by aesthetic standards. Consequently, many amateurs make eccentric opening moves in the belief that they will thereby get "interesting" positions. Curiously enough these interesting positions which they try so hard to get — where everything hangs by a hair — are frequently found in standard opening practice.

As a case in point, here is a game which is as tense and nerve-racking as anyone would want. In the course of twenty-six moves, White offers his opponent a Bishop, a Knight, a Rook, his other Knight and then his remaining Rook. Not to be outdone in generosity, Black offers a Knight, an exchange, a Queen and a Rook.

Tiflis, 1937

FRENCH DEFENSE

V. PANOV   M. YUDOVICH
White   Black

	White	Black
1	P - K4	P - K3
2	P - Q4	P - Q4
3	N - QB3	N - KB3
4	B - KN5	B - K2
5	P - K5	KN - Q2
6	P - KR4	P - KB3
7	B - Q3	P - QB4!
8	Q - R5 ch	K - B1
9	N x P	P x B

Better than 9 .... P x N, *10* P - K6, Q - K1, *11* Q x Q ch, as White gets his piece back with an even game.

| 10 | R - R3 | .... |

Everybody wants to get into the act!

| 10 | .... | P - N5 |
| 11 | N - B4 | N x P |

Not *11* .... P x R as *12* N x P ch wins Black's Queen, and with mating threats (*11* .... P x R, *12* N x P ch, K - N1, *13* N x Q and the threat of mate at B7 prevents Black's *13* .... P - R7, regaining his Queen, while *13* .... P - KN3 doesn't help much after *14* B - B4 ch).

12	P x N	P x R
13	B x P	R x B
14	Q x R	P - R7

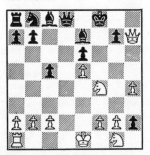

Lisitsyn says at this point, "The originality of this opening system, devised by Black, is expressed in the career of this Pawn, which has crossed three files and six ranks, captured two pieces and becomes a Queen on the fifteenth move!"

| 15 | K - K2 | P - R8 (Q) |
| 16 | N - N6 ch | K - B2 |

17	N - R8 ch	Q x N
18	Q x Q	N - B3
19	Q - R5 ch	K - N1
20	N - R3	Q x P!
21	Q - K8 ch	B - B1
22	N - N5	....

White threatens mate in two.

22	....	N x P
23	P - B4	Q - N5 ch
24	K - B1	Q x P ch
25	K - N1	Q - N5 ch
26	K - B1	B - Q2!

Resigns

The last offer was more than White could take. If 27 Q x R, B - N4 ch decides.

JACQUES MIESES must have taken a sip or two at the Fountain of Youth so fruitlessly sought by Ponce de León. How else can one explain the energy and intensity of his attacks? In the following game, played when he was eighty-three, Mieses produces a beautiful specimen of brilliant and imaginative chess.

Oxford, 1947

NIMZOWITSCH DEFENSE

J. MIESES   DR. H. G. SCHENK

	White	Black
1	P - K4	N - QB3
2	P - Q4	P - Q4
3	P x P	Q x P
4	N - KB3	P - K4
5	N - B3	B - QN5
6	B - K3	B - N5
7	B - K2	O - O - O
8	O - O	Q - R4
9	N x P	B x B
10	Q x B	N x N
11	P x N	N - R3

At this point, the conscientious commentator is beset by doubts. If he fails to explain what happens after *11* .... Q x KP, he neglects his duty. On the other hand, if he does explain, the erudite reader will point out that a note on a simple refutation of a blunder is superfluous.

12	N - N5!	P - R3
13	P - QR4!	B - K2
14	P - QN4!	B x P
15	KR - N1	P - QB3
16	P - QB3!	RP x N
17	P x B	Q - R3

On *17* .... Q - B2, White opens the position with *18* P x P.

| 18 | P - R5 | .... |

The average player would clear a file for his Rook with *18* P x P, but Mieses is not an average player.

| 18 | .... | N - B4 |
| 19 | B - N6! | .... |

White imprisons Black's Queen!

19	....	R - Q4
20	R - Q1	N - K2
21	Q - N4 ch	K - N1
22	Q x P	R - QB1

How unfortunate! The Rook must go to this square which Black had hoped to use for his Knight (to drive away the White Bishop).

23	Q - B6	R x R ch
24	R x R	N - Q4
25	Q - Q6 ch	K - R1
26	R x N	P x R
27	P - N3	Resigns

Black recognizes the futility of further resistance. He is reduced to Rook moves on the first rank and is helpless to prevent Q x QP and Q x BP followed by the march of the King Pawn to its coronation.

♕

IN OUR next curio, there is an amusing mimicking of captures. Black's King Knight removes in order a Pawn,

Knight, Queen, King Bishop Pawn, King Rook and King Knight Pawn. White's King Knight matches this by removing in the same order a Pawn, Knight, Queen, King Bishop Pawn, King Rook and King Knight Pawn. Then, to finish off this remarkable game, White makes use of two moves commonly reserved for the opening – P - Q4 and P - K4!

Correspondence, 1945
ENGLISH OPENING

G. KOSHNITSKY   W. HEWITT
White   Black

1	P - QB4	P - K4
2	N - QB3	N - QB3
3	N - B3	N - B3
4	P - KN3	B - K2
5	B - N2	P - Q4
6	P x P	N x P

| 7 | N x P | .... |

White wins a Pawn by his Bishop's discovered attack on the Knight.

| 7 | .... | N x QN |
| 8 | N x N | N x Q |

Both Knights now run amok.

9	N x Q	N x BP
10	N x BP	N x R
11	N x R	N x P
12	P x N	P - B3

Black prevents *13* B - Q5 and the escape of White's Knight via B7.

13	B - K4	P - KN3
14	N x P	P x N
15	B x NP ch	K - Q1
16	P - Q4	B - KN5
17	P - K4	Resigns

♚

MOST of us like to play over games of twenty to thirty moves. We avoid the longer games because we are afraid they might be boring. And thereby we deprive ourselves very often of a good deal of pleasure. Here for example is a sixty-mover which is completely fascinating from start to finish. The opening is original; the mid-game features a King wandering as early as the eleventh move; and the ending includes an exciting Pawn race. A pretty stalemate try is thrown in for good measure.

Munich, 1942

ENGLISH OPENING

P. KERES   K. RICHTER
White   Black

1	P - QB4	P - K4
2	N - QB3	N - KB3
3	N - B3	N - B3
4	P - Q4	P x P
5	N x P	B - N5
6	B - N5	P - KR3!
7	B - R4	P - KN4
8	B - N3	P - Q3
9	R - B1	N x N
10	Q x N	B - KB4
11	P - KR4	K - Q2!

At one stroke, Black takes the edge off the threat of *12* P x P, unpins his Knight, establishes communication between his major pieces and brings his King into the field for the end game!

12	R - Q1	N - K5

Apparently just to prevent *13* P - B5; but there is a deeper purpose behind the Knight's move.

13	Q - K5	B x N ch
14	P x B	N x B
15	P x N	....

The Knight was instrumental in the double exchange which resulted in White having two doubled Pawns. If Black can simplify further, say into a King and Rook ending, he will have the advantage.

15	....	B - N3
16	P x P	Q x P
17	Q - B4	QR - K1

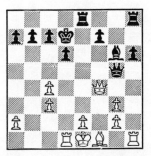

White must do something about developing his Bishop, but how? If *18* P - K3, or *18* P - K4, R x P ch wins on the spot.

18	R - Q5	Q x Q
19	P x Q	P - N3

Just so White doesn't get any ideas about moving either Bishop Pawn! If *20* P - KB5, then Black wins a Pawn by *20* .... P - QB3.

20	K - B2	P - KR4
21	P - K3	P - R5
22	R - KN5	B - K5
23	B - K2	QR - KN1!
24	B - N4 ch	K - B3
25	R x R	R x R
26	R x P	K - B4

In return for his Pawn, Black has gained two tempi for his King. How would a chess-playing machine weigh such values?

27	B - B3	B x B
28	K x B	K x P
29	R - R7	R - KB1
30	P - N4	K x P
31	K - K4	P - QB4
32	K - Q5	P - B5
33	P - K4	K - N5
34	P - N5	P - B6
35	R - R2	R - B1
36	R - QB2	P - N4
37	P - B5	P - R4
38	K x P	K - B5
39	P - K5	P - N5
40	K - Q7	R - QR1
41	P - K6	P x P
42	P - B6	P - R5
43	P - B7	P - N6
44	P x P ch	P x P
45	R x P ch	K x R

| 46 | P - N6 | P - N7 |
| 47 | P - N7 | P - N8 (Q) |

An interesting position. Which Pawn should White promote to a Queen? If *48* P - N8 (Q), Q - N2 ch, *49* K - Q6, Q - N5 ch, *50* K - K5 (K - Q7, R - R2 ch, *51* K x P, Q - K2 ch, followed by *52* .... Q x P ch), Q - Q5 ch, *51* K x P, R x Q, *52* P x R (Q), Q - B5 ch, and Black wins White's remaining Queen.

48	P - B8 (Q)	Q - N2 ch
49	K x P	R - R3 ch
50	K- B5	Q - Q2 ch
51	K - B4	R - R5 ch
52	K - N3	Q - Q6 ch

Black misses *52* .... Q - N5 ch, with a mate in four.

| 53 | Q - B3! | R - R1 |

And here he transposes moves light-heartedly and almost loses half a point! The simple way is *53* .... Q x Q ch, *54* K x Q, R - R1, followed by *55* .... R - KN1.

| 54 | P - N8 (Q) | R x Q ch |
| 55 | K - R2! | .... |

Take the Queen if you dare!

55	....	R - R1 ch
56	K - N1	R - N1 ch
57	K - R2	K - B7
58	Q - B2 ch	K - Q8
59	Q - B3 ch	....

A last try.

| 59 | .... | Q - K7 ch |
| | Resigns | |

♛

EXTRA! EXTRA!
CAPABLANCA GETS QUEEN ODDS!!
Havana, 1893
PETROFF DEFENSE
Remove White's Queen

DON RAMON	JOSÉ
IGLESIAS	CAPABLANCA
White	Black
1 P - K4	P - K4
2 N - KB3	N - KB3
3 N x P	N x P
4 P - Q4	P - Q3
5 N - KB3	B - K2
6 B - Q3	N - KB3
7 P - B4	O - O
8 N - B3	N - B3
9 P - QR3	P - QR3
10 B - Q2	P - QN3
11 O - O - O	B - Q2

Black brings his minor pieces into play and secures himself against sudden assault on either wing. Apparently these are routine developing moves such as any other master would make. Nevertheless, as we shall see, this is astonishing position play.

12	K - N1	N - QR4
13	R - QB1	N - N6
14	R - B2	P - B4
15	P - Q5	R - K1
16	P - KR4	P - QN4

In accordance with Nimzowitsch's precepts, Black undermines the base of White's Pawn chain.

| 17 | P - KN4 | .... |

17 ....   N - Q5

Correct strategy; White's wing attack is met by play in the center.

| 18 | N x N | P x N |
| 19 | N - K4 | P x P |

Black forces exchanges and simplification. If now *20* R x P, B - N4, *21* R x P (or *21* N x N ch, B x N and Black wins the exchange) B x B ch, 22 R x B, N x N wins a piece.

20	N x N ch	B x N
21	B x BP	B x NP

Black threatens 22 .... B - B4.

22	B - Q3	B - B6
23	R - R3	B x QP
24	P - R5	B - K3
25	R - N3	P - N3
26	P - B4	B - R5
27	R - N1	K - R1
28	P - B5	B x P
29	B x B	P x B
30	B - R6	R - KN1
31	R(B2) - N2	R x R
32	R x R	....

Black's Queen has been just a spectator up to this point. Now she makes a brief but effective entrance.

32	....	Q - B3
33	B - N7 ch	Q x B
34	R x Q	K x R
35	K - B2	K - B3
36	K - Q3	K - K4
37	P - R6	P - B5
38	K - K2	K - K5

Resigns

Now for the explanation. Believe it or not, Capablanca *did* get Queen odds in this game. It was played when he had not yet reached the age of five! For a performance by a boy four years and ten months old, where a strong sense of position play is combined with cool defense, it eclipses by far the achievements of the other famous prodigies — Morphy, Reshevsky, Pomar and Fischer.

AHEAD OF THEIR TIME

ELIJAH WILLIAMS — never heard of him? Well, he played in only one tournament and that was back in 1851. He was a slow player; and that exasperated Howard Staunton, who organized the tournament, was the favorite for first prize and wrote the book of the tournament. It is true that there was no time limit, but Mr. Williams was slow, real slow.

In his introduction to the games between Williams and Mucklow, Staunton says: "In some respects, these players are well paired, not for equality of force, indeed, Mr. Williams being by far the stronger, but because each, in his degree, exhibits the same want of depth and inventive power in his combinations and the same tiresome prolixity in maneuvering his men. It need hardly be said that the games, from first to last, are remarkable only for their unvarying and unexampled dullness."

Later on, commenting on his own set of games with Williams, he says: "There are positions, every one knows, occurring occasionally in a game, where even the clearest and farthest-seeing head requires a long time to unravel all the intricacies of a maze. In such cases, deliberation is a duty, and none, except a very unreasonable opponent, would object to it; but, when a player, *upon system,* consumes hours over moves when minutes might suffice and depends, not upon out-maneuvering, but out-sitting his antagonist, patience ceases to be a virtue. . . ."

I was curious about Williams's score. He finished third, next to Adolf Anderssen and Marmaduke Wyvill. I was curious about his meditations. Was his prolonged thinking part of a plan

to infuriate his opponents? Or was it because he was slowly evolving a new system of play?

The terms "Double Pawn Complex" and "*Zugzwang*" could have had no meaning for Williams, but here, in two games, we have this Nimzowitsch of a hundred years ago demonstrating these concepts.

London, 1851
DUTCH DEFENSE

LOWENTHAL WILLIAMS

White		Black
1	P - Q4	P - K3
2	P - K3	P - KB4
3	P - QB4	N - KB3
4	N - KB3	B - N5 ch
5	N - B3	B x N ch
6	P x B	P - B4!
7	B - Q3	Q - K2
8	0 - 0	0 - 0
9	P - QR4	....

White threatens 10 P x P, Q x P, 11 B - R3.

9	....	P - Q3
10	Q - B2	N - B3
11	B - R3	P - QN3
12	KR - K1	B - R3

Black's development and his planned attack against the doubled Pawn (.... QR - B1, ... N - QR4 and .... P x P) are in line with the system evolved by Nimzowitsch about seventy-five years later!

13	P - K4	P x KP
14	KB x P	B - N2
15	B x N	B x B
16	P - Q5	B - Q2
17	P x P	B - B3

At the cost of a Pawn, Black isolated White's Queen-side Pawns and made them permanently weak.

18	N - N5	P - KR3
19	N - R3	N - N5
20	Q - K2	N - K4

21	P - B4	N - N3
22	P - N3	R - B3
23	Q - R5	R x P
24	R x R	Q x R
25	N - B2	....

Disaster follows upon 25 P - B5 (25 .... Q - K6 ch, 26 K - B1, B - B6).

25	....	R - K1

Now Black threatens 26 .... Q - K8 ch and mate next.

26	P - R3	Q - K6
27	Q - N4	....

Of course not 27 Q x N, Q - B6.

27	....	Q x QBP
28	R - KB1	Q x B
29	K - R2	Q - KB6

No false pride. The exchange of the Queens might not be artistic, but it is the quickest way to win.

30	Q x Q	B x Q
31	P - B5	N - K4
32	R - B1	B - B3
33	P - N4	R - K2

Black aims to save his Queen Rook Pawn after 34 .... B x P, 35 R - QR1.

34	K - N3	B x P
35	R - B3	B - B3
36	P - R4	P - QR4
37	N - Q3	N x BP

With the fall of his last miserable Queen-side Pawn, White is convinced.

Resigns

♔

LEST you think that Black's strategy was just lucky coincidence, watch the ease with which he handles Staunton.

London, 1851
DUTCH DEFENSE

STAUNTON	WILLIAMS
White	Black
1 P - QB4	P - K3
2 P - K3	P - KB4
3 P - KN3	N - KB3
4 B - N2	B - K2
5 N - QB3	O - O
6 KN - K2	B - N5
7 O - O	P - Q3
8 P - Q4	B x N
9 P x B	Q - K2
10 B - QR3	P - B4

The strategy as before. If Black can induce 11 P x P or 11 P - Q5, White will be left with a badly doubled Pawn.

11	R - N1	P - K4

Now we have the V-shaped formation of which Nimzowitsch was so fond.

12	R - N5	P - QR3
13	R - N6	QN - Q2
14	R - N1	P - K5
15	Q - Q2	Q - B2
16	P - B3	....

"Throwing away a Pawn," says Staunton. But how can he save it? If 16 P x P, P x P, 17 Q - Q6, Q x P or 16 P - Q5, N - K4, he is worse off than in the game.

16	....	Q x P
17	P x KP	P x KP
18	B - R3	P - QN4
19	N - B4	N - N3
20	B - KN2	Q - B2

Black leaves QB5 for the Knight, which will exert tremendous pressure there.

21	P x P	N - B5
22	Q - B1	Q - R2!

Now Black is ready to reply to 23 P x P with 23 .... N x KP, winning the Exchange.

23	R - K1	P x P
24	B - N2	P - N4
25	N - K2	B - N5
26	P - KR3	B - B6
27	K - R2	....

Not 27 B x B, P x B as White's Knight is then hemmed in by Black and White Pawns!

27	....	QR - Q1
28	B - QR1	....

White is almost in *zugzwang!* — e.g., 28 B x B, P x B, 29 N - N1, P - B7, or 28 N - N1, R - Q7, and Black wins.

28	....	R - Q7
29	R - N2	KR - Q1
30	N - Q4	....

Rendered desperate by the threat of 30 .... N x R, 31 B x N, B x N, White gives up a piece. Against the alternative 30 R - B2, Black has a choice of two pretty wins of the Queen: 30 .... B x N, 31 R x B, R -

Q8 or *30* .... R x R, *31* Q x R, B x
B, *32* K x B, N x P ch. All this in
typical Nimzowitsch style!

30	....	R x R
31	B x R	P x N
32	BP x P	B x B
33	K x B	N - Q4
34	K - R2	....

White cannot play such moves as *34*
R - B1 or *34* Q - B2, either of which
loses to *34* .... N x P ch. But now
Black seizes the file.

34	....	R - KB1
35	Q - B2	Q - KB2
36	R - K2	Q - B8
37	B - B1	N - N5!

Resigns

Staunton's final comment was: "Mr.
Williams conducts this attack all
through the close with great judgment, while the defense is propor-
tionately imbecile."
Staunton is unnecessarily harsh on
himself. He was simply a victim of a
hypermodern system.

IN THE good old days of Morphy and
Anderssen, everybody played brilliant
chess. There was – to speak with
some poetic license – only one style
of play, and that was to attack and
keep on attacking. You either won
gloriously, or you succumbed to a
counterattack and lost gloriously. Defense was an unknown art to those
gallant knights. The Philidors and
Stauntons were very rare. And, after
Morphy, it took a long time even for
such a strong personality as Steinitz
to convince the chess world that defensive play could be beautiful, and
that a strategic retreat was not necessarily a cowardly flight from the
enemy.
Nobody, they say, before Steinitz, deliberately played a defensive game of
chess. Well, hardly anybody. So it is
all the more remarkable that a comparatively unknown amateur played a

game in a style decades ahead of his
time – a game studded with preventive moves against the King of Attack
himself, Paul Morphy. It is only poetic
justice that the first tilt between Attack and Defense should end in a
draw!

Paris, 1858
CENTER COUNTER

P. MORPHY	GUIBERT
White	Black
1 P - K4	P - Q4
2 P x P	Q x P
3 N - QB3	Q - Q1
4 P - Q4	P - K3

An augury of what is to come.

5	N - B3	B - Q3
6	B - Q3	N - K2
7	0 - 0	P - KR3!!

Anybody else would have castled and
fallen into the trap, *8* B x P ch, K x B,
9 N - N5 ch, etc. An old trap to you
and me, but it was invented twenty-
five years after this game was played!

8	B - K3	P - QB3

Black prevents White from even *thinking* about P - Q5.

9	N - K5	N - Q2
10	P - B4	N - B3
11	N - K4	N - B4
12	B - B2	B - B2
13	P - B3	N - Q4
14	Q - B3	Q - K2
15	QR - K1	B x N!

Black forces White to recapture with
a Pawn and so keep the King file
closed to White's Rook.

16	QP x B	P - KR4!

Another preventive move! Black anticipates the threat of *17* P - KN4, driving off his Knight.

17	B - B5	Q - Q1
18	N - Q6 ch	N x N
19	B x N	P - KN3!

Black stops *20* P - B5. It must be remembered that this sort of preventive
move, which Nimzowitsch dignified
by calling "prophylaxis," was as unknown in 1858 as television.

20	Q - N3	N - K2!

Just some more protection for his King Knight Pawn.

21	R - Q1	B - Q2
22	R - Q2	P - R5
23	Q - N4	N - B4
24	B x N	KP x B
25	Q - B3	Q - N3 ch
26	K - R1	0 - 0 - 0
27	P - B4	P - R6
28	P - KN3	....

Now Black exerts pressure of his own, on White's KN2.

28	....	B - K3
29	Q - B3	R - Q2
30	KR - Q1	P - B4
31	K - N1	KR - Q1
32	Q - R3	P - R3
33	B x P	....

Of course not 33 Q x P ch, Q x Q, 34 B x Q, R x R — as White loses a Rook!

| 33 | .... | Q - B3 |

Black threatens not only 34 .... R x R but also 34 .... Q - N7 ch, 35 R x Q, R x R ch, 36 K - B2, R(Q1) - Q7 ch, 37 K - K3, P x R, 38 K - B3, R - Q 6 ch, and Black wins easily.

| 34 | B - Q6 | P - B3 |

A little undermining; if now 35 P x P, R x B wins at once. Notice the power of Black's KRP!

| 35 | R - Q5! | .... |

Morphy could smell trouble. He offers a sacrifice which must be accepted, as he threatens 36 R - B5 and 35 .... P - N3 permits 36 Q x P ch.

| 35 | .... | B x R |
| 36 | R x B | .... |

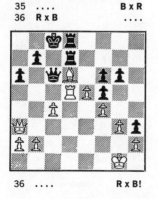

| 36 | .... | R x B! |

"Two can play at this game, Jack Dalton!"

| 37 | P x R | .... |

Of course not 37 R x R, Q - N7 mate. Or 37 R - B5, R - Q8 ch, 38 K - B2, R (Q1) - Q7 ch, 39 K - K3, R - Q6 ch, and Black wins.

37	....	K - N1
38	Q - Q3	R x P
39	Q - Q2	Rx R
40	P x R	Q - B4 ch
41	K - B1	Q - B5 ch
42	K - B2	Q - B4 ch
	Drawn	

It is a tribute to Morphy's prowess to point out that this was one of eight games played blindfold simultaneously by him at the Café de la Régence.

♛

LOUIS PAULSEN, one of the earliest masters to discover something about position play, was little appreciated in his lifetime, and less later. Early in his career, he was overshadowed by Morphy and Anderssen, who played brilliant combinative chess, and not plodding, tortuous, dull chess. Even his blindfold exploits suffered by comparison with those of Morphy. He played more games simultaneously than Morphy, but his performance might take a full day or two, while Morphy mowed them down in a few hours. Later on, he was neglected when Steinitz and Tarrasch came to the forefront.

The popular concept is that Steinitz is the father of the modern school of strategy, the discoverer of the elements of position play. Tarrasch then refined these theories of Steinitz and fashioned a technique based on principles by means of which a player could be guided in the conduct of his game. Admittedly, this is more dependable than awaiting the caprices of inspiration.

Generally, this is true, but Paulsen made one important contribution in the field of end-game strategy which is attributed to Steinitz. He was the first to discover the superiority of two Bishops to two Knights in the ending! In the game which follows he anticipates by eleven years the Vienna, 1873, encounter between Rosenthal and Steinitz, about which Réti says, "This is perhaps the oldest game in which we find the practical application of the theory *created by Steinitz* (italics mine) to demonstrate the advantage of the combined Bishops. . . . The method, created by Steinitz to turn the advantage of two Bishops to the fullest possible account, is applicable only to positions like the above which are neither closed nor completely open, but in which there are still to be found some points of support for the Knight protected by Pawns. The method, then, consists in advancing the Black Pawns in such a way that these points of support become unsafe for the Knight, which thereby is condemned to a passive role and becomes quite ineffectual."

As we shall see, Paulsen keeps his Bishops for the ending and plays in accordance with precept, driving the Knights off from good squares with his Pawns and obtaining more space for his Bishops.

London, 1862

RUY LOPEZ

HANNAH White	PAULSEN Black
1 P - K4	P - K4
2 N - KB3	N - QB3
3 B - N5	N - B3
4 P - B3	N x P
5 Q - K2	N - Q3
6 B x N	QP x B
7 Q x P ch	Q - K2!
8 P - Q4	P - B3
9 Q x Q ch	B x Q
10 B - B4	B - N5
11 QN - Q2	0 - 0 - 0
12 0 - 0	P - KN4
13 KR - K1	QR - K1

14 B - N3	B - Q1
15 B x N	P x B
16 N - K4	K - B2
17 N(B3) - Q2	P - KB4
18 N - KN3	P - B5
19 N(N3) - B1	P - KR4
20 P - B3	B - B4
21 K - B2	P - Q4

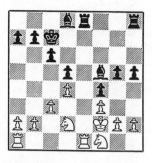

22 R x R		....

Either Hannah lacks patience, or he has confidence in his Knights.

22	....	R x R
23	R - K1	R x R
24	K x R	B - B3
25	N - QN3	P - N3
26	K - K2	P - R4
27	N - B1	K - Q3
28	N - Q3	P - B4
29	P x P ch	P x P
30	K - Q2	P - B5
31	N - B1	P - N5
32	K - K2	P - QR5
33	P - QR3	K - B4
34	K - Q2	P x P
35	P x P	P - Q5
36	N - K2	B - R6
37	K - K1	B - R5 ch
38	N(B1) - N3	P x N
39	P x P ch	K - Q4
40	P x P	B - N4
41	P - B4	B - B3
42	N - B3 ch	K x P
43	N x P	K - Q6
44	K - Q1	B - Q5
45	N - B3	B x N
46	P x B	K x P
47	P - R4	K - N5
48	K - Q2	K x P
49	K - B3	K - N4
50	K - N2	K - N5

Resigns

Historically important, this game is an instructive example of this form of ending. Later masters, of course, have polished this technique, notably in these encounters: Rosenthal–Steinitz, Vienna, 1873; Englisch–Steinitz, London, 1883; Richter–Tarrasch, Nuremberg, 1888; Walbrodt–Charousek, Nuremberg, 1896; Tarrasch–Rubinstein, San Sebastian, 1912; and Flohr–Botvinnik, 6th match game, 1933.

Apart from their didactic value, these games are eminently worth playing over, as they are extremely entertaining.

ANOTHER little idea that Paulsen anticipated is the ritual sacrifice of B x P ch in the French Defense. Credit is usually given to Fritz, who surprised Mason with it in the Nuremberg tournament of 1883. So, here to dispute the claim is an entry from a match played in 1879.

Leipzig, 1879
FRENCH DEFENSE

PAULSEN	SCHWARZ
White	Black
1 P - K4	P - K3
2 P - Q4	P - Q4
3 P - K5	P - QB4
4 P - QB3	N - QB3
5 N - B3	Q - N3
6 P - QR3	B - Q2
7 P - QN4	P x QP
8 P x P	KN - K2
9 N - B3	N - B4
10 N - QR4	Q - B2
11 B - N2	B - K2
12 R - B1	P - QR3
13 N - B5	B x N
14 R x B	0 - 0
15 B - Q3	N(B4) - K2
16 B x P ch!	K x B
17 N - N5 ch	K - N3
18 Q - N4	P - B4
19 Q - N3	Q - B1
20 R - B3	P - B5
21 Q - N4	N - B4

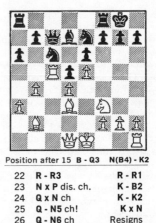

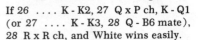
Position after 15 B - Q3   N(B4) - K2

22	R - R3	R - R1
23	N x P dis. ch.	K - B2
24	Q x N ch	K - K2
25	Q - N5 ch!	K x N
26	Q - N6 ch	Resigns

If 26 .... K - K2, 27 Q x P ch, K - Q1 (or 27 .... K - K3, 28 Q - B6 mate), 28 R x R ch, and White wins easily.

IN THE past few years,* death has taken from us some of the most illustrious names in the history of chess.

First, there was Tarrasch in 1934, the man whose games fascinated the world with their classic, clear-cut, logical, positional planning. Tarrasch formulated a science out of a rude art, and his teachings made masters out of amateurs.

Then in 1935 followed his archrival, Nimzowitsch, whose original over-the-board strategy thoroughly bewildered his opponents, and whose hypermodern ideas revolutionized chess theory.

In 1941 Lasker died. Lasker had held the title of world's champion for twenty-seven years, and his exploits and triumphs had been legendary.

One year later came the shocking news of Capablanca's sudden death from a cerebral hemorrhage. In his passing, we lost the greatest chess genius that ever lived.

Just as two of the game's preeminent teachers, Tarrasch and Nimzowitsch, died within a year of each other, and just as two of the world's greatest

* This was written in 1951.

masters, Lasker and Capablanca, left this life a year apart (coincidentally at the same hospital), so, too, did we lose two of our most celebrated exponents of attack at almost the same time. These two were Spielmann in 1943 and Marshall in 1944. We could ill spare all these, but the worst was yet to come.

In 1946, news flashed from Spain that one of the greatest chess masters of all time had died of a heart attack. The brilliant Alekhine had been snatched away at a most dramatic moment — on the eve of a match with Botvinnik for the world's championship.

And now it is Grandmaster Maróczy who joins these giants of the chessboard.

Géza Maróczy was a fine position player when knowledge of such strategy was the property of just a handful of masters. It was a pleasure to see Maróczy beating back a premature King-side attack. He sat back coolly, quietly strengthened his center, patiently defended his King against any wild onslaught, and methodically turned back the invading forces. The whole process was completely delightful — it seemed so quiet and painless. Offhand, I can think of only five other masters who excelled at this style of unruffled defense: Schlechter, Tarrasch, Rubinstein, Lasker and Capablanca.

Here is how Maróczy parried Bird's attacks when they first crossed swords. At the time when this game was played, Maróczy had not yet won his spurs, while Bird had been recognized as a master for almost a half century before. Bird had all the experience in the world, having met in tournament and match play such stars as Anderssen, Steinitz, Blackburne, Zukertort, Tarrasch and countless others. Bird had even been a contestant in the first tournament of modern chess history, far back in 1851!

Hastings, 1895
FRENCH DEFENSE

H. E. BIRD G. MARÓCZY
White Black

1	P - K4	P - K3
2	N - KB3	P - Q4
3	B - Q3	....

Why waste good moves on an unknown?

3	....	N - KB3
4	P - K5	N(B3) - Q2
5	P - QB3	P - QB4
6	B - B2	N - QB3
7	P - Q4	B - K2
8	P - KR3	....

Steinitz would shudder at this. White prepares to attack when there is not the slightest possible justification for doing so; Black has no weaknesses in his position to attack!

8	....	P - QR3
9	B - K3	P - QN4
10	P - QN3	B - N2
11	QN - Q2	P x P
12	P x P	O - O
13	P - KR4	....

White hopes to win by *14* B x P ch, K x B, *15* N - N5 ch in bang-bang style.

| 13 | .... | P - B3 |
| 14 | Q - N1 | .... |

To induce a weakening Pawn move.

14	....	P x P!
15	B x P ch	K - R1
16	N - N5	....

Never underestimate the power of an attack! White threatens *17* N x P as well as *17* B - N8.

| 16 | .... | R - B3 |

Now *17* B - N8 fails after the simple *17* .... Q x B.

| 17 | Q - Q1 | .... |

Trying to get in by *18* Q - R5.

| 17 | .... | Q - K1 |
| 18 | P - R5 | P x P! |

Nimzowitsch says that a wing attack is best met by play in the center. But here is Maróczy playing what Nimzowitsch had not yet discovered!

| 19 | B - N6 | .... |

This can become dangerous!

19	....	Q - KB1!
20	N - R7	P x B!!
21	N x Q	P x N ch
22	K - B1	QR x N
23	P - B3	N(Q2) - K4
24	Q x P	N x P!

Black breaks open the position for the powerful doubled Rooks!

| 25 | P x N | R x P ch |
| 26 | K - N2 | .... |

What's left? If 26 K - K1, B - N5 pins the Queen; or, if 26 K - N1, B - B4 ch wins the Queen or 26 .... R - N6 ch, followed by 27 .... B - Q3, leaves White helpless.

| 26 | .... | B - N5! |
| 27 | Q - B1 | .... |

White still hopes to get 28 P - R6 in.

| 27 | .... | R - B7 ch |
| 28 | K - N1 | .... |

No better is 28 K - R3, R(B1) - B6 ch, 29 K - N4, N - K4 ch, 30 K - N5, B - K2 mate.

28	....	N - Q5
29	B - Q3	B - Q7
30	Q - B5	B - K6
	Resigns	

CURIOUS CONCLUSIONS

IN a book featuring the pleasures of chess, these sprightly games belong in *The Department of Curious Conclusions*.

Melbourne, 1929
ALEKHINE DEFENSE

W. F.	B. W.
COULTAS	STENHOUSE
White	Black
1 P - K4	N - KB3
2 P - K5	N - Q4
3 N - QB3	N - N3
4 P - B4	P - QB4
5 N - B3	N - B3
6 P - Q4	P x P
7 N x P	P - N3
8 B - K3	B - N2
9 B - Q3	P - Q3
10 N x N	P x N
11 P x P	P x P
12 0 - 0	P - Q4
13 B - QB5!	B - K3
14 P - B5	P x P
15 B x P	Q - N4
16 Q - K2!	K - Q1

On *16 .... 0 - 0 - 0*, the continuation might be: *17* Q - R6 ch, K - N1, *18* B x B, P x B, *19* R - B7, R - Q2, *20* R x R, N x R, *21* B - Q6 ch, K - R1, *22* Q x BP mate.

17 B x B	P x B
18 Q x P	R - K1
19 Q x BP	R - QB1
20 B x N ch	P x B
21 Q - Q6 mate	

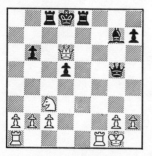

A pretty picture! Strangely enough, the winner of this game came in last in the tournament, while the victim of the epaulet mate won first prize!

EVEN the great Houdini could not have wriggled out of this paralyzing *zugzwang*.

Prague, 1927
SICILIAN DEFENSE

J. SCHULZ	B. THELEN
White	Black
1 N - QB3	P - QB4
2 P - K4	N - QB3
3 N - B3	P - K3
4 P - Q4	P x P
5 N x P	P - QR3
6 P - QR4	Q - B2
7 B - K2	N - B3
8 0 - 0	B - K2
9 B - K3	0 - 0
10 Q - Q2	P - Q3
11 N - N3	K - R1

Black isn't falling for any "book" traps such as *11 ....* N - QR4, *12* N x N, Q x N(R4), *13* N - Q5, Q x Q, *14* N x B ch, etc.

12 P - R5	N - Q2
13 N - R4	B - Q1
14 N - N6	N x N
15 P x N	Q - N1
16 KR - Q1	B - K2
17 P - QB4	N - Q1
18 P - B5!	P x P
19 QB x P	N - B3
20 B x B	N x B
21 Q - N4	N - N3

Of course not *21 ....* R - K1, *22* Q x N.

| 21 R - Q6! | .... |

Limiting Black's defensive resources. His Queen is out of play and, if *21 ....* P - K4 (to free his Bishop), *22* R x N costs him a piece.

21	....	P - R3
22	QR - Q1	K - R2
23	P - N3	....

White's last curbs the Black Knight's movements.

23	....	N - K2
24	N - R5	P - B4
25	R - Q8	R x R
26	R x R	N - N3

Black sidesteps loss by 26 .... N - B3, 27 N x N, P x N, 28 R x B, Q x R, 29 P - N7.

27	P x P	P x P
28	P - B4	Resigns

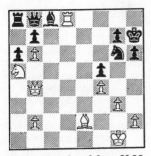

Black is tied hand and foot. If 28 .... P - R4, 29 B x KRP, K - R3, 30 Q - K7! K - R2, 31 Q - K8, White soon mates. Or, if 28 .... N - R1 (what a miserable move to be left with!), 29 Q - B8, N - N3, 30 Q - N8 is mate.

AND this pleasant little game, I would have relished seeing in *The Bright Side of Chess.*

Lausanne, 1947

ALEKHINE DEFENSE

POST	LOB
White	Black
1 P - K4	N - KB3
2 P - K5	N - Q4
3 P - QB4	N - N3
4 P - Q4	N - B3?
5 P - B4?	P - Q4
6 P - B5	N - Q2
7 N - KB3	P - K3
8 B - N5	N - K2
9 N - B3	P - QB3

10	B - Q3	P - QR4
11	O - O	P - QN3
12	N - KN5	P - R3
13	N x KP	P x N
14	Q - R5 ch	P - N3
15	B x P ch	N x B
16	Q x N ch	K - K2
17	P - B5	....

Threatening mate on the move.

17	....	Q - K1
18	Q x P ch	K - Q1
19	Q x BP	R - QN1
20	N x P	....

Now he intends 21 Q - B7 mate.

20	....	R - N2
21	P x P	....

White has snipped off no less than six Pawns for the piece he sacrificed.

21	....	R - KN1
22	Q - B7 ch!	R x Q
23	P x R mate	

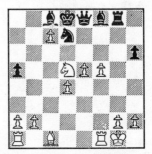

A pretty finish! The triumph of the passed Pawns is in keeping with White's winning method.

TYPICAL of Tarrasch's style, even in his salad days, is this example in which he ties up his opponent and leaves him helpless. This he does without so much as taking a Pawn off the board.

Berlin, circa 1880

SICILIAN DEFENSE

TARRASCH	MUNCHOFF
White	Black
1 P - K4	P - QB4
2 N - KB3	N - KR3

3	P - Q4	P - K3
4	P - Q5	P - Q3
5	P - B4	P - K4
6	B - Q3	N - N5
7	N - B3	N - QR3
8	P - QR3	B - K2
9	O - O	P - R3
10	P - R3	N - B3
11	N - KR2	P - KN4
12	P - QN4	B - Q2

Certainly not *12 .... P x P, 13 P x P, N x P* after which *14 Q - R4 ch* wins the Knight.

13	P - N5	N - B2
14	B - Q2	B - KB1
15	P - QR4	B - N2
16	P - R5	O - O
17	N - K2	N - R2
18	N - N3	P - B3
19	R - K1!	....

White makes room for N(R2) - B1 - K3 - B5 for a death grip on the white squares.

19	....	Q - K2
20	N(R2) - B1	K - R1
21	N - K3	N - K1
22	P - N6!	....

Now he prevents .... N - B2.

22	....	P - R3
23	N(K3) - B5	Q - B2
24	B - K2	R - KN1
25	B - R5	Q - B1

Black is driven to the wall.
Now Tarrasch has time, as he says, to prepare the sacrifice at Q6, to cut the Gordian knot.

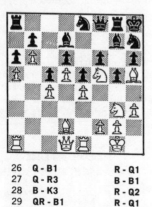

26	Q - B1	R - Q1
27	Q - R3	B - B1
28	B - K3	R - Q2
29	QR - B1	R - Q1

30	KR - Q1	B - Q2
31	N x QP!	N x N
32	B x BP	B - B1
33	B - KN4	B x B
34	P x B	R - Q2
35	N - B5	Q - Q1
36	B x N	N - B1
37	P - B5	N - N3
38	P - B6	P x P
39	P x P	R x B

Black runs (as little as his cramped space will allow) amok.

| 40 | Q x R | Q x Q |
| 41 | R x Q | Resigns |

♛

WINNING a game by a slashing, smashing attack never appealed to Nimzowitsch. Some masters reveled in sacrificial combination play, but not the Crown Prince of Chess. He preferred to tie up his opponent in knots. He paralyzed them with the *Blockade*, his name for the system by which his pieces got a stranglehold on one square after another, advancing with crushing effect until there was no retreat for the enemy army.

Arnstadt, 1926

DUTCH DEFENSE

HAGE	NIMZOWITSCH
White	Black
1	P - Q4	P - KB4
2	P - K3	P - Q3
3	B - Q3	P - K4
4	P x P	P x P
5	B - N5 ch	P - B3
6	Q x Q ch	K x Q
7	B - B4	B - Q3
8	N - KB3	N - B3
9	N - B3	K - K2
10	P - QR3	R - Q1
11	B - Q2	P - QN4

This P - QN4 move comes up with remarkable frequency in Nimzowitsch's games, and with striking effect.

12	B - R2	P - QR4
13	O - O	P - N5
14	N - N1	P - B4
15	B - B4	P - K5
16	N - N5	B - R3

Black challenges White's best-posted piece.

17	B x B	R x B
18	P x P	RP x P
19	R x R	N x R
20	P - QB3	P - R3
21	N - R3	N - N5

Now he attacks the Rook Pawn and forces 22 P - KN3.

| 22 | P - KN3 | .... |

And now, with all his Pawns on black squares, White has condemned his Bishop to life imprisonment.

22	....	N - K4
23	K - N2	P - N4
24	B - B1	....

The useless Bishop retires, making room for the Knight who may have a more illustrious career.

24	....	P - N6
25	N - Q2	P - QB5
26	N - KN1	N - B4
27	N - K2	R - KN1
28	N - Q4	P - B5
29	N - B5 ch	K - K3
30	N x B	P - B6 ch
31	K - N1	K x N
32	R - Q1	K - K3
33	N - N1	N(B4) - Q6
34	N - R3	K - Q4
35	N - N5	R - N1
36	N - R3	....

What a life! This poor Knight has done nothing but advance a bit and then retreat.

36	....	R - QR1
37	P - R3	K - B4
38	K - B1	....

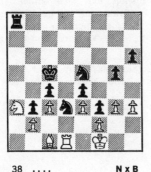

38 ....   N x B

Simplification so that Hage can see clearly how helpless he is!

39	R x N	N - Q6
40	R - N1	N x NP
41	R x N	R x N

Mate on the move practically is threatened.

| 42 | R - N1 | P - N7 |
| | Resigns | |

White cannot prevent the fatal 43 .... R - R8.

DESPITE the sophistication of the modern player and his amazing absorption of book knowledge, he may still find himself in an embarrassing situation. The game that follows shows Keres tying up his opponent in the style made famous by Tarrasch. Here is the sad story:

Gothenburg, 1955
SICILIAN DEFENSE

KERES	PANNO
White	Black
1 P - K4	P - QB4
2 N - KB3	P - Q3
3 P - Q4	P x P
4 N x P	N - KB3
5 N - QB3	P - QR3
6 B - KN5	P - K3
7 P - B4	....

This move is more troublesome to meet than the usual 7 Q - B3.

| 7 .... | Q - N3 |
| 8 Q - Q2 | N - B3 |

"The complications following 8 .... Q x P defy exact analysis," says Keres. The rule is simple enough, though, in such cases: Never capture Keres's Queen Knight Pawn!

9 0 - 0 - 0	Q x N
10 Q x Q	N x Q
11 R x N	N - Q2

An awkward move, but the plausible 11 .... B - Q2 would be met by 12 P - K5, to which there is no favorable reply.

| 12 B - K2 | P - R3 |
| 13 B - R4 | P - KN4 |

Panno sacrifices a Pawn to get some play for his pieces. The natural development by *13* .... B - K2 would cost a Pawn after *14* B x B, K x B, *15* KR - Q1, and the Queen Pawn falls.

| 14 | P x P | N - K4! |

This is better than *14* .... B - K2, *15* B - N3. With the next move Black is ready to meet *15* P x P with *15* .... B x P ch, *16* K - N1, B - K6, and two of White's pieces are attacked.

| 15 | N - R4! | .... |

The Knight is headed for N6, where it will get a powerful grip on Black's position. The full import of the threat may not have been appreciated by Black, or he would have forced its exchange by *15* .... P - N4, *16* N - N6, R - QN1, *17* N x B, R x N.

15	....	B - K2
16	N - N6	R - QN1
17	B - N3	P x P
18	KR - Q1	....

The situation is getting difficult. Black cannot develop his Bishop, as after *18* .... B - Q2, *19* B x N, P x B, *20* R x B removes the Bishop from the board. Meanwhile he is threatened with *19* B x N, P x B, *20* R - B4, and the Bishop is lost.

| 18 | .... | P - B3 |
| 19 | P - B4! | .... |

Ready to reply to *19* .... B - Q2 with *20* P - B5.

19	....	0 - 0
20	R(Q4) - Q2	P - B4
21	P - B5!	P - B5
22	P x P	B x P
23	R x B	P x B
24	P x P	R - B2
25	K - N1!	....

Quiet but powerful! The threat is winning the Bishop by *26* R - Q8 ch, or by *26* R - QB1. The impulsive *25* R - Q8 ch would not do, as after *25* .... K - N2, *26* R x B, R x R ch, *27* N x R, there follows *27* .... R - B2 ch, and Black regains his piece.

25	....	R - B2
26	R - Q8 ch	K - N2
27	R - QB1	N - B3

No better is *27* .... R x R ch, *28* K x R, and White wins a piece.

| 28 | P - K5! | .... |

Nails down Black's King Pawn and with it Black's hope of P - K4 and the emergence of the Bishop into daylight.

| 28 | .... | K - N3 |
| 29 | B - Q3 ch | K - B2 |

Or *29* .... K - R4, *30* R - R8 ch, K - N5, *31* R - R3, and mate follows by *32* R - B4.

| 30 | R - R8 | .... |

Threatens *31* R - R7 ch winning a Rook.

| 30 | .... | K - K2 |
| 31 | B - N6!! | .... |

Black is completely helpless! None of his pieces (two Rooks, a Knight and

a Bishop) can move without instant loss of material, and his King, now in a stalemate position, is threatened with *32* R - K8 — mate on the move.

| 31 | .... | Resigns |

A game played by Keres with accuracy and artistry. Who can say, "Chess is a minor art," after seeing such a masterpiece?

THERE are many unusual checkmates, but this one must be in a class by itself! To say any more would give away the plot, so here is the story from the beginning:

Melbourne, 1928

FRENCH DEFENSE

GAUDERSEN	PAUL
White	Black
1 P - K4	P - K3
2 P - Q4	P - Q4
3 P - K5	P - QB4
4 P - QB3	P x P
5 P x P	B - N5 ch
6 N - B3	N - QB3
7 N - B3	KN - K2
8 B - Q3	0 - 0
9 B x P ch	....

Almost any decent player would make this sacrifice instinctively, without bothering to calculate the consequences.

9	K x B
10 N - N5 ch	K - N3
11 P - KR4	....

Threatens to subdue Black by *12* P - R5 ch, K - R3 (if *12* .... K - B4, *13* Q - B3 mate) *13* N x P dbl. ch, and White wins the Queen.

11	N x QP
12 Q - N4	P - B4
13 P - R5 ch	K - R3

| 14 N x KP dis. ch | P - N4 |

Or *14* .... K - R2, *15* Q x NP mate.

| 15 P x P e.p. mate! | |

An extraordinary finish — checkmate by capturing a Pawn *en passant!*

BLINDFOLD BEAUTIES

BRILLIANCIES just flowed from Blackburne's mind in his displays of blindfold chess. From an abundance of gems, it is easy to select a few sparklers, but which shines the brightest of all?

Critics are practically agreed that his game against Ballard is the finest effort of his career in the field of blindfold play – a masterpiece any way you look at it!

London, 1871
SCOTCH GAMBIT

	J. H. BLACKBURNE White	DR. BALLARD Black
1	P - K4	P - K4
2	N - KB3	N - QB3
3	P - Q4	P x P
4	B - QB4	B - B4
5	N - N5	N - R3
6	Q - R5	Q - K2
7	O - O	N - K4
8	B - N3	P - Q3
9	P - KR3	N - N1
10	P - KB4	P - Q6 dis. ch
11	K - R2	N - KB3
12	Q - Q1	N(K4) - N5 ch
13	P x N	N x P ch
14	K - N3	P - KR4

Black threatens 15 .... P - R5 ch, 16 K - B3 (or 16 K - R3, N - B7 ch), N - R7 mate.

15	P - B5	B - K6
16	B x P ch	K - B1
17	Q x N!	....

Remarkable in view of the circumstances: Blackburne was playing ten games at once, blindfold!

17	....	P x Q
18	B x B	Q - K4 ch
19	B - B4	Q x NP
20	N - Q2	P x P
21	N - B4	Q - B6 ch
22	N - K3	B - Q2
23	K x P	B - R5
24	N - Q5	Q - Q6
25	B - N6	....

White threatens 26 N - K6 ch, K - N1, 27 N - K7 mate.

25	....	R - R3
26	N - K6 ch	K - N1
27	N - K7 ch	K - R1
28	R - R1	Q - Q8 ch
29	QR x Q	P x R (Q) ch
30	R x Q	B x R ch
31	K - N3	R - R8

Blackburne could keep track of the weirdest positions! Now, with a couple of vigorous moves, he forces the win.

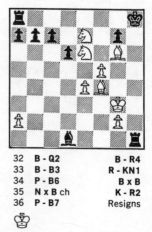

32	B - Q2	B - R4
33	B - B3	R - KN1
34	P - B6	B x B
35	N x B ch	K - R2
36	P - B7	Resigns

THOSE who saw Pillsbury in action considered him the greatest blindfold player who ever lived. It was not from the number of boards he faced (or more properly, turned his back to) but for the ease and grace with which he mentally manipulated his pieces throughout even the most bewildering complications.

In his day, it was customary for even the best of blindfold artists to give displays of their skill on eight or ten boards. To Pillsbury, an exhibition on sixteen boards was a routine affair.

It is from one of these sixteen-game performances that we select this beauty, which deserves to be rescued from the Department of Neglected Masterpieces.

Vienna, 1902

QUEEN'S GAMBIT DECLINED

H. N. PILLSBURY   A. WOLF

	White	Black
1	P - Q4	P - Q4
2	P - QB4	P - QB3
3	N - QB3	N - B3
4	P - K3	P - K3
5	N - B3	B - Q3
6	B - Q3	QN - Q2
7	P - K4	P x KP
8	N x P	N x N
9	B x N	N - B3
10	B - B2	B - Q2

The position has a distinctly modern look, which is not to be wondered at, as Pillsbury played the sort of chess which never gets out of date.

11	0 - 0	N - N5
12	R - K1	P - KR4
13	P - KR3	Q - K2
14	P - B5	B - B2
15	B - N5	N - B3
16	N - K5	0 - 0 - 0
17	Q - B3	K - N1
18	P - QN4	B - B1
19	KR - Q1	....

The proper way to protect the Pawn. White's Queen Rook is to be used to support the advance of his Queen Knight Pawn. Meanwhile Black must not snap at *19 .... R x P; 20 R x R, B x N*, as *21 B - B4* is the refutation.

19	....	K - R1
20	QR - N1	B - N1
21	P - QR4	R x P

Black sacrifices the exchange to get some freedom for his pieces. Better that than to be slowly crushed to death.

22	R x R	B x N
23	R - QB4	B - N1
24	P - N5	Q - B2
25	B - B4	P - K4
26	B - R2	N - Q4
27	B - K4	B - K3
28	P x P	P x P
29	R - Q4!	....

A pretty move which threatens *30 R x N.*

29	....	Q - Q1
30	R(Q4) - N4!	Q - B2

Of course not *30 .... N x R, 31 B x P ch.*

31	R(N4) - N2	P - N3
32	B x N	P x B
33	Q - B6	R - QB1
34	P - B6!	Q x P
35	B x P	B - B2

There is no relief in *35 .... B x B, 36 Q x B(K5), Q - K1, 37 P - R5,* followed by *38 P - R6* and *39 R - N7.*

36	B x B	Q x B
37	Q - Q4	Q - Q3
38	R - N7	R - B8 ch
39˙	R x R	K x R
40	P - R5	K - R1
41	R - N1	....

There is a little threat of *42 Q - R8 ch.*

41	....	Q - B2
42	P - R6	.....

Now White aims at *43 R - N7.*

42	....	Q - B3
43	Q - K5	Q - B1

44	Q - Q6!	....

The quiet move which forces resignation. The threat of *45 R - N8 ch, Q x R, 46 Q - B6 ch,* followed by mate can be stopped only by *44 .... B - Q2,* but then *45 R - N8 ch, Q x R, 46 Q x P ch* leads to the same finish.

It is worth repeating that this was one of sixteen blindfold games played simultaneously!

SOME years ago, I came across a game of Pillsbury's which I clutched to my heart. The play was intricate but pretty, the opposition strong and the occasion noteworthy.

The game was one of twenty conducted simultaneously blindfold (a world's record at the time) by the young genius against a redoubtable field which included seven competitors in the championship tournament of the Franklin Chess Club.

This was the team that faced him:

Board	1	S. W. Bampton
Board	2	M. Morgan
Board	3	D. S. Robinson
Board	4	C. J. Newman
Board	5	J. F. Magee
Board	6	J. A. Kaiser
Board	7	A. C. Baclay
Board	8	W. Mimmelsbach
Board	9	W. P. Shipley
Board	10	L. S. Landreth
Board	11	J. F. Roeske
Board	12	(identity unknown)
Board	13	F. W. Doerr
Board	14	J. H. Rhoads
Board	15	W. O. Dunbar
Board	16	J. T. Wright
Board	17	W. J. Ferris
Board	18	R. R. Deardon
Board	19	S. R. Stadelman
Board	20	O. Hesse

In the amazingly quick time of 6½ hours Pillsbury had finished the exhibition, winning fourteen games, drawing five and losing only one! The lone winner was Landreth, and the drawn games were secured by Magee, Baclay, Shipley, Rhoads and Wright. To my mind this, and not Pillsbury's performance at Hanover two years later, was his greatest feat as a blindfold artist.

The game which follows has never

been sufficiently appreciated, as the annotators cast doubts on the soundness of Pillsbury's combination. But let us see for ourselves:

Philadelphia, 1900

RUY LOPEZ

PILLSBURY	BAMPTON
White	Black
1 P - K4	P - K4
2 N - KB3	N - QB3
3 B - N5	N - B3
4 0 - 0	N x P
5 P - Q4	N - Q3
6 B - R4	P - K5
7 R - K1	B - K2
8 N - K5	0 - 0
9 N - QB3	B - B3
10 B - B4	R - K1
11 N - N4!	....

White boldly sacrifices a second Pawn.

11	B x P
12 N - Q5	B - K4
13 N x B	N x N
14 Q - R5	P - KB3
15 B - QN3	K - R1

"Even the laziest King," says Nimzowitsch, "flees wildly in the face of a double check."

16 R - K3	P - KN3
17 Q - R4	R - K3

Black guards his King Bishop Pawn. If instead 17 .... P - KN4, White gains the edge with 18 B x N.

18 R - R3	P - KR4
19 N x KBP!	....

There is more to this than the fact that capturing the Knight costs Black the exchange — e.g., 19 .... Q x N, 20 Q x Q ch, R x Q, 21 B x N or 19 .... R x N, 20 B x N.

19	N - B4
20 Q - N5	N - B2
21 Q x NP	Q x N

Taking with the Rook succumbs to 22 B - K5, N x B, 23 R x P ch, and mate next.

| 22 R x P ch | .... |

This is the position (and how Pillsbury mastered its intricacies in his mind, as well as those of the other nineteen games, Heaven only knows).

At this point, say the critics, Black should play 22 .... N(B4) - R3, and White then has no winning line: e.g.,

23 Q x Q ch, R x Q, 24 B x N(B7), R x B(B5), 25 R x N ch, K - N2, and Black retains his piece.

Let us consider this hypothetical line, however, before continuing with the actual game: (Start from diagram.)

22	N(B4) - R3
23 B - K5	Q x B

Obviously if 23 N x B, 24 R x N mate. Or 23 .... R x B, 24 Q x Q ch, and White wins.

24 Q x N(B7)	Q - N2

Black's last is forced in view of the threat (25 R x N ch, R x R, 26 Q - N8 mate).

25 B x R!	P x B
26 R x N ch	Q x R
27 R - Q1	Q - N4

Or 27 .... Q - R5 (to guard against mate by the Rook) 28 P - KN3, Q - N4, 29 P - KR4, Q - N2, 30 R - Q8 ch, K - R2, 31 Q - R5 ch, Q - R3, 32 R - R8 ch, and White wins.

28 P - KR4	Q x RP
29 P - KN3	Q - N4
30 K - N2	....

And now the threat of mate by 31 R - R1 ch is impossible to meet.

Now back to the diagram and the actual game — with Pillsbury vindicated!

22	N(B2) - R3
23 Q x Q ch	R x Q
24 B - K5	K - N2
25 P - KN4	....

White strikes at one piece and also threatens to push on and attack two others.

25	N x P
26 R - N5 ch	K - R3
27 B x R	N x B
28 R x N	K - N3

Black must have had a faint hope that Pillsbury might move R - B4, after which 29 .... K - N4 wins the exchange.

29 R - K5	P - Q3
30 R - K7	B - R6
31 K - R1	R - KB1
32 R - N1 ch	N - N5
33 R x KP	K - B4

Ostensibly, Black adds a protector to his Knight, but there is more. He has quietly unpinned the Knight and actually threatens mate on the move.

34 R - K2	R - K1

Black kindly offers a Rook.

35 R(N1) - K1	....

Black would love to play 35 .... N x P ch and, after his Knight is taken, capture by 36 .... R x R with check and mate. Unfortunately for him White would take the Knight with check!

35	N - K4
36 P - KB4	K x P
37 R - B2 ch	K - N4
38 B - Q5	P - B3
39 R - N1 ch	N - N5
40 B - B3	R - K6
41 B x N	B x B
42 R(B2) - N2	Resigns

The pin is irresistible. If 45 .... R - K5 to help the Bishop, 43 P - KR3 puts on the extra bit of pressure needed to win the pinned piece.

♛

ALEKHINE may well have been the greatest blindfold player that ever lived. In number of games conducted simultaneously, his records have been broken, notably by Najdorf who set a blazing mark of 45 at Sao Paulo in 1947, whereas Alekhine never tried to exceed his own record of 32 at a time.

In quality of performance, though, nobody, but nobody, surpassed Alekhine. His sensitive position play was a joy to behold, while his combinations lit up the whole board with their radiance. This pleasing, graceful blending of profound strategy and lively tactics is particularly manifest in the game which follows and moves me to nominate it to occupy the niche reserved for "The Immortal Blindfold Game" in Caissa's Hall of Fame.

London, 1926

KING'S INDIAN DEFENSE

ALEKHINE   SCHWARTZ
White   Black
	White	Black
1	P - Q4	N - KB3
2	P - QB4	P - KN3
3	P - KN3	B - N2
4	B - N2	0 - 0
5	N - QB3	P - Q3
6	N - B3	N - B3
7	P - Q5	N - QR4
8	Q - Q3	P - N3

Black prepares to retreat his Knight. The threat was 9 P - QN4.

9	N - Q4	N - N2
10	N - B6	Q - Q2
11	0 - 0	P - QR4
12	P - N3	N - B4
13	Q - B2	B - N2
14	P - KR3	....

White prevents Black from swinging his King Knight over to K4 via N5.

14	....	QR - K1
15	P - R3	....

White intends to follow with P - QN4 to evict the Knight.

15	....	B x N
16	P x B	Q - B1
17	P - QN4	P x P
18	P x P	N - R3

The alternative, 18 .... QN - K5, 19 N - N5, Alekhine says, "is anything but pleasant."

19	R - R4	N - N1
20	P - N5	P - R3
21	R - R7	P - K4
22	K - R2	....

More of this preventive stuff; after P - B4, White does not want to be bothered by .... N - R4 in reply.

22	....	K - R2
23	P - B4	R - K2
24	P x P	R x P
25	B - B4	R(K4) - K1

After 25 .... R - R4, 26 N - Q5, N x N, 27 P x N, the Rook never gets out alive.

26	N - Q5	N x N
27	B x N	Q - Q1
28	P - R4	Q - K2
29	P - K3	K - R1

Black prepares for .... P - N4, thinking he will win a piece.

30	K - N2	....

Two can play at that game: if now 30 .... P - N4, 31 P x P, P x P, 32 R - R1 ch. White wins at once.

30	....	P - B4
31	R - K1	K - R2
32	P - K4	B - K4
33	P x P	P x P

Now comes a brilliant twelve-move combination which wins a piece and the game.

34	P - B5!	NP x P

Black's last is forced, as White threatened 35 P x NP. 34 .... QP x P, of course, is out because of 35 R x B.

35	P - N6	R - B1
36	Q - B3!	KR - K1
37	B x B	P x B
38	Q x KP!	....

This temporary Rook sacrifice, and its sequel, had to be foreseen at the 34th move, or else the whole combination had no point.

38	....	Q x Q
39	R x Q	R x R
40	R x P ch	R x R
41	P x R	R - K1

42	P x N (Q)	R x Q
43	B - K6!	....

White controls the queening square and so wins the Rook for a Pawn. This is the kick which so often comes at the end of an Alekhine inspiration.

43	....	K - N3
44	P - B7	R - KB1
45	P - B8 (Q)	R x Q
46	B x R	P - QB5
47	B - R6	P - B6

48	B - Q3	K - B3
49	K - B3	K - K4
50	K - K3	P - R4
51	B - B2	K - B3
52	K - B4	K - N2
53	K x P	K - R3

Black hopes for 54 K - B6, as he is then stalemated.

54	K - B4!	Resigns

♛

PERIPATETIC PAWNS
The Soul of Chess

ABOUT a century and a half ago Philidor made the immortal observation, "The Pawns are the soul of chess." Have you ever wondered how Philidor himself handled the Pawns?

London, 1788

ODDS OF PAWN AND TWO MOVES

Remove Black's KBP

BOWDLER	PHILIDOR
White	Black
1 P - K4	....
2 P - KB4	P - K3
3 N - KB3	P - Q4
4 P - K5	P - B4
5 P - Q4	N - QB3
6 P - B3	Q - N3
7 Q - N3	N - R3
8 B - Q3	P - B5
9 Q x Q	P x Q
10 B - B2	B - Q2
11 N - N5	P - N3
12 N x RP	R x N
13 B x P ch	R - B2
14 B x R ch	K x B
15 P - KR3	N - B4
16 P - KN4	N - N6
17 R - N1	N - K5
18 N - Q2	N x N
19 B x N	P - N4
20 B - K3	P - N5
21 P - KR4	P - N4
22 P - R5	P - N6
23 P - R3	P - N5!
24 B - B1	P x BP
25 P x P	N x QP

Clearing the way for his Pawns.

| 26 P x N | P - B6 |

And now they do look menacing!

27 R - N1	B x P
28 R x P	B x B
29 R x P	B x P
30 R - B3	....

How will Black save himself?

30	R - R8 ch
31 K - B2	R - R7 ch
32 K - B1	R - R8 ch
33 K - N2	R - R7 ch
34 K - B1!	....

The point! White cannot escape the checks by 34 K - R3 or 34 K - R1 as mate by 34 .... R - R7 would follow.

| 34 .... | R - R8 ch |

Drawn by perpetual check

ONCE a year, Napier says, he plays through all the eighty-odd games of the Labourdonnais–McDonnell matches. It is easy to understand the fascination of these exciting battles after playing through the score of their 62d game, one of my favorites.

London, 1834

SICILIAN DEFENSE

McDONNELL	LABOURDONNAIS
White	Black
1 P - K4	P - QB4
2 N - KB3	N - QB3
3 P - Q4	P x P
4 N x P	P - K4
5 N x N	NP x N
6 B - QB4	N - B3
7 B - KN5	B - K2
8 Q - K2	P - Q4

9	B x N	B x B
10	B - N3	0 - 0
11	0 - 0	P - QR4
12	P x P	P x P
13	R - Q1	P - Q5
14	P - QB4	Q - N3
15	B - B2	B - N2
16	N - Q2	QR - K1
17	N - K4	B - Q1
18	P - B5	Q - QB3

Black threatens *19* .... P - B4, and the Knight dares not move away.

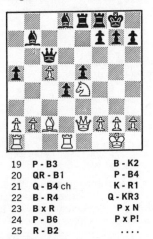

19	P - B3	B - K2
20	QR - B1	P - B4
21	Q - B4 ch	K - R1
22	B - R4	Q - KR3
23	B x R	P x N
24	P - B6	P x P!
25	R - B2	....

If *25* P x B, Black forces mate by 25 .... Q - K6 ch, *26* K - R1, P x P ch, *27* K x P, R - B7 ch, *28* K - N1, R - K7 dis. ch, *29* K - R1, Q - B6 ch, *30* K - N1, Q - N7 mate.

25	....	Q - K6 ch
26	K - R1	B - B1
27	B - Q7	P - B7

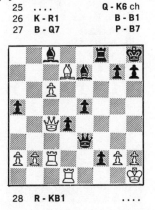

| 28 | R - KB1 | .... |

But not *28* Q - B1, B - R3, *29* Q x B, P - Q6, *30* Q x QP (or *30* R x BP, R x R, and Black wins), Q x Q, *31* R x Q, P - B8 (Q) mate.

28	....	P - Q6
29	R - B3	B x B
30	P x B	P - K5
31	Q - B8	B - Q1
32	Q - B4	Q - K8
33	R - B1	P - Q7
34	Q - B5	R - N1
35	R - Q1	P - K6

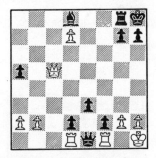

Such a pretty group picture!

36	Q - B3	Q x R(Q8)
37	R x Q	P - K7
	Resigns	

And the final position is remarkable.

BACK in 1940, Marshall played a game against Rogosin where he defied all the conventions for opening procedure. Instead of developing his pieces, Marshall pushed six of his eight Pawns into the flanks of his enemy's Knights, won a piece after ten moves, and shortly thereafter the game. It was a remarkable feat and one not likely to be duplicated — but it was!

Milwaukee, 1950

SICILIAN DEFENSE

R. KUJOTH   FASHINGBAUER

	White	Black
1	P - K4	P - QB4
2	P - QN4	P x P
3	P - QR3	N - QB3
4	P x P	N - B3
5	P - N5	N - QN1
6	P - K5	Q - B2
7	P - Q4	....

White doesn't fall for 7 P x N, Q - K4 ch.

7	....	N - Q4
8	P - QB4	N - N3
9	P - B5	N - Q4
10	P - N6!	....

Black resigned, as the loss of a piece was inevitable. Continuing would have enabled Kujoth to score neatly: *10* .... Q - Q1, *11* R x P, R x R, *12* P x R, Q - R4 ch, *13* N - B3! N x N, *14* P x N (Q), N x Q dis. ch, *15* B - Q2! Q - Q1, *16* K x N — and Black will have most of his pieces set up for the next game.

♛

IMMORTAL games feature all kinds of sacrifices, but none so strange as here. Before White achieves his objective, he gives away — well, let's see.

KING'S GAMBIT

Remove White's Queen Knight

BALLARD   FAGAN

	White	Black
1	P - K4	P - K4

2	P - KB4	P x P
3	N - B3	B - K2
4	B - B4	B - R5 ch
5	P - N3	P x P
6	0 - 0	N - KR3
7	P - Q4	0 - 0
8	P x P	B x P
9	K - N2	B - Q3
10	R - R1	Q - B3
11	P - K5	Q - N3 ch
12	K - B1	N - B4
13	R - KN1	N - N6 ch
14	K - B2	N - K5 ch
15	K - K1	B - N5 ch
16	P - B3	N x P
17	P x N	B x P ch
18	K - B2	Q - QB3

Black is pretty aggressive for a Knight-odds player.

19	B - Q3	B x R
20	P - Q5	Q - N3 ch
21	B - K3	Q - N7 ch
22	K - B1	P - KB4
23	B - Q4	Q x P
24	B x B	Q x P
25	P - K6	P - KN3
26	P - K7	R - K1

This is a strange position! White has one solitary Pawn, but it's a passed Pawn on the seventh rank; Black meanwhile has seven passed Pawns!

27	Q - K2	Q - B4
28	Q - QN2	....

White threatens — need we tell?

28	....	R x P

If *28* .... Q x P, then White has *29* Q - R8 ch, K - B2, *30* B - B4 ch, P - Q4, *31* B x P ch, B - K3, *32* N - K5 mate.

29	Q - R8 ch	K -B2
30	N - N5 mate	

The diagram shows that White has given away all eight of his Pawns — a world's record which cannot be broken!

COULD a candidate for "the Pawn least likely to succeed" become the star of the show? Let's see!

Ostend, 1937

INDIAN DEFENSE

A. DUNKELBLUM   P. KERES

White	Black
1 P - Q4	N - KB3
2 N - KB3	P - B4
3 P - K3	P - KN3
4 B - K2	B - N2
5 0 - 0	0 - 0
6 P - B4	P - Q4
7 P x QP	N x P
8 P x P	N - R3
9 B x N	P x B

White cheerfully gives up his long-range Bishop for a short-stepping Knight, as he thereby gives Black an isolated, hence weak, doubled Pawn. How is he to know that Black's Queen Knight Pawn, which he shunts off to the Rook file, will be the chief cause of his later troubles?

10 N - Q4	Q - B2
11 N - N3	R - Q1
12 Q - K2	P - QR4!

To dislodge the Knight.

13 B - Q2	P - R5
14 B - R5	Q - B3
15 B x R	B - QR3

It's fun to play over positions in which half a dozen pieces are *en prise*, but only a Keres could enjoy such complications in a tournament game.

16 N - R5	Q - K3
17 Q - Q2	B x R
18 N - B3	B x P!

Threatening *19 ....* B - B6, followed by *20 ....* Q - R6.

19 K x B	R x B

Now White must guard against loss of his Queen by 20 N - B5 ch. His best recourse seems to be 20 N x N, R x N, 21 Q - N4 (but not 21 Q - K2, R x P, 22 N - N7, Q - K5 ch, 23 Q - B3, R - N4 ch).

20 K - R1	P - R6!

Have you forgotten me, Mr. Dunkelblum?

21 R - Q1	....

Something has to be done about the threat of *21 ....* P x P, followed by *22 ....* B x N.

21	P x P

"He just keeps rolling along."

22 N x N	R x N
Resigns	

If 23 Q x R, Q x Q ch, 24 R x Q, P - N8 (Q) ch, winning the Rook next move. Or, if 23 Q - B2, R x R ch (even 23 .... Q - K5 ch at once is decisive) 24 Q x R, Q - K5 ch, 25 P - B3, P - N8 (Q), and Black wins.

OUR last is the Story of the Three Passed Pawns.

Kaschau, 1892

EVANS GAMBIT

BERGER   CHAROUSEK

White	Black
1 P - K4	P - K4
2 N - KB3	N - QB3
3 B - B4	B - B4
4 P - QN4	B x P
5 P - B3	B - R4
6 0 - 0	P - Q3
7 P - Q4	B - Q2

8	P x P	P x P
9	B - R3	Q - B3
10	Q - N3	B - N3
11	B- Q5	KN - K2
12	P - B4	N - R4
13	Q - B3	P - B3
14	P - B5	B - B2
15	B - N3	N x B
16	P x N	N - N3
17	B - B1	B - N5
18	B - N5	Q - K3
19	QN - Q2	P - KR3
20	B - K3	O - O
21	P - R3	B x N
22	N x B	N - B5
23	B x N	P x B
24	KR - K1	KR - Q1
25	P - QN4	P - R3
26	K - B1	R - Q2
27	Q - B2	QR - Q1
28	K - N1	R - Q6
29	QR - N1	R x N!

This is not a sacrifice on impulse, just to be brilliant. The position which results after White forces an exchange of Queens and Rooks looks quite lost for Black. The saving move (for there is a happy ending) had to be seen 'way ahead by young Charousek.

| 30 | P x R | Q x RP |
| 31 | Q - K2 | P - KN4 |

32	Q - B1	Q x P
33	Q - N2	Q x Q ch
34	K x Q	P - N5
35	QR - Q1	P - B6 ch
36	K - B1	P - KR4
37	R x R ch	B x R
38	R - Q1	B - N4
39	R - Q7	P - R5
40	R x NP	P - R6
41	K - N1	. . . .

41	. . . .	B - K6!
42	P x B	P - N6

Aren't those Pawns a lovely sight?

43	R - Q7	P - B7 ch
44	K - B1	P - R7
	Resigns	

HAPPY ENDINGS

IN HIS invaluable treatise, *My System*, Nimzowitsch makes this cryptic statement: "Tartakower is, in my opinion, without question the third best endgame artist of all living masters." One wonders who his two superiors were. Whom did Nimzowitsch have in mind?

There was Lasker, former world's champion, whose consummate endgame skill was almost legendary. There was another ex-champion, the mighty Capablanca, who deliberately steered for the ending in his games, as it was there that he could display his fabulous technique to best advantage. There was the reigning champion himself, the peerless Alekhine, who played the endings with dazzling brilliance. Then, to complicate matters, there was Rubinstein, who was — to quote Dr. Hannak — "the sublime end-game virtuoso of all time." And what about Nimzowitsch himself? He must have had a leaning toward his own abilities in that branch of the game. If so, there were five eligible candidates for the positions which only two could fill. Which two did Nimzowitsch mean? Poor Nimzowitsch is gone, and we, alas, will never know.

Apropos of the above, the game which follows features a Queen ending, conducted by Tartakower in exquisite style. As an added attraction, Tartakower has his King take a charming little walk.

Semmering, 1926
QUEEN'S GAMBIT DECLINED

DR. S.
TARTAKOWER

MARQUIS
ROSSELLI

	White	Black
1	P - Q4	P - Q4
2	P - QB4	P - QB3
3	N - KB3	N - B3
4	P - K3	P - K3
5	QN - Q2	QN - Q2
6	B - Q3	B - Q3
7	O - O	O - O
8	P - K4	P - K4
9	KP x P	BP x P
10	BP x P	P x P
11	N - K4	N - K4
12	B - KN5	B - KN5
13	B x N	B x N
14	B x Q	B x Q
15	QR x B	QR x B
16	B - K2	....

The reason for all the exchanges — White now wins a Pawn. "The rest," as annotators are apt to say, "is a matter of technique." But, as we shall see, it requires the technique of a magician to win this ending.

16	....	B - N1
17	R x P	N - B3
18	R - Q2	B - B5
19	R(Q2) - Q1	N - K2
20	B - B4	P - QN4
21	B - N3	P - QR4
22	P - QR3	N - B4
23	KR - K1	N - Q3
24	P - N3	KR - K1
25	P x B	R x N
26	R x R	N x R

Both players have gained something. Black has broken up his opponent's King-side Pawns, and White is happy too, as he can now seize an open file.

27	R - QB1	P - N3
28	R - B7	K - N2
29	B - R2	....

So that White's King can go to B3 without fear of .... N - Q7 ch.

29	....	K - B3
30	K - N2	P - R4
31	K - B3	N - Q3
32	K - K3	R - K1 ch
33	K = Q3	R - K8

Clearly, passive defense is hopeless.

34	R - Q7	N - B5
35	B x N	P x B ch

36	K x P	R - K7
37	P - N4	P x P
38	P x P	R x P
39	P - N5	R x RP

This may look like a Rook ending to you, but honestly it isn't!

40	P - N6	R - QN7
41	K - B5	P - R5
42	P - N7	P - R6
43	R - Q6 ch	K - N2
44	R - N6	R x R
45	K x R	P - R7
46	P - N8 (Q)	P - R8 (Q)
47	Q - K5 ch	P - B3
48	Q - K7 ch	K - N1
49	Q - K6 ch	....

White cannot win with 49 Q x P, Q x P, 50 Q x P ch, K - B1. Some pretty ideas arise after 49 P - Q6, a plausible enough winning attempt: 49 P - Q6, Q - QN8 ch, 50 K - B7, Q - B8 ch, 51 K - Q8, Q x P, 52 K - K8 (of course not 52 P - Q7, Q - N1 mate!), Q - R5 ch, 53 P - Q7, Q - R1 ch, 54 P - Q8 (Q), Q - R5 ch, 55 Q(K7) - Q7, Q - K5 ch, 56 Q(Q8) - K7, Q - R1 ch, and Black, who is a Queen behind, draws by perpetual check.

49	....	K - N2
50	P - Q6	Q - QN8 ch
51	K - B7	Q - B8 ch
52	K - Q8	Q x P

| 53 | K - K8!! | .... |

White avoids sui-mate by 53 P - Q7, Q - N1 ch, 54 K - K7, Q - B1 mate.

53	....	P - N4
54	P - Q7	Q - QR5
55	Q - K7 ch	K - N1
56	Q - B7 ch	K - R1
57	K - B8	Resigns

After 57 .... Q - R1 ch, 58 Q - K8, Q - B6 (to stop 59 Q - R5 mate) 59 K - B7 dis. ch, K - R2, 60 Q - N8 ch and mate next move follows.

♚

"THE most distinguished end-play performance of a great end-game artist," says Foldeak of this beautiful Maróczy game. "It is a filigree work that is unique in the literature of chess." Marco, the victim of this brilliancy, expressed his admiration by saying that the ending was reminiscent of the classic compositions of Kling and Horwitz.

Vienna, 1899

FRENCH DEFENSE

MARCO	MARÓCZY
White	Black
1 P - K4	P - K3
2 P - Q4	P - Q4
3 P x P	....

Marco explains that he simplified because he was not in the mood for hard chess. Little did he know what he was in for!

3	....	P x P
4	N - KB3	B - Q3
5	B - Q3	N - KB3
6	0 - 0	0 - 0
7	P - B3	P - B3
8	B - KN5	B - KN5
9	QN - Q2	QN - Q2
10	Q - B2	Q - B2
11	KR - K1	QR - K1
12	B - R4	B - R4
13	B - N3	B x B
14	RP x B	B - N3
15	R x R	R x R
16	B x B	RP x B
17	R - K1	P - R3
18	Q - N1	K - B1
19	R x R ch	N x R
20	P - R3	Q - Q1
21	Q - K1	Q - K2
22	Q x Q ch	K x Q
23	K - B1	N - Q3
24	K - K2	P - B3
25	N - K1	P - QN4
26	P - QN4	N - N3

| 27 | P - B3 | N(N3) - B5 |
| 28 | N - N1 | .... |

Exchanging Knights is better; but Marco wanted to avoid analyzing the variations arising from Black's choice of recapture.

28	....	N - B4
29	P - N4	N(B4) - K6
30	K - B2	P - N4
31	K - K2	P - N3
32	K - B2	K - Q3

"One is often asked," says Maróczy, "how many moves ahead a master calculates. Réti is of the opinion that two moves are enough to play as a master does; but his dictum holds only in situations where one does not seek an immediate decision. But, if one spies a combination or an idea, then the ability to look ahead must be increased enormously. In this position, I saw clearly before my eyes *in one second* the winning position that I would obtain at the seventeenth move, and at the same moment my opponent knew that he was irretrievably lost. What now follows is nothing but the precise, systematic exemplification of the winning idea."

33	K - K2	K - B2!
34	K - B2	K - N3
35	K - K2	P - R4
36	K - B2	P - R5

Black eliminates the weakness of his Rook Pawn. White's Knights dare not stir (if 37 N - Q3, N - B7) and his King must stick to K2, B2 and N1 (if 37 K - N3 or R2, N - B8 ch and 38 .... N(B8) - Q7).

37	K - K2	K - B2
38	K - B2	K - Q3
39	K - K2	K - K2
40	K - B2	K - B2
41	K - K2	K - N2
42	K - B2	K - R2
43	P - N3	K - R3
44	K - K2	P - KB4
45	P x P	P x P
46	K - B2	K - R4
47	K - K2	P - B5!
48	P x P	P x P
49	K - B2	K - N4

| 50 | K - K2 | K - R5 |
| 51 | K - B2 | K - R6! |

The last move, on the King side, wins the Rook Pawn away over at the other end of the board; for White is out of King moves! — e.g., 52 K - K2, K - N6, 53 K - Q3, K - B7!

52	N - Q3	N - B7
53	N x P ch	K - R5
54	N - Q3	N(B7) x RP
55	N x N	N x N

Now the threat is 56 .... N - N8, followed by 57 .... P - R6.

56	N - B1	N - N8
57	N - R2	K - R6
58	K - K3	K - N6
59	P - KB4	K - N5
60	P - B5	K x P
61	K - Q3	K - B5
62	N - B1	K - B6
63	K - B2	N - R6 ch
64	K - Q3	K - B7
65	K - Q2	N - B5 ch
66	K - Q1	K - K6
67	K - B2	P - R6!
68	N - R2	N - N7
69	N - B1	....

| 69 | .... | N - Q6!! |
| 70 | N - N3 | .... |

Naturally, if 70 N x N, Black wins with 70 .... P - R7, 71 K - N2, K x N.

On 70 N - R2, Hoffer's analysis in *The Field* runs as follows: 70 .... N - K8 ch, 71 K - Q1, K - Q6, 72 K x N, K - B7, 73 K - K2, K - N7, 74 K - Q2, K x N, 75 K - B2, K - R8, 76 K - B1, P - R7, 77 K - B2, P - B4, 78 NP x P, P - N5, 79 P x P — Stalemate!

212

THE CHESS COMPANION

Marco, who loved to deflate lesser critics, refutes the suggested defense by 70 .... K - K7, 71 K - N3, K - Q7, 72 K x P, K - B7 and concludes: 'White is crushed to death."

	70	....	N - K8 ch
	71	K - Q1	K - Q6!
	72	K x N	K x P
	73	N - R1	K x QP!

"The play is piquant to the finish. Black avoids the trap: 73 .... K - N7, 74 K - Q2, K x N, 75 K - B1 and Black's King never emerges."

	74	N - B2 ch	K - B6
	75	K - Q1	....

If 75 N x P, K - N7 catches the Knight.

	75	....	P - R7
	76	K - B1	P - Q5
	77	N - R1	P - Q6
	78	N - B2	....

Hoping desperately for a hasty 78 .... P x N as White draws by stalemate.

	79	....	P - B4!
		Resigns	

For, if 79 P x P, P x N, 80 P - B6, P - R8 (Q) mate.

IN THE course of a tournament, all manner of prizes are offered to spur imaginative, colorful chess. Largesse has been given in dollars, rubles, pounds, crowns, florins and francs for the most brilliant game, for the best-played game, for the best attack, for the best defense, for the most aggressive opening and for the most delicate ending. Generally, the *bonne bouche* would go to the player who won the tournament, but it was possible for a master to receive an award for one solitary, shining achievement, though the rest of the games he played might have been humdrum affairs.

But how about giving a prize to the master who creates the most beautiful set of games in one tournament? Had such a custom prevailed in the past, who would have been the most likely recipients of the accolades? I imagine that these would be plausible candidates:

Lasker at London, 1899
Lasker at St. Petersburg, 1909
Lasker at St. Petersburg, 1914
Lasker at New York, 1924
Tarrasch at Hamburg, 1885
Tarrasch at Vienna, 1898
Pillsbury at Hastings, 1895
Pillsbury at Vienna, 1898
Rubinstein, St. Petersburg, 1909
Alekhine at Carlsbad, 1923
Alekhine at Baden-Baden, 1925
Spielmann at Carlsbad, 1929
Capablanca at New York, 1927
Capablanca at Carlsbad, 1929
Botvinnik at Leningrad-Moscow, 1941
Tal at Bled-Zagreb, 1959

Long before these great men exhibited their skills, Johannes Zukertort played a set of games in the London Tournament, 1883, which compares favorably with any of the above performances. Consider if you will his beautiful defense to Tchigorin's Ruy Lopez, as well as his conduct of the Black side of the Evans Gambit against the same formidable adversary. Play over his long (but not too long) wins from Mason, his two fine victories over Blackburne (one of them a famous immortal and the other a positional jewel, not understood then and not sufficiently appreciated now), his fascinating struggle with Englisch (a tough man to beat) and his protracted, though exciting encounters with Bird and Winawer (a Giuoco Piano and a Queen's Pawn Game, respectively).

If you are lucky enough to have the Book of the Tournament, I recommend that you follow Zukertort's notes faithfully as they were (for the time, of course) a revelation.

To whet your appetite, here is a sample of his style. Watch him toy with Mason!

London, 1883

ENGLISH OPENING

JAMES MASON	J. H. ZUKERTORT
White	Black
1 P - QB4	P - K3
2 P - K3	N - KB3
3 N - KB3	P - Q4
4 P - Q4	B - K2
5 N - B3	O - O
6 B - Q3	P - QN3
7 P x P	P x P
8 N - K5	B - N2
9 O - O	P - B4
10 B - Q2	N - B3
11 N x N	B x N
12 R - B1	P - B5
13 B - N1	P - QN4
14 N - K2	P - N5
15 N - N3	P - QR4
16 R - K1	P - R5
17 N - B5	....

White initiates a King-side attack, the current cure-all.

| 17 .... | P - R6 |
| 18 P - K4 | .... |

White cannot afford *18* P x P, P - B6, as he loses a piece.

18	RP x P
19 R - B2	B - R5
20 P - K5	N - K1
21 Q - N4	B x B
22 B x B	R - R3
23 N - R6 ch	R x N
24 B x R	Q - R4!
25 R - KB1	....

White avoids the threat of double attack on his Rook and Bishop by *25* .... P - N6. Note that the reply to *25* B - Q2 is still *25* .... P - N6 as *26* B x Q loses to *26* .... P x B, following by queening a Pawn.

25	Q x P
26 Q - B5	P - N3
27 Q - Q7	P - N6
28 Q x B	N - N2
29 B - N1	P - B6!
30 Q - B5	....

If *30* B x Q, Black wins with *30* .... P x B, *31* Q - N4, P - R8 (Q), *32* Q x BP, Q x R ch (not *32* .... P - N8 (Q) as *33* Q x Q lets White win) *33* K x Q, P - N8 (Q) ch.

| 30 .... | P - B7 |

| 31 B x P | N - K3 |

"Overfinessing," says Zukertort. He could have continued with *31* .... P x B, *32* Q x BP, R - R1! *33* P - N4, N - K3, *34* K - N2, N x P, *35* Q - N1, Q - N6, after which the threats of *36* .... R - R8 as well as *36* .... Q - B6 ch, followed by mate, are decisive.

32 Q x P	P x B
33 Q x Q	R - N1
34 P - Q5!	....

On *34* R - N1, P - N4 prevents *35* B - B1, and Black's Bishop Pawn queens.

34	P - N8 (Q)
35 Q - B4	N - N2
36 P - K6	....

Mason violates his own precept: "Do not make a strong move too soon." He ought to play *36* P - N4, "blocking the egress of the hostile Knight," to quote Zukertort again, and then continue with *37* R - B1.

36	P x P
37 P x P	Q - N6
38 Q - B7	....

Not content with exchanging Queens for a probable draw, Mason stakes everything on his attack.

| 38 .... | N x P |
| 39 Q - K7 | Q - Q4 |

Black has an eye on *40* .... P - N4, cutting off the Bishop.

40 P - R4	Q - B3
41 R - K1	R - K1
42 Q - R3	R - Q1
43 Q - N3	K - B2
44 B - K3	R - QB1
45 B - B1	Q - B5
46 Q - KB3 ch	K - N1

47	Q - B6	N - N2

Certainly not 47 .... R - K1, 48 B - N2, threatening 49 Q - R8 ch.

48	B - N2	Q - KB2
49	Q - Q4	P - R4
50	R - QB1	K - R2
51	Q - Q3	Q - B4
52	Q - Q4	Q - B2
53	Q - K5	Q - B2
54	Q - B6	R - Q1

Ready to meet 55 Q x N ch with 55 .... Q x Q, 56 B x Q, R - Q8 ch, and Black wins.

55	Q - KB3	N - B4
56	Q - K2	R - QB1
57	P - N3	N x NP!

"Take first and philosophize afterwards!" says Tartakower.

58	Q - Q3	....

Naturally, 58 P x N is answered by 58 .... Q - N3 ch and 59 .... Q x B.

58	....	N - B4
59	Q - K4	Q - QB5
60	Q - N7 ch	R - B2
61	Q - N8	Q - N5 ch
62	K - R1	Q x P ch
63	K - N2	Q - N5 ch
64	K - R1	Q - Q8 ch
65	K - N2	N - R5 ch
66	K - R2	....

Or 66 K - N3, Q - N5 ch, 67 K - R2, Q - N7 mate

66	....	Q - Q3 ch
67	K - N1	N - B6 ch
68	K - B1	....

On 68 K - N2, Q - R7 ch, 69 K x N, R - B2 ch, and Black wins the Queen or 69 K - B1, N - Q7 ch, 70 K - K2, R - K2 ch, ditto.

68	....	Q - R3 ch
69	K - N2	N - R5 ch
70	K - R2	Q - B1

Definitely not 70 .... Q - N2 (threatening mate at N7 or forcing an exchange of Queens) as Mason then crosses him up with 71 Q - KR8 mate!

71	Q - N6	....

"Enough of slow torture. Take me!"

71	....	N - B6 ch
72	K - N2	Q - N5 ch
73	K - B1	R - K2

Black indicates that it is time to yield; he has four threats of mate on the move.

Resigns

♛

ALL SORTS OF ODDS!

THE IDEA of giving odds is to help equalize the contest for players of disparate skills. The master chess player concedes his opponent anything from a Pawn to a Queen. And sometimes the handicaps take exceedingly strange forms, as we may see.

HERE Max Lange undertakes to force checkmate with his Queen Knight.

Ring White's Queen Knight

MAX LANGE	SCHIERSTEDT
White	Black
1 P - K4	P - K4
2 N - QB3	N - QB3
3 P - B4	P x P
4 N - B3	P - KN4
5 B - B4	P - N5
6 0 - 0	P x N
7 P - Q4	P x P
8 B x P ch	K x B
9 Q - R5 ch	K - N2
10 R x P	N - R3
11 B - K3	P - Q3
12 N - K2	Q - K2
13 K x P	B - K3
14 QR - KB1	B - B2
15 Q x N ch!	K x Q
16 R - N4 dis. ch	K - R4
17 N - N3 ch	K x R
18 R - B5	P - KR3

White announced mate in three with the ringed Knight: *19* P - R3 ch, K - R5, *20* R - R5 ch, B x R, *21* N - B5 mate.

WHITE gave his Queen in this one, for the privilege of making six moves.

Olmütz, 1901

Remove White's Queen

K. ANDREASCHEK	DR. R. M.
White	Black
1 P - K4	....
2 P - Q4	....
3 N - QB3	....
4 P - KB4	....
5 N - B3	....
6 B - B4	P - Q3
7 P - KR3	N - Q2
8 B x P ch	K x B
9 N - N5 ch	K - B3
10 N - Q5 ch	K - N3
11 P - B5 ch	K - R3
12 N - B7 ch	K - R4
13 P - N4 ch	....

Yes, Virginia, there is a quicker mate.

13	K - R5
14 K - B2	P - K4
15 N - K3	any
16 N - N2 mate	

FROM a 1955 match at Progressive Blitz. "Progressive" means that the winner takes on and increases the odds with each win. "Blitz" means an instantaneous rate of play.

Remove White's Queen, Queen Rook and King Knight

ELIOT HEARST	R. E.
White	Black
1 P - QN3	P - KN3
2 B - N2	N - KB3
3 P - K4	B - N2

4	P - KR4	P - KR4
5	P - KN4	P x P
6	P - R5	N x RP
7	B x B	N x B
8	R x R mate	

PLAYED about a century ago.

Remove both White Rooks

J. A. LEONARD	JOSEPH LEONARD
White	Black
1 P - Q4	P - Q3
2 P - QB4	P - K4
3 P - K3	P - QB4
4 P - Q5	N - KB3
5 N - QB3	B - N5
6 P - B3	B - R4
7 N - N5	N - K5
8 Q - R4	N - KB3

White mated in two moves: 9 N x P dbl. ch, K - K2, 10 N - B5 mate.

IN 1878, Paris and Marseilles played a game by correspondence as remarkable as any in the field of queer odds-giving. Marseilles (Black) was to get Queen odds. In return, Black undertook to force self-mate — would compel White to give mate!

Remove White's Queen

PARIS	MARSEILLES
White	Black
1 P - Q4	P - Q4
2 N - QB3	P - QB3
3 N - B3	P - KN3

4	P - K4	P - K3
5	P - K5	B - N5
6	B - Q2	B x N
7	B x B	P - QN4
8	P - KR4	P - KR4
9	0 - 0 - 0	P - QR3
10	N - N5	P - KB4
11	P - KN3	N - R3
12	B - Q3	N - B2
13	B x BP	NP x B
14	N x N	K x N
15	B - Q2	N - Q2
16	KR - K1	P - B4
17	P x P	N x BP
18	B - N5	Q - N1
19	R - K3	B - N2
20	R - QB3	R - B1
21	B - K3	N - Q2
22	B - Q4	R x R
23	P x R	P - R4
24	K - Q2	P - R5
25	R - QN1	B - R3
26	R - N1	Q - N5
27	R - N1	R - QB1
28	R - N4	R - B5
29	R x R	QP x R
30	P - R3	P - B5
31	K - B1	P x P
32	P x P	Q x NP
33	K - N2	Q x RP
34	K - B1	Q - K8 ch
35	K - N2	Q - Q8
36	B - R7	N x P
37	B - B5	P - R5
38	B - Q4	N - B3
39	B - K3	P - K4
40	B - B2	P - R6
41	B - N3	P - K5
42	B - B4	K - B3
43	B - N3	P - K6
44	B - B4	P - K7
45	B - N3	K - Q2
46	B - R2	P - K8 (Q)
47	B - B4	Q(K8) - K7
48	B - N3	Q(Q8) x P ch
49	K - R1	Q - KB8 ch
50	B - K1	Q - Q7
51	K - N1	P - R7
52	K - R1	P - R8 (Q)
53	K - N1	Q - B1
54	K - R1	Q x RP ch
55	K - N1	Q(R6) - Q3
56	K - R1	Q - B3
57	K - N1	K - B2
58	K - R1	P - N5
59	K - N1	P - N6
60	K - R1	K - N3

61	K - N1	K - R4
62	K - R1	N - K2
63	K - N1	N - B1
64	K - R1	B - N4
65	K - N1	Q - QR3
66	K - R1	N - N3
67	K - N1	....

67	....	Q - R2 ch
68	K - R1	Q x P ch!
69	B x Q mate	

And Black, who is checkmated, wins!

♚

ONE of Morphy's little-known brillian-cies is the following, remarkable odds game. Despite the fact that he is a piece or two down, Morphy does not seek to avoid exchanges if the mobil-ity of his remaining pieces is thereby increased.

Paris, 1863

KING'S GAMBIT

Remove White's Queen Knight

MORPHY	ST. LEON
White	Black
1 P - K4	P - K4
2 P - KB4	P x P
3 N - B3	P - KN4
4 B - B4	P - N5
5 P - Q4	....

"Have another piece!"

5	....	P x N
6	Q x P	B - R3
7	0 - 0	Q - B3
8	P - K5	Q - N2
9	QB x P	B x B
10	Q x B	N - KR3
11	R - B3	R - N1
12	R - KN3	Q - B1

13	R x R	N x R
14	R - KB1	N - KR3
15	P - KN4	....

White aims to dislodge the Knight.

| 15 | .... | P - Q3 |
| 16 | P - K6 | P - KB3 |

Of course not 16 .... B x P, 17 B x B, and Black dares not recapture.

| 17 | P - N5 | Q - N2 |

Black pins the Pawn. Is this the end of White's attack?

18	Q x P!	Q x Q
19	R x Q	N - N1
20	R - B7	P - B3

| 21 | R - N7 | N - K2 |

On 21 .... K - B1, White wins by 22 R x N ch, K x R, 23 P - K7 dis. ch.

| 22 | R x P | K - Q1 |

Black still cannot play 22 .... P - Q4 on account of 23 R - R8 ch.

23	R - R8 ch	K - B2
24	R - K8	P - Q4
25	R x N ch	K - Q3
26	R - K8	P x B
27	R x B	K x P
28	P - KR4	K - B4
29	R - N8	Resigns

The finish could be 29 .... K - N5, 30 P - N6, K - R4, 31 K - N2, K - R3, 32 K - B3, K - R4, 33 K - B4, K - R3, 34 K - B5, P - R4, 35 K - K6, P - R5, 36 K - B7, winning.

♚

218

PAUL MORPHY was a marvelous odds-giver. This is not surprising, as Morphy was one of the first masters to realize the importance of rapid opening development. Add to that his genius for handling wide-open positions, and his eminence in the art of odds-giving is clear. What is surprising is that he had a rival in that field in Tarrasch. Tarrasch was a cold-blooded, precise position player. Not for him the realm of imaginative, speculative combinations. Rather for him the slower but surer methods — the steady relentless crushing of all resistance. And yet he could adapt his style to suit the occasion, as we shall see from the following games.

Nuremberg, 1892

Remove White's Queen Knight

S. TARRASCH   CH. SCHROEDER

White	Black
1 P - K4	P - Q4
2 P - K5	P - QB4
3 P - KB4	P - K3
4 N - B3	N - QB3
5 P - B3	Q - N3
6 B - Q3	B - Q2
7 B - B2	P - B5
8 P - QN3	P x P
9 P x P	P - Q5

Hey! Knight-odds players aren't supposed to make good moves.

10 Q - K2	P x P
11 P x P	N - R3
12 N - Q2	B - K2
13 N - K4	O - O
14 Q - Q3	P - N3!

Schroeder sees that White's threat is not *15* Q x B but *15* N - B6 ch and mate next.

| 15 Q - R3 | .... |

Of course not *15* Q x B, QR - Q1 as White loses his Queen.

| 15 .... | N - B4 |
| 16 P - KN4 | N - N2 |

Not *16* .... N - R5, *17* N - B6 ch, as White wins a piece.

17 N - B6 ch	B x N
18 P x B	N - K1
19 P - N5	K - R1

20 Q - R6	R - N1
21 P - R4	N - Q3
22 P - R5	N - B4

White now forces mate in three moves.

23 Q x P ch	K x Q
24 P x P dbl. ch	K x P
25 R - R6 mate	

IN the next game, we see a blend of two styles. Tarrasch regains his Rook by a combination in mid-game but is left with a two-Pawn deficit for the ending. Despite that, he brings about a remarkable conclusion. He gets a half nelson on his opponent's Knight and then throws him with a hold unknown to wrestlers — the *Zugzwang.*

Nuremberg, 1892

Remove White's Queen Rook, and place his Queen Rook Pawn at R3

S. TARRASCH   H. ROMBERG

White	Black
1 P - K4	P - K3
2 P - Q4	P - Q4
3 P - KB3	P - QB4
4 P - B3	N - QB3
5 B - K3	P x QP
6 BP x P	Q - N3
7 Q - Q2	N - R4
8 N - B3	P x P
9 P x P	N - KB3
10 N - B3	B - K2
11 P - Q5	Q - Q1
12 B - N5 ch	B - Q2
13 P - Q6	B x B
14 N x B	N x P
15 P x B	Q x Q ch

16	N x Q	N x N
17	B x N	N - B3
18	N - B7 ch	K x P
19	N x R	R x N

Despite the recovery of almost all the material he was behind, White faces a disheartening scene. He cannot hope to swindle even a Rook-odds player in such a serene, transparent position.

20	R - B1	P - B4
21	B - B3	P - KN4
22	P - QN4	P - N4

Please try not to shudder! I have seen worse moves.

23	B - Q2	R - KN1
24	R - B3	K - B3
25	R - B3	N - K4

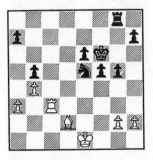

26   R - B7!   ....

Ostensibly to attack the Rook Pawns, but in reality a camouflage for his actual threat — a paralyzing pin.

26	....	R - N2
27	R x R	K x R
28	B - B3	K - B3
29	P - N3!!	....

A quiet but irresistible waiting move which forces quick surrender. If 29 .... P - B5, 30 P - N4 and, after Black's Pawn moves are exhausted, his King must abandon the Knight!

| 29 | .... | P - KR4 |
| 30 | P - R3 | Resigns |

If 30 .... P - N5, 31 P - KR4, P - B5, 32 P x P, and White wins; or, if 30 .... P - R5, 31 P - N4, P x P, 32 P x P, P - R6, 33 K - B2, again Black's

King will be forced to desert the Knight.

♛

AND for dessert a brevity at tremendous odds.

Nuremberg, 1889

Remove White's Queen

S.	CH.
TARRASCH	SCHROEDER
White	Black
1 P - K4	P - K4
2 P - KB4	P - Q3
3 P - Q3	P - KB4
4 N - QB3	BP x P
5 QP x P	P - QR3
6 P x P	P x P
7 N - B3	B - QN5
8 B - N5	Q - Q3
9 R - Q1	Q - KN3?

One of the most important things for an odds-player to learn is to give back *some* of his booty in order to simplify the position. For example, 9 .... Q x R ch, 10 K x Q, B x N leaves Black a Rook up and no dangerous attacking enemy in sight. After the text move, Tarrasch winds up the game nicely.

10	R - Q8 ch	K - B2
11	B - B4 ch	B - K3
12	N x P mate	

♔

THE GALLOPING KNIGHTS

ONE of the chief prejudices against problems is that they are not true to life. The positions they depict are artificial and bear no resemblance to those which occur in everyday chess. Yet all sorts of picturesque situations and weird designs have appeared on the chessboards of practical players. Here are a few in which the Knights are the protagonists. Their dancing and prancing is a joy to behold.

Budapest, 1942

SICILIAN DEFENSE

KHLOYBER	NAGY
White	Black
1 P - K4	P - QB4
2 N - KB3	N - QB3
3 P - Q4	P x P
4 N x P	N - B3
5 N - QB3	P - Q3
6 B - KN5	P - QR3
7 Q - Q2	N - Q2
8 B - K2	P - KN3
9 N - Q5	....

White prevents 9 .... B - N2, as then 10 N x N, P x N, 11 B x KP snags the Queen.

9	P - B3

But this is the wrong medicine!

10 N - K6!	....

A powerful move. The ring-around-a-rosy position of the Knights is purely incidental, but very pretty.

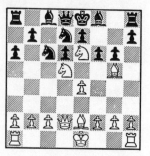

10	Q - R4
11 N(Q5) - B7 ch	K - B2
12 N - Q8 ch	K - N2
13 N - K8 ch	Resigns

An amusing, final scene. King and Queen have fled, and the White Knights occupy their thrones.

TURNING back our history books a hundred years, we find a beautiful specimen of a Knight cluster in a game which Schiffers called immortal.

Dorpat, 1862

EVANS GAMBIT

CLEMENS	EISENSCHMIDT
White	Black
1 P - K4	P - K4
2 N - KB3	N - QB3
3 B - B4	B - B4
4 P - QN4	B x P
5 P - B3	B - B4
6 P - Q4	P x P
7 P x P	B - N3
8 O - O	P - Q3
9 N - B3	B - Q2
10 P - K5	P x P
11 R - K1	KN - K2
12 N - KN5	B - K3
13 B x B	P x B
14 N x KP	Q - Q3

15	N x NP ch	K - B1
16	Q - N4	B x P
17	N - K4	Q - N5
18	N - K6 ch	K - K1
19	N - B6 ch	K - B2
20	N - N5 ch	K - B1
21	B - R3!	....

Ordinarily you would find a diagram after a brilliant sacrifice, but we are saving our diagram for an artistic grouping.

| 21 | .... | Q x B |
| 22 | Q - K6 | N - Q1 |

Black prevents mate by 23 Q - B7 but, at the same time, gives us a pretty picture of the Knights in diagonal alignment.

23   Q - B7 ch!   ....

A sacrifice of the Queen which must be accepted, and in a flash the whole design changes!

| 23 | .... | N x Q |
| 24 | N - K6 mate | |

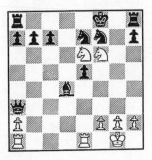

IN OUR next game, we shall see the Knights arrange themselves in even more remarkable formations.

Somewhere at the front, 1941

FRENCH DEFENSE

PATSCHURKOWSKI   RHODE

	White	Black
1	P - K4	P - K3
2	P - Q4	P - Q4
3	P x P	P x P
4	N - QB3	N - KB3
5	N - B3	P - B4
6	B - N5 ch	B - Q2
7	0 - 0	B x B
8	N x B	P - QR3
9	N - B3	B - K2
10	B - K3	P - B5
11	P - QR4	Q - B2
12	R - K1	0 - 0
13	B - B4	B - Q3
14	B - K5	QN - Q2
15	B x B	Q x B
16	N - K5	KR - K1
17	P - B4	N - B1
18	Q - B3	Q - N3
19	N x QP	Q x P ch
20	N - K3	N - K3
21	Q x P	N x P
22	Q x P ch	K - R1
23	N - B3	....

23 N(K5) x P fails after 23 .... R - R2.

23	....	Q - N3
24	P - R5	Q x NP
25	N - B5!	....

White threatens 26 Q x P mate. The four Knights stand like soldiers on the King Bishop file.

| 25 | .... | N - K7 ch! |
| 26 | K - R1 | N - N5 |

Black guards his Knight Pawn and, in turn, threatens mate on the move.

27	P - R3	N - B7 ch
28	K - R2	Q - N1 ch
29	P - N3	R - R2
30	Q x BP	R - QB2
31	QR - N1	Q - B1
32	Q - Q5	R - B4
33	R - N8!	R x Q
34	R x Q	R x R
35	N - K7	R x BP
36	N x R	N - Q6
37	R - Q1	N - Q5 dis. ch
38	N - Q2	....

And now, just before the axe falls, look at the way the Knights are all lined up in a row!

| 38 | .... | R x N ch |
| | | Resigns |

♛

MR. PRATTEN regales us with this fine specimen of a two-Rook sacrifice. To differentiate it from its rivals, he tops it off with a Queen sacrifice! Then his Knights waltz in merrily, crying, "Check, check and mate!" So delighted was the *British Chess Magazine* with this sprightly bit of play that they suggested it be called —

THE ENGLISH IMMORTAL
Portsmouth, 1948
GIUOCO PIANO

MACZYNSKI	PRATTEN
White	Black
1 P - K4	P - K4
2 N - KB3	N - QB3

3	B - B4	B - B4
4	P - B3	Q - K2
5	O - O	P - Q3
6	P - Q4	B - N3
7	P - QN4	B - N5
8	P - QR4	P - QR4
9	P - N5	N - Q1
10	B - R3	P - KB3
11	R - R2	N - K3
12	P x P	BP x P
13	Q - Q5	B x N
14	Q x NP	....

If *14* P x B, N - B5 attacks White's Queen and also threatens mate in two. He might just as well play *va banque*.

14	....	Q - N4
15	Q x R ch	K - K2
16	P - N3	N - B5

Black's Knight heads for R6 and mate.

| 17 | R - K1 | Q - R4 |
| 18 | N - Q2 | .... |

There is no relief in *18* B - KB1, as the reply *18* .... N - R6 ch forces *19* B x N and leaves White helpless after *19* .... Q x B.

| 18 | .... | N - B3! |
| 19 | Q x R | .... |

Now for the grand *coup!*

19	....	Q x P ch!
20	K x Q	N - N5 ch
21	K - N1	N - R6 ch
22	K - B1	N - R7 mate

♛

QUEEN SACRIFICES

IT WAS games like this one, played in his younger days, that earned Steinitz the title of the "Austrian Morphy."

Liverpool, 1872
BISHOP'S OPENING

FISHER	STEINITZ
White	Black
1 P - K4	P - K4
2 B - B4	P - KB4
3 B x N	R x B
4 P x P	P - Q4
5 Q - R5 ch	P - N3
6 P x P	R x P
7 N - K2	N - B3
8 O - O	B - KN5
9 Q x RP	R - R3
10 Q - Q3	P - K5
11 Q - K3	Q - R5
12 P - KR3	B x N
13 Q x B	N - Q5
14 Q - Q1	....

A quick knockout would follow on *14 Q - N4 – Q x Q, 15 P x Q, N - K7 mate.*

| 14 .... | N - B6 ch |
| 15 K - R1 | .... |

15	Q x P ch
16 P x Q	R x P ch
17 K - N2	R - R7 ch
18 K - N3	B - Q3 ch
19 K - N4	R - R5 ch
20 K - B5	R - R4 ch
21 K - N6	....

Or *21 K - B6, B - K2 ch, 22 K - K6, R - K4 mate.*

21	R - N4 ch
22 K - R6	B - B1 ch
23 K - R7	K - B2
24 R - R1	B - N2

Resigns

♔

KNOWING just when to sacrifice your Queen is important. Had Black chosen the right moment to offer his Queen, he might have saved the game below. Instead, he lost – by a Queen sacrifice!

Vienna, 1924
IRREGULAR OPENING

SOYKA	KOLTA
White	Black
1 P - K4	P - K4
2 P - KN3	P - KN3
3 B - N2	B - N2
4 N - K2	N - K2

Both players are avoiding *PCO* and any other books on openings you can name.

5 P - Q3	QN - B3
6 O - O	O - O
7 P - KB4	P x P
8 B x P!	....

Considering the early stage of the game, this is surely a remarkable sacrifice of the exchange.

8	B x P
9 N - Q2	B x R
10 Q x B	....

The Queen exerts enormous pressure on the long diagonal. The immediate threat is *11 B - R6, P - B3, 12 R x P, R - B2, 13 R x R, K x R, 14 Q - N7 ch, K - K3, 15 N - QB4, P - Q4, 16 B - R3 ch, N - B4, 17 N - B4 mate.*

10	P - B3
11 B - R6	R - B2
12 R x P	Q - K1

Black hopes to get his Queen into the fight.

223

13 N - KB3   ....

The plan is now to continue with *14 N - N5, R x R, 15 Q x R.*

13	....	R x R
14	Q x R	Q - B2
15	Q - B3	....

White renews the threat of N - N5.

15	....	P - Q4
16	N - N5	P - Q5
17	N x QP	Q - B3

Black now pins the Knight at Q4 — he thinks! The best defense is *17 .... N x N!* The game might then go *18 Q x P* (not *18 N x Q, N - K7 ch* — nor *18 Q x N, N - B3), N - K3, 19 Q - Q6, Q - K1, 20 N x N,* with approximately even chances.

18 N x N!!   ....

The rebellion of a pinned piece! The Knight tears loose by main force to deliver the *coup de grâce.* Or, as Alvin C. Cass would say, it was not a safety pin! On *18 Q x Q, 19 N x N ch, K - R1, 20 N - B7* is checkmate. *18 .... Q x N* permits mate on the move; so there is nothing left but to resign gracefully.

RARELY did Capablanca heed the call of the wild. But such was his genius that he could take an eccentric opening and fashion from it a thing of beauty. Regard, if you will, his incredible third move!

Simultaneous, New York, 1922
KING'S GAMBIT

CAPABLANCA	CHASE
White	Black
1 P - K4	P - K4
2 P - KB4	P x P
3 Q - B3	QN - B3
4 P - B3	N - B3
5 P - Q4	P - Q4
6 P - K5	N - K5
7 B x P	P - KN4
8 B - K3	P - KR4
9 N - Q2	B - KN5

I had the temerity to ask Capa if he had overlooked this move or whether he really intended to sacrifice his Queen. He smiled and said, "Wait and see."

10 N x N	B x Q
11 N - B6 ch	K - K2
12 N x B	B - R3
13 N x NP	B - N2
14 B - Q3	B x N

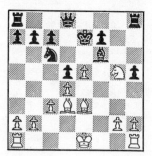

15 0 - 0!   ....

An elegant touch!

15	....	Q - KN1
16	R x B	R - KB1
17	QR - KB1	N - Q1
18	P - QN4	Q - N2
19	P - KR4	K - K1
20	P - N5	P - N3
21	B - K2	N - K3
22	B - B3	N x N
23	B x N	Q - R2
24	B x QP	Q - Q6
25	B - B6 ch	Resigns

Or Black can walk into a discovered check and a quick mate.

And, if I too lost my game to Capa, it was with the consolation that I was in distinguished company, as the player at my right was Sergei Prokofiev.

THE TERM *amateur* in any sport has a connotation of dilettantism. It is assumed that the amateur has a certain amount of skill but that, pitted

THE CHESS COMPANION

against a professional, he would find himself hopelessly outclassed. In the main this is true. The professional must of necessity — by the law of the survival of the fittest — be at the top of his form at all times. In the world of chess, he must supplement his own ability with an encyclopedic knowledge of the games, analyses and discoveries of his contemporaries. In addition, he must be fairly conversant with what has gone before.

Occasionally there is a glorious exception, when the amateur plays with the inspiration of genius — and then we are presented with a coruscating brilliancy, such as the masterpiece that follows, wherein Adams offers his Queen to Torre six times in succession!

New Orleans, 1920
PHILIDOR DEFENSE

	ADAMS	TORRE
	White	Black
1	P - K4	P - K4
2	N - KB3	P - Q3
3	P - Q4	P x P
4	Q x P	N - QB3
5	B - QN5	B - Q2
6	B x N	B x B
7	N - B3	N - B3
8	O - O	B - K2
9	N - Q5	B x N

Black cannot keep both his Bishops. If for example, 9 .... N x N, 10 P x N, B - Q2 (if 10 .... B - B3, 11 Q - K4 ch wins a piece) 11 Q x NP, R - KB1, 12 R - K1 threatening 13 B - R6 or 13 B - N5 wins at once.

10	P x B	O - O
11	B - N5	P - B3
12	P - B4	P x P
13	P x P	R - K1
14	KR - K1	P - QR4

In order to be able to continue with 15 .... QR - B1, or possibly with 15 .... P - R5 and 16 .... R - R4.

| 15 | R - K2 | QR - B1 |

Instead of this, 15 .... P - R3 would have given Black's King an escape square — and deprived the world of a work of art!

| 16 | QR - K1 | Q - Q2 |

| 17 | B x N! | .... |

The first move in the combination seems harmless enough!

| 17 | .... | B x B |

If 17 .... P x B, White plays 18 P - KR3!, and there is no satisfactory defense to the threat of 19 R x B!, R x R, 20 R x R, Q x R, 21 Q - N4 ch, and the unprotected Rook falls.

| 18 | Q - KN4! | Q - N4 |

On 18 .... Q x Q, 19 R x R ch, R x R, 20 R x R is mate. Black's Queen must stay on the diagonal Q2 to R5 to protect the King Rook.

| 19 | Q - QB4! | Q - Q2 |

Once again, if 19 .... Q x Q, 20 R x R ch forces mate, and if 19 .... R x Q, 20 R x R ch, followed by mate. Finally, if 19 .... R x R, 20 Q x R ch, Q - K1, 21 Q x Q ch, R x Q, 22 R x R mate. Black's Queen must still stay on the vital diagonal.

| 20 | Q - B7! | Q - N4 |

Here, too, 20 .... Q x Q or 20 .... R x Q succumbs to 21 R x R ch, while 20 .... R x R loses prosaically by 21 Q x Q.

| 21 | P - QR4!! | .... |

White avoids 21 Q x NP — which would lose brilliantly by 21 .... Q x R!

21	....	Q x RP
22	R - K4!	Q - N4
23	Q x NP!	Resigns

A splendid performance.

SEVEN world champions (Alekhine, Capablanca, Euwe, Botvinnik, Smyslov, Tal and Petrosian) have fallen victims of Keres's brilliancies!

From the many beautiful games played by Keres, there is one, a favorite of mine, which features a magnificent Queen sacrifice against a former holder of the world's championship.

Match, 1940
QUEEN'S INDIAN DEFENSE

EUWE	KERES
White	Black
1 P - Q4	N - KB3
2 P - QB4	P - K3
3 N - KB3	P - QN3
4 P - KN3	B - N2
5 B - N2	B - K2

A modest move, but actually stronger than the aggressive 5 .... B - N5 ch.

6 0 - 0	0 - 0
7 N - B3	N - K5
8 Q - B2	N x N
9 Q x N	P - Q3
10 Q - B2	....

Threatening positionally, *11* P - K4 and White has a powerful center — and tactically, *11* N - N5, which wins the exchange by the threat of mate.

| 10 .... | P - KB4 |
| 11 N - K1 | Q - B1 |

Better than *11* .... B x B, *12* N x B, and White's Knight is back in the game.

12 P - K4	N - Q2
13 P - Q5	BP x P
14 Q x P	....

Not *14* B x P, as *14* .... N - B3 is a good enough reply. Besides, White wants to be able to play B - R3, to concentrate on Black's K3, the weak point.

14	N - B4
15 Q - K2	B - KB3!
16 B - R3	....

Pinning the Pawn.

| 16 .... | R - K1 |

Pins and counterpins follow each other in dramatic succession! Black's King Pawn was pinned, but now it is he who threatens *17* .... P x P.

| 17 B - K3 | .... |

Prevents *17* .... P x P, and in turn threatens *18* B x N followed by *19* B x P ch.

| 17 .... | Q - Q1! |

A fiendishly ingenious move, as will be seen.

| 18 B x N | P x P! |
| 19 B - K6 ch | .... |

Of course, if *19* B - K3, Black gets his piece back by *19* .... P - Q5.

| 19 .... | K - R1 |
| 20 R - Q1 | .... |

If *20* B - QR3, Q - K2, *21* P x P, B x QP, and Black recovers his piece with a winning position.

| 20 .... | QP x B |
| 21 N - N2 | .... |

Black was prepared to refute *21* P x P with *21* .... B x QP, *22* R x B, Q - K2. Another possibility was *21* .... B x NP, *22* Q x B, R x B.

| 21 .... | P - Q5 |

The weak Pawn at K3 has now become a powerful protected passed Pawn on the Queen file!

| 22 P - B4 | .... |

This is the position, with Black to move:

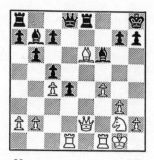

| 22 .... | P - Q6! |

Sacrificing his beautiful passed Pawn!

| 23 R x P | Q x R! |

And now a Queen sacrifice as the prelude to a superb combination! Hasn't he any respect for a former world's champion?

| 24 | Q x Q | B - Q5 ch |
| 25 | R - B2 | .... |

No better is 25 K - R1, R x B followed by the doubling of the Rooks, and then .... R - K7. Or if 25 N - K3, R x B, 26 R - K1, QR - K1, 27 K - B2, R x N, and Black wins.

| 25 | .... | R x B |
| 26 | K - B1 | QR - K1! |

Much more elegant than the brutal 26 .... B x R.

| 27 | P - B5 | R - K4 |
| 28 | P - B6 | .... |

Trying to free himself by force. Black was threatening to win by 28 .... B - K5, as well as by 28 .... B x R, 29 K x B, R - K7 ch, 30 K - N1 (if 30 Q x R, R x Q ch, 31 K x R, B x N) B x N, followed by 31 .... B - R6.

| 28 | .... | P x P |
| 29 | R - Q2 | .... |

Of course, not 29 R x P, B x N ch, 30 K x B, R - K7 ch, etc.

| 29 | .... | B - B1! |

Intending 30 .... B - R6, 31 R - Q1 (to stop 31 .... R - K8 mate) R - B4 ch, and White must give up his Queen.

| 30 | N - B4 | .... |

Preventing 30 .... B - R6. White's regrouping makes it appear for a moment as though Keres had overplayed his hand. However:

30	....	R - K6!
31	Q - N1	R - B6 ch
32	K - N2	R x N!

Another sparkling sacrifice!

| 33 | P x R | R - N1 ch |
| 34 | K - B3 | .... |

If 34 K - R1, B - N2 ch is deadly, while 34 K - B1 is answered by 34 .... R - N8 ch, winning the Queen.

| 34 | .... | B - N5 ch |
| 35 | Resigns | |

For if 35 K - N3, B - B4 ch wins the Queen, and if 35 K - K4, R - K1 ch, 36 K - Q5 (36 K - Q3, B - B4 mate) B - B6 ch forces mate.

An exquisite game by Keres.

THE MASTER AT HIS BEST

WHICH is the most brilliant of all chess masterpieces? What is "the most famous game of all time"? Which game is the best example of furious sustained attack? What is the finest specimen of defensive play? Who played "the immortal game"? Who thrilled the spectators (and many future generations) with "the evergreen game"? Who astonished the world with "the immortal *zugzwang* game"? Which of Morphy's brilliants is the nonpareil? Which game did Nimzowitsch regard as "the Pride of the Family"? Which combination did Steinitz say was "one of the most charming poetical chess compositions that have ever been devised in practical play"? Which did Capablanca himself choose as his "most finished and artistic game"? From his treasury of breathtaking beauties, what did Alekhine select as the *crème de la crème*? What marvelous inspiration impelled the *cognoscenti* to agree unanimously that a certain move was "the most beautiful move ever played"?

Critics and connoisseurs have come up with some answers in the past and are still trying to do so now. I want to give you some of their opinions as well as some of my own. To these, I will add games that the masters themselves considered their outstanding creative and imaginative efforts. I will include further miscellanea which belong in the category of all-time greats: such affairs as wondrous Queen endings, artistic (and instructive) performances by the Rooks, *tours de force* of the Knights, Kings wandering and Pawns peripatetic. I plan to include some of the strangest games ever played,

the most surprising moves ever made and some of the quietest and subtlest moves ever to gladden the heart of the *aficionado* – and terrorize the opponent. These, and many, many more things.

THE great fiftieth battle in the series of matches between Labourdonnais and McDonnell is the first of chess history's immortal games.

Summing up critical opinion of the time, Franklin Young says, "Connoisseurs hold that the annals of chess produce no higher flight of genius than the play of McDonnell in this game."

If this praise seems fulsome to us it is because we compare the game with the dazzling inspirations of Alekhine or Keres or Spielmann or Marshall. But their brilliancies had not yet enchanted the world, nor, to go further back, had those of Morphy and Steinitz and Blackburne and Tarrasch. Their golden masterpieces that are so familiar to us had not yet seen the light of day, nor for that matter had their creators! Yes, there was one great player alive then, the legendary wizard of combination play, Anderssen. But his name meant nothing when this immortal game was being played, as he was still going to school!

London, 1834

QUEEN'S GAMBIT

LABOURDONNAIS McDONNELL

	White	Black
1	P - Q4	P - Q4
2	P - QB4	P x P
3	P - K4	P - K4
4	P - Q5	P - KB4
5	N - QB3	N - KB3
6	B x P	B - B4

7	N - B3	Q - K2
8	B - KN5	....

A surprising mistake for such a tactician as Labourdonnais.

8	....	B x P ch
9	K - B1	....

On 9 K x B, Q - B4 ch regains the piece.

9	....	B - N3
10	Q - K2	P - B5
11	R - Q1	....

"Preparing to lose," says Fine humorously.

11	....	B - N5
12	P - Q6	P x P
13	N - Q5	....

13	....	N x N!
14	B x Q	N - K6 ch
15	K - K1	K x B

Black has only Knight and Bishop for his Queen, but his pieces come into play quickly, while White is still getting himself organized.

16	Q - Q3	R - Q1

Better than 16 .... N x R, 17 Q - Q 5, N - B3, 18 Q - B7 ch, K - Q1, 19 Q x KNP, as White will still need a lot of subduing.

17	R - Q2	N - B3
18	P - QN3	B - QR4
19	P - QR3	QR - B1
20	R - N1	P - QN4
21	B x P	B x N
22	P x B	....

If 22 B x N, R x B, 23 P x B, R - B8 ch, 24 K - B2, B x R, 25 Q x B, R - B7, and White can turn down his King.

22	....	N - Q5
23	B - B4	N x BP ch
24	K - B2	N x R(Q7)

25	R x P ch	K - B3
26	R - B7 ch	K - N3
27	R - QN7	N(Q7) x B
28	P x N	R x P
29	Q - N1	B - N3

Squelching any ambitions White might have of checking at N1, as the retort 30 .... N - N5 dbl. ch would be more than he could stand.

30	K - B3	R - B6
31	Q - R2	N - B5 dis. ch
32	K - N4	R - KN1
33	R x B	....

Desperation, but otherwise White gets mated by 33 .... P - R4 ch, 34 K - R4, B - Q1 ch, 35 R - K7, B x R mate.

33	....	P x R
34	K - R4	....

White could resign, but while there's a check, there's hope.

34	....	K - B3
35	Q - K2	R - N3
36	Q - R5	N - K6

Resigns

White cannot prevent the check at N7, which wins the Queen or mates.

THE CRITICS went wild over the way Anderssen beat Kieseritzky and tried to outdo each other in praise of what they called "The Immortal Game." Franklin K. Young said, "All authorities agree that this *partie* is the most brilliant game of which there is any record." Steinitz said that it was "a continuity of brilliancies, every one of which bears the stamp of intuitive genius that could have been little assisted by calculation, as the combination point arises only at the very end of the game, with a final sacrifice of the Queen after Anderssen had already given up two Rooks and a Bishop." Bird called it "the most beautiful game on record," while Galbreath had recourse to Shakespeare with "Age can not wither, nor custom stale its infinite variety."

A hundred years have passed since this game was played, and its impact is still terrific. In their fine collection, *500 Master Games of Chess*, Tartakower and du Mont say of it, "Universally known as 'The Immortal Game,' this magnificent example of Anderssen's combinative powers is still without a peer in the annals of chess."

London, 1851

KING'S GAMBIT

ADOLF ANDERSSEN	L. KIESERITZKY
White	Black
1 P - K4	P - K4
2 P - KB4	P x P
3 B - B4	Q - R5 ch
4 K - B1	P - QN4
5 B x P	N - KB3
6 N - KB3	Q - R3
7 P - Q3	N - R4
8 N - R4	Q - N4
9 N - B5	P - QB3
10 P - KN4	N - B3
11 R - N1!	P x B
12 P - KR4	Q - N3
13 P - R5	Q - N4
14 Q - B3	....

White has two powerful threats: 15 B x P, winning the Queen, and 15 P - K5, uncovering an attack on the Rook while the Pawn stabs at the Knight.

| 14 .... | N - N1 |

A humiliating retreat.

15 B x P	Q - B3
16 N - B3	B - B4
17 N - Q5!	Q x P

The stage is now set for the sacrifices which made this game immortal.

18   B - Q6!   ....

As Gottschall says, *"Ganz grossartig gespielt!"*

| 18 .... | B x R |

Or *18 ....* B x B, *19* N x B ch, K - Q1, *20* N x P ch, K - K1, *21* N - Q6 ch, K - Q1, *22* Q - B8 mate.

Or *18 ....* Q x R ch, *19* K - K2, Q x R, *20* N x P ch, K - Q1, *21* B - B7 mate.

19   P - K5!   ....

Offering another Rook! Black's Queen is kept from returning to the defense in general and to that of the King Knight Pawn in particular, so that White now has a threat of mate in two, beginning with 20 N x P ch.

| 19 .... | Q x R ch |
| 20 K - K2 | .... |

Black is now two Rooks and a Bishop ahead, but his game is hopeless. If he tries 20 .... B - N2, then 21 N x P ch, K - Q1, 22 Q x P, N - KR3, 23 N - K6 ch, K - B1, 24 N - K7 mate.

20	N - QR3
21 N x P ch	K - Q1
22 Q - B6 ch!	....

Anderssen throws in his Queen, too!

| 22 .... | N x Q |

A recapitulation shows that Anderssen has given away his Queen, two Rooks and a Bishop for one single, solitary Pawn! All this to be able to play his next move:

23   B - K7 mate!

"A glorious finish," says Lasker.

WHEN the critics saw this game, they turned handsprings with joy. Crusty old Steinitz waxed poetic, calling it "the blossom in Anderssen's wreath of laurel," and proceeded to name it the "evergreen *partie*." Cordel said the game was one of the most beautiful ever played. Franklin K. Young (more cautious) called it "the most brilliant Evans Gambit ever played." Gottschall said that the winning combination was one of the most wonderful of Anderssen's conceptions, such as only a genius could have discovered. And Zukertort was of the opinion that the game was "even finer than the celebrated game between Anderssen and Kieseritzky." In 1952, exactly one hundred years after this immortal game was played, Tartakower and du Mont found the combination to be "second to none in the literature of the game." So here it is, laden with encomia.

THE EVERGREEN PARTIE

Berlin, 1852

EVANS GAMBIT

A. ANDERSSEN   J. DUFRESNE

White	Black
1 P - K4	P - K4
2 N - KB3	N - QB3
3 B - B4	B - B4
4 P - QN4	B x P
5 P - B3	B - R4
6 P - Q4	P x P
7 O - O	P - Q6

Black's last was a popular idea; it is intended to prevent White's Queen Knight from developing at B3.

| 8 Q - N3 | Q - B3 |
| 9 P - K5 | Q - N3 |

On *9 .... N x P, 10 R - K1, P - Q3, 11 Q - N5 ch*, White wins a piece.

| 10 R - K1 | KN - K2 |

On *10 .... B - N3*, White can reply with the insidious *11 Q - Q1*, threatening to win the Queen by *12 N - R4*.

| 11 B - R3 | P - N4 |

Castling is safer; but players were not so materialistic a century ago.

| 12 Q x P | R - QN1 |
| 13 Q - R4 | B - N3 |

Now Black would love to castle, but the penalty is *13 .... O - O, 14 B x N, N x B, 15 Q x B*.

| 14 QN - Q2 | B - N2 |

Apparently, Black is not interested in safety but prefers the excitement of counterattack.

| 15 N - K4 | Q - B4 |
| 16 B x QP | .... |

White threatens the Black Queen, by *17 N - B6 ch*.

16	Q - R4
17 N - B6 ch!	P x N
18 P x P	R - N1

This is the position in which Anderssen made the wonderful first move of a combination which made chess history.

| 19 QR - Q1!! | .... |

"This subtle and apparently harmless move is the quiet key to the magnificent sacrifices which follow."

Gottschall.

"One of the most subtle and profound moves on record."   *Lasker.*

"A magnificent conception, probably the most profound ever seen in over-the-board chess at that time."   *Fine.*

19	Q x N
20 R x N ch!	N x R
21 Q x P ch!!	....

A million-dollar move!

| 21 .... | K x Q |
| 22 B - B5 dbl. ch | K - K1 |

22 .... K - B3, 23 B - Q7 is mate.

| 23 B - Q7 ch | K - Q1 |
| 24 B x N mate | |

♛

MORPHY's brilliant win against Paulsen, his chief rival in the First American Chess Congress, is one of the classics of chess literature. Steinitz thought so highly of the game that he reproduced its critical position in gold on the covers of his book *The Modern Chess Instructor*. The winning combination, he said, was "one of the

most poetical chess compositions that
has ever been devised in practical
play."

New York, 1857

FOUR KNIGHTS' GAME

PAULSEN   MORPHY
White   Black
1 P - K4   P - K4
2 N - KB3   N - QB3
3 N - B3   N - B3
4 B - N5   B - B4

It took fifty-five years for the best defense (4 .... N - Q5) to be discovered. Rubinstein was the master who
had the courage to move the same
piece twice in the opening.

5 0 - 0   0 - 0
6 N x P   R - K1
7 N x N   QP x N
8 B - B4   P - QN4

Black weakens his Queen side, but he
wants to regain his Pawn. Capturing
by 8 .... N x P at once would not
do, as after 9 N x N, R x N, 10 B x P
ch, K x B, 11 Q - B3 ch, White wins
the exchange.

9 B - K2   N x P
10 N x N   ....

If 10 B - B3, N x BP! 11 R x N, Q -
Q5, 12 Q - B1, Q x R ch! 13 Q x Q, R
- K8 mate.

10 ....   R x N
11 B - B3   ....

This is inferior to 11 P - QB3 followed
by 12 P - Q4.

11 ....   R - K3
12 P - B3   ....

Preparing the advance 13 P - Q4, but
he gets a rude shock.

12 ....   Q - Q6!

Paralyzes White's position! Paulsen
cannot free his game by P - Q4, nor
is there any easy way to dislodge the
unwelcome Queen.

13 P - QN4   B - N3
14 P - QR4   P x P
15 Q x P   B - Q2
16 R - R2   ....

The idea of this is evidently to continue with 17 Q - B2, to evict Black's
Queen. But why not play 16 Q - R6
immediately?

16 ....   QR - K1

Threatens 17 .... Q x R ch, 18 K x
Q, R - K8 mate.

17 Q - R6   ....

17 ....   Q x B!

Morphy took twelve minutes over this
move, probably to assure himself that
his combination was sound and that
he had a forced win in every variation. Nowadays, masters of the caliber of Alekhine, Tal, Keres, and a
good many lesser lights would take
less than a minute to see all the consequences of the Queen sacrifice. *But
they couldn't do this without the pio-
neer work in combination play by
such masters as Morphy and Anderssen.*

18 P x Q   R - N3 ch
19 K - R1   B - R6
20 R - Q1   ....

If 20 R - N1, R x R ch, 21 K x R, R -
K8 ch, and mate next move. Or if 20
Q - Q3, P - KB4, 21 Q - B4 ch, K - B1,
and Black wins.

20 ....   B - N7 ch
21 K - N1   B x P(B6) dis. ch
22 K - B1   B - N7 ch

Zukertort discovered a quicker win
by 22 .... R - N7 (threatening 23
.... R x RP) 23 Q - Q3, R x P ch, 24
K - N1, R - N7 dbl. ch, 25 K - B1 (or
R1), R - N8 mate.

23 K - N1   B - R6 dis. ch

A quicker line (pointed out by Bauer)
is 23 .... B - K5 dis. ch, 24 K - B1,
B - KB4, 25 Q - K2, B - R6 ch, 26 K -
K1, R - N8 mate.

24 K - R1   B x P
25 Q - B1   B x Q

26	R x B	R - K7
27	R - R1	R - R3
28	P - Q4	....

Finally the freeing move, but it's too late!

28	....	B - K6!
29	Resigns	

For if 29 B x B, R(R3) x P ch, and mate next move.

Now as to the quicker wins — Morphy has been blamed (even by his idolators) for not finding the decisive lines of play pointed out by Zukertort and Bauer. Morphy didn't find these lines *because he was not looking for them.* He saw one line of play that would win and stuck to it. The Queen sacrifice was sound and led to a sure win, and that was all that mattered.

ONE of Morphy's most brilliant games is the one that took place in the Duke of Brunswick's box at the Paris Opera House, during a performance of *The Barber of Seville.* This game has been printed and reprinted thousands of times in hundreds of chess books and periodicals. It has been played over with pleasure by millions of people, and its practical value in rapid development and the forming of simple combinations have increased the strength of countless amateurs.

It has been called by Frank J. Marshall

THE MOST FAMOUS GAME OF ALL TIME

Paris, 1858

PHILIDOR DEFENSE

DUKE OF
BRUNSWICK AND
MORPHY   COUNT ISOUARD

White	Black
1 P - K4	P - K4
2 N - KB3	P - Q3
3 P - Q4	B - N5

"Bring your Knights out before developing the Bishops, especially the Queen Bishop," said Lasker, and "do not pin the adverse King Knight [by B - KN5] before your opponent has castled." The allies with their one last move violated two of Lasker's four rules of development in the opening. It is only fair to say that these rules were stated long after this game was played.

4	P x P	B x N

This is forced, as after 4 .... P x P, 5 Q x Q ch, K x Q, 6 N x P wins a Pawn for White.

5	Q x B	P x P

Now we see how Morphy has taken advantage of his opponents' little error. Black's Bishop is off the board completely. White's Knight has disappeared, but another piece has taken its place. After Morphy's next move he will have two pieces in play to none of Black's.

6	B - QB4	....

Threatens mate on the move. But the threat is incidental to Morphy's real purpose, which is simply to develop his pieces quickly.

6	....	N - KB3
7	Q - QN3!	....

What's this? Morphy moving a piece twice in the opening? Yes, if thereby he can make his opponent lose time defending, or if he can hamper his opponent's development. Morphy threatens 8 B x P ch, K - Q2, 9 Q - K6 mate, as well as 8 Q x P, winning a Pawn.

7	....	Q - K2
8	N - B3	....

Morphy prefers the bringing of more pieces into the field to the mere winning of a Pawn. Indeed, after 8 Q x P, Q - N5 ch would force an exchange of Queens and rule out the prospect of a quick victory.

8	....	P - B3

Black is reduced to a Pawn move, the natural development by 8 .... N - B3 losing instantly after 9 Q x P.

9	B - KN5	....

Paralyzes Black's only properly developed piece.

9	....	**P - N4**
10	**N x P!**	....

A sound sacrifice! Morphy is so far ahead in development that he can afford to give up a Knight to keep his opponent on the run.

10	....	**P x N**
11	**B x NP** ch	**QN - Q2**
12	**0 - 0 - 0!**	

Much stronger than castling on the King side. Now a Rook bears down on the open file *without any loss of time*.

Morphy has various threats:

a] *13* B x N(Q7) ch, and Black dares not recapture;

b] *13* B x N(B6), P x B (or *13* .... Q x B), *14* B x N ch, and again Black is helpless to recapture;

c] *13* R x N, and three of Black's pieces may not take the Rook with impunity.

12	....	**R - Q1**

Black may not castle into safety, as after *12* .... 0 - 0 - 0, *13* B - R6 ch, K - B2, *14* Q - N7 mate would be the penalty.

This is the position:

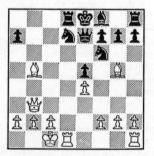

Let us compare the positions:

Morphy's Queen, Queen Rook and both Bishops are in active play.

His King, having castled, is out of any immediate danger.

His King Rook is free to come into the game.

The allies' King is still in the center of the board and, consequently, in danger.

Their King Rook cannot come into play until the Bishop moves away.

The Bishop is blocked by the Queen.

The Queen must stay at K2 to help guard the King.

Both Knights are pinned and cannot move without exposing King or Queen.

The Queen Rook must not leave Q1 and the protection of the Queen Knight.

With Black's pieces boxed in as they are, it's time to look for a decisive combination — and Morphy, of course, finds it!

13	**R x N!**	....

Stronger than the obvious *13* B x N (Q7) ch, as we shall see.

13	....	**R x R**
14	**R - Q1**	....

The point of White's 13th move. The King Rook is brought into the attack without loss of time, striking at Black's Queen Rook, which is pinned.

14	....	**Q - K3**

Unpins the Knight, so that it now protects the Rook.

White can now win neatly by *15* B x N, P x B (if *15* .... Q x Q, *16* B x R mate!) *16* B x R ch winning the Queen; but White, being Morphy, finds a brilliant and more effective conclusion.

15	**B x R** ch	**N x B**
16	**Q - N8** ch!	**N x Q**
17	**R - Q8** mate	

VERY few masters in Steinitz's time were familiar with the games of their contemporaries. But Steinitz kept well informed on the achievements of his rivals, studied and analyzed their play, and improved on their discoveries. His pronouncements always deserved consideration, as they were based on profound if sometimes egregious thought. He could be severe in his censure, but he never withheld praise when it was deserved.

Of the following game he said, "The design of Mr. Blackburne's attack, especially from the 21st move, in combination with the brilliant finish, belongs to the finest efforts of chess genius displayed in match play."

Berlin, 1881

FRENCH DEFENSE

BLACKBURNE   SCHWARZ

White	Black
1	P - K4	P - K3
2	P - Q4	P - Q4
3	N - QB3	N - KB3
4	P x P	P x P
5	N - B3	B - Q3
6	B - Q3	P - B3
7	O - O	O - O
8	N - K2	B - KN5
9	N - N3	Q - B2
10	B - K3	QN - Q2
11	Q - Q2	KR - K1
12	QR - K1	N - K5
13	Q - B1	B(N5) x N
14	P x B	N x N

Such is the perversity of human nature that Blackburne refused an offer of a draw at this point, although that would have assured him of first prize in the tournament.

| 15 | RP x N | B x P |
| 16 | K - N2 | .... |

Naturally, *16 P x B* lets Black get a draw by perpetual check.

16	....	B - Q3
17	R - R1	N - B1
18	R - R3	P - KN3
19	QR - R1	QR - Q1
20	B - KN5	R - Q2
21	P - QB4	P x P
22	B x P(B4)	P - KR4
23	R - R4	P - N4
24	B - N3	N - K3
25	B - B6	N - B5 ch

Upon which Herr Schwarz gets the shock of his young life.

26	Q x N!	B x Q
27	R x P	P x R
28	R x P	Resigns

In unmistakable clarity, there appears on the board a design for checkmate.

THERE are masters who never reach the heights. In tournaments, first prize always eludes them, and in matches they manage to lose more games than they win. They carve out undistinguished careers, leaving behind them a legacy of uneventful, interminable gropings on the chessboard. They would be easily forgotten were it not for one glorious moment which lit up their march to obscurity. But this moment of truth enshrines them in our hearts and inscribes them in our anthologies.

So is it with this happy creation, which deserves to be known as follows.

SCHIFFERS'S IMMORTAL GAME

Frankfurt, 1887

GIUOCO PIANO

SCHIFFERS   HARMONIST

White	Black
1	P - K4	P - K4
2	N - KB3	N - QB3
3	B - B4	B - B4
4	P - B3	N - B3
5	P - Q4	P x P
6	P x P	B - N5 ch
7	B - Q2	B x B ch
8	QN x B	P - Q4!

| 9 P x P | KN x P |
| 10 Q - N3! | .... |

A triple-action move: (a) White's Queen comes into play; (b) more pressure is exerted against Black's centrally posted Knight; (c) Black's Bishop is tied down to the defense of the Queen Knight Pawn.

10	QN - K2
11 O - O	O - O
12 KR - K1	P - QB3

Black cannot dispute the open file with 12 .... R - K1, as 13 B x N then wins a piece. So he supports his Knight first.

| 13 P - QR4 | .... |

To prevent an attempt to drive off the Bishop by 13 .... P - QN4.

| 13 .... | Q - B2 |

Guarding the Knight Pawn and preparing to develop the Bishop.

| 14 QR - B1 | .... |

The best kind of move! White brings a piece into play with a threat to win a piece: 15 B x N, N x B, 16 Q x N, P x Q, 17 R x Q.

| 14 .... | N - B5 |
| 15 N - N5 | .... |

Now three pieces menace Black's King Bishop Pawn.

| 15 .... | N(K2) - N3 |

| 16 R - K8! | .... |

A beautiful sacrifice which must have come as a surprise to the opponent.

| 16 .... | R x R |
| 17 B x P ch | K - R1 |

On 17 .... K - B1, 18 N x P ch, K - K2, 19 R - K1 ch, B - K3, 20 R x B ch,

White wins without any further fireworks.

| 18 B x R | N - K7 ch |

Has Schiffers overlooked this reply?

19 K - R1	N x R
20 N - B7 ch	K - N1
21 N - R6 dbl. ch	....

Uh-uh! Don't touch the Queen. It's *double check*.

21	K - B1
22 Q - N8 ch	K - K2
23 B x N	P x B

On 23 .... P x N, White wins by 24 Q - B7 ch, followed by mate.

| 24 Q x P ch | K - Q1 |

Black must protect his Queen and, on the alternative 24 .... K - Q3, 25 N - K4 ch forces the King away.

| 25 Q - B8 ch | K - Q2 |

| 26 N - K4! | .... |

White threatens mate on the spot, the spot being QB5.

| 26 .... | Q - Q1 |
| 27 Q - Q6 ch | K - K1 |

With the exception of the adventurous Knight, Black's pieces are all at home, but not safe at home.

| 28 N - B6 ch | Resigns |

IT WAS in the twilight of his career, when he was no longer world champion, that Steinitz played this, his immortal masterpiece. Of this golden game, the critics said:

"It is a gem of a game, which for brilliancy combined with absolute soundness has never been surpassed and rarely, if ever, equalled." *Galbreath.*

"A game with a combination which ranks among the most profound ever made." *Fine.*

"A jewel in the treasury of chess, one of the most beautiful sacrificial attacks in all chess literature." *Foldeak.*

"One of the most beautiful and aesthetically satisfying combinations ever devised on the chess board."
                        Tartakower and du Mont.

"A gem of the first water (afterwards awarded first prize for sound brilliancy) and the final picture is a *chef d'oeuvre* of an old master." *Cheshire.*

And, if Chernev may have a voice, "The whole game is played in the grand manner, and the combination is of a magnificence worthy enough to place it among the most brilliant ever played."

Hastings, 1895

GIUOCO PIANO

STEINITZ BARDELEBEN

	White	Black
1	P - K4	P - K4
2	N - KB3	N - QB3
3	B - B4	B - B4
4	P - B3	N - B3
5	P - Q4	P x P
6	P x P	B - N5 ch
7	N - B3	P - Q4
8	P x P	KN x P
9	O - O	B - K3
10	B - KN5	B - K2

11 B x N   ....

Beginning a series of exchanges the object of which is to prevent Black from castling.

11	....	B(K3) x B
12	N x B	Q x N

If 12 .... B x B, 13 N x P ch wins a Pawn.

13	B x B	N x B
14	R - K1	P - KB3

Black prepares for 15 .... K - B2, 16 .... KR - K1 and 17 .... K - N1, castling by hand.

15	Q - K2	Q - Q2
16	QR - B1	P - B3
17	P - Q5!	P x P
18	N - Q4	K - B2

Black's last is forced, in view of the threats of 19 N - B5 and 19 N - N5.

19	N - K6	KR - QB1

If 19 .... QR - B1, White has 20 Q - N4, P - KN3, 21 N - N5 ch, K - K1, 22 R x R ch, Q x R, 23 Q x Q mate.

20	Q - N4	P - KN3
21	N - N5 ch	K - K1

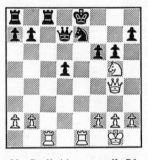

22 R x N ch!   K - B1

If 22 .... Q x R, 23 R x R ch wins at once. If 22 .... K x R, White wins by 23 R - K1 ch, K - Q3 (23 .... K - Q1, 24 N - K6 ch, K - K2, 25 N - B5 dis. ch wins the Queen) 24 Q - N4 ch, K - B2, 25 N - K6 ch, K - N1, 26 Q - B4 ch, R - B2, 27 N x R.

As it is, White is threatened with mate and all four of his pieces are *en prise.*

23 R - B7 ch!   K - N1

If 23 .... Q x R, 24 R x R ch wins

easily; and, if 23 .... K - K1, 24 Q
x Q is mate.

    24   **R - N7** ch!   **K - R1**

Here, too, if 24 .... Q x R, 25 R x R
ch simplifies into a won ending, while
24 .... K x R loses to 25 Q x Q ch.
Finally, if 24 .... K - B1, White finishes a Queen up with 25 N x P ch,
K x R (or 25 .... K - K1, 26 Q x Q
mate) 26 Q x Q ch.

    25   **R x P** ch!   Resigns

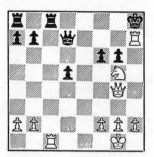

After 25 .... K - N1, there is a remarkably brilliant mate in ten, or a
win of Black's Queen (as Steinitz
demonstrated at the time):

    26   **R - N7** ch   **K - R1**

On 26 .... K - B1, 27 N - R7 ch wins
as in the note to the 24th move.

	27	Q - R4 ch	K x R
	28	Q - R7 ch	K - B1
	29	Q - R8 ch	K - K2
	30	Q - N7 ch	K - K1
	31	Q - N8 ch	K - K2
	32	Q - B7 ch	K - Q1
	33	Q - B8 ch	Q - K1
	34	N - B7 ch	K - Q2
	35	Q - K6 mate	

MARÓCZY was known as one of the
great defensive players of all time,
but that he could attack brilliantly
when the occasion warranted it is an
exemplification of his consummate
mastery of tactics as well as strategy.

Vienna, 1903

MUZIO GAMBIT

G. MARÓCZY   M. TCHIGORIN

White	Black
1 **P - K4**	**P - K4**
2 **P - KB4**	**P x P**
3 **N - KB3**	**P - KN4**
4 **B - B4**	**P - N5**
5 **N - B3**	**P x N**
6 **Q x P**	**P - Q3**

Years ago, discussions raged on the
merits of 6 .... P - Q3 as against 6
.... P - Q4. Now no one dares to play
the Muzio even in an offhand game!

7 **P - Q4**	**B - K3**
8 **N - Q5!**	....

Sacrificing another piece.

8	**P - QB3**
9 **0 - 0**	**P x N**
10 **P x P**	**B - B4**
11 **B x P**	**B - N3**

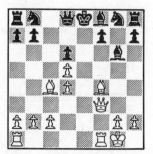

Black protects his King Bishop Pawn,
the usual sore spot in King's Gambits.

12 **B - N5** ch	**N - Q2**
13 **QR - K1** ch	**B - K2**
14 **B x P**	....

With the simple but powerful threat
of *15* B x B, N x B, *16* P - Q6.

    14 ....   **K - B1**

To get out of the pin. Whether *14*
.... Q - N3 would have saved the
game is one of those questions on
which pages and pages of analysis
have been written.

    15   **R x B!**   ....

Marco acidly says that this sort of
move would gladden the heart of any
Rook-odds player.

15	....	N x R
16	R - K1	K - N2
17	B(Q6) x N	Q - R4
18	Q - K2	N - B1
19	B - B6 ch	K - N1

Not 19 .... K x B, 20 Q - K5 mate.

20	Q - K5	P - KR3
21	B x R	P - B3
22	Q - K7	K x B
23	Q x P ch	K - N1
24	R - K7	Resigns

♔

MY FRIEND Mannis Charosh once asked me, "Which *one* game of each great master is your favorite? Which *one* masterpiece would you select to take to a desert island?"

"All right," I replied, "let's try Alekhine as a starter. All I have to do is pick one of these games and eliminate the rest."

Tarrasch - Alekhine, *Pistyan 1922*
Alekhine - Yates, *Hamburg 1910*
Alekhine - Wolf, *Pistyan 1922*
Gruenfeld - Alekhine, *Carlsbad 1923*
Alekhine - Yates, *London 1922*
Rubinstein - Alekhine, *London 1922*
Réti - Alekhine, *Baden 1925*
Nimzowitsch - Alekhine, *Vilna 1912*

"Clearly this won't do," I thought, while a corner of my mind was still busy listing.

Alekhine - Alexander, *Nottingham 1936*
Tarrasch - Alekhine, *Carlsbad 1923*
Bogolyubov - Alekhine, *Hastings 1922*
Alekhine - Sterk, *Budapest 1921*
Mieses - Alekhine, *Mannheim 1914*

"Well then, let's try Pillsbury —"
Pillsbury - Tarrasch, *Hastings 1895!!*

Stop right there! That is *the* game. But my conscience whispered, "Have you considered these others?"

Pillsbury - Lasker, *Nuremberg 1896*
Janowski - Pillsbury, *Paris 1900*

Pillsbury - Tarrasch, *Vienna 1898* (Second Game, Tie Match)
Pillsbury - Wolf, *Monte Carlo 1902*
Pillsbury - Marco, *Paris 1900*
Pillsbury - Gunsberg, *Hastings 1895*
Pillsbury - Lasker, *Cambridge Springs 1904*

Obviously I would have the same sort of trouble in selecting one favorite game from the hundreds of masterpieces produced by Capablanca, Lasker, Keres, Botvinnik, Nimzowitsch, Rubinstein, Marshall, Spielmann, Euwe, Tarrasch and Tartakower.

Embarras de richesses! Just too many masterpieces!

But the challenge intrigued me, and I decided to meet it, master by master. I began with Janowski. To refresh my memory I played through all of the brilliant Polish-Frenchman's games.

From all his efforts, one performance stands out as his supreme achievement. The game, which now follows, is a marvelous blending of clear-cut positional planning with inspired combination in attack. The opening is simple and logical, the mid-game is a wonderful demonstration of a King-side attack, and the ending with a quiet Pawn push as the *coup de grâce* is the artistic fillip which adds the cherry to the icing.

Barmen, 1905

QUEEN'S GAMBIT DECLINED

	D. JANOWSKI	S. ALAPIN
	White	Black
1	P - Q4	P - Q4
2	P - QB4	P - K3
3	N - QB3	B - K2
4	N - B3	N - KB3
5	B - N5	P - KR3
6	B - R4	P x P
7	P - K3	P - R3
8	B x P	P - QN4
9	B - QN3	QN - Q2
10	Q - K2	P - B3
11	0 - 0	0 - 0
12	QR - B1	B - N2
13	KR - Q1	R - B1
14	N - K5!	....

White prevents 14 .... P - B4, as then 15 P x P, R x P (on 15 .... B x BP, White has choice of winning by 16 B x N or 16 N x N or 16 R x N) 16 B x N, followed by 17 N x N, leaves Black's whole game *en prise*.

14	....	N x N
15	P x N	N - Q4
16	B x B	N x N

Black snaps off White's Knight as it might otherwise anchor itself at Q6.

| 17 | R x N | Q x B |
| 18 | R(B3) - Q3! | .... |

The proper caper! The natural 18 R - Q6 loses time as, after 18 P - QB4, 19 R(B3) - Q3, the Pawn fork by 19 .... P - B5 is annoying.

| 18 | .... | KR - Q1 |
| 19 | R - Q6! | R x R |

Can't let the Rook stay there.

| 20 | P x R | Q - Q2 |

The passed Pawn is dangerous, and must be kept under restraint.

| 21 | P - K4 | .... |

White aims for 22 P - K5, to give himself a protected passed Pawn.

| 21 | .... | P - QB4 |

If instead 21 .... P - B3, 22 Q - N4, R - K1, 23 B x P ch, R x B, 24 Q x R ch!, Q x Q, 25 P - Q7 wins. Or 22 .... K - B2, 23 P - K5, P x P, 24 Q - B5 ch, K - K1, 25 B x P and Black is helpless.

| 22 | P - K5 | P - B5 |
| 23 | B - B2 | Q - B3 |

Not so much to threaten mate as to switch blockaders. The Queen is much too important; so first the Rook, then the Bishop will stand guard at Q2.

24	P - B3	Q - B4 ch
25	K - R1	R - Q1
26	Q - K1	R - Q2
27	P - KR3	B - B3

Black prepares to relieve the Rook.

28	P - B4	R - R2
29	P - B5!	B - Q2
30	P - B6!	P - N3

If 30 .... P x P, 31 Q - N3 ch, K - B1, 32 Q - B4, P - B4 (32 .... Q x KP, 33 Q x RP ch, K - N1, 34 Q - R7 ch, K - B1, 35 Q - R8 mate) 33 Q x P ch, K - N1, 34 Q - N5 ch, K - B1, 35 Q - B6, K - N1, 36 P - KR4 and White wins.

| 31 | Q - N3 | .... |

Already threatening 32 B x P.

| 31 | .... | K - R2 |
| 32 | P - KR4 | Q - B1 |

Of course not 32 .... P - KR4, 33 Q - N5, K - N1 (otherwise 34 Q x RP ch follows), as 34 Q - R6 wins.

33	P - R5	Q - KN1
34	R - Q4	B - K1
35	R - R4	....

White plans 36 P x P ch, P x P, 37 R x P ch, K x R, 38 Q - R4 mate.

| 35 | .... | Q - B1 |
| 36 | R - N4 | .... |

Quadruple attack on the Knight Pawn.

| 36 | .... | Q - N1 |
| 37 | Q - K3! | .... |

Hitting out in V-style against Rook and King Rook Pawn.

| 37 | .... | R - Q2 |
| 38 | R - R4 | .... |

New threat: 39 P x P ch, P x P, 40 Q x P mate.

38	....	Q - B1
39	P - KN4	K - R1
40	P x P	P x P
41	R x P ch	R - R2
42	R x R ch	K x R
43	Q - N5	Q - B2

No better is 43 .... Q - R3 ch, 44 Q x Q ch, K x Q, 45 P - B7, B x P, 46 P - Q7 and White gets a new Queen.

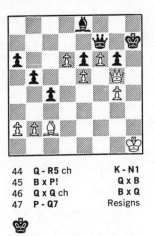

44	Q - R5 ch	K - N1
45	B x P!	Q x B
46	Q x Q ch	B x Q
47	P - Q7	Resigns

then comes *11* .... B x P ch, and he
loses his Queen.

9	....	0 - 0
10	Q - Q2	Q - K2!
11	B - Q3	P x P
12	B x P	P - QN4
13	B - Q3	R - Q1
14	Q - K2	....

White gets his Queen away from the
pressure of the adverse Rook.

14	....	B - N2
15	0 - 0	N - K4!
16	N x N	B x N

Black threatens to win material by
17 .... Q - Q3.

17	P - B4	B - B2
18	P - K4	QR - B1
19	P - K5	....

White's last is an aggressive move
which opens another line (for Black)
and paves the way (says Fine) for
one of the most magnificent combinations of all time.

19	....	B - N3 ch
20	K - R1	N - N5
21	B - K4	....

TARTAKOWER defined Rubinstein as
"The Rook ending of a game of chess
begun years ago by the Gods." In less
mystic prose, others have paid tribute
to Rubinstein's genius as an end-
game artist. Especially with the right
materials, such as a field with a Rook
rampant, five or six Pawns trippant
and the King (gules) couchant.
One is apt to forget Rubinstein's wizardry in the middle game, but he
could fashion combinations to make
the soul ache. Of all his beautiful
creations, there is none equal to the
splendor of this, known to us now as
"RUBINSTEIN'S IMMORTAL."

Lodz, 1907
QUEEN'S GAMBIT DECLINED
ROTLEVI   RUBINSTEIN
White   Black
1	P - Q4	P - Q4
2	N - KB3	P - K3
3	P - K3	P - QB4
4	P - B4	N - QB3
5	N - B3	N - B3
6	QP x P	B x P
7	P - QR3	P - QR3
8	P - QN4	B - Q3
9	B - N2	....

White can win a Pawn with *9* P x P,
P x P, *10* N x P, N x N, *11* Q x N, but

White tries to remove by exchange
one of those terrifying Bishops. If, instead, *21* N - K4, Black wins neatly
by *21* .... R x B, 22 Q x R, B x N,
23 Q x B, Q - R5 (with mate threat)
24 P - R3, Q - N6 (again with mate
threat) 25 P x N, Q - R5 mate!

| 21 | .... | Q - R5! |
| 22 | P - N3 | .... |

On 22 P - R3, Black winds up brilliantly with 22 .... R x N, 23 B x R
(if 23 B x B, R x P ch forces mate),
B x B, 24 Q x N (on 24 Q x B, Black
mates by 24 .... Q - N6, 25 P x N,

Q - R5), Q x Q, 25 P x Q, R - Q6, and the threat of 26 .... R - R6 mate leaves White no time to save his Bishop.

22   ....   R x N!!!

It's only the beginning. You ain't seen nothin' yet.

Kmoch gives this move three exclamation marks. We can hardly do less.

23   P x Q   ....

The alternative 23 B x R runs into 23 .... B x B ch and quick mate (e.g., 24 R - B3, B x R ch, 25 Q - N2, Q x P mate!), while 23 B x B is met by 23 .... R x NP after which the threat of 24 .... N x RP is too much to bear.

23   ....   R - Q7!!!

"A wonderful sequel to the sacrifice of the Queen."   *Chernev.*

24   Q x R   ....

Or 24 B x B, R x Q (with mate threat) 25 B - N2, R - KR6!

Or 24 B x R, R x Q, and Black's threats (25 .... R x P mate and 25 .... B x B ch) cannot be parried.

Or, finally, 24 Q x N, B x B ch, 25 R - B3, R x R wins at once.

24   ....   B x B ch
25   Q - N2   R - R6!!

And mate will come by .... R x RP.

♛

IT IS not always their greatest masterpieces that the masters love best. Sometimes it is an airy trifle, a light conceit or improvisation that captures their fancy. Sometimes it is the public that insists on identifying a bagatelle with its creator to his everlasting annoyance. Paderewski regretted his "Minuet in G" as did Rachmaninoff his "confounded 'Prelude,'" which never ceased to haunt him. Réti is remembered as an end-game artist for a composition which he regarded

as froth, and Morphy by an offhand encounter played in an opera box. Heifetz must be as tired of "Hora Staccato" as Nelson Eddy was of "Shortenin' Bread."

So it is that our hero Nimzowitsch played many wonderful games, but his favorite was this, which he called The Pride of the Family:

Riga, 1913
FRENCH DEFENSE
NIMZOWITSCH   ALAPIN

White		Black
1	P - K4	P - K3
2	P - Q4	P - Q4
3	N - QB3	N - KB3
4	P x P	N x P
5	N - B3	P - QB4
6	N x N	Q x N
7	B - K3	P x P
8	N x P	P - QR3
9	B - K2	Q x NP
10	B - B3	Q - N3
11	Q - Q2	P - K4
12	O - O - O!	P x N
13	B x QP	N - B3

14   B - B6!   ....

"Travels by express," says Nimzowitsch.

14   ....   Q x B
15   KR - K1 ch   B - K2

If 15 .... B - K3, 16 Q - Q7 is mate.

16   B x N ch   K - B1

Or 16 .... P x B, 17 Q - Q8 mate.

17   Q - Q8 ch!   B x Q
18   R - K8 mate!

♛

FRANK MARSHALL once asked Capablanca what he thought was his (Capablanca's) best game. He replied, "It is difficult to say; so much depends on the point of view. There are three possible types of best game — a fine attack, a brilliant defense, or a purely artistic treatment." Marshall then asked which he considered his best game from the artistic point of view, and Capablanca's answer was, "I think my most finished and artistic game was the one I played against Dr. Bernstein on February 4, 1914."

Here is the game:

Moscow, 1914

QUEEN'S GAMBIT DECLINED

BERNSTEIN   CAPABLANCA

	White	Black
1	P - Q4	P - Q4
2	P - QB4	P - K3
3	N - QB3	N - KB3
4	N - B3	B - K2
5	B - N5	O - O
6	P - K3	QN - Q2
7	R - B1	P - QN3
8	P x P	P x P
9	Q - R4	B - N2
10	B - QR6	B x B
11	Q x B	P - B4
12	B x N	N x B
13	P x P	P x P

Black has two "hanging Pawns." Are they strong or weak? No one knows for sure, any more than anyone knows whether an isolated Pawn is strong or weak, or whether two Bishops are better than two Knights. Perhaps it's just as well, or chess would be played only by I.B.M. machines.

14	O - O	Q - N3
15	Q - K2	P - B5!

Capablanca explains that the advance of the Bishop Pawn lets his Bishop take an active role in the game, instead of being tied down to the defense of the Pawn. It also gives Black a point of attack in the fixed and weakened Queen Knight Pawn. "The fact that the text move opens Q4 for one of White's Knights is of small consequence," says Capablanca, "since by posting a Knight there the attack on the Queen Pawn is blocked for the moment, and thus Black has time to assume the offensive."

16	KR - Q1	KR - Q1
17	N - Q4	B - N5!
18	P - QN3	....

The purpose of this move is to saddle Black with a weak, isolated Pawn. Dr. Bernstein was completely unsuspicious of any danger in the position, or he would have played *18* Q - B2, followed by *19* N(Q4) - K2 and *20* N - B4.

18	....	QR - B1
19	P x P	P x P

Bernstein has accomplished his object, but the "weak isolated Pawn" is also a passed Pawn, and apt to be dangerous.

20	R - B2	B x N
21	R x B	N - Q4
22	R - B2	....

Of course not 22 R x P, N - B6 and Black wins the exchange.

22	....	P - B6

"As White is forced to retreat, the Black Pawn advances, and being well supported and far advanced it becomes a source of great strength."

Capablanca.

23	KR - QB1	R - B4
24	N - N3	R - B3
25	N - Q4	R - B2
26	N - N5	R - B4
27	N x BP	....

Fatal, although it isn't obvious why the Knight should not capture a Pawn that is attacked three times and defended only twice.

27	....	N x N
28	R x N	R x R
29	R x R	Q - N7! What a move!

This is the position:

White must lose a Rook or be mated!

If *30* Q x Q, R - Q8 mate.

If *30* R - B2, Q - N8 ch wins a Rook.

If *30* R - Q3, Q - N8 ch wins a Rook.

If *30* R - B8, Q - N8 ch, *31* Q - B1, Q x Q ch wins a Rook.

If *30* Q - K1, Q x R, *31* Q x Q, R - Q8 ch forces mate.

If *30* Q - B2, Q x Q, *31* R x Q, R - Q8 mate.

If *30* Q - Q3, Q - R8 ch!, *31* Q - B1, Q x R wins a Rook.

"One of the prettiest combinations involving the last rank ever played."
                              Dr. Euwe.

Bernstein tried none of these lines. He resigned, as playing even one more move would have been an anti-climax.

THIS is the brilliancy which outshines nearly all its rivals and does so without appealing to the sensational. There are no flamboyant Queen or Rook sacrifices, no flashy, no startling moves. The game just moves along with easy grace and simple elegance. It finishes with a subtle *coup de repos,* the quietest little move ever seen on a chessboard! Nimzowitsch threatens nothing, not even a Pawn, and yet his opponent dares not stir King, Queen, Rook, Bishop, Knight or Pawn! This is the "Immortal *Zugzwang* Game!" It was played at Copen-

hagen in 1923 against a worthy and veteran opponent.

QUEEN'S INDIAN DEFENSE
F. SÄMISCH   A. NIMZOWITSCH

	White	Black
1	P - Q4	N - KB3
2	P - QB4	P - K3
3	N - KB3	P - QN3
4	P - KN3	B - N2
5	B - N2	B - K2
6	N - B3	0 - 0
7	0 - 0	P - Q4
8	N - K5	P - B3
9	P x P	BP x P
10	B - B4	P - QR3!

Black prepares for .... P - QN4, followed by .... N - B3, ... N - QR4 and .... N - B5, so that the Knight can exert pressure on the Queen side.

11	R - B1	P - QN4
12	Q - N3	N - B3
13	N x N	....

White breaks up that plan but at the cost of exchanging off his own strongly posted Knight.

13	....	B x N
14	P - KR3	Q - Q2
15	K - R2	N - R4
16	B - Q2	P - B4!

Black tightens his grip on K5 and threatens to occupy the spot with his Knight. Meanwhile White is prevented from making the freeing move, P - K4.

| 17 | Q - Q1 | .... |

White hopes to continue with P - K4, as his attack on the Knight gives the King Pawn time to exchange or advance.

| 17 | .... | P - N5! |
| 18 | N - N1 | .... |

How sad! The Knight must go home again.

| 18 | .... | B - QN4 |

Still preventing *19* P - K4.

| 19 | R - N1 | B - Q3!! |

Deep, dark and devious! Black lets White make the move he's dying to make and free himself by advancing.

| 20 | P - K4 | .... |

Certainly, it looks attractive, as *20*

.... N - B3 costs a piece by 21 P - K5, and 20 .... P - N3, 21 P x QP, P x P, 22 B x P ch loses the exchange.

| 20 | .... | BP x P! |
| 21 | Q x N | R x P |

Materially, Nimzowitsch has only two Pawns for his piece; but his Rook has a grip on the seventh rank, his other Rook will come in on the open Bishop file and his Bishops overlook two fine diagonals.

| 22 | Q - N5 | QR - KB1 |
| 23 | K - R1 | .... |

White unpins his Bishop to avert 23 .... R(B1) - B6 and 24 .... R x P.

| 23 | .... | R(B1) - B4 |
| 24 | Q - K3 | B - Q6! |

Black closes in on the Queen, indicating his desire for 25 .... R - K7!

| 25 | QR - K1 | .... |

| 25 | .... | P - R3!! |

Quiet, and fiendishly clever! White, with nearly all his pieces still on the board, has no move left! These are the plausible tries:

a] 26 N - B3 (or R3), P x N;

b] 26 B - QB1, B x N;

c] 26 B - KB1, R(B4) - B6, winning the Queen;

d] 26 R - Q1, R - K7, winning the Queen;

e] 26 R(N1) - B1, B x R;

f] 26 K - R2, R(B4) - B6, winning the Queen;

g] 26 P - N4, R(B4) - B6, 27 B x R, R - R7 mate.

After such a stroke, *noblesse oblige* actuated White to make the only move compatible with such a situation. He turned down his King in token of surrender!

OF ALEKHINE's game against Réti, Dr. Euwe, former world's champion, said: "A peerless example of Alekhine's attacking skill. The position is incredibly complicated, and everything is suspended in mid-air; but Alekhine dominates the proceedings. He pulls the wires, and it is to his bidding that the marionettes dance."

Chess World called the game "the gem of gems," and commented further "Alekhine's chess is like a god's. One can revere but never hope to emulate."

In the *American Chess Bulletin*, C. S. Howell, in his introduction to the game, said: "The game is a wonderful one, and the amateur who fails to study it or, studying it, learns naught would do well to give up chess and try another game — say mah-jongg."

Alekhine himself considered it one of the two most brilliant games he had ever played — the other being one against Bogolyubov (the last game in this book).

To these songs of praise, I can only add my own small voice. It is truly a game of bewildering beauty, one of the greatest masterpieces in the entire literature of chess.

Baden-Baden, 1925

KING'S FIANCHETTO

RÉTI	ALEKHINE
White	Black
1 P - KN3	P - K4
2 N - KB3	P - K5
3 N - Q4	P - Q4
4 P - Q3	P x P
5 Q x P	N - KB3
6 B - N2	B - N5 ch
7 B - Q2	B x B ch
8 N x B	0 - 0
9 P - QB4	N - R3

10	P x P	N - QN5
11	Q - B4	N(N5) x QP
12	N(Q2) - N3	P - B3
13	O - O	R - K1
14	KR - Q1	B - N5
15	R - Q2	....

On *15* P - KR3, Black brings his Bishop to K5, via R4 and N3.

15	....	Q - B1
16	N - QB5	B - R6!

A brilliant offer of a Pawn. If *17* B x B, Q x B, *18* N x NP, N - KN5, *19* N - B3, N(Q4) - K6, *20* P x N, N x KP (threatening mate at N7, as well as the Queen) *21* Q x P ch, K - R1! (not *21* .... K x Q, *22* N - N5 ch) *22* N - R4, R - KB1, and Black wins the Queen, as a Queen move is answered by *23* .... R - B8 ch.

17	B - B3	B - N5
18	B - N2	B - R6
19	B - B3	B - N5
20	B - R1	P - KR4!

Now that Réti has refused his tacit offer of a draw, Alekhine begins his King-side attack. His immediate intention is to advance his KRP to weaken White's KN3.

21	P - N4	P - R3
22	R - QB1	P - R5
23	P - R4	P x P
24	RP x P	Q - B2

The start of Alekhine's second combination.

25	P - N5	RP x P
26	P x P	....

Never suspecting Black's spectacular next move.

26	....	R - K6!

As startling as it is beautiful. The Rook cannot be taken, as after *27* P

x R, Q x P ch, *28* B - N2 (*28* K - B1, N x P mate) N x P, and White cannot parry both threats — *29* .... Q x B mate, and *29* .... N x Q. Meanwhile, Black's threat is *27* .... R x P ch.

27	N - B3	P x P
28	Q x P	N - B6!
29	Q x P	Q x Q
30	N x Q	N x P ch
31	K - R2	....

If *31* K - B1, N x P ch, *32* P x N, B x N, *33* B x B, R x B ch, *34* K - N2, R (R1) - R6, *35* R - Q8 ch, K - R2, *36* R - R1 ch, K - N3, *37* R - R3, R(B6) - N 6, and wins the Knight, as White must guard against the mating threat.

31	....	N - K5!
32	R - B4	....

But not *32* P x R, N(K5) x R, *33* R - B2, N x N ch, and Black wins.

32	....	N x BP

32 .... N x R would be countered by *33* N x N!, and two of Black's pieces are attacked, while if *32* .... B x N, *33* R(B4) x N.

33	B - N2	....

Black's threat was *33* .... N x B, *34* K x N, B x N ch followed by *35* B x N.

33	....	B - K3!
34	R(B4) - B2	N - N5 ch
35	K - R3	....

Of course not *35* K - R1, as the reply *35* .... R - R8 ch is murderous.

35	....	N - K4 ch
36	K - R2	R x N!
37	R x N	

Obviously, *37* B x R, N x B ch, followed by *38* .... N x R wins for Black.

37	....	N - N5 ch!

White does not even get a breathing spell!

38	K - R3	....

Here, too, *38* K - R1 (or N1) loses at once by *38* .... R - R8 ch.

38	....	N - K6 dis. ch
39	K - R2	N x R
40	B x R	N - Q5!

The sting at the tail end of the combination! If now *41* R - K3 (or KB2), then *41* N x B ch, *42* R x N, B - Q4, and Black wins the unfortunate Knight, which cannot be protected by the Rook.

41 Resigns

Inimitable wizardry on the part of Alekhine. No adjective short of "wonderful" can begin to describe it!

ALEKHINE says of his game against Thomas at Baden-Baden, in 1925, "The late Nimzowitsch – who was rather reluctant to comment on games of his colleagues – distinguished this one by including it as an example in his remarkable book, *My System*."

Alekhine spoke truth, as it is indeed rare to find a great master (and this applies equally to Alekhine himself) giving unstinted praise to the works of a contemporary. Consequently, when Lasker says of the following game that it is the finest played in ten years, one may be pardoned for venturing that his appraisal was conservative. It is the finest game played in almost any ten years!

Dresden, 1926
NIMZO-INDIAN DEFENSE

JOHNER   NIMZOWITSCH

White	Black
1 P - Q4	N - KB3
2 P - QB4	P - K3
3 N - QB3	B - N5
4 P - K3	0 - 0
5 B - Q3	P - B4
6 N - B3	N - B3
7 0 - 0	B x N
8 P x B	P - Q3
9 N - Q2	P - QN3
10 N - N3	P - K4
11 P - B4	P - K5
12 B - K2	Q - Q2!

Echt Nimzowitsch! Who else would prevent 13 P - N4 by blocking his Bishop with his Queen?

| 13 P - KR3 | N - K2 |
| 14 Q - K1 | P - KR4! |

Blockade work by the master of the art himself.

| 15 B - Q2 | .... |

On the ambitious 15 Q - R4, Black intends 15 .... N - B4 and, if then 16 Q - N5, N - R2 forces 17 Q x RP, after which 17 .... N - N6 wins the exchange.

| 15 .... | Q - B4! |

Of this, Nimzowitsch says, "The Queen is bound for KR2!, where she will be excellently placed, for then the crippling of White's King side by .... P - R5 will at once be threatened." Then he adds, with understandable pride. It must be conceded that the restraint maneuver, Q - Q2 - B4 - R2, represents a remarkable conception."

| 16 K - R2 | Q - R2! |
| 17 P - QR4 | N - B4 |

With this immediate threat: 18 .... N - N5 ch, 19 P x N, P x P dis. ch, 20 K -N1, P-N6, and Black wins.

18 P - N3	P - R4
19 R - KN1	N - R3
20 B - KB1	B - Q2
21 B - B1	QR - B1
22 P - Q5	....

This locking-up of the position is what Nimzowitsch wants. But he could have forced it by .... B - K3, anyway, threatening to exchange Pawns and then win the Queen Bishop Pawn (or make its life miserable).

22	K - R1
23 N - Q2	R - KN1
24 B - KN2	P - KN4
25 N - B1	R - N2
26 R - R2	N - B4
27 B - R1	QR - KN1
28 Q - Q1	P x P
29 KP x P	B - B1
30 Q - N3	B - R3

Very, very deep! If *31* B - Q2, R - N3, *32* B - K1, N - N5 ch, *33* P x N, P x P dis. ch, *34* K - N2, B x P! *35* Q x B, P - K6! This last quiet move threatens *36* .... Q - R6 mate, and the only way to prevent that is by *36* N x P, walking into a devastating Knight fork!

| 31 | R - K2 | N - R5 |

Black is prepared to answer *32* N - Q2 with *32* .... B - B1 and then, if *33* N x P, Q - B4, *34* N - B2, Q x P ch! *35* N x Q, N - N5 mate!
Or *33* Q - Q1, B x P, *34* K x B, Q - B4 ch, *35* K - R2, N- N5 ch, *36* K - R3, N - B7 dbl. ch, *37* K - R2, Q - R6 mate.

32	R - K3	B - B1
33	Q - B2	B x P!
34	B x P	....

Or *34* K x B, Q - B4 ch, *35* K - R2, N - N5 ch and mate in two more.

| 34 | ..... | B - B4! |

Beginning the clearance which will enable Black's Rook Pawn and Queen to get at the opposing King.

35	B x B	N x B
36	R - K2	P - R5
37	R(N1) - N2	P x P dis. ch
38	K - N1	Q - R6
39	N - K3	N - R5
40	K - B1	R - K1!
	Resigns	

Black threatens *41* .... N x R, *42* R x N (if *42* N x N, Q - R8 mate), Q - R8 ch, *43* K - K2, Q x R ch, followed by the exchange of Queens and .... P - N7.
If *41* K - K1, N - B6 ch, *42* K - Q1 (or B1), Q - R8 ch and quick mate.
"This," says Nimzowitsch, "is one of the best blockading games that I have ever played."

THE ONE branch of chess in which Spielmann excelled was the art of at-

tack. Almost from the very beginning of the game Spielmann would lash out with a burst of fury that had one single purpose — checkmate! His guiding principle seemed to be: "Attack, attack, attack! Sacrifice, if necessary to keep the initiative, but keep on attacking! Get your opponent on the defense, and keep him on the run!" Evidently the policy paid off, as Spielmann won a great many very fine games with it.
Ordinarily, choosing one from the many beautiful Spielmann gems might be difficult, but there is one flawless, magnificent specimen of blinding brilliance, which outshines all the others.

Match, 1929

CARO-KANN DEFENSE

SPIELMANN   HONLINGER

White		Black
1	P - K4	P - QB3
2	P - Q4	P - Q4
3	N - QB3	P x P
4	N x P	N - B3
5	N - N3	P - K3
6	N - B3	P - B4
7	B - Q3	N - B3
8	P x P	B x P
9	P - QR3	....

To prevent *9* .... N - QN5, and as a prelude to *10* P - QN4.

9	....	0 - 0
10	0 - 0	P - QN3
11	P - N4	B - K2
12	B - N2	Q - B2
13	P - N5	....

White chases the Knight, so that he can occupy or control K5.

13	....	N - QR4
14	N - K5	B - N2
15	N - N4	....

With mating threats! The idea is *16* N x N ch, B x N (on *16* .... P x N, *17* Q - N4 ch, K - R1, *18* Q - R4 and it's all over), *17* B x B, P x B, *18* Q - N4 ch, K - R1, *19* Q - R4, P - B4, *20* Q - B6 ch, K - N1, *21* N - R5, and mate follows.

15 ....   Q - Q1
16 N - K3!   N - Q4

17   Q - R5!   P - N3

On 17 .... P - R3, White breaks through with 18 B x P, K x B, 19 N (K3) - B5 ch, P x N, 20 N x P ch, K - N1, 21 Q x P, B - B3, 22 N - K7 ch and 23 Q - R7 mate. The defense 17 .... P - B4 is refuted by 18 N(N3) x P, P x N, 19 N x P, N - KB3, 20 Q - N5, P - N3, 21 KR - K1, B - B4, 22 R - K6, Q - Q4, 23 N - R6 ch, K - N2, 24 R x N!, Q x Q, 25 Rx KNP mate!

18   N - N4!   ....

Not merely a flashy brilliancy (18 .... P x Q, 19 N - R6 mate) but in order to get a grip on the black squares weakened by 17 .... P - N3.

18   ....   B - KB3

The Bishop's diagonal must be blocked in order to stop mate. If instead 18 .... P - B3, 19 B x NP, P x B, 20 Q x P ch, K - R1, 21 N - R5 wins, while 18 .... N - KB3 leads to a pretty White win by 19 Q - K5, K - N2, 20 N x N, B x N, 21 N - R5 ch!, P x N, 22 Q - N5 ch, K - R1, 23 Q - R6! (even stronger than 22 B x B ch), and quick mate follows.

Or 18 .... N - KB3, 19 Q - K5, Q - Q4, 20 Q x Q, B x Q (if 20 .... N x Q, 21 N - R6 is mate), 21 N x N ch, and White wins a piece.

19   N x B ch   N x N
20   Q - R6   ....

Now 20 Q - K5 does not work, as Black replies 20 .... Q - Q4 threatening mate, and saves himself by forcing an exchange of Queens.

20   ....   R - B1
21   QR - Q1   ....

Developing with tempo. The threat is 22 B x P, Q - K2, 23 B x N, and Black must give up his Queen to stop mate.

21   ....   Q - K2
22   KR - K1   ....

Another developing move that gains time by threatening. White's plan is 23 N - B5!, attacking the Queen and aiming for mate at N7. On 23 .... NP x N in reply, 24 B x N wins at once.

22   ....   N - K1

Guards against mate at his N2.

23   N - B5!   ....

He goes there anyway! Spielmann never runs out of ideas.

23   ....   Q - B4

If 23 .... NP x N, 24 B x P, P - B3, 25 B x KP ch, K - R1, 26 R - Q7, and White wins.

24   R - K5   B - Q4

Now comes a stunning mating combination! This is the scene:

25   N - K7 ch!   ....

A sacrifice in order to sacrifice again! Spielmann is in his element.

25   ....   Q x N

The Knight must be taken, as 25 .... K - R1 allows 26 Q x R mate.

26   Q x RP ch!   K x Q
27   R - R5 ch   K - N1
28   R - R8 mate!

A fine example of furious, sustained attack.

PLAN your game according to the principles which underlie sound chess strategy, and you will be a strong (and perhaps dull) player. Deviate from accepted theory, and you will probably be thoroughly shellacked. That is, unless you are a genius like Botvinnik, in which case you may break rules and thereby produce masterpieces.

In the game which follows, Botvinnik springs these little surprises:

At his 13th move, he gives up his advantage of the two Bishops, meanwhile releasing the pin on his opponent's Knight.

On his 16th move, he exchanges Pawns, leaving himself with a doubled, isolated Pawn.

On his 21st move, he can undouble his Pawns and obtain a passed Pawn — but he chooses not to do so!

Leningrad, 1938

NIMZO-INDIAN DEFENSE

BOTVINNIK   CHEKHOVER

White		Black
1	P - Q4	N - KB3
2	P - QB4	P - K3
3	N - QB3	B - N5
4	N - B3	O - O
5	B - N5	P - Q3
6	P - K3	Q - K2
7	B - K2	P - K4
8	Q - B2	R - K1
9	O - O	B x N
10	P x B	....

Capturing with the Queen permits 10 .... N - K5 in reply, whereby Black breaks the pin by force.

10	....	P - KR3
11	B - R4	P - B4
12	QR - K1	B - N5

Black's last is a shrewd counter to White's threat of 13 N - Q2 followed by 14 P - B4 or 14 N - K4. Now, if White plays 13 N - Q2, B x B, 14 R x B, KP x P, 15 BP x P, P x P, then 16 P x P would cost a Rook.

13   B x N!   ....

As strong as it is unexpected. White will concentrate his attack on the Q5

square; and, to do so, he must first remove the guardian Knight.

| 13 | .... | Q x B |
| 14 | Q - K4! | .... |

White threatens Knight Pawn and the Bishop simultaneously. Black can defend by 14 .... B - B1, but such a retreating move is not something to relish.

14	....	B x N
15	B x B	N - B3
16	P x BP!	P x P

Here Botvinnik takes on weak, doubled, isolated Pawns; but, as compensation, he has the open file for his heavy pieces and full control of the strong point on Q5.

17	R - Q1	QR - Q1
18	R - Q5	P - QN3
19	KR - Q1	N - R4
20	P - KR3	R x R

21   R x R!!   ....

One would expect 21 P x R, undoubling the Pawns and setting up a passed Pawn. Botvinnik explains that the reply is 21 .... Q - Q3, blockading the dangerous Pawn, after which White can make little progress.

21   ....   Q - K2

If 21 .... R - Q1 (to dispute the open file), then 22 R x KP; for, if then 22 .... N x P, 23 R - K8 ch, R x R, 24 Q x R ch, K - R2, 25 Q - K4 ch, and White wins the Knight.

22   B - N4!   ....

White threatens to take the seventh rank with his Rook.

22   ....   Q - N2
23   B - B5!!   ....

White defends his Queen, and renews the threat.

23   ....   Q - N1

If 23 .... P - N3, White wins by 24 B x P!, P x B, 25 Q x P ch, K - B1, 26 R - Q6, followed by 27 R - B6 ch.

24   R - Q7   ....

In taking the seventh rank, White already plans annihilation by 25 B - R7 ch, K - B1, 26 Q - Q5, R - K2, 27 R - Q8 ch.

24   ....   R - Q1
25   Q x KP   ....

No exclamation marks for this move, as such brilliant moves come of themselves in a strategically superior position.

25   ....   N x P
26   Q x Q   R x Q
27   B - K4!   ....

Centralization, in preference to capturing the Rook Pawn. The consequences (after 27 R x RP) could be 27 .... N - Q3, 28 B - Q3, P - B5, 29 B - B1, N - N4, 30 R - R6, R - QB1, after which Black can breathe more easily.

27   ....   N - R6
28   B - Q5   ....

Note how cleverly White has utilized Q5 first for both his Rooks and now for his Bishop.

28   ....   R - KB1
29   P - K4   P - QR4
30   P - QB4   P - QN4

Black aims not only to simplify (by exchanging instead of losing Pawns) but also to get his Knight back into the fray.

31   P x P   N x P
32   P - K5   P - R5
33   P - B4!   ....

Now White builds to create a passed Pawn.

33   ....   N - Q5
34   K - B2   P - N4
35   P - N3   P x P
36   P x P   N - K3
37   K - K3   P - B5
38   P - B5   N - B4
39   R - B7   N - Q6
40   P - K6   P x P

41   P x P   Resigns

The continuation would be 41 .... R - K1, 42 P - K7 dis. ch, K - N2, 43 B - B6, and Black must give up his Rook.

"THE COMBINATION, or rather series of combinations," says Reuben Fine of the game that follows, "is in my opinion the most remarkable tactical conception in chess history."

Margate, 1938

QUEEN'S GAMBIT

ALEKHINE	BOOK
White	Black
1 P - Q4	P - Q4
2 P - QB4	P x P
3 N - KB3	N - KB3
4 P - K3	P - K3
5 B x P	P - B4
6 0 - 0	N - B3
7 Q - K2	P - QR3
8 N - B3	P - QN4
9 B - N3	P - N5
10 P - Q5!	N - QR4

If 10 .... P x P, 11 N x P, N x N, 12 R - Q1, B - K3, 13 P - K4, N(B3) - K2, 14 P x N, B - N5, 15 P - Q6, White wins a piece.

11 B - R4 ch	B - Q2
12 P x P!	P x P
13 R - Q1!	P x N
14 R x B!	N x R
15 N - K5	R - R2

Now watch this!

16   P x P!   ....

"This," says Alexander, "is played with extraordinary coolness! A Rook behind, White calmly stops to recapture a Pawn. *16* Q - R5 ch would not have been good, because of *16* ....
P - N3, *17* N x P, P x N, *18* Q x R, K - B2, and Black should win."

| 16 .... | K - K2 |
| 17 P - K4! | .... |

White releases his Queen Bishop, thus preventing *17* .... N x N; for *18* B - N5 ch then wins Black's Queen.

| 17 .... | N - KB3 |

Black cannot frighten the Knight away by *17* .... K - B3, as *18* B - N 5 ch, K x B, *19* N - B7 ch removes his Queen.

| 18 B - KN5 | Q - B2 |
| 19 B - B4 | Q - N3 |

Alekhine refutes *19* .... Q - N2 by *20* Q - K3, N x P, *21* B - N5 ch, N x B, *22* Q x N ch, K - Q3, *23* R - Q1 ch, K - B2, *24* Q - Q8 mate — and *20* ....
K - Q1, *21* Q - Q3 ch, K - B1, *22* R - N1, Q x P, *23* N - B7! Q x Q, *24* R - N8 mate.

| 20 R - Q1 | .... |

White holds the King fast and threatens *21* B - KN5, followed by *22* Q - R5 and mate at B7 or K8.

| 20 .... | P - N3 |

Not only to prevent that line but to get his Bishop and King Rook into play as his Queen side is almost paralyzed.

| 21 B - KN5 | B - N2 |

| 22 N - Q7! | .... |

Striking at the Queen and the pinned

Knight simultaneously. He also (as if that were not enough) clears the way for the Pawn stab by P - K5.

22	R x N
23 R x R ch	K - B1
24 B x N	B x B
25 P - K5!	Resigns

If *25* .... B - N2, *26* Q - B3 ch and mate at B7; and, if *25* .... B - K2, White wins with *26* Q - B3 ch, K - N1, *27* R x B, Q - N8 ch, *28* B - Q1, Q - B4, *29* Q - R8 ch, Q - B1, *30* R - K8.

♛

NAJDORF sacrifices a Bishop, a Knight, another Bishop and another Knight in this beautiful game and then checkmates with a Pawn! So lovely a game deserves a distinguished title, and Tartakower gave it one —

THE POLISH IMMORTAL

Warsaw, 1935

DUTCH DEFENSE
Stonewall Variation

GLUCKSBERG	NAJDORF
White	Black
1 P - Q4	P - KB4
2 P - QB4	N - KB3
3 N - QB3	P - K3
4 N - B3	P - Q4
5 P - K3	P - B3
6 B - Q3	B - Q3
7 O - O	O - O
8 N - K2	QN - Q2
9 N - N5	B x P ch!

Quick as a flash!

| 10 K - R1 | N - N5 |
| 11 P - B4 | .... |

On *11* N x KP, Q - R5, White could resign.

11	Q - K1
12 P - KN3	Q - R4
13 K - N2	....

Not only to escape the discovered check but also to steal the Bishop by *14* R - R1 and *15* N - KB3.

| 13 .... | B - N8! |
| 14 N x B | .... |

On *14* K x B, Black mates instantly; and, on *14* R x B, Black mates in two.

| 14 | .... | Q - R7 ch |
| 15 | K - B3 | P - K4! |

Black threatens 16 .... P - K5 ch, 17 B x P, BP x B ch, 18 N x P (or 18 K x N, N - B3 mate), N(Q2) - K4 ch, 19 P x N, N x P mate.

16	QP x P	N(Q2) x P ch
17	P x N	N x P ch
18	K - B4	N - N3 ch
19	K - B3	P - B5!

Now Black threatens 20 .... N - K4 mate as well as a deadly discovered check.

| 20 | KP x P | .... |

On 20 NP x P, N - K4 is instant mate; and, if 20 B x N, B - N5 ch!, 21 K x B, Q x P ch, 22 K - R5, P x B ch, 23 K x P, R - B3 ch, 24 K - R5, R - R3 mate. A sparkling variation.

| 20 | .... | B - N5 ch! |

This is the position as Black gives up his third piece.

| 21 | K x B | N - K4 ch! |

Another kindly gift.

| 22 | P x N | P - R4 |
| | | mate! |

STILL another candidate for undying fame is this brilliant, honored by Hans Mueller. "An immortal game!" is the way he sums it up simply in his book, *Praktische Schachstrategie*.

Gruzinske, 1941

QUEEN'S GAMBIT DECLINED

MIKENAS	LEBEDEV
White	Black
1 P - Q4	N - KB3
2 P - QB4	P - K3
3 N - QB3	P - Q4
4 B - N5	B - K2
5 P - K3	P - KR3
6 B - R4	O - O
7 R - B1	P - B3
8 B - Q3	QN - Q2
9 N - B3	P x P
10 B x P	N - Q4
11 B - KN3!	N x N
12 P x N	P - QB4
13 O - O	P - R3
14 B - Q3	N - B3
15 N - K5	B - Q3
16 B - R4	B - K2
17 B - N1!	Q - K1

Black prepares to meet 18 Q - Q3 (threatening 19 B x N) with .... P - KN3 without fear of 19 N x NP in reply.

18	P x P	P - KN4
19	B - N3	B x P
20	P - KB4!	B x P ch
21	K - R1	B x R
22	P x P	B x P

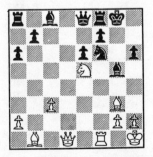

| 23 | R x N! | K - N2 |

On 23 .... B x R, 24 Q - Q3 wins at once.

| 24 | Q - Q3! | P - KR4 |

And now 24 .... K x R is penalized
by 25 N - N4 ch, K - K2, 26 Q - Q6
mate.

| 25 | P - KR4! | .... |

Threatening the brutal 26 P x B.

25	....	K x R
26	N - N4 ch!	P x N
27	B - K5 ch!	....

Simply beautiful!

| 27 | .... | K x B |
| 28 | Q - Q4 mate | |

HANS KMOCH called this victory of
thirteen-year-old Bobby Fischer over
Donald Byrne in the 1956 United
States Championship Tournament the
"Game of the Century." It is indeed
a remarkable game, surpassing in
depth of strategy and brilliance of
execution any of the productions of
Morphy or Reshevsky at a similar
age.
It is the only game by a chess prodigy
worthy of being classed with the
Capablanca-Corzo masterpiece. Both
games are wonderful.

New York, 1956

GRUENFELD DEFENSE

D. BYRNE	FISCHER
White	Black
1 N - KB3	N - KB3
2 P - QB4	P - KN3
3 N - B3	B - N2
4 P - Q4	0 - 0
5 B - B4	P - Q4
6 Q - N3	P x P
7 Q x BP	P - B3
8 P - K4	QN - Q2
9 R - Q1	N - N3
10 Q - B5	B - N5
11 B - KN5	....

This innocent-looking move gets White
into trouble. The safer course would
be 11 B - K2, followed by 12 0 - 0, to
complete his development.

| 11 | .... | N - R5! |
| 12 | Q - R3 | .... |

If 12 N x N, N x P, 13 Q - B1, Q - R4
ch, 14 N - B3, B x N, 15 P x B, N x B,

and Black regains his piece and wins
a Pawn as well.

| 12 | .... | N x N |
| 13 | P x N | N x P! |

And now this Knight makes a surprise
move!

| 14 | B x P | Q - N3! |
| 15 | B - B4 | .... |

White refuses the offer of the exchange, as after 15 B x R, B x B, 16
Q - N3, N x QBP gives Black a winning attack (if 17 Q x N, B - N5 pins
the Queen).

| 15 | .... | N x QBP! |
| 16 | B - B5 | .... |

Here, if 16 Q x N, KR - K1 wins the
piece back and leaves Black with an
extra Pawn.

| 16 | .... | KR - K1 ch |
| 17 | K - B1 | B - K3! |

Fischer has an endless fund of surprise moves, and this one includes an
offer of the Queen.

| 18 | B x Q | .... |

Byrne decides to accept the Queen
sacrifice. Two other alternatives are:
18 Q x N, Q x B, 19 P x Q, B x Q, and
18 B x B, Q - N4 ch, 19 K - N1, N - K
7 ch, 20 K - B1, N - N6 dbl. ch, 21 K
- N1, Q - B8 ch, 22 R x Q, N - K7 mate
— the well-known but always pleasing
smothered mate.
This is the position, with Black to
play:

18	....	B x B ch
19	K - N1	N - K7 ch
20	K - B1	N x P dis. ch
21	K - N1	....

If 21 R - Q3, P x B, 22 Q - B3, N x N!, 23 Q x B, R - K8 mate!

21	....	N - K7 ch
22	K - B1	N - B6 dis. ch
23	K - N1	P x B

After this, White must abandon his Rook, as 24 Q - B1 loses Queen and Rook by 24 .... N - K7 ch, 25 K - B1, N x Q dis. ch, 26 K - N1, N - K7 ch, 27 K - B1, N - B6 dis. ch, followed by 28 .... N x R.

| 24 | Q - N4 | R - R5 |
| 25 | Q x P | N x R |

Fischer is now ahead in material, "and the rest is a matter of technique." Byrne plays on, though, apparently unconvinced that a thirteen-year-old boy could beat him so brilliantly, until he is forced into a mating net.

26	P - KR3	R x P
27	K - R2	N x P
28	R - K1	R x R
29	Q - Q8 ch	B - B1
30	N x R	B - Q4
31	N - B3	N - K5
32	Q - N8	P - QN4
33	P - R4	P - R4
34	N - K5	K - N2
35	K - N1	B - B4 ch
36	K - B1	N - N6 ch
37	K - K1	B - N5 ch

Fischer is having fun, or he would shorten the agony by 37 .... R - K7 ch, 38 K - Q1, B - N6 ch, 39 K - B1, B - R6 ch, 40 K - N1, R - K8 mate.

38	K - Q1	B - N6 ch
39	K - B1	N - K7 ch
40	K - N1	N - B6 ch
41	K - B1	R - B7 mate

♚

ROBERT BYRNE turns out a sparkler which may well be the most brilliant game played by an American in the last ten years.

New York, 1966
SICILIAN DEFENSE

R. BYRNE	EVANS
White	Black
1 P - K4	P - QB4
2 N - KB3	P - QR3

3	N - B3	P - Q3
4	P - Q4	P x P
5	N x P	N - KB3
6	B - KN5	P - K3
7	P - B4	Q - N3
8	Q - Q2	Q x P
9	R - QN1	Q - R6
10	P - K5	P x P
11	P x P	KN - Q2
12	B - QB4	B - N5
13	R - N3	Q - R4
14	0 - 0	0 - 0
15	B - B6!	....

Threatens to win by 15 R x B (not at once 15 Q - N5, N x B, 16 R x N, and White has nothing) Q x R, 16 Q - N5, P - KN3, 17 Q - R6, and mate soon follows.

| 15 | .... | P x B |
| 16 | Q - R6! | .... |

Now the threat is 17 B - Q3, P - B4, 18 R x P, P x R, 19 B x BP, R - Q1, 20 B x P ch, K - R1, 21 B - N6 dis. ch, and mate in two more moves.

| 16 | .... | Q x KP |

There is no relief in 16 .... B x N, 17 B - Q3, B x N ch, 18 K - R1, P - B4, 19 B x BP, P x B, 20 R - N3 ch, and mate next move.

| 17 | N - B5! | .... |

Another sacrifice! The threat of 18 Q - N7 mate forces Black to capture the beast, and gains a tempo for White, whose purpose is to swing the Queen Rook over to the King side.

| 17 | .... | P x N |

The position is now ripe for a third sacrifice! This is the picture on the board:

| 18 | N - K4! | B - Q7 |

The alternatives are:

a] 18 .... P x N, 19 R - KR3, R -
Q1, 20 Q x P ch, K - B1, 21 Q x P
mate.

b] 18 .... Q x N, 19 R - N3 ch,
Q - N5, 20 R x Q ch, P x R, 21 B - Q3,
and White forces mate.

c] 18 .... R - Q1, 19 R - KR3, N -
B1, 20 N x P ch, winning the Queen,
and shortly thereafter, the game.

19	N x B	Q - Q5 ch
20	K - R1	N - K4
21	R - N3 ch	N - N5

But not 21 .... N - N3, which succumbs to 22 R - KR3.

| 22 | P - KR3 | Q - K4 |
| 23 | R - B4! | .... |

Byrne summons up another combination!

23	....	Q - K8 ch
24	N - B1	Q x R
25	R x N ch	....

Of course not the hasty 25 N x Q,
when 25 .... N x Q wins for Black!

| 25 | .... | Q x R |
| 26 | P x Q | N - Q2 |

Black has no time for 26 .... P x P,
as 27 N - N3 followed by 28 N - R5
would ruin him.

27	N - N3	K - R1
28	B - Q3	R - KN1
29	B x P	R - N3
30	B x R	P x B
31	N - K4	P - QN4
32	P - N5	B - N2

If 32 .... P x P, 33 N x P, N - B3,
34 Q - B8 ch, N - N1, 35 N - B7 mate.

33	N x P	N - B1
34	Q - R2!	B - B1
35	Q - K5	N - K3

This guards against 36 N - K8 dis. ch,
K - N1, 37 Q - N7 mate. There was no
escape by 35 .... K - N2 as 36 Q -
K7 ch, K - R1, 37 Q x N is mate.

| 36 | N - Q7 dis. ch | Resigns |

Pity! White is deprived of this finish:
36 .... N - N2, 37 N - N6, B - N2, 38
N x R, B x N, 39 Q - N8 ch, and
Black's last two pieces come off the
board!

THE AMAZING GENIUS OF PETROSIAN

TIGRAN PETROSIAN is not the first great master to mystify his contemporaries by the originality of his play. To go back a bit in chess history, Steinitz's strategy was not understood by his fellow masters. Such concepts of his as the exploitation of weak Pawns, or turning to account a Queen-side majority of Pawns, or fixing pieces on the opponent's weakened squares, had no meaning for them. They were interested only in sacrificial combinations that would lead to a direct attack on the King. They would then either win brilliantly, or go down to glorious defeat in the inevitable counterattack.

After Steinitz's theories had been absorbed, adopted and perfected by such world-beaters as Tarrasch and Lasker, other masters came along with refinements in technique that were also regarded with astonishment. Réti tells us, for example, of a consultation game in which he and Capablanca were playing against Fahndrich and Kaufmann. At one stage Réti and Capablanca had an opportunity to develop their King Rook with gain of tempo. The Rook not only would seize control of the important King file, but would also gain additional time by driving the opposing Queen off the file. "This move," says Réti, "was in accordance with the principles prevailing when I grew up, and corresponded almost entirely with Morphy's principles, for he would without considering have chosen that move."

To Réti's amazement, *"Capablanca would not even consider the move at all."*

Some years later, when Nimzowitsch appeared on the chess scene, his strategic ideas (overprotection, prophylaxis, attack on the base of a Pawn chain, etc.) not only were little understood by the world's leading masters, but actually were ridiculed by Tarrasch, chief exponent of the theories of Steinitz, and founder of the classical school of play.

And now we have Petrosian, *who plays like no other great master, past or present.*

Petrosian does not play for the attack; you get the impression that he regards a King-side attack as a primitive attempt to force a win. Nor does he try to improve his position at every turn, or play to weaken that of his opponent. Very often he seems to be devoting his time to maneuvering his pieces back to the first rank, or even into a corner of the board.

Only recently have the other masters and a few chess critics realized the depth and subtlety of Petrosian's play. Euwe says, for example, "The Petrosian style shows great analogy with that of Capablanca, who too was famous for his almost faultless play, spiced with small venomous pinpricks." Commenting on a quiet move of Petrosian's in the same game, Euwe says, "White is not in a hurry. Petrosian never is!"

Summing up a game between Petrosian and Spassky, Cozens makes this observation, "One watches Spassky take the initiative and mount lordly attacks on both wings. Nothing decisive emerges, and around moves 25–30 it begins to dawn that most of the good squares on the board are occupied by Petrosian's pieces. A few more moves, and Spassky can see nothing for it but to resign."

John Hammond in an interesting article says, "Petrosian's ideas are a further development of those of Nimzowitsch." Further on, he says, "The time for the eventual realization of Petrosian's chess vision may be centuries away."

Petrosian's style is unique unto himself. In his games we shall see him using such ideas as these to win:

1] Opening moves which seem to contradict established principles.

2] Late development of several pieces.

3] Long-delayed castling.

4] Castling to a wing where the King seems exposed to danger.

5] Retreat of seemingly well-placed pieces, developing backward to the first rank, or into a corner.

6] Early advance of the King Rook Pawn, a step which seems premature and makes castling on the King side dangerous.

7] A series of strange, apparently purposeless moves.

8] Unexpected *zwischenzüge* – in-between moves.

9] Little stabbing Pawn pushes, alternating from one side of the board to the other, which nibble away at the enemy position.

10] Subtle defensive touches, when his position seems in no danger of attack.

Small wonder, then, that Petrosian's opponents are often bewildered by his mysterious maneuvers and seem at times to put up insufficient resistance. Now let us look at some games, and see the one and only Petrosian fashion a win in his own inimitable style:

The originality of Petrosian's play in this game might have impressed even the great Nimzowitsch, and made him pause to wonder.

Moscow, 1961
RÉTI DEFENSE
PETROSIAN   ARONIN

	White	Black
1	N - KB3	P - QB4
2	P - KN3	N - QB3
3	B - N2	P - Q4
4	O - O	N - B3
5	P - Q3	B - N5
6	P - B4	P - K3
7	Q - R4	....

Threatens 8 N - K5, Q - N3, 9 N x B, N x N, 10 P x P, and both Black Knights are *en prise*.

7	....	Q - Q2
8	N - B3	P - Q5
9	N - QN5	B - K2
10	P - KR3	B x N
11	P x B	O - O
12	Q - Q1	....

The Queen undevelops. This is the first retreat. There will be more!

12	....	KR - K1
13	P - B4	B - Q1
14	N - R3	....

Now the Knight returns.

14	....	B - R4
15	N - B2	....

The Knight continues its retreat.

15	....	B - B2
16	P - R3	P - QR4
17	R - N1	....

Apparently preparing to advance the Queen Knight Pawn.

17	....	B - Q3

Which, of course, Black prevents.

18	B - Q2	P - K4
19	P x P	N x P
20	P - B4	N - B3

Of course not 20 .... N x QP, 21 Q - B3, and the Knight is trapped.

21	Q - B3	P - R4

To stop 22 P - KN4. Note how Black has been forced to weaken his Pawn position on both sides of the board.

22	KR - K1	R x R ch
23	R x R	R - K1
24	R x R ch	Q x R
25	N - K1	....

The Knight is now happily posted on the back rank!

25	....	Q - Q1
26	Q - Q1	....

Now the Queen comes back from her aggressive position!

| 26 | .... | Q - N3 |
| 27 | B - QB1 | .... |

Another piece returns home!

27	....	N - K2
28	Q - B3	Q - N6
29	P - N4	....

An attacking move?

29	....	P x P
30	P x P	P - KN3
31	B - B1	....

Now the King Bishop returns to its home base. Petrosian (unlike any other player in the world) can prepare a decisive attack by posting most of his pieces on the back rank! What would Morphy think?

31	....	Q - N3
32	P - B5	P x P
33	P x P	K - B1

Would you believe that White, with only one piece in play, now wins this in about half a dozen moves? Here is the position:

34	B - N2	N - B3
35	Q - R3	N - KN1
36	Q - R8	....

Threatens 37 B - R6 ch, winning the Knight.

| 36 | .... | B - N6 |

Or 36 .... P - B3, 37 B - Q5, N(B3) - K2, 38 B - R6 ch, and White wins a piece.

Black's idea (with 36 .... B - N6) is to force 37 N - B3, blocking the Bishop. This would allow Black time to defend by 37 .... N - K2.

| 37 | P - B6! | .... |

But Petrosian doesn't bother to save his Knight!

37	....	B x N
38	Q - N7 ch	K - K1
39	Q x N ch	K - Q2
40	B - R3 ch	Resigns

The continuation would be: 40 .... K - Q3, 41 B - B4 ch, N - K4, 42 Q - N 8 ch, K - B3 (if 42 .... Q - B2, 43 B x N ch wins the Queen), 43 Q - K8 ch, K - B2, 44 Q - B8 ch, K - Q3, 45 Q - Q7 mate — a pretty exploitation of the pin motif.

♚

NOW comes another remarkable game, where the Petrosian touch brings some fantastic positions into being.

Tiflis, 1949

ENGLISH OPENING

PETROSIAN	ARANOVICH
White	Black
1 P - QB4	N - KB3
2 N - QB3	P - B4
3 P - KN3	P - Q4
4 P x P	N x P
5 B - N2	N x N
6 NP x N	P - KN3
7 Q - R4 ch	....

"Don't move your Queen in the opening" and "don't check unnecessarily" — so we were taught in school.

| 7 | .... | N - Q2 |
| 8 | P - KR4 | .... |

Lasker says, "Do not move any Pawns in the opening of a game but the King and Queen Pawns."
Further exception might be taken to Petrosian's advance of the Rook Pawn by pointing out that he seems to be embarking on a premature attack, and that his King might find it dangerous to castle on the King side.

| 8 | .... | B - N2 |
| 9 | P - R5 | .... |

Continuing in the same vein.

| 9 | .... | Q - B2 |
| 10 | R - N1 | .... |

Petrosian switches his play from one side of the board to the other. Incidentally, this last move rules out Queen-side castling, but Petrosian is not worried about sticking to the conventional.

| 10 | .... | P - QR3 |
| 11 | P x P | .... |

Now he shifts to the King side.

11	....	RP x P
12	R x R ch	B x R
13	N - R3	....

Again quoting Lasker, "In my practice I have usually found it strongest to post the Knights at B3, where they have a magnificent sway."
But Petrosian has his own ideas!

13	....	R - N1
14	N - B4!	P - QN4
15	N - Q5!	....

A fine centralization, which the Knight could not have achieved by the routine development at B3. (This does not cast any reflection on Lasker's principles of development, as they were meant for the guidance of average players, and not for geniuses).

15	....	Q - K4
16	Q - R5	B - QN2
17	P - Q4	....

These little in-between moves are also characteristic of Petrosian's style, and are seen frequently in his games.

| 17 | .... | P x P |
| 18 | P x P | .... |

And not the plausible 18 B - B4, when 18 .... Q - B4, 19 P - K4, P x P e.p. leaves Black with the advantage.

18	....	Q - R4
19	N - B7 ch	K - B1
20	N x RP	B x N

Forced, as 20 .... B x B loses material after 21 N x R, N x N, 22 Q - Q8 ch, K - N2, 23 Q x N.

| 21 | Q x B | B x P |
| 22 | B - B4 | N - B4 |

But not 22 .... P - K4, 23 Q - Q6 ch, K - K1, 24 B - B6, R - Q1 (if 24 .... Q - B4, 25 B x N ch, Q x B, 26 Q x R ch), 25 R x P, and White has too many threats — 26 B x P, or 26 R - N7, or 26 R - N8, R x R, 27 B x N ch.

| 23 | Q - B6 | R - N3 |
| 24 | Q - B8 ch | .... |

Clearly, if 24 Q x R, N - Q6 ch wins the Queen.

| 24 | .... | K - N2 |
| 25 | K - B1 | R - K3 |

Black's position looks imposing, with four of his pieces poised for attack. Despite this, Petrosian is not perturbed. He makes two unassuming little Pawn moves, drives off the protectors of the Knight — and wins a piece!
This is the position, with White to play:

26	P - K3	B - B3
27	P - N4	Q x P
28	Q x N	R - R3
29	Q x NP	R x P
30	Q - B4!	....

Attacks the Rook, and also threatens to win the Queen by discovered attack (31 B - R6 ch).

| 30 | .... | Q - K3 |
| 31 | Q x Q | P x Q |

The rest is a matter of technique, of which Petrosian has a plentiful supply.

32	R -N6	B - R5
33	B - N3	R - R8 ch
34	K - K2	R - R7 ch
35	K - B3	B - B3
36	R x P	....

Another Pawn falls.

36	....	K - B2
37	R - B6	R - R4
38	B - R3	R - QN4
39	B - K6 ch	K - N2
40	B - KB4	R - QR4
41	P - K4	R - R6 ch

| 42 | K - N4 | R - R5 |
| 43 | B - B4 | .... |

Threatens to win the Bishop by 44 P - K5.

43	....	R - R4
44	B - K3	R - R6
45	R - B7	....

With this pretty threat: 46 P - K5, B x P, 47 R x P ch, K - B3, 48 R - B7 mate (or 48 B - N5 mate).

| 45 | .... | R - R4 |
| 46 | P - B4 | Resigns |

The advance 47 P - K5 will win at least a Pawn. If 46 .... K - B1 (to protect the King Pawn, and give the Bishop elbow room) the continuation 47 R - B8 ch, K - N2, 48 P - K5 traps the Bishop.

♛

THAT Petrosian's style does not preclude sparkling play can be seen from this brilliant little game.

Tiflis, 1949

GRUENFELD DEFENSE

PETROSIAN   POGREBYSSKY

White	Black
1 P - Q4	N - KB3
2 P - QB4	P - KN3
3 N - KB3	B - N2
4 P - KN3	0 - 0
5 B - N2	P - Q4
6 P x P	N x P
7 0 - 0	P - QB4

An attack on the center — the proper strategy for Black in most Queen Pawn games.

| 8 P - K4 | N - KB3 |
| 9 P - K5 | .... |

The books say that advancing the Pawns beyond the fourth rank weakens them, but Petrosian can reply (as Alekhine once did), "The books say? *I* make the books!"

| 9 | .... | KN - Q2 |
| 10 | N - N5! | .... |

The books also say, "Move each piece only once in the opening," and "Do not start an attack until most of your pieces have been brought into play."

10	....	P x P
11	P - B4	N - B4
12	P - QN4	....

Another wild-looking attacking move, of the sort that only a beginner (or perhaps a genius) would play.

12	....	P - B3
13	P x P!	P x P
14	N x P	....

Rather unexpected!

14	....	K x N
15	P x N	N - B3
16	B - N2	Q - B2
17	N - Q2	B - K3
18	N - K4	QR - Q1
19	P - KR4!	Q - Q2
20	P - R5	B - N5
21	P x P ch	K x P

This is the position, before the fireworks were set off:

| 22 | P - B5 ch! | .... |

A surprise move! The Pawn is attacked by three pieces, and defended only once.

| 22 | .... | B x P |

If 22 .... Q x P, 23 Q - N1! (a beautifully subtle move) forces the win. For example, 23 .... Q - K3, 24 N - N5 dis. ch, K x N (if 24 .... B - B4, 25 N x Q, B x Q, 26 N x R ch wins) 25 B - B1 ch, K - R4, 26 Q - R7 ch, B - R3, 27 Q x B mate.

Or if 22 .... K - R5, 23 Q x B ch!, K x Q, 24 R - B4 ch, K - R4, 25 R - R4 mate.

| 23 | N - Q6! | .... |

"This quiet move is the key to the combination," says Petrosian.

| 23 | .... | B - N5 |
| 24 | B - K4 ch | K - R4 |

Of course not 24 .... P - B4, 25 Q x
B ch, and White wins.

| 25 | R - B4! | .... |

A bit of a shock! Now if 25 .... B x
Q, 26 R - R4 ch, K - N4, 27 B - B1 is
checkmate.

25	....	P - B4
26	R x B	P x R
27	Q - Q2	....

Another quiet little move — with
power behind it! The threat is 28 Q -
R2 ch, K - N4, 29 Q - R4 mate.

| 27 | .... | R - KR1 |
| 28 | K - N2! | .... |

The third quiet little move — and
Black is rendered helpless! The threat
is instant mate by 29 R - R1 ch.
So . . .

| 28 | .... | Resigns |

A delightful specimen of Petrosian's
skill, and one that is sure to find a
place in the anthologies.

♛

ANOTHER attractive little game with
some characteristic strategic touches.
Petrosian makes a few innocuous-
looking moves, first on one side of
the board and then on the other, and
Barendregt's game just falls apart!

Beverwijk, 1960

BENONI DEFENSE

PETROSIAN   BARENDREGT

White		Black
1	P - QB4	P - KN3
2	P - Q4	B - N2
3	N - QB3	P - Q3
4	P - K4	P - QB4
5	P - Q5	P - K4
6	B - K2	N - KR3

There is nothing wrong with 6 ....
N - KB3 followed by castling, but
Black evidently intends to support the
thrust .... P - B4.

| 7 | P - KR4 | .... |

The players of an earlier generation
would regard this move with horror.
It initiates a premature attack, moves

a Pawn instead of a piece, and makes
castling on the King side hazardous.

7	....	P - B4
8	B - N5	Q - N3
9	R - N1	....

And this makes Queen-side castling
impossible, but that does not bother
Petrosian.

| 9 | .... | N - B2 |
| 10 | B - Q2 | P - QR4 |

A preventive measure against the
threat of 11 P - R3 followed by 12 P
- QN4. But it weakens his game ever
so slightly, and Petrosian will see to
that little weakness.

| 11 | N - B3 | P - R3 |
| 12 | P - KN3 | .... |

To stop 12 .... P - B5 followed by 13
.... P - N4.

12	....	N - R3
13	P - R3	Q - Q1
14	Q - B2	P - R4
15	P x P	P x P
16	N - KN5	....

This Knight attacks on the King side —

| 16 | .... | Q - B3 |
| 17 | N - R4 | .... |

— and the other Knight attacks on the
Queen side.

| 17 | .... | P - B5 |

If 17 .... Q - Q1 (to save the Queen
Rook Pawn), 18 N - K6, B x N, 19 P
x B, N - R3, 20 B x P ch, K - K2, 21 B
x N, B x B, 22 Q x P, and White wins.

18	N - N6	B - B4
19	B - Q3	B x B
20	Q x B	R - QN1
21	N - K4	Q - Q1
22	B x RP	O - O

This is the situation:

23 **Q - Q1**   ....

The Queen retreats – in order to attack!

23 ....   **P - B6**

The Rook Pawn could not be saved. Black offers his Bishop Pawn to get some counterplay after 24 Q x P by 24 .... N - N4, 25 Q - K2, N - B6 ch.

24 **P - QN4**   ....

Switch attack – once more. White supports his Bishop (in order to free the Queen Knight) and prepares to bring his Queen Rook into the game.

24 ....   **N - R3**
25 **R - N3**   **N - N5**
26 **0 - 0**   ....

Long delayed (and unexpected) castling – the hallmark of Petrosian.

26 ....   **B - B3**
27 **Q x P!**   ....

Again unexpected, and superior to 27 R x P. Now if 27 .... B x P, 28 Q - R1, B - K2, 29 Q x P, and the Queen comes strongly into the adverse position. A plausible continuation could be: 29 .... N - B3, 30 Q - N6 ch, K - R1, 31 K - N2, and check by the Rook will be fatal.

27 ....   **Q - K2**

If 27 .... R - B2 (to protect the Rook Pawn), 28 Q - B5, R - R2, 29 P - B3 wins a piece.

28 **Q - B5**   **R - B2**
29 **Q x RP**   **R - N2**
30 **P - B3**   ....

Steals the Knight.

30 ....   **B x P**
31 **P x N**   **R - R2**
32 **Q - B5**   ....

And now the Bishop.

32 ....   Resigns

HOW does the Petrosian technique work with the Black pieces? Let's begin with this interesting specimen:

Moscow, 1955

QUEEN PAWN OPENING

TERPUGOV   PETROSIAN
White   Black
1 P - Q4   N - KB3
2 N - KB3   P - Q3
3 N - B3   B - N5

"Do not pin the adverse King Knight before your opponent has castled," says Dr. Lasker. Hasn't Petrosian read *Common Sense in Chess*?

4 P - K4   P - B3
5 P - KR3   B x N

And now he lets Terpugov have the two Bishops, as well as helping him bring his Queen into play.

6 Q x B   QN - Q2
7 B - K3   P - K3
8 P - KN4   P - Q4
9 P - K5   N - KN1

The Knight is forced to retreat, but such things don't trouble Petrosian.

10 0 - 0 - 0   P - QN4

This would be termed a premature attack by theorists of the old school, but the wily Petrosian knows what he is doing. His opponent has the two Bishops, but their mobility will gradually be cut down.

11 B - Q3   N - N3
12 K - N1   N - B5
13 B - QB1   Q - N3
14 P - N5   N - K2
15 P - KR4   P - QB4
16 P x P   Q x P
17 KR - K1   P - N3

This strengthens Petrosian's grip on the white squares, nips any incipient King-side attack in the bud, and prepares the development of the King Bishop. What more can be done by one little Pawn push?

18 P - N3   B - N2!

A passive Knight sacrifice. Quite unexpected, and the first in a series of brilliant moves.

19 P x N   NP x P

20   **B - B1**   ....

Now both of White's Bishops have been reduced to impotence. This is the position, with Black to play:

20   ....   **O - O!**

Delayed castling — here an aggressive gesture, and not to assure the safety of the King.

The King Rook is now in position to seize the open Knight file.

21	K - R1	KR - N1
22	N - N1	N - B3
23	Q - N3	R x N ch!

Black is a piece down, but he sacrifices the exchange!

| 24 | K x R | R - N1 ch |
| 25 | K - R1 | P - B6 |

Threatens to force mate by 26 .... Q - N5.

26   **B - Q2**   ....

White offers his Bishop, hoping to save himself by 26 .... P x B, 27 R x P, Q - N5, 28 P - QB3, but our hero is not to be tempted. He has another surprise or two in store!

26   ....   **N - N5**

Threatens 27 .... N x BP mate.

27   **B - Q3**   ....

White guards against this threat.

27   ....   **Q - B5!**

The last surprise, and to this there is no reply. The threat is 28 .... Q x RP mate.

28   Resigns

An enchanting little game.

PETROSIAN can smell danger a mile off, and defend a position with the tenacity of a Steinitz. But, unlike Steinitz, Petrosian does not tie his game up in knots to resist an invasion. His pieces, though cramped, are ready to spring into action at a moment's notice.

Moscow, 1951

INDIAN DEFENSE

TERPUGOV	PETROSIAN
White	Black
1 P - Q4	N - KB3
2 N - KB3	P - B4
3 P - Q5	P - QN4
4 B - N5	Q - N3
5 N - B3	P - KR3
6 B x N	KP x B

Geniuses do not have to capture toward the center.

| 7 P - K4 | P - QR3 |
| 8 P - QR4 | P x P |

One might expect 8 .... P - N5, but in Petrosian's games one must always be prepared for the unexpected.

9   N x P   ....

A natural recapture, as it forces Black to lose a move with his Queen. How could the poor Knight know that its doom was sealed with this move, and that it would die on this square?

9	Q - B2
10 B - K2	P - Q3
11 0 - 0	B - K2
12 N - Q2	N - Q2
13 B - N4	0 - 0
14 R - R3	R - N1
15 R - KN3	K - R1

The first subtle move in preparing an airtight defense.

| 16 B - B5 | Q - Q1 |

More of the same.

17 Q - N4	R - N1
18 Q - R5	Q - K1
19 P - N3	B - B1

Now all is secure. The Steinitzian position of the pieces on the back rank is misleading, as these pieces have a great deal of latent power.

| 20 Q - K2 | P - N3 |

The beginning of counterplay. "The real criterion by which to appraise closed positions," says Réti, "is the possibility of breaking through."

| 21 | B - R3 | P - B4 |
| 22 | P - KB4 | .... |

Of course not 22 P x P, as the King Pawn is pinned.

22	....	N - B3
23	R - K1	P x P
24	B x B	Q x B
25	N x KP	N x N
26	Q x N	B - N2

What a beautiful view the Bishop has!

| 27 | R - Q3 | R - N5 |
| 28 | Q - B3 | P - B5 |

To undermine the support of the Knight.

29	R - Q2	P x P
30	P x P	Q - KB4
31	P - N3	....

Black is now ready to launch the final attack. This is the position:

| 31 | .... | P - N4 |
| 32 | Q - Q3 | .... |

White could not save his Bishop Pawn. If 32 R - KB1 (on 32 R - KB2, B - Q5 wins the exchange for Black) P x P, 33 P x P, R x BP, 34 Q x R, B - Q5 dbl. ch, 35 K - R1, Q x Q, 36 R x Q, R - N8 is mate.

32	....	Q x Q
33	R x Q	P x P
34	R - K7	....

Of course not 34 P x P, because of 34 .... B - B6 dis. ch, and Black wins the exchange.

| 34 | .... | P x P |
| 35 | P x P | R(N1) - QN1 |

After all the fuss on the King side,

the decision will come on the Queen side!

36	R x P	R x P
37	R x R	R x R
38	K - N2	R - N5
39	R - B4	B - Q5

Suddenly the Knight is lost! If 40 N - N6, R - N7 ch followed by 41 .... B x N. Or if 40 N - N2, R x N ch wins at once.

| 40 | Resigns |

♚

PETROSIAN's winning ways are weird and wonderful. In this game, for example, Petrosian's opening moves seem to violate every principle in the book — yet he manages to reduce his opponent to helplessness easily and painlessly!

The entire game is one of the most amazing I have ever seen.

Belgrade, 1954

FRENCH DEFENSE

JOPEN	PETROSIAN
White	Black
1 P - K4	P - K3
2 P - Q4	P - Q4
3 N - QB3	B - N5

"Knights before Bishops!" say the authorities.

| 4 P - K5 | P - QN3 |

Now he prepares to fianchetto the Bishop on a closed diagonal.

| 5 Q - N4 | B - B1 |

Two violations: moving the same piece twice in the opening, and undeveloping the Bishop.

| 6 N - B3 | Q - Q2 |

Two more violations: bringing his Queen out early in the game, and blocking the path of the Bishop.

| 7 N - QN5 | N - QB3 |

And this move obstructs the Bishop Pawn. "You will sometimes, especially in Queen-side openings, find it a better plan to advance the Queen Bishop Pawn two squares before obstructing it with your Knight," says Dr. Lasker. True, this is not a Queen-side opening, but the strategy recommended for Black in the French Defense is to attack the center by .... P - QB4.

8	P - B3	P - QR3
9	N - R3	P - B4
10	Q - N3	B x N

Not only does Petrosian exchange his long-range Bishop for a Knight posted at the side of the board, but he allows his opponent to have the advantage of the two Bishops.

| 11 | P x B | B - N2 |

Black's remaining Bishop bites on granite — commanding a diagonal that is blocked by his own Queen Pawn.

| 12 | N - N5 | O - O - O |

"Castle as early as possible, preferably on the King side," says everybody, beginning with Howard Staunton.

| 13 | P - KR4 | N - R3 |

The Knight develops sideways, there being no other choice.

14	B - Q3	K - N1
15	Q - B3	N - B2
16	N - R3	P - N3
17	Q - K2	K - R2
18	B - KN5	N x B
19	N x N	P - R3
20	N - R3	....

The Knight could have returned to B3, but what was its future? From B3 the Knight could move to Q2 and to N3, and then what? The Knight could find no secure foothold anywhere. From R3, though, the Knight envisioned a possibility of getting into the game by way of B4.

| 20 | .... | Q - K2 |

Suddenly the Queen strikes in two directions at once, and menaces both of White's Rook Pawns!

| 21 | N - B4 | P - KN4 |
| 22 | N - R3 | .... |

The alternatives are not inviting: If 22 N - N6, Q x P, 23 N x R, Q x BP ch, 24 Q - Q2, Q x R ch, and Black

wins a piece. Or if 22 P x P, P x P, 23 R x R, R x R, 24 N - R3, P - N5, 25 N - N1, R - R8, 26 K - B1 (if 26 Q - B1, Q x P wins) Q - R5, and White is lost.

| 22 | .... | Q x P |
| 23 | Q - Q2 | Q - K2 |

White cannot now regain his Pawn by 24 P x P, as, after 24 .... P x P in reply, he dares not recapture with either Queen or Knight.

24	O - O - O	QR - KN1
25	K - N1	N - R4
26	P x P	P x P
27	P - B4	....

Of course not 27 N x P, as 27 .... R x R, 28 R x R, Q x N wins a piece for Black.

| 27 | .... | P - N5 |
| 28 | N - N5 | .... |

The Knight's third visit to this square!

28	....	B - B3
29	Q - N2	N - B5
30	Q - N4	Q - Q2

This seems to lose a Pawn, but Petrosian is never caught napping. This is the position, with White to play:

| 31 | B x N | P - R4 |

An in-between move to drive the Queen away from the protection of the Bishop.

| 32 | Q - N2 | .... |

But not 32 Q - N3 (guarding the Bishop) as 32 .... B - R5 in reply would be painful.

| 32 | .... | P x B! |

Suddenly new vistas are opened to Petrosian's Bishop!

| 33 | Q - Q2 | B - Q4 |
| 34 | R(Q1) - N1 | Q - B3 |

| 35 | R x R | R x R |
| 36 | P - N3 | .... |

Otherwise, 36 .... R - R7 wins another Pawn for Black.

36	....	Q - K1
37	K - N2	Q - R4
38	K - B2	Q - R7
39	Q x Q	....

Forced, as a move by the Rook costs the Knight Pawn.

39	....	R x Q ch
40	K - N1	K - R3
41	Resigns	

White is helpless:

A move by his Rook allows *41 ....* R - N7 in reply, winning the Knight Pawn, and allowing Black a passed Pawn.

The Knight can move only to B7 and Q8, and back again — to no avail.

Meanwhile, Black's King is free to wander down to R6, capture the Rook Pawn, and win as he pleases.

A characteristic Petrosian game, unconventional and thoroughly captivating.

INTERLUDE

BASEBALL has long been America's most popular game. Popular, that is, with men. Women tolerated it; children ignored it. Almost overnight, though, everybody was converted to the cause. Men, women and children now sit glued to a television set, safely out of the harmful sunshine, watching their favorite team. Those who have no television sets go down to the ball park with their radios. There they can see the Dodgers play and, at the same time, tune in on the Yankee game.

What caused this sudden frenzy for baseball? Radio, a little; television, a great deal — but more powerful than these two mediums of modern civilization was the influence of one of the oldest sciences — mathematics. It was the fascination of numbers — the excitement of statistics. So intense is the interest in players' records that the fans hardly watch the game at all.

The pitcher whips the ball over the plate, and the batter swings into it. As soon as his bat connects and the ball starts its flight, they turn away. They never see its graceful, beautiful flight over the fence. They are too busy writing down statistics. Or telling the world at large: "This makes Musial's 28th home run, and he's batted in 109 runs. He's leading the league now with a percentage of .346. Hey, did you know that he's gotten hits in 24 consecutive games?"

Wonder what would happen if the bug for statistics bit chess followers? Just to start the ball rolling, here are a few which I have compiled. Some of these are genuine, so you might try separating fact from fiction.

1] In a forty-year chess career, Steinitz captured a total of 47,963 Pawns.

2] Kieseritzky in one day's play against all comers sprang the Scholar's Mate 19 times.

3] In offhand games alone, Morphy sacrificed 52 Queens, 97 Rooks, 136 Knights and 263 Bishops.

4] Buckle wrote two chapters of the *History of Civilization* while waiting for Williams to make his 25th move in the fourth game of their 1851 match.

5] Colonel Moreau holds the record for the worst score in any one tournament. At Monte Carlo in 1903, he lost twice to every opponent, winding up with 26 zeros.

6] Mason made 144 moves in succession with his Queen, against Mackenzie at London in 1882.

7] In ten years of tournament and match play, Capablanca lost only one game.

8] The world's record for checkmating on the unprotected last rank is held by Paolo Boi, who won 9,647 games by this maneuver.

9] Nimzowitsch doubled Rooks on the 7th rank in 167 tournament games, beating the former mark of 152 held by Zukertort.

10] In the Ostend tournament of 1937, Grob won three games in a row on the time-limit.

11] The record holder of *en passant* captures in one game is Paulsen, who had four such captures out of six possible in his game against Anderssen at Baden-Baden in 1870.

12] The under-promotion record is still Mackenzie's: he advanced three Pawns to the eighth rank and promoted them to Knight, Rook and Bishop in his masterpiece against Winawer at Paris, 1878.

13] Against Bogolyubov at Hastings in 1922, Alekhine sacrificed his Queen, promoted a Pawn to Queen, sacrificed his new Queen, queened another Pawn and sacrificed his third Queen. He was preparing to advance a Pawn for his fourth Queen when Bogolyubov resigned.*

14] Réti has fianchettoed both Bishops in 42 games in succession. His lifetime total of fianchettoed Bishops is 2,486.

15] Rubinstein has played a grand total of 1,985 games, of which 1,763 were Rook and Pawn endings.

16] Steinitz accepted and held on to 6,327 gambit Pawns offered by his opponents.

17] A. N. Other has snatched 8,645 Pawns in the opening. His lost games total (by sheer coincidence) 8,645 games.

18] World's record for resigning by sweeping away the pieces and breaking the board over his opponent's head is held by Ahmed Ben Jussof, whose seven in one tournament is still unapproached.

19] In Sumatra, where the natives bet money, clothing and even parts of their bodies, the championship is held by a young man whose name in our language would be "Lefty."

20] Total number of victims of the Noah's Ark trap (including last year's casualties) is now 7,653,186.

* See the last game in the book!

Here are some interesting quotations. How many can you identify?

1] This little man has taught us all to play chess.
2] After the first move, 1 P - K4, White's game is in the last throes.
3] I want to be quiet; I mean to win this tournament.
4] I shall have to play a championship match with this man some day.
5] Young man, you play well!
6] It is not enough just to be a good player; one must also play well.
7] I cannot play well in England.
8] The East threatens us.
9] I am going to be world champion.
10] I never read a (chess) book until I was already a master.
11] I wish I could do what he has done in chess.
12] I was wrong in supposing that I could bottle up my chess and put it in a glass case.
13] It is no easy matter to reply correctly to Lasker's bad moves.
14] That boy understands as much of chess as I do of rope dancing!
15] It is remarkable; you never seem to make a mistake.

Answers to quiz

1] Schwarz said this of Steinitz, during the Vienna Tournament of 1882.
2] Julius Breyer, in a monograph on hypermodern chess.
3] Pillsbury, before the great Hastings Tournament of 1895, which he won.
4] Lasker, speaking of Charousek.
5] Lasker to Fine, after losing to him in the Nottingham Tournament of 1936.
6] Tarrasch, after a poor showing in the Leipzig Tournament of 1888.
7] Bogolyubov.
8] Maróczy, while watching young Tartakower play in 1905.
9] Najdorf in an interview in 1947.
10] Reuben Fine.
11] Vidmar, of Botvinnik, during the Nottingham Tournament of 1936.
12] Anderssen, after his defeat by Paul Morphy in 1858.
13] Pollock.
14] Janowski, referring to his game with the prodigy Reshevsky. P. S. Reshevsky won the game.
15] Lasker, of Capablanca, after the latter beat him in a ten-game match at lightning chess.

Did you know that ...

Reshevsky made his debut on the radio by singing a love song?

Capablanca was never checkmated?

Steinitz was the thirteenth child in his family?

Neumann won a tournament in 1865 with a score of 34 wins, no losses, no draws?

James Mason's real name is still a mystery?

Charousek copied out by hand the gigantic *Handbuch des Schachspiels*?

To accustom himself to all conditions of tournament play, Botvinnik in practice matches would have his opponent blow smoke at him?

For more than a thousand years more people have played chess than any other game?

Paul Morphy once conducted a chess column at the fantastic salary (for 1859) of $3,000 a year?

Michael Tal won the world's championship at the age of twenty-three?

Moving one square at a time, a Bishop may go from K1 to K7 in eight moves in 483 ways?

In successive rounds, Reuben Fine once beat Botvinnik, Reshevsky, drew with Capablanca, beat Euwe, Flohr and Alekhine?

It takes a Knight three moves to check a King that is two squares away on the same diagonal?

Paul Morphy, King of Chess, once lost a game in twelve moves?

Two lone Knights cannot force mate?

Chess players for more than five hundred years used a pair of dice to determine their moves?

THE ALCHEMISTS OF OLD devoted their lives to the search for a philosopher's stone which would turn base metals into gold. In another metier, writers of chess books indulge themselves by their efforts to make a science of an art. They try to show how games can be won and positions may be analyzed by a series of mathematical symbols (or a reasonable facsimile thereof).

An interesting example of one such explanation is the following characteristic algebraic demonstration by Franklin K. Young of a position which appears in his book *The Major Tactics of Chess*.

Defended Piece

With or without the move, the White Queen Bishop Pawn is defended.

SOLUTION

X = Any piece employed in the given evolution.

Y = Piece attacked.

$B + R + Q + R$ = Attacking pieces.

$B + R + R$ = Supporting pieces.

$B + R + Q + R > B + R + R$ = Construction of the inequality.

$4X$ = Number of terms on left side.

$3X$ = Number of terms on right side.

$4X - 3X$ = Excess of left-side terms.

$(B + R) - (B + R)$ = Value of like terms.

$Q - R$ = Value of first unlike term.

Thus the given piece is defended; for, although the number of terms contained in the left side of the inequality exceeds by one the number of terms contained in the right side, the third term of the inequality is an unlike term, of which the initial contained in the left side is greater than the initial contained in the right.

How many of these chess books can you identify?

1] This book gives lessons in chess and love.

2] This one has a record of the games of a master player from his youth up to the age of fourteen!

3] This is a record of the games of a former world champion — but only the games which he lost!

4] This one has a pun in its title.

5] This book (on chess) was written by two checker masters.

6] This one has a diagram after every single move.

7] The games in this book are all annotated by literary quotations.

8] These two books have contradictory titles.

9] So do these two!

10] This one illustrates the Battle of Waterloo on the chess board.

11] The notes to the games in this book are in English, Dutch, French and German.

12] The author of this one tells you how to become a master — something he could never do himself!

13] The pages of this book are watermarked with the name and year of the tournament which it describes.

14] Nobody resigns in this book!

15] The author of this one began by saying: "This is a book in which the analysis is accurate."

Answers to literary quiz

1] *The Passionate Game*, by Schenk.

2] *Mis Cinsuenta Partidas con Maestros* (Pomar's Games).

3] Capablanca's *Sämtliche Verlustpartien*.

4] *Chess Pieces*, by Norman Knight.

5] *Chess*, by Grover and Wiswell.

6] *Chess Rendered Familiar*, by Pohlman.

7] *Chesslets*, by Dr. J. Schumer.

8] *Chess the Easy Way*, by Reuben Fine, and *Chess the Hard Way*, by Dan Yanofsky.

9] *How to Play Chess*, by Emanuel Lasker, and *How Not to Play Chess*, by Znosko-Borovsky.

10] *Chess Strategetics*, by Franklin K. Young.

11] Kessling's *International Archives*.

12] *Der Weg zur Meisterschaft*, by Franz Gutmayer.

13] *Sixth American Chess Congress, 1889*.

14] *Every Game Checkmate*, by Watts and Hereford.

15] *The St. Petersburg 1909 Tournament Book*, annotated by Dr. Lasker.

EPIGRAMS AND ADVICE

Epigrams on Chess and Its Players

AN ANCIENT writer said that, if there were no flowers and moon and beautiful women, he would not want to be born into the world. I might add that, if there were no pen and ink and chess and wine, there was no purpose in being born a man.

Chang Chao

FOR surely, of all the drugs in the world, Chess must be the most permanently pleasurable.

Assiac

THERE is no other game so esteemed, so profound and so venerable as chess; in the realm of play it stands alone in dignity.

Ely Culbertson

THERE is a certain nobility about chess that appertains to no other game . . . to imagine a great player otherwise than respectable is difficult; he gives the impression, while at work, of being a stoic philosopher.

James Payn

THERE are two classes of men; those who are content to yield to circumstance, and who play whist; those who aim to control circumstances, and who play chess.

Mortimer Collins

CHESS has this in common with making poetry, that the desire for it comes upon the amateur in gusts.

A. A. Milne

BLESSED be the memory of him who gave the world this immortal game.
A. G. Gardiner

THE WORLD is not likely to tire of an amusement which never repeats itself, of a game which presents today features as novel and charms as fresh as those with which it delighted, in the morning of history, the dwellers on the banks of the Ganges and the Indus.

Willard Fiske

IN ANSWERING the question, "Which is the greater game, Chess or Checkers," I must, in all frankness, favor Chess.

Newell W. Banks
Blindfold Checker Champion of the World

CHESS is a sea in which a gnat may drink and an elephant may bathe.

Indian Proverb

THE POOREST chess player is more to be envied than the most favored servant of the Golden Calf; for the latter grovels all his life long in the mire of materialism; while the former dwells high aloft, in the bright realms of imagination and poetry.

Weiss

CHESS is as much a mystery as women.

Purdy

OTHERS may talk of the Round Table with its fifty Knights, but I greatly prefer the Square Table with only four Knights.

Fiske

CHESS holds its master in its own bonds — fetters and in some ways shapes his spirit, so that under it the inner freedom of the very strongest must suffer.

Albert Einstein

NATURE supplies the game of chess with its implements; science with its system; art with its aesthetic arrangement of its problems; and God endows it with its blessed power of making people happy.

Weiss

THE WAY he plays chess demonstrates a man's whole nature.

Stanley Ellin

WHEN chess is reduced to mere mathematics, chess will lose its charm.

Robert J. Buckley

IT IS hopeless to try to make a machine to play perfect chess.

Norbert Wiener

COULD we look into the head of a chess player, we should see there a whole world of feelings, images, ideas, emotion and passion.

Alfred Binet

THE CHESS master today must have courage, a killer instinct, stamina and arrogance.

Evans

IT IS plain that the unconscious motive actuating the players is not the mere love of pugnacity characteristic of all competitive games, but the grimmer one of father-murder.

Ernest Jones

THE GAME possesses a literature which in contents probably exceeds that of all other games combined.

H. J. R. Murray

I NOW see myself (after fifty years of tournament play) compelled to change my concepts of chess strategy during the years which may still lie ahead.

Dr. Tartakower

"YOU MAY learn much more from a game you lose than from a game you win. You will have to lose hundreds of games before becoming a good player."

Capablanca

I AM hopelessly in love with the game.

Assiac

THE REAL lives of dazzlingly brilliant chess geniuses are sometimes hopelessly dull.

Fine

IT IS remarkable, and deserves special mention, that the great masters, such as Pillsbury, Maróczy and Janowski, play against Lasker as though hypnotized.

George Marco

AT NO time in the history of chess have there been more than fifteen ranking first-class masters, and most of the time ten or twelve would be nearer the truth.

Capablanca

YOU CANNOT play at chess if you are kind-hearted.

French Proverb

SOME of Capablanca's finest games remind me of the compositions of de Falla in their blend of intricacy, elusiveness, dignity and basic simplicity.

Gilbert Highet

ONE OF the most curious facts found in the by-paths of chess research is the affected dread of brain ruin on the part of men whom the Fates have made absolutely immune from any such calamity.

Anonymous

FORTUNE favors the bold, especially when they are Alekhines.

Prins

MORPHY was an artist; and the best way to enjoy an artist is not to dissect him.

Sergeant

THOU shalt not shilly-shally!

Nimzowitsch

A MAN that will take back a move at chess will pick a pocket.

Fenton

I KNOW at sight what a position contains. What could happen? What is going to happen? You figure it out. I know it!

Capablanca

A MASTERPIECE is a masterpiece though a million people say so.

Quiller-Couch

RUBINSTEIN stands as the greatest end-game player of all time.

Winkelman

ALL SULI's play at chess is more beautiful than this garden, and everything that is in it.

Anonymous

THE GREATEST compliment one can pay a master is to compare him with Capablanca.

Chernev

TO FREE your game, take off some of your adversary's men, if possible for nothing.

Captain Bertin
The Noble Game of Chess (1735)

THE SCHEME of a game is played on positional lines; the decision of it, as a rule, is effected by combinations.

Réti

THE GREAT master places a Knight at K5; checkmate follows by itself.

Tartakower

FIRST restrain, next blockade, lastly destroy!

Nimzowitsch

. . . P - Q4 is the antidote for the poison in gambits.

Anonymous

IT IS not a move, even the best move, that you must seek, but a realizable plan.

Znosko-Borovsky

WHOEVER sees no other aim in the game than that of giving checkmate to one's opponent will never become a good chessplayer.

Max Euwe

WHEREAS the tactician knows what to do when there is something to do, it requires the strategian to know what to do when there is nothing to do.

Gerald Abrahams

THE DELIGHT in gambits is a sign of chess youth. . . . In very much the same way as the young man, on reaching his manhood years, lays aside the Indian stories and stories of adventure, and turns to the psychological novel, we with maturing experience leave off gambit playing and become interested in the less vivacious but withal more forceful maneuvers of the position player.

Emanuel Lasker

THE BLUNDERS are all there on the board, waiting to be made.

Tartakower

GIVEN a Geometric Symbol Positive or a combination of Geometric Symbols Positive which is coincident with the Objective Plane; then, if the'

Prime Tactical Factor can be posted at the Point of Command, the adverse King may be checkmated.

Franklin K. Young

PAWN endings are to chess what putting is to golf.

Purdy

PROPERLY taught, a student can learn more in a few hours than he would find out in ten years of untutored trial and error.

Emanuel Lasker

THE GREATEST GAME OF CHESS EVER PLAYED

THERE is an epic grandeur about the following game which inspires awe as well as admiration. Alekhine's subtle strategy involves maneuvers which encompass the entire chessboard as a battlefield. There are exciting plots and counterplots. There are fascinating combinations and brilliant sacrifices of Queens and Rooks. There are two remarkable promotions of Pawns, and a third in the offing, before White decides to capitulate.

It is the writer's deeply considered opinion, based on a fifty-year study of master chess, that this brilliant effort of Alekhine's is the greatest masterpiece ever created on a chessboard.

Hastings, 1922

DUTCH DEFENSE

BOGOLYUBOV ALEKHINE

	White	Black
1	P - Q4	P - KB4
2	P - QB4	N - KB3
3	P - KN3	P - K3
4	B - N2	B - N5 ch
5	B - Q2	B x B ch
6	N x B	N - B3
7	KN - B3	0 - 0
8	0 - 0	P - Q3
9	Q - N3	K - R1
10	Q - B3	P - K4!

Black insists on his share of the center. The King Pawn is indirectly protected, as after 11 P x P, P x P, 12 N x P, there would follow 12 .... N x N, 13 Q x N, Q x N, and Black has won a piece.

| 11 | P - K3 | P - QR4! |

This prevents any counteraction on the Queen side by 12 P - QN4.

| 12 | P - N3 | .... |

If *12* P - QR3 preparing for *13* P - QN4, then *12* .... P - R5!

| 12 | .... | Q - K1! |
| 13 | P - QR3 | Q - R4! |

Black mobilizes his forces with a view to a King-side attack. He does not fear 14 P x P, P x P, 15 N x P, as after 15 .... N x N, 16 Q x N, N - KN5! the threat of mate by 17 .... Q x P wins the Queen. Or if 14 P - QN4, P - K5, 15 N - K1, P x P, 16 P x P, R x R wins a Pawn for Black.

| 14 | P - KR4 | .... |

Now White threatens 15 P x P.

14	....	N - KN5
15	N - N5	B - Q2
16	P - B3	N - B3
17	P - B4	....

Necessary, to prevent a break by 17 .... P - B5.

17	....	P - K5
18	KR - Q1	P - R3
19	N - R3	P - Q4!

Intending to consolidate his center before embarking on a flank attack.

| 20 | N - B1 | N - K2 |

In order to follow with 21 .... P - R5, and weaken the Pawn support of the Bishop Pawn. Then if 22 P - QN4, P x P, 23 Q x P, N(K2) - Q4 establishes a Knight in the center permanently, as no Pawns can drive it away.

| 21 | P - R4 | N - B3! |

Now that White's Queen Rook Pawn is at R4, Black's Knight is free to invade the enemy territory by way of QN5 and Q6.

| 22 | R - Q2 | N - QN5 |
| 23 | B - R1 | Q - K1! |

Again with an eye to dominating the center. The immediate threat is 24

.... P x P, 25 P x P (or 25 Q x P, KN - Q4) B x P winning a Pawn.

Notice that Black's strategy ranges over the entire chessboard. It is not confined to the King side or the Queen side.

24   R - KN2   ....

The blockade by 24 P - B5 is not satisfactory, as the reply 24 .... P - Q N4 breaks open a file for Black.

24   ....   P x P
25   P x P   ....

White gives up a Pawn rather than let the other Knight into his game.

25   ....   B x P
26   N - B2   ....

Trying for 27 P - N4.

26   ....   B - Q2

This attempt is promptly stopped.

27   N - Q2   P - QN4!

Again prepared to meet 28 P x P or 28 P - B5 with 28 .... N(B3) - Q4, dominating the center.

28   N - Q1   N - Q6
29   R x P   P - N5!

The beginning of a magnificent combination, in Alekhine's most imaginative style.

30   R x R   ....

If 30 Q - R1, R x R, 31 Q x R, Q - R1! 32 Q x Q, R x Q, and the Rook will swoop down to the seventh or eighth rank with telling effect.

30   ....   P x Q!
31   R x Q   ....

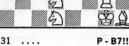

31   ....   P - B7!!

The point of Alekhine's combination.

The Pawn cannot be prevented from queening, and a new phase begins.

32   R x R ch   K - R2
33   N - B2   ....

Any other move loses a piece.

33   ....   P - B8 (Q) ch
34   N - B1   N - K8!

Threatens 35 .... N - B6 — a picturesque smothered mate!

35   R - R2   Q x BP

Now the threat is 36 .... B - N4, 37 N - Q2 (or 37 B - N2, N x B, winning a piece) Q - QB8, 38 N - B1, N - B6 ch and mate next move.

36   R - QN8   B - N4
37   R x B   Q x R
38   P - N4   N - B6 ch!

Another surprise move, and there's more where that came from!

39   B x N   P x B
40   P x P   ....

Forced, for if 40 P - N5, N - N5, 41 N x N (on 41 R - R3, Q - K7 wins) P x N, and Black has two connected passed Pawns.

40   ....   Q - K7!!

Ties White up completely. Any move by one of his pieces loses at once. If, for example, 41 N - R3, N - N5, 42 R x Q, P x R, and Black gets a new Queen. Or if 41 R - R3, N - N5! is again the winning move.

41   P - Q5   K - N1!

The natural continuation 41 .... P - R4 allows White to escape cleverly by 42 N - R3, N - N5, 43 N - N5 ch!, K - N1, 44 R x Q, P x R, 45 N - B3!

42   P - R5   K - R2

Alekhine waits for Bogolyubov's Pawn moves to be exhausted.

43   P - K4   N x KP
44   N x N   Q x N
45   P - Q6   P x P
46   P - B6   ....

Unable to save his Pawns, White sells their lives dearly by breaking up his opponent's Pawns.

46   ....   P x P
47   R - Q2   Q - K7!

"A pretty finish, worthy of this fine game," says Alekhine himself, pardonably proud of a great creation. The Queen's occupation of the fatal square forces a delightful simplification, and offers a fine illustration of the dictum that "Pawn endings are the easiest to win." The sign of a great master is his ability to win a won game quickly and painlessly.

48	R x Q	P x R
49	K - B2	P x N (Q) ch
50	K x Q	K - N2

| 51 | K - B2 | K - B2 |
| 52 | K - K3 | .... |

On 52 P - B5, K - K2, 53 K - K3, P - Q 4, 54 K - Q4, K - Q3, and Black wins easily.

52	....	K - K3
53	K - K4	P - Q4 ch
54	Resigns	

Bogolyubov does not care to see the continuation: 54 K - Q4, K - B4, 55 K x P, K x P, 56 K - Q4, P - B4, 57 K - Q3, K - N6, and Alekhine will soon have a fourth Queen on the board!

INDEX TO THE COMPOSERS OF THE
PROBLEMS, PUZZLES AND ENDINGS

Adamson   167

Bron   157
Brown   162

Chernev   163
Cheron   151
Clausen   156

Dawson   152
Dobrusky   151

Fabel   169
Flatt   162
Fritz   156

Gereben   168
Gilberg   151
Grasemann   171

Halumbirek   153
Hanneman   165, 169
Heuacker   161
Horwitz   170

Kemp   170
Kipping   151
Korteling   160
Kovacs   163, 168
Kuznetzov   158

Lazard   160
Leathem   165

Libiurkin   158
Libiurkin and Bondarenko   159
Lommer   164
Loyd   152, 153, 164, 165

Mendheim   162
Moravec   168
Mortimer   171

Orlimont   167

Piltz   154
Prokes   157

Reichhelm   168
Rinck   155, 156
Rubin   170

Sarychev   159, 169
Selesniev   155, 161
Selman   155, 157
Shinkman   152, 171, 172

Terho   161
Tolosa   167

Unknown   162, 163, 164, 165

Valvo   158
Vlk   159

Wolff   171
Wurzburg   152

INDEX TO THE PLAYERS AND THEIR GAMES

	Page
Adams-Torre, New Orleans, 1920	225
Alekhine-Book, Margate, 1938	251
Alekhine-Schwartz, London, 1926	202
Anderssen-Dufresne, Berlin, 1852	231
Anderssen-Kieseritzky, London, 1851	230
Andreaschek-R. M., Olmütz, 1901	215
Ballard-Fagan	206
Berger-Charousek, Kaschau, 1892	207
Bernstein-Capablanca, Moscow, 1914	243
Bird-Maróczy, Hastings, 1895	190
Blackburne-Ballard, London, 1871	198
Blackburne-Schwarz, Berlin, 1881	235
Bogolyubov-Alekhine, Hastings, 1922	281
Botvinnik-Chekhover, Leningrad, 1938	250
Bowdler-Philidor, London, 1788	204
Byrne, D.-Fischer, New York, 1956	254
Byrne, R.-Evans, New York, 1966	255
Capablanca-Botvinnik, Leningrad, 1925	173
Capablanca-Chase, New York, 1922	224
Capablanca-Corzo, Havana, 1900	175
Clemens-Eisenschmidt, Dorpat, 1862	220
Coultas-Stenhouse, Melbourne, 1929	192
Dunkelblum-Keres, Ostend, 1937	207
Euwe-Keres, Match, 1940	226
Fisher-Steinitz, Liverpool, 1872	223
Gaudersen-Paul, Melbourne, 1928	197
Gerassimov-Smyslov, Moscow, 1935	176
Glucksberg-Najdorf, Warsaw, 1935	252
Hage-Nimzowitsch, Arnstadt, 1926	194
Hannah-Paulsen, London, 1862	188
Hearst-R. E., New York, 1955	215
Iglesias-Capablanca, Havana, 1893	182
Janowski-Alapin, Barmen, 1905	239
Johner-Nimzowitsch, Dresden, 1926	247
Jopen-Petrosian, Belgrade, 1954	265
Keres-Panno, Gothenburg, 1955	195
Keres-Richter, Munich, 1942	181
Khloyber-Nagy, Budapest, 1942	220
Koshnitsky-Hewitt, Correspondence, 1945	180

	Page
Kujoth-Fashingbauer, Milwaukee, 1950	206
Labourdonnais-McDonnell, London, 1834	228
Lange-Schierstedt	215
Leonard, J. A.-Leonard, J.	216
Lowenthal-Williams, London, 1851	184
McDonnell-Labourdonnais, London, 1834	204
Maczynski-Pratten, Portsmouth, 1948	222
Marco-Maróczy, Vienna, 1899	210
Maróczy-Tchigorin, Vienna, 1903	238
Mason-Zukertort, London, 1883	213
Mieses-Schenk, Oxford, 1947	179
Mikenas-Lebedev, Gruzinske, 1941	253
Morphy-Brunswick and Isouard, Paris, 1858	233
Morphy-Guibert, Paris, 1858	186
Morphy-St. Leon, Paris, 1863	217
Nimzowitsch-Alapin, Riga, 1913	242
Panov-Yudovich, Tiflis, 1937	179
Paris-Marseilles, Correspondence, 1878	216
Patschurkowski-Rhode, 1941	221
Paulsen-Morphy, New York, 1857	232
Paulsen-Schwarz, Leipzig, 1879	189
Petrosian-Aranovich, Tiflis, 1949	259
Petrosian-Aronin, Moscow, 1961	258
Petrosian-Barendregt, Beverwijk, 1960	262
Petrosian-Pogrebyssky, Tiflis, 1949	261
Pillsbury-Bampton, Philadelphia, 1900	200
Pillsbury-Wolf, Vienna, 1902	199
Post-Lob, Lausanne, 1947	193
Réti-Alekhine, Baden-Baden, 1925	245
Rotlevi-Rubinstein, Lodz, 1907	241
Sämisch-Nimzowitsch, Copenhagen, 1923	244
Schiffers-Harmonist, Frankfurt, 1887	235
Schulz-Thelen, Prague, 1927	192
Soyka-Kolta, Vienna, 1924	223
Spielmann-Honlinger, Match, 1929	248
Staunton-Williams, London, 1851	185
Steinitz-Bardeleben, Hastings, 1895	237
Tarrasch-Munchoff, Berlin, 1880	193
Tarrasch-Romberg, Nuremberg, 1892	218
Tarrasch-Schroeder, Nuremberg, 1889	219
Tarrasch-Schroeder, Nuremberg, 1892	218
Tartakower-Rosselli, Semmering, 1926	209
Terpugov-Petrosian, Moscow, 1951	264
Terpugov-Petrosian, Moscow, 1955	263
Tresling-Benima, Winschoten, 1896	177

About the Editor

IRVING CHERNEV is a chess master who has taken part
in state and national championship tournaments. He has
written about the game, with charm and wit, for nearly
thirty years and has served as Associate Editor of *Chess
Review*. Able to write amusingly and with wide knowledge of the famous players themselves, he is at his best
when analyzing a brilliant move or a magical ending.

Despite the time he gives to chess, he does have other
interests: travel (if it's to London or Paris), reading (if
it's something by Perelman), music (if it's by the three
B's — Bach, Beethoven, the Beatles), and magic (if it includes card manipulation). Ping-Pong, poker and track-
ing down three-star restaurants (with an assist from
Michelin) occupy his remaining time.

He has written fourteen books, including the remarkable *Logical Chess, Move by Move*, which has been called
the most instructive chess book ever written. He is also
co-author of the best seller *An Invitation to Chess*, a
complete guide for the beginner.